FURTHER TO FALL

CATHERINE COWLES

FURTHER TO FALL

Editor: Susan Barnes
Copy Editor: Chelle Olson
Proofreading: Grahame Claire & Emma Renshaw
Paperback Formatting: Stacey Blake, Champagne Book Design
Cover Design: Hang Le

DEDICATION

For my Dad.
The best dad there ever was. I know if he were still with us today
he'd be shouting from the rooftops that his daughter wrote a book,
even if that said book had sex scenes. Miss you every day, Dad,
and am eternally grateful to be your daughter.

ONE

Carter

"**W**HERE ARE ALL YOUR BOOB SHIRTS?" TAYLOR'S muffled voice came from between racks of clothing in my closet.

"My boob shirts?" I asked, my eyebrows creeping their way up my forehead.

"Yeah. You know, the shirts that are going to give the guys we meet tonight a nice sneak peek at the killer set of girls you're currently hiding under that ruffled school teacher top."

I glanced down at my shirt. I thought it looked cute. "You know I *am* a teacher, right? And that you are, too?"

"Duh. But we're not currently on duty. New teacher training is over, and school doesn't start for another week. So, I'm letting my freak flag fly while I can, sister!"

Taylor and I had met a week ago during new teacher orientation. We had quickly bonded over our Southern roots, love of cheesy, made-for-TV movies, and our need to mainline caffeine to get through our early-morning training sessions. Taylor could crack me up even before my double shot of espresso had taken effect, and I thanked my lucky stars that Teach For Our Youth had placed us both in Los Angeles county. Taylor emerged from my closet, shaking something victoriously. "We have a winner!"

My eyes narrowed on the item. "That's a camisole. I wear it *under* other shirts, not by itself."

"Honey, I don't have a lot to work with in there. This is just going to have to do. Thank goodness I brought an extra skirt with me." Taylor crossed the room and started unbuttoning my blouse.

"Whoa there, cowgirl," I said, pushing her overzealous hands away.

Taylor pinned me with a stare I was sure worked wonders on her students. "Carter, you are not in Georgia anymore. This is Los Angeles, and we need to look the part." My shoulders curved in on themselves, and I plopped back on my bed, sighing.

"Come on, girl, this should be fun! We'll get all gussied up, have a few cocktails, get our flirt on, maybe even get our make-out on."

I let out a laugh as Taylor waggled her eyebrows in my direction. "Sorry, Taylor. No, no, no. I'm just not comfortable showing that much skin."

Taylor's eyes narrowed as she drummed her fingers across her berry pink lips. "I'll make you a deal. You let me pick your outfit, and I'll do your lunchroom duty for two weeks."

I scoffed. Lunchroom duty was nobody's idea of fun, but I wasn't going out with my boobs on display for a measly two weeks' reprieve. Taylor's eyes narrowed further as she studied my face. "Okay, I see you've come to play. One month of lunchroom duty."

A smile crept over my face. "Do your worst, Miss Lawson."

She covered her heart with her hand. "I thought you'd never ask. Stay right there and don't move a muscle. I'm going to get my makeup bag so I can punch up your look, just a little." I twisted my fingers in my lap, but Taylor was back before my second thoughts could spur me out of my sitting position.

Just as Taylor dumped the contents of her bag on my bed, a

knock sounded at my bedroom door. "Come in," I called.

A head of gorgeous brown hair that caught the light appeared from around the corner. "Hey, just wanted to see what you were up to before I head out for the night."

"Taylor, meet my roommate Lexi. Lexi, this is my friend Taylor. She'll be teaching at the same school I am."

"Nice to meet you," Lexi said, extending a perfectly manicured hand. Her eyes traveled over Taylor, taking in every detail of her appearance before seeming to dub her no threat.

When I started the search for apartments, one of my sorority sisters had said she had a friend from home who lived in LA and was looking for a roommate. It had seemed like the perfect setup at the time, especially since I couldn't really afford to live by myself on my teacher's salary. But there was something about Lexi that had never really sat right with me. She was nice enough on the surface, and always invited me to go out with her and things like that, but she was constantly judging and evaluating the women around her. The things she said about her so-called friends behind their backs made me cringe.

"Nice to meet you, as well," Taylor responded with forced politeness.

"What are you guys up to tonight?" Lexi asked.

"Just grabbing a drink," I answered quickly, the last thing I needed was Lexi finding out I was friends with Liam Fairchild.

"Nice. Where?"

"Oh, I don't know, just some neighborhood bar, I think."

"Oh, well I'm going to Chateau with the girls. You should go there instead, much chicer than whatever you have planned. I know you don't have connections there, but I can get you on the list." This was exactly the kind of comment that was typical Lexi. Kindly inviting you out with her, while insulting your plans and lack of cool friends at the same time. I don't think it was even a conscious dig, she was just used to the cutthroat world of

Hollywood public relations.

I forced a smile. "Thanks, Lexi, but I think we're going to stick with our plans."

She shrugged. "Suit yourself. I'll see you tomorrow."

"Bye," I called at her retreating back.

The door to the apartment slammed, and Taylor giggled. "She's something."

"I know. She works in PR, so she doesn't really understand when people don't want to get into the hottest party on any given night."

"I guess that makes sense," Taylor said as she searched through her various tubes, tins, and palettes. "Close your eyes for me."

The soft bristles of a makeup brush danced across my lids while Taylor hummed along to a familiar song. "I can't believe you grew up next door to Liam Fairchild. Lordy, he is sex on a stick! And that voice! That rasp could make me orgasm on the spot."

I snorted. "When you've lived through all of each other's awkward phases, including a particularly rough case of the chicken pox, no one is sex on a stick."

Liam's voice continued to croon over the speakers. "You can't tell me he doesn't make your lady parts tingle just a little bit."

I cracked one of my eyes open. "Not even a little bit." It was true. As handsome and talented as he was, Liam had entered brother status during our childhood and never left.

"That's so disappointing," she said with a forlorn sigh.

I chuckled at her obvious devastation. "Why?"

"It would just be such a great love story. Childhood best friends separated by thousands of miles, and the dream a small-town Georgia girl could never contain. The girl was left brokenhearted, weeping into her pillow every night. The boy, while sowing his wild oats, compared every girl to her, and they all came up short. Suddenly, they're thrown back into each other's orbit when the girl gets a job in the City of Angels. Cue the swelling of the romantic score!" Taylor's Texas twang had gotten stronger with each word, and by the end, she was using her makeup brush like a conductor's baton.

"I'm pretty sure you should have gone into movies instead of teaching," I said with a roll of my eyes. Why did no one ever believe that Liam and I were only ever friends?

She collapsed onto the mattress next to me, bringing her forearm to her brow. "I know. It's a loss for the theatrical community."

"That's for dang sure." Taylor's desire for a true love connection between me and Liam cemented my high opinion of her. Typically, when girls found out that I was childhood besties with one of the most famous musicians in the world, the first thing they wanted to know was if I could hook them up with him.

I didn't blame them. I knew Liam was handsome, I just wasn't attracted to him. But after I caught one of my sorority sisters going through my phone to find his number, I'd started being a lot more careful with who I shared the knowledge of our friendship with. But from the moment I met Taylor, there was just something in her spirit that let me know I could trust her.

She eyed the clock on my bedside table. "What time did Liam want us to meet him at the bar? I don't want to be late for my first LA celebrity meeting."

"Ten thirty."

Taylor bolted to a sitting position. "Shit! We gotta hurry," she said, riffling through the duffle bag she'd brought with her.

Taylor shoved a black piece of spandex into my hands along with the camisole she'd hijacked from my closet earlier. "Here, go put this on quick, and I'll do your eyeliner after."

"Fine," I huffed and headed for the bathroom.

Taylor's skirt was creeping up my thighs, I could feel it. I surreptitiously inched my hand between my body and the bar to try and pull it down. Taylor bounced on the balls of her feet. "This place is awesome! No name on the front door, extra cool points."

Glancing over my shoulder, I took in the room. It screamed old Hollywood speakeasy, with tufted leather banquettes and gilded mirrors lining the walls. People were everywhere, but my eyes caught sight of a familiar head of longish, brown hair. Warmth filled my chest, a swell that felt like comfort and home. I grabbed Taylor's arm, leaning in so she could hear me above the music. "Liam's over there."

Taylor followed the incline of my head. "You head on over, I'll wait for our drinks."

"Okay, next round's on me."

"No, next round is on whichever handsome gentlemen we meet," Taylor said with a lascivious grin.

My head tipped back as I let out a laugh. "Sounds like a plan." I wove my way through bodies, dodging precariously balanced drinks and couples making out, trying to keep an eye on Liam. As I got closer, my steps faltered, and I toddled on my heels as heat swept through my body.

Next to Liam was the most gorgeous man I had ever seen. And that's what he was, a man. Not a boy, not a guy. He was a man. Square jaw dusted with stubble, and dark hair cropped close to his skull in a way that had my hands itching to run my fingers over it.

God, he was hot. Hot and apparently upset, because when I approached, the mountain of a man stood, and there was definitely anger blazing in his deep blue eyes. He stepped between me and the table, his incredibly broad shoulders effectively blocking any view I had of Liam. "Not tonight, sweetheart. Move along," he said with a dismissive shooing motion. My spine stiffened, and my eyes narrowed. But before I could open my mouth, I was suddenly lifted off the ground in a bear hug.

"It is so damn good to see you," Liam said into my ear as he lowered me back to my feet. He kept a hold on my shoulders as he pulled back. "You look gorgeous. I'm going to have to beat guys away from you with a stick." I felt my cheeks heat and I tugged on the hem of my skirt.

Throwing an arm over my shoulder, Liam turned me to face angry mountain man. "Austin, this is Carter. My old next-door neighbor I told you was moving to LA. Carter, this is my good friend and old bodyguard, Austin."

I swallowed my irritation and extended a hand. "It's nice to meet you."

Austin's hand engulfed mine. It was warm and rough and sent tingles up my arm. "Sorry about that. I thought you were a groupie." As apologies go, it was a pretty cruddy one. One-part half-hearted amends, one-part insult. Not to mention his jaw was locked so tight, I was pretty sure he was going to crack a molar.

Liam let out a bellow of laughter as he squeezed my rigid frame into his side. Austin tracked the movement with narrowed eyes. "Definitely not a groupie. Other than my mom, no one gives me a harder time than Carter."

I tilted my face up to meet Liam's eyes. "I'm not that bad."

"Sure," Liam replied, drawing out the vowel sound.

Feeling a nudge at my back, I turned to see Taylor holding up two drinks. "Thanks for getting those," I said. "Liam, Austin, this is my friend, Taylor."

"Nice to meet y'all." She sent them both her most dazzling smile. Liam returned it with one of his own, while Austin gave more of a grimace. What was his deal?

Before the awkward introductions could continue, a tall man with artfully disheveled blond hair and lean muscles appeared at Austin's side. "Well, who are these two stunners? And how did you trick them into hanging out with the sorry likes of you?"

Taylor giggled, and a smile came to my own lips. Liam

gestured towards the handsome man. "Ladies, this is Ford. He owns this place. Ford, this is Carter and her friend, Taylor."

"Ah, the infamous Carter. Nice to finally meet you." Ford reached out, grabbing my hand and pressing it to his lips. While handsome, no flush of heat stopped me in my tracks.

I found my eyes seeking out Austin's, but the fierce scowl on his face had me quickly averting my gaze and coming back to Ford. I forced a smile, trying to shake off the negative vibes Austin was sending my way. "It's nice to meet you, too."

The next hour proceeded in much the same way. Ford cracked jokes, and both he and Liam gave Taylor and me the lowdown on all the restaurants we needed to try, where to find the best coffee, and a list of bars and clubs we needed to avoid. But I couldn't relax.

Somehow, I had ended up sitting between Austin and Liam. There wasn't a whole lot of room on the banquette, and Austin was acting like I might have Ebola—one touch and he would be a dead man. As the minutes ticked on, my body grew more and more rigid. I was aware of every small movement I made. This was ridiculous. So, Austin and I had gotten off on the wrong foot, I just needed to change our course. If he was friends with Liam, he couldn't be that bad.

I turned to face Austin and was again held captive by those incredible eyes. They seemed to dance between shades under the lights. I shook myself out my hot guy stupor. "So, how did you and Liam meet?"

"Work."

"Work?" I parroted, unsure how else to respond to his overly verbose answer.

"Yeah. I was on his security detail at one of his first big gigs."

"Oh, that's cool. Is that still what you do?" I asked, drumming my fingers on the tops of my thighs.

The scowl was back, and it was even more ferocious than

before. "No. I fight MMA. Mixed martial arts. I just used to do security to pay the bills."

Clearly asking what he did for work was the wrong question. I tried a different tack. "So, what are some of your favorite things to do in LA? There are so many exciting things to do and see here. I don't want to miss anything."

Austin tipped his chin, looking down his nose at me. "I don't think I do the kinds of things you would be interested in."

What was this jerk's deal? I balled my hands into fists, attempting to take slow breaths to ease my frustration. "You have no idea what I'm interested in because you've barely said ten words to me."

He shrugged. I wanted to scream.

I searched out Taylor and widened my eyes at her, the universal help-me signal in girl world. She sent a perplexed look back at me, clearly not understanding my intent.

I needed out of here. Something about angry mountain man Austin had my nervous system fraying. Even though he was beyond rude, my attraction to him was a sharp and visceral thing. I hated myself a little for that.

I pushed off the leather bench, but when I did, the edge of my palm skimmed the side of Austin's muscular thigh. He jerked back as if he had been burned. "Sorry," I mumbled. Turning to Taylor and the rest of the group, I asked, "Do you mind if we head out? I feel a killer headache coming on." It wasn't a total lie. The tension I'd been feeling for the past hour was bound to give me a migraine if I stayed put any longer.

Taylor's brow furrowed, and she stood. "Of course, sweetie."

Liam's gaze traveled over my face, and his eyes narrowed. He *always* knew when I was lying. But he didn't call me out on it this time, he just wrapped me in a warm and familiar hug. "I'll text you later, and we'll plan a day for you to come hang out at the Malibu house."

"Sounds good," I said. I skirted around the table, avoiding Austin's eyes and body like he was a bomb that could detonate at any moment. "Nice to meet you guys," I mumbled without looking in Austin's direction.

"You too, gorgeous," Ford said with a devastating smile. I was able to give a weak one back as I grasped Taylor's hand and turned towards the door.

The cool night air felt like heaven on my overheated skin as I marched towards the car. Taylor tugged on my arm. "What the hell is going on?"

"I just needed to get out of there. That guy was such a jerk." He *was* a jerk, but something in my gut told me I might be overreacting just a little.

"I just thought he was a little dull. Hot, but dull."

I let out an exasperated huff. "Hotness does not compensate for rudeness." While I firmly believed that, I had never felt such a strong instant attraction to someone. And to have that same person dismiss me at every turn...it wounded my pride.

Taylor linked arms with me and started us moving again. "No, it does not. But it doesn't hurt to have something pretty to look at right before you knee him in the balls."

TWO

Austin

FOCUS. INCREASED TRAINING. NO DISTRACTIONS. I HIT ON
each point as my feet pounded the pavement. Those were
the things I could count on, the tools that would keep me
in control. This is how I could prevent another loss, how I could
achieve what I had dreamed of for most of my life.

I would do whatever it took to keep my mind free of the stuff
that shouldn't be there. Right now, that meant running five miles
before meeting up with the guys for our weekly flag football
game. Five miles to cleanse my brain of the mental images that
had awoken me from a dead sleep at 4:30 a.m. with a pounding
heart and a pulsing dick. Five miles to forget about that straw-
berry blonde with the innocent smile and laugh that hit me right
in the solar plexus.

When I caught sight of Carter in the bar last night, I'd had a
stirring in my gut that I'd only felt once before. That last encounter had left me bitter and broken. I needed another stirring like I
needed a hole in the head. I'd just have to avoid Carter, it couldn't
be that hard. She was one girl, and this was a city of thousands.
Famous last words.

Ripping my shirt over my head, I wiped the sweat that was
pouring down my brow. I came up short, my steps stuttering as

I reached the park's bleachers. Sitting on the second metal rung, long hair pulled through the back of a Georgia Bulldogs' cap, was Carter. The way Liam had described this girl, I had pictured her as a klutzy tomboy, almost masculine-looking.

There was nothing boyish about Carter, she was all long lines and smooth curves. Today, those dips and valleys were on full display as she wore ragged cutoff jean shorts that had my mind wondering if I could pull one of those loose threads and have them disappear altogether. Fuck. I did not need this.

Striding purposely forward, I barked, "What are you doing here?"

Carter jumped a little in her seat, but then she rolled her shoulders back and stiffened her spine. "I'm watching a football game. What are you hoping to do, make small children on the playground cry?"

My teeth ground together, and my hand fisted my t-shirt. "This is a guys-only league."

Carter made a show of glancing around. "Is it a guys-only park? I must have missed the sign."

A snicker came from beside her, and my eyes shot to the same girl Carter had been with last night. I hadn't even noticed her sitting there. Before I could respond, an arm slung over my shoulders, and a familiar voice started, "Ladies, how nice of you to come cheer us on."

Carter's cool eyes suddenly turned warm, and she smiled—fucking beamed—up at Ford. I needed to hit something. Why couldn't this be full-contact football instead of this pussy flag shit? "I'm going to go find Liam," I muttered, extricating myself from under Ford's arm.

He sent me a wicked grin. "Sure thing. Just leave these ladies in my capable hands." Carter and her friend giggled. I scowled and took off towards the parking lot.

The game helped. Physical exertion helped. Imagining

slamming Ford into the dirt helped, even though he was on my team. Seconds before the end of the second half, an opposing player snagged Liam's flag just after he'd let a beautiful pass sail down the field. Before I could turn to the ref to dispute his lack of call, I heard yelling from the bleachers. Carter was on her feet, hands flailing about, full-out screaming at the ref and his lack of vision.

Liam sauntered up next to me. "She's something, huh?" I grunted in response. He continued on, "She gets real fiery about injustice. Anything she thinks is unfair, she'll raise hell. One time, when she was in third grade, there was this bully of a sixth-grader, who picked on every kid younger or smaller than him." A grin was spreading across Liam's face as he got lost in the memory. "Shit, A, she sent him home in tears using words alone. He never picked on another kid again."

I said nothing as we stood there and watched as Carter argued her point with the ref, arms still waving in the air. She almost toppled over at one point, but her friend caught her elbow, steadying her. Finally, the ref threw up his hands and blew his whistle, calling an illegal flag removal and giving us ten yards. I fought back a smile. Shit, the poor guy probably knew we'd never get out of here if he didn't give the woman her way.

We took the field and finished out the last minute with a win. The backslapping and chest bumping commenced. Making our way off the field, I saw Carter bouncing up and down on her Converse-covered feet. She launched herself at Liam, throwing her arms around his neck. "Amazing job! You killed 'em!"

He grinned down at her, and I felt a prickling sensation at the back of my neck. "Thanks for your assist."

"That ref was blind!" she said, scowling in the black-and-white-clad man's direction.

Liam tapped the brim of her hat. "I can always count on you to have my back."

Turning back to face him, her face shone with that devastating smile. "Always." I grabbed my water bottle with more force than necessary, and the plastic crinkled as I slugged down the cool liquid. The noise must have caught Carter's attention because her eyes darted in my direction, and then they began to travel over my bare chest. My eyes narrowed, and I crushed the empty bottle, breaking her stare-off with my nipples.

"Do you and Taylor want to come back to Malibu with us? Austin and Ford are going to come over to hang on the beach and have a few beers," Liam said, tossing a few things into his gym bag.

Carter's eyes bounced between Liam and me and back again. "Uh, I actually need to go get a few things for work. Maybe another day?"

Thank fuck. I needed distance from this girl, and I needed it now.

Liam studied Carter carefully, and she began to squirm under his gaze. Finally, he shrugged, and Carter seemed to relax. "All right. I'll text you later, and we'll figure out a day for you to come out to the house."

"Sounds like a plan." Carter stood on her tiptoes and planted a smacking kiss on Liam's cheek. My stomach churned.

"I want a kiss. Where's my kiss?" Ford reached out his arms to Taylor, who swatted him away with a laugh.

"See you later, boys!" Taylor called.

"Bye," Carter echoed, avoiding my eyes.

I watched her perky little ass until she was halfway to the parking lot when a hand smacked me upside the head. "What the hell is wrong with you, man?" Liam was glaring at me.

"What?"

"I know you've got this whole brooding thing down to a science at this point, but you're being a real dick."

"I'm not being a dick, I'm just not real eager to play

buddy-buddy with your childhood bestie. So, sue me," I said, cracking my neck, trying to alleviate the growing pressure.

"You don't have to be her best friend, but you do need to be cordial. Grow up already. Not every girl is Hailey."

My jaw hardened. "This has nothing to do with Hailey."

Liam slung his bag over his shoulder. "If you really think that, you're more delusional than I thought."

"What's that supposed to mean?"

"It means that Hailey was a manipulative, cheating bitch, but not every single girl has a heart of pure evil. You need to move on."

My back molars ground together. "I have." It was true, I had moved on to dozens of women of all shapes, sizes, colors, and creeds. "I'm just not looking for a girlfriend. I need to focus on training and my fights. I don't have time or energy for more than a quick fuck."

"Whatever you say, man." And with that, Liam turned and took off for the parking lot.

THREE

Carter

THE SUN BEAT DOWN ON MY BACK, AND AS I LISTENED TO the crashing of the waves below, I could feel the stress of the last few days melting away. Rolling over, I grabbed the sunscreen to slather on another layer. I did not need to start the school year as a lobster. "This is a pretty nice setup you've got."

Liam sent me a devilish grin. "Not too bad for a country boy from Georgia, is it?"

I snorted. He made it sound as if he'd grown up without running water and was forced to use an outhouse when, really, Liam's dad was a lawyer and his mom a librarian. But they didn't have Malibu beach houses, that was for sure. Liam's current home sat on a private street that required a security guard lifting a gate for anyone to access it. Every house in the row sat right above the waves, and Liam said that during high tide, the waves actually crashed under the house. It was heaven.

"So, when does school start?" Liam asked after taking a pull on his beer.

"Next Monday."

"You ready?"

"Almost. I just have to decorate my classroom." I twirled the bottle of sunscreen in my hands, twisting and untwisting the cap. "I'm nervous," I admitted.

Liam's face gentled. "You're going to be great. You were born to do this."

"I'm glad you think so." His support really did mean the world to me. "I can't believe we're both doing what we always dreamed of." I let out a small chuckle. "Although your rise to glory is a bit more impressive than mine."

"Don't belittle all you've accomplished. Getting accepted into Teach For Our Youth is no joke."

"All right, brother bear."

Liam's phone buzzed on the side table, causing the remnants of my sparkling water to vibrate. He grabbed it and tapped at the screen while I lay back on my lounge and turned my face towards the sun. I could get used to the Southern California life. "Austin's on his way over." Liam's words were a bucket of ice water on my blissfully warm skin.

"Great," I said, drawing out the word in a super mature manner.

Liam raised himself to a sitting position, swinging his legs over his lounge chair so that he was facing me. "What is it with you two?"

"He's a jerk," I said, setting the sunscreen back on the table with a clang. "I'm sorry. I know he's your friend, but he's rude."

Liam sighed. "I know he didn't give the best first impression, but he did apologize."

"And oh, so convincingly."

Rubbing the back of his neck, Liam trudged on. "Look, he's had a rough go of it. He got burned by his ex pretty bad. Do me a favor and give him another chance?"

I nibbled on the corner of my lip. "Fine," I said. What I really wanted to ask was what Austin's ex could have done that had turned him into such a bitter Betty.

"Thank you. He should be here any minute."

"Super," I replied.

"Love the enthusiasm," Liam shot back.

I stuck out my tongue, I was grown-up like that.

About fifteen minutes later, Austin strode out onto the deck, looking unfairly gorgeous in workout shorts and a worn tee that clung to his broad shoulders and well-defined chest. Crud. His steps faltered when he caught sight of me, and his jaw hardened. Suddenly, my bikini had me feeling very exposed. I quickly stood and wrapped the towel I had been lying on around myself. "I'm going to grab some more water. You need anything, Liam?"

"No, I'm good," he answered as I scurried past.

I let out a quiet "hey" as I passed Austin. He, of course, said nothing, simply glared in my direction as if I had run over his puppy. What a freaking jerk. Sliding open the glass door, I made my way into the kitchen and grabbed a Perrier from the ridiculously fancy fridge.

The large picture window over the kitchen sink looked out onto the deck, and I could see that the guys were in a heated discussion. Liam was standing now, gesturing in an aggravated manner towards the house, while Austin just shook his head. Great. A few tense moments later, Austin said something and turned to head back inside. I had to fight the urge to sink to the kitchen floor or look for a pantry to hide in. Double crud.

I heard the door slide open, and then there he was, filling up every inch of the doorway with his giant, angry, mountain man body. "Hey." The word was low and clipped.

"Hi." Of course, my voice came out in a squeak.

Austin gripped the doorframe, forearms bulging, and I found myself wondering if he could rip the wood out with his bare hands. His hands were very large. "Look," he started, and I tore my eyes away from his hands and moved my gaze towards his face. "I'm sorry I was a dick at the club. I just got the wrong impression because of how you were dressed."

My heart stuttered, and I felt my blood start to boil. "Excuse me?"

"Come on," he said with a smirk. "You were wearing one of those stretchy miniskirts and hooker heels, I was supposed to assume you were Mother Theresa?"

I was moving before I knew what was happening, and then I was poking him in his rock-hard chest. "You are a misogynistic piece of work, you know that? If some guy had groped me, would I have been asking for it?" The smirk he had been wearing fell from his face, and his eyes went stormy. "It's guys like you that give your gender a bad name. But it's clear to me that you're just trying to overcompensate for some serious shortcomings." I eyed his crotch with my last words, and before he had a chance to reply, I sidestepped him and bolted for the front door.

FOUR

Austin

"DUDE, WHAT IN THE ACTUAL FUCK? WHAT DID YOU say to her?" Liam's face was getting redder by the second, but I was just standing there slack-jawed. I hadn't meant the words the way they had come out. I was just trying to explain how I could have mistaken Carter for a groupie. But something about this girl just brought out my inner asshole.

Clearing my throat, I straightened. "I'm sorry. I was just trying to explain why I got the wrong impression of her at the bar. I apologized, she just took it the wrong way."

"She just took it the wrong way? Let me guess, her *taking it the wrong way* had nothing to do with you insulting her in some way."

I grimaced. "Come on, she looked like a groupie! I saw her swiveling her hips over your way, and I jumped to the wrong conclusion."

Liam's eyes bore into mine. "What is going on with you? Is your head really in that much of a fucked-up place? You assume every girl has their cat claws out, using whatever it takes to snag a man and then rake him over the coals?"

"Not every woman. Just most. I'm not saying Carter's that way, but I don't know she's not."

"Carter is one of the kindest and most genuine people I've ever known. Do you know why she moved here?"

I shrugged. "You said she got a job."

"Yeah, a job that pays next to nothing teaching little kids in the ghetto." I swallowed down the guilt that was starting to take root in my stomach. "She's had one boyfriend in her whole damned life, and I'm almost positive she's still a virgin. She might be a little naïve, but she has a good heart. And you have made her feel like dog shit on the bottom of your shoe."

I took a deep breath, rolling my shoulders back to alleviate some of the tension there. "I fucked up. I'm sorry." Apparently, the ghost of Hailey was still alive, well, and wreaking havoc on my life. I knew that when she cheated the way she did and fucked up my life so royally, it had changed the way I looked at women. I didn't want to let someone close enough to cause that kind of damage again, especially when it knocked me off my fighting game for so long. But that was no excuse for being such an ass to an innocent bystander. I was a dick. "I'll fix it."

Liam let out a breath that whistled between his clenched teeth. "You better fix this. And soon." With that, he headed upstairs, leaving me alone with my guilty conscience.

I wiped a palm on my jeans as I balanced three boxes of cupcakes with my other arm. Were three boxes overkill? Probably. But the cupcake place that Liam said was Carter's favorite had like fifty-two different flavors. How was I supposed to know what she liked? I bit the bullet, reached out, and knocked on her door.

She lived in a decent area, but her building's security was shit. I could walk right up to her front door without buzzing at a gate or anything. Not smart for a single girl. I heard muted footsteps, and the door swung open. There stood Carter in some super ugly, fuzzy sock-looking things, short-ass shorts, a slouchy shirt that hung off one shoulder, glasses perched on her nose, and her strawberry-blonde hair piled on the top of her head. I tried not to think about my gaze lingering on those legs that seemingly went on forever.

"You shouldn't open your door without checking to see who it is first," I blurted.

Carter wrapped an arm around her middle, looking past me as though she expected someone else to be behind me. When she didn't find anyone, she straightened and brought her emerald eyes back to mine. "Uh, hi."

"Hi, sorry to be pushy, you should just be careful. LA isn't the safest place in the world."

"Well, thanks. I guess." Her eyes roamed over my face, then she gave a slight shake of her head as though scolding herself. "What are you doing here?"

"I, uh, brought you cupcakes."

She pushed her glasses up her nose and stared at me. "Are they poisoned?"

I let out an uncomfortable chuckle. "I know I've been an asshole to you, but do you really think I'd poison you?"

She shrugged sheepishly. "I don't know, maybe." I turned at the sound of a door opening and saw an older woman peeking her head out of another apartment. Carter waved at the woman, who scowled in return, and then turned back to me. Hesitating for a moment and then taking a deep breath, she started speaking. "Look, why don't you come in." Stepping back, Carter ushered me over the threshold.

A blast of cool air hit me as I took in my surroundings. Carter's apartment was one of those shabby chic deals: white, overstuffed couch with a million throw pillows and a brand new wooden coffee table that was purposely scuffed up. I'd always thought that look was stupid, but it somehow worked for her. I also noticed that there was paper, glue, glitter, scissors, and the like everywhere.

"Sorry about the mess, I'm making decorations for my classroom." She bent down, clearing the craft explosion, and I tried not to stare at her ass. Carter's eyes darted from the paper she was trying to put into piles, to me, to the cupcakes, and back to her piles again. "You can set those down here, I guess," she said, gesturing to the cupcake boxes with an incline of her head. "Do you want one?"

I cleared my throat. "Uh, no thanks. I start training again tomorrow so I can't eat any refined sugar."

Her head snapped in my direction as she lost a few of the papers on her pile. "You can't eat *any* sugar? Like, at all?" She seemed appalled, as if I'd just told her I murdered little, fluffy kittens.

"Not while I'm training."

"That's awful. Why don't I put these in the kitchen so you're not being tortured by the smell?" She took the boxes from my outstretched arms, careful not to touch me in the process. Fumbling just a little, she managed to get them safely to the kitchen counter. "Thanks, by the way. Sprinkles makes my favorite cupcakes. Please, sit down."

I sat back on her girlie, white couch and prayed I didn't get any stains on it. "Yeah, that's what Liam said. He also set me straight on a few things." I cleared my throat and rushed through my next words without meeting Carter's eyes. "Look, I'm really sorry I've been an ass to you. I had the total wrong impression of who you were, but that was my fault, it had nothing to do with you."

Carter walked back over with two bottles of water. Handing me one, she plopped down on the opposite end of the couch and eyed me suspiciously. "And who exactly did you think I was?"

I felt a bead of sweat roll down my back. Cracking the bottle of water, I took a swig, buying time to come up with an answer that was truthful but didn't make me seem like the judgmental asshole I definitely was. "I see a lot of girls come around Liam. Most of them are looking for someone with a big bank account who can buy them designer clothes. Or someone who can make them famous. Or, even better, someone who can do both."

Carter's forehead wrinkled slightly as she studied me. Why did it feel as if she could see into the depths of my soul? I shifted uncomfortably. "I get the feeling that's not the whole story," she said.

I let out a half-laugh, half-cough. "Well..." I started to peel the label off my water bottle. "You also kind of remind me of someone."

A hint of a smile played at Carter's lips. "An ex?"

"Bingo." It burned to admit that I had been such an ass to a girl who might actually be Mother Theresa in a smoking-hot body, just because something about her had reminded me of Hailey. God, I was such a dick.

"She screwed you over?"

I hesitated in answering, my vision stalling on Carter's long-ass legs all twisted around like she was a fucking pretzel. Her skin was creamy white, and I found myself wanting to reach out to see if it was as smooth as it looked. When I pulled my eyes away from her legs and towards her face, a flush was staining her cheeks. I forced myself back to the conversation at hand. "Yeah. She did."

"Geez, don't talk my ear off or anything."

I grinned back at her, but it had a slightly feral edge. "It's not something I enjoy talking about. And, honestly, there's not much to say. She cheated. Repeatedly. I ended it. Now, I avoid that shit."

Lines formed between Carter's brows. "What stuff?"

She wouldn't even say the word *shit*. I fought the laugh that wanted to surface. "I don't date."

Her jaw dropped. "At all? Like the sugar?"

This time, I couldn't hold in my laugh, she looked like someone told her Santa wasn't real. "Just like the sugar. No chicks during training. Well, other than for relieving some tension."

Carter's cheeks flamed. "Um, well, whatever works for you."

I grinned. She was so fucking innocent, I really hoped this city didn't ruin her. "Listen, I really am sorry, and I'd love it if we could start over."

"Start over?" She said it as though she were speaking a foreign language and was unsure of what the words meant.

"Yeah, fresh slate. You're like Liam's sister, and I think it would mean a lot to him if we got along." Carter worried her bottom lip as she silently took my measure. It didn't seem like things were going to go in my favor, so I reached out, awkwardly patting her hand. Damn, her skin was even softer than I had imagined. Her eyes jolted to mine. "Please, give me a chance. I promise I'm not usually this much of an ass."

"Okay." The word came out as a whisper.

"Great." I forced myself to remove my hand from the warmth of her skin. "Why don't you let my first act of goodwill be teaching you some self-defense?"

Carter quirked her head to the side. "Self-defense?"

"Yeah. Liam said you're going to be working in a not-so-great area, so it couldn't hurt." I threw it out there casually, but I was going to make sure this girl could defend herself. The neighborhood her school was in was no joke.

"Ummmmm…" She nibbled on her bottom lip as her eyes traveled over my shoulders and torso. My dick twitched in response. I needed to tamp that bastard down. Carter was not a hit-and-quit type of girl, and that was all I had room for in my life. "I really don't think that's necessary," she continued.

I tilted my head down to make sure she met my eyes. "Please. It's something I can do for you to make up for being such a jerk."

Her shoulders slumped just the tiniest bit. "Okay, fine. But fair warning, I'm not the most coordinated person."

"You don't have to be, most of the moves are super simple."

"Okay." She was still gnawing on the side of her lip, and I had to stop myself from tugging it from between her teeth.

"It'll be awesome, you'll see." I tried to reassure her. "My training is always hellish this first week, so how about a week from Thursday?"

"Yeah, that should work. Classes start on Monday, so it'll have to be after school."

"That's fine, we can meet at my gym." I slipped my phone from my pocket and handed it to Carter, a zap of electricity coursing through my arm at the contact of our fingers. Being in such close physical proximity to this girl was going to mean playing with fire. "Program your number in, and I'll text you the address."

"'Kay. Thanks—for the cupcakes, the apology, and teaching me to kick booty," she said as she tapped the screen of my phone.

"Just never call it teaching you to 'kick booty' again, and you are most welcome."

Carter handed back my phone. "Deal." She blushed again. "And I'm sorry for insulting the size of your manhood, I was really mad."

I let out a choked laugh. "We're all good, Firecracker."

"Firecracker?" she asked, her head tilted to the side in that cute-as-fuck way of hers.

"I think Firecracker is a fitting nickname. You've got some fire in you."

Her lips tipped up. "Firecracker, I like it."

As I walked to my car, I realized that my cheeks hurt from smiling so much, and I couldn't remember the last time that had happened.

FIVE

Carter

THE CAR RADIO CUT OUT AS MY PHONE RANG THROUGH the speakers. I glanced at the screen and tapped accept. "Hi, Liam."

"Hey, how was school today?"

I grinned even though Liam obviously couldn't see me. The first few days of classes had been exhilarating and exhausting, and I had loved every second of it. "It was great, I think I'm starting to get the hang of things. I don't feel like I want to barf before starting a lesson anymore."

Liam chuckled, "Sounds like a win to me. So, what are you up to right now? Want to meet up for an after-work drink?"

I grimaced, glad Liam couldn't see my face. I didn't want him to make a big deal of me getting self-defense lessons from Austin, so I hadn't told him. But there was no way around telling him now. "I'm actually going to the gym to get some self-defense pointers from Austin."

I was met with silence. After about thirty seconds, I heard a throat clearing and then, "Austin? Austin Lyons?"

"One and the same." I turned my car into the parking lot my Prius's navigation system pointed me towards and slid into an empty spot.

"Last time I checked, you guys had a strong dislike vibe going."

I drummed my fingers against the steering wheel. "We did. But he showed up at my house last week with a million cupcakes and an apology for having misjudged me. I'm guessing you talked to him."

"I might have had a word."

"Did that word come with the threat of bodily harm?" I asked.

"Hell no! He's an MMA fighter, I love you like you're my own sister, but I don't have a death wish."

I couldn't help the snort that escaped. "I guess that's fair." Now that Liam knew what was going on, I couldn't resist digging for a little more information on Austin. "So, what's the deal with his ex?"

"He told you about her?" The shock was evident in Liam's voice.

"A little. He said she cheated and that I reminded him of her. That's why he was a jerk to me."

Liam let out a humming noise from the back of his throat. "That girl raked him over the coals, so I get it, but he needs to stop letting someone from his past ruin his present."

I gripped the wheel. Now I had to know. "What happened?"

Liam was quiet for a few moments. "I'm going to share, so you understand where he's coming from."

"Okay." The word came out hesitantly because my conscience was at war with itself. Half of me was dying to know what the story was, and the other half felt like it was a total invasion of privacy.

"Austin comes from a pretty poor community. He didn't have much money, but he scrimped and saved and worked his ass off to get enough money to move him and Hailey out to LA. He kept working his ass off when he got here. Nightshift security gigs so he could train during the day."

"That's admirable."

"It is. Hailey did not get a job. Said she wanted to model, but I never saw any evidence of her actually pursuing that. One night, I was having a party at my place. Austin couldn't come because he was working as usual, but Hailey showed up. I didn't think much of it at first, but then she followed me into my bedroom and proceeded to make a hard pass at me. I kicked her ass out and called A immediately."

I couldn't help the small gasp that escaped my lips. "That witch, you're his closest friend out here."

"I know." Liam's voice sounded defeated, and if I wasn't mistaken, it carried a note of guilt. "After he did a little recon, he found out she'd been sleeping around pretty much the whole time they were together. Austin was working so hard, he didn't see the signs. When he ended things with her, she emptied their joint bank account and stole his emergency cash and anything she thought she could sell from the apartment. She had also applied for a bunch of credit cards in both of their names, which she maxed out and didn't pay off, tanking his credit."

"That's awful." My words came out as a whisper. I felt slightly nauseous at the revelation of how badly Austin had been treated. I had a lot more empathy for his view of women now, that was for sure.

"It threw him for a loop. He dealt with it by turning off his emotions a bit, not letting anyone new in, especially women." My heart softened even further towards the angry mountain man. Between the softening of my heart and the way my body tingled at Austin's proximity, I was going to be a mess during this workout. Liam kept talking. "I'm glad you're hanging out with him. I think you'll do him some good. Shine some of that Carter sunshine on him."

I let out a light laugh. "I don't know, I might accidentally give him a black eye. You know how I am with physical activity that requires coordination."

"Oh, boy."

"On that note, I better get in there."

"All right, I'll talk to you later."

"Later, Liam."

I switched off my car and made my way across the parking lot. The fluttering in my stomach increased the closer I got. I looked up at the faded sign that read *Boxing Gym* in peeling paint. This was the place. Shifting the bag on my shoulder, I pushed open the door. I was so not sure about this particular exercise in new friendship. The smell of stale sweat that greeted me did nothing to help convince me.

Tiptoeing a few steps forward, I took in the rows of punching bags swinging back and forth as sweaty dudes grunted each time they made contact. This was certainly not the swanky West Hollywood gym I had joined a few weeks ago. This was the real deal, and I could not feel more out of place in my teacher get-up of pencil skirt, blouse, and heels.

This was such a bad idea, why had I thought this was a good idea again? Oh, yeah, because of sheepish, adorable Austin with his apologies and cupcakes and broken-heart stories. Ugh, I had no way out of this one.

A wolf-whistle cut through the steady beat of gloves beating heavy bags. "*Mamí*, are you lost? Or have I died and gone to librarian heaven?" A sweaty but handsome guy swaggered towards me, licking his lips and removing his gloves as he walked. As he moved forward, I moved back. Part of me wanted to laugh, but the other part was just a little bit nervous.

"Leave her alone, Carlos, she's here for me." Relief swept through me at the sound of Austin's voice.

"Shit, man, why you gotta crush my dreams like that? I swear she's the future Mrs. Rodriguez!"

Austin grabbed one of Carlos's gloves and smacked him over

the head with it. "Get back to training, Casanova."

"Yeah, yeah. Bye, wifey, I'll miss you!" he called with a massive grin on his face as he headed back to his punching bag, swagger still in full effect.

"Sorry about that, he comes on strong, but he's harmless."

I laughed out a shaky breath. "No problem. Thanks again for offering to do this."

"Happy to. Learning how to defend yourself will give you the confidence to handle situations like that one."

I groaned and shifted from foot to foot. "I'm not really a big fan of violence."

"We'll get you used to necessary force, Firecracker. Do you have clothes to change into?" His eyes raked over my body in what felt like a physical caress. Uh-oh, this was not good. "Because as much as I dig the sexy school teacher look, I don't think it's going to work for what we'll be doing."

I swallowed thickly and squeaked out, "In my bag."

"Come on, I'll show you where you can change."

My eyes darted around, taking in everything I could as we walked through the gym. Beyond the heavy bags was a row of treadmills and mats where men—and one bad-A-looking woman—were jumping rope. Past that was two boxing rings with sparring going on inside. It was actually pretty darn cool, and my nose had already grown somewhat accustomed to the stale sweat smell.

"We don't have many women who train here, so the locker room is just a bathroom with a few lockers, but your stuff will be safe there for the hour we're training," Austin said as he stopped at a door.

"Okay, cool. Thanks again."

He smiled. "You don't have to keep thanking me."

"Right." I reached for the door handle and tripped over my own feet in the process.

Austin let out a low chuckle that hit me in all the wrong places for a platonic almost-friend. "Careful, don't want you getting injured before we even get started."

I gulped and shut the door quickly. Cruddy McCrudderson, this was so not good. I needed to put Austin in the brother-like friend category and stat. Why couldn't I see him like Liam? Or Ford? I mean, I could objectively see that they were handsome, but they were my friends. They didn't make my stomach hollow out as if I hadn't eaten in days, nor did they give me the shakes as if I'd given up coffee cold turkey. I hit myself in the forehead repeatedly while I set my bag down on the bench, hoping that would miraculously knock some sense into me.

I quickly slipped out of my skirt and blouse and into my cropped workout pants, sports bra, and hot pink tank top, while reassuring myself that I could do this. I was simply reacting to a good-looking man. Once I got used to his hotness, these feelings would pass. I grabbed my water bottle, shoved my bag into an empty locker, steeled myself to face Hottie McHotterson again, and pushed open the door.

Austin leaned against the wall opposite the locker room, looking like a *Men's Health* cover model, and I stifled a sigh. This was going to be a long adjustment period. Looking up, I caught Austin's scan of my body and fought a pleasant shudder. "You ready?"

"Yup." I did not sound convincing.

Austin led me down the hall to what looked like a private workout room. "This room is usually used for classes, but it's free Thursday evenings, so we can have some privacy while you're starting out." He walked over to a cabinet in the corner and grabbed a couple of towels, tossing me one.

"Thanks. I'm not the most athletic person, so I'd rather a whole gym of finely tuned machines not see me falling on my butt repeatedly."

Austin grinned. "Why don't we start with you telling me what experience you *do* have."

"Like sports experience?"

"Sure. Sports, working out, yoga, whatever."

I looked down, twisting the ring on my water bottle. "Well, no real sports experience. I mean other than when my parents forced me to play soccer in the fourth grade. Three trips to the ER later—two for me, one for a teammate I took out—and they really regretted that decision. Like I said, I'm not the most coordinated. I belong to a gym, and I make myself go at least twice a week. But mostly for beginner Pilates and the elliptical." I sucked in a breath.

Austin looked as if he were trying really hard not to laugh, he coughed instead. "We'll take it slow, then. Start with light stretching, work into some conditioning, and then maybe work on a few basic drills."

I was unsure about this plan, really freaking unsure. With my luck, I'd end up giving him a concussion or permanently damaging his little swimmers. Shoot, don't think about his swimmers. I could feel my cheeks getting hot. "Sure, sure, that sounds great."

Austin walked me through a couple of easy stretches, and I tried to take some deep breaths to calm my rapidly beating heart. Then he grabbed a mat from the pile in the corner and brought it over. "Lay down."

"What?" I choked.

He smirked. "Lay down on the mat. I have to stretch out your hamstrings, and then we can get started."

"I don't think that's necessary. I feel super limber," I said, backing away from the mat. I did not need this gorgeous man fondling any part of my body.

Austin's smirk turned into a grin. "Carter. I don't want you pulling a muscle or injuring yourself in some other way." He pointed at the mat.

I felt hot, and sweat pooled between my breasts. I hadn't even done anything strenuous yet, this was just embarrassing. "Okay, sure." I laid back on the mat.

Austin knelt by my feet, and I swallowed hard. He gently grabbed my left ankle and slowly lifted it as he worked his way forward until his knees were almost touching my butt. I gulped. "You need to breathe, Firecracker. Just breathe."

I let out a whoosh of air. It was so much easier to ignore these threads of chemistry when Austin was being a big, fat jerk. I needed to get over it and quick. Austin was not for me, he wasn't the boyfriend type, and even if he were, it was too complicated. He was best friends with one of my only friends in LA, that could only end messily.

Austin leaned over me as he pushed me deeper into the stretch. All I could think about was dry humping with my high school boyfriend. This was basically the same thing, except totally different. Different because Austin was all broad shoulders and raw masculinity, and my high school boyfriend was all lanky limbs and nerdiness. Think about something else, Carter, literally *anything* else.

"Are you okay?"

My eyes flew open to find Austin staring down at me. "I'm fine," I squeaked.

"You're doing great, just let me get the other leg."

I sang the alphabet backwards in my head until he was done.

"Okay." Austin jumped up and then reached down to offer me a hand. I winced as I put my surely sweaty palm in his and got up. "Let's start with some jumping rope to get your heart rate up." He handed me a super thin jump rope that looked nothing like the plastic-beaded ones I remembered from elementary school.

I gingerly took the rope from him, like it was a snake that might bite me. "I'll give it my best try, but if I break my neck, just promise me you'll make up a cooler story to tell our friends than…she died tripping over her own feet."

"I promise. Now, stop stalling and start jumping."

After a few false starts and one almost collision with the mirrored wall, I started to get the hang of it. I also realized I was ridiculously out of shape. I knew I wasn't sporty, but I went to the gym, I thought I was in average shape. Not so much. "Holy shitake mushrooms, are you trying to kill me?" I wheezed. "I thought you said you wanted to get along. You could have just poisoned the cupcakes, it would have been quicker. And far less painful."

Austin's muscular chest shook with laughter. "Holy shitake mushrooms?"

Thankfully, my face was so red I was sure the blush that came to my cheeks couldn't be seen. "I, um, make up my own versions of cuss words so I won't accidentally drop an F-bomb in front of my students."

"Your word choice is making a lot more sense now. Come on, you've got one more minute to go. We really need to work on your cardio, maybe get you on a jogging regimen."

I shot him a dirty look and then stuttered and wheezed my way through the rest of jumping rope, a ridiculous amount of ab exercises, and my pathetic attempt at push-ups. I now lay on the floor while Austin again stretched my hamstrings, too tired to be embarrassed by the sexual-like positions. "But when do I learn how to take down a grown man with my pinky?" I asked.

"Patience, young grasshopper. One thing at a time. We have to build up your muscles, but I'll start showing you some things next time."

That brought a big dumb grin to my face. I think I was high from all the activity; my brain wasn't used to this.

"The biggest thing to remember is to trust your instincts. They don't call it women's intuition for nothing. Women have this sixth sense that, if they listen to it, will almost always steer them right. If something is niggling in the back of your brain or a situation doesn't feel right, *always* listen to that." Austin had the most serious look I had ever seen on his face, so I nodded. "Also, scream, act crazy, and no matter what, never let them get you into a car or to a second location. Even if they have a gun or knife."

I bit my lip and nodded again. "I'm not sure I like kick-butt lessons anymore."

Austin pulled me up to standing and tugged on my long ponytail. "Sorry, but the world isn't all sunshine and roses."

I scowled, "I know that. I just don't like being reminded of it."

"I just want you to be prepared and remind you to always listen to your gut."

I pushed at his shoulder. "Okay, okay."

"Come on, let's grab your bag and I'll walk you to your car."

I popped into the locker room and pulled my bag from my locker. I paused at the mirror long enough to be briefly horrified at the face looking back at me, I was as red as a tomato. Oh well, there was nothing I could do about it now, and it wasn't as if I hadn't looked like this for the past hour. *Groan.*

I pushed open the door and found Austin talking to a graying grizzly of a man. "Ready to go?" Austin asked.

The older man turned to me, and his face gentled. "Now, who is this pretty lady, and what is she doing with your ugly mug?"

"Mel, this is my friend, Carter. Carter, this grumpy bastard is my trainer, Mel."

I beamed up at Mel and offered him my hand. "Nice to meet you, Mel. Anyone who puts up with training Austin must have the patience of a saint."

A rumbling laugh erupted from Mel. "Knows you well, huh, Bulldog?"

I looked at Austin. "Bulldog?"

"My fighting name."

"He's like a dog with a bone, and bullheaded...Bulldog," Mel said with a fond smile.

I smiled back. "Makes total sense."

"Well, since you two have now bonded over my stubborn ass, I need to get Carter to her car so she can get home. She'll be back next week."

"I will be?" I asked, surprised.

"Yes, you will be. Every week until I'm convinced you can defend yourself."

"Until I can take down a grown man with my pinky?" I asked with a hopeful smile.

"I'll settle for not tripping over the jump rope."

I threw up my hands. "That was only one time!"

"Uh-huh, sure." He smirked.

I hit him in the stomach with the back of my hand. "Ow! Why do your muscles have to be so hard?"

Austin just shook his head and grinned.

"Well, little lady, it was great to meet you, and I'll be happy to see you around here more often. It's nice to see this fella smiling again." Mel patted my shoulder in a grandfatherly gesture as he walked away.

"I like him."

"You would like anyone who gave me shit."

"This is true," I said, smiling to myself as we headed towards the front doors.

Austin opened my car door when we reached it. "Drive safe, and text me when you get home so I know you made it okay."

"All right, *Mom*." Austin grimaced, and I smiled. "Thanks again for doing this, it's really nice of you."

"No thanks needed."

I tossed my gym bag onto the passenger seat as I climbed behind the wheel. "I'll thank you anyway."

"Whatever you say, Firecracker," he said and gently shut my door.

I was going to murder Austin. Everything hurt. Muscles I didn't even know I had were aching, and I could barely walk. It was more of a waddle. Mentally cursing Austin with all the non-swear curse words I could think of, I shuffled around my desk to face my class.

Michael, the world's most adorable fourth-grader, raised his hand with the kind of enthusiasm I wished I could muster this morning. I know I wasn't supposed to have favorites, but Michael was totally my favorite. He had cemented that status day one of class when he stayed behind at lunch to tell me all of his classmates' life stories, even the new girl's. "Yes, Michael?"

"Why are you walking funny, Miss McCarthy? You fall down or something?" His brow was furrowed, and his eyes were filled with concern. So totally my favorite. The rest of the class giggled.

"Well, can I let you guys in on a secret?"

There were titters and a few "yeahs."

I smiled at all the precious faces. "I'm training to be a superhero."

Michael and the rest of the class laughed at my dorkiness, just what I was going for.

"Okay, maybe not a superhero, but my friend is teaching me self-defense. Kind of like martial arts. Do any of you take karate or anything like that?" Only two kids raised their hands. I shouldn't have been surprised. Families in this area didn't typically have money for extracurriculars, and funding for such programs was seriously lacking. It broke my heart. "Well, I'm learning some martial arts moves so that I can defend myself in case any bad guys come my way, but I have to get my muscles stronger first."

Michael's hand shot up again, and I nodded at him. "Maybe after you learn, you can teach all of us!" He looked so freaking excited that my heart just about burst.

"Maybe, if I get good enough. But that might take a while," I said with a little smile. He looked so dejected. Perhaps I could get Austin to come in and do a demonstration or something. "Okay, away from superheroes and onto something even more exciting…book reports!" The entire class groaned.

The rest of the morning crawled by with my muscles protesting every little move. I eventually had to just stay seated in my chair and point when necessary. Michael stopped by my desk on the way to lunch and said, "Miss McCarthy? I think it's real great that you're learning how to defend yourself."

My heart warmed. This was one of the best parts of being a teacher, getting to know awesome little humans like Michael. "Thanks, Michael, I think so, too."

He hustled out of the classroom, seemingly embarrassed by his comment. I reached for my cell phone and typed out a message to Austin.

Me: *I think you broke me. All of my muscles hurt, and one of my students called me out for walking funny. I kind of hate you.*

I grimaced as I reached under my desk to pull out my lunch and heard my phone buzz.

Austin: *Not the first time I've been accused of making a pretty girl walk funny…*

My jaw dropped.

Me: *Not even sure how to respond to that.*

Austin: *Sorry, you made it too easy. What'd you tell your class?*

Me: *That I was training to be a superhero.*

Austin: *You didn't.*

Me: *I did. And they want me to teach them after I learn. I told them maybe.*

I unwrapped my turkey sandwich, opened my chips, and slugged down some water.

Austin: *You kill me, you are too cute.*

I wasn't sure if any girl wanted to be thought of as *cute* past the fifth grade, but we were friends—forever to be just friends, so it didn't matter. My phone buzzed again.

Austin: *Don't murder me, but we need to get you moving again tonight.*

My sandwich fell from my hand.

Me: *You said next week.*

Austin: *If you don't loosen those muscles up today, you'll feel even worse tomorrow. I'll meet you at your apartment at 6 tonight. We can go for a short run and then I'll stretch you out. You'll be golden by tomorrow, promise.*

I groaned and let my head fall to my desk for a moment.

Me: *The life of a superhero, the work never ends.*

Austin: *See you tonight, superhero.*

Me: *Tonight, torture master.*

I popped four Advil in preparation.

SIX

Austin

THE SUN GLINTED OFF LIAM'S POOL AS I TOOK A PULL OF my water. No beer for me since training was back in full swing. The sound of Carter's laugh had my eyes searching her out. Her head was tipped back, a look of pure delight on her face as she clutched Taylor's arm in reaction to a story Liam was telling them. Her strawberry-blonde hair cascaded down her back in waves, stopping short of her delectable ass in miniscule bikini bottoms. I gripped my bottle of water tighter. This girl would be the death of me.

"Careful, don't want Liam to catch you looking at the girl he thinks of as a baby sister that way," Ford said from the lounger next to me.

I hid my grimace by taking another drink. "I don't know what you're talking about."

Ford chuckled. "Sure, you don't. You two seem to be getting awfully chummy."

"We're friends." It surprised me more than anyone that the statement rang true. Carter and I had been spending more and more time together. Our weekly training sessions were often extended into getting a quick bite to eat afterwards. We ran together two or three times a week. I enjoyed her company. I just needed to remind myself not to ruin it by trying to fuck her.

"Looks like you've got a little drool there from staring at your friend's ass," Ford replied, pointing at the corner of my mouth.

I smacked his hand away. "Like you're one to talk. You're constantly ogling those two."

Ford tipped his head and let his sunglasses slide down his nose as he studied Carter and Taylor with a mischievous grin. "Fair point, well made."

His leer caused a burning in my gut that I didn't want to study too closely, so I got to my feet. "I need another water, you want anything?"

"Naw, I'm good, man," he responded with a devilish smile in my direction.

Such a dick. One of my best friends in this world but still a dick. I slid open the door to the house and went in search of the coldest water I could find. If all else failed and Carter's ass kept tempting me all damn day, I'd have to jump into the freezing-cold Pacific to calm my cock down.

Ice-cold water in hand, I headed back outside and towards the girl who had my body rebelling against my brain. She was gesturing animatedly while recounting some tale from her first month as a teacher. All that smooth, ivory skin on display, I couldn't resist. I reached out my almost-frozen bottle, touching it to Carter's bare back.

She shrieked at a decibel that might have caused my eardrums to rupture and whirled on me. "What in the world?!" Her eyes narrowed on the offending item in my hand. "That was just cruel!"

I chuckled in response. "Come on, it's just a little water."

"I'll show you just a little water!" And with that, she shoved at my chest with all her slender-framed might.

The chilly pool water was a shock to my system, but I came up to the surface with a grin, pulling at my lips. "You little minx!"

Hands on her slightly flared hips, she met my gaze dead-on with a smile of her own. "Come on, Austin, it's just a little water."

"Yeah, yeah. At least help me out, would you?"

Carter reached a hand down to me. No matter how often I tried to drill into her head in our training sessions not to trust everyone she came across, she just couldn't help her innocent and slightly naïve nature. As soon as my hand closed around hers, I gave a firm tug.

Carter's eyes widened as she catapulted into the pool beside me. She came up spluttering and hissing like a drenched kitten. Just as adorable, too. "Austin Lyons, I am going to murder you, and no one is going to find the body because I listen to too many true crime podcasts!"

I couldn't help the rumbling laugh that escaped my throat. "I told you not to trust so easily—" My words were cut off by a wave of water Carter sent splashing into my open mouth. The fit of choking coughs was immediate.

When I regained composure, my eyes narrowed on Carter. Her hands were covering her mouth, but her eyes danced with silent laughter. "I'm so sorry," she said, her words muffled by the fingers still covering her lips.

"You are going to pay for that, Firecracker."

Carter let out a yelp and made a break for the opposite end of the pool, but I was too quick for her. My fingers latched onto her ankle, and I pulled. Grabbing her around the waist, I yanked her back flush against my front. "Now, are you going apologize like a good girl?"

"Never!" Carter couldn't contain her laughter, and each echo sent vibrations through my body, ending at my dick. Before she had a chance to feel my body's reaction to her, I sent her flying through the air toward the opposite end of the pool. I needed to stop touching her. Maybe I just needed to get laid, it had been a couple of weeks. I could hit a bar for a quick fix after I left Liam's tonight. Whatever the solution was, it wasn't the green-eyed goddess emerging from the water at the other end of the pool. I needed to get a grip and fast.

∽

Later in the day, as the sun danced low in the sky, Liam and I kept an eye on the meat grilling while Ford and the girls sat around the firepit sipping cocktails. "I'm really glad you and Carter ironed things out," Liam said as he flipped a steak. "It would've really sucked to have two of my best friends always at each other's throats."

I swallowed thickly at the reminder of what an ass I'd been to Carter. "She's a great girl. I admit it, I was totally wrong about her."

"Can you say that one again? I'm not quite sure I heard you correctly."

I gave a half-hearted jab to Liam's shoulder. "Yeah, yeah. You were right. I was wrong." I had never been more wrong about someone in my life.

"I feel like that should at least earn me a bottle of my favorite whiskey."

"Your favorite whiskey is too rich for my blood, rock star."

"Not for long, man. Those prizes are getting larger and larger. You'll be one of the Ultimate Fighting League's top dogs before you know it."

"I hope so. I really fucking hope so." It was true that I was winning bigger and bigger paydays, but I wanted top billing with the UFL. I wanted to claim the world heavyweight title so badly I could taste it. I was getting closer, paving the road with my sweat and blood. It was worth every drop. I just had to stay focused, and that meant ignoring the delicious temptation sitting twelve feet away.

SEVEN

Carter

MY LUNGS WERE BURNING WITH THE FIRE OF A thousand blazing suns. Almost two months of running, and it hardly felt any easier than the first night Austin had forced my poor, pitifully sore muscles into a jog after our training session. I'm sure one of the reasons the running didn't feel any easier was that Austin had recently decided he needed to add hills into our regime. Hills that felt like Mount Kilimanjaro to my out-of-shape self.

"Stop," I pleaded, placing a hand on Austin's forearm. I was too exhausted to even relish the feel of his taut muscles. "I. Need. A. Minute," I said, gasping for breath between each word.

"All right, let's walk for a bit."

Even walking was difficult at first, but eventually it no longer felt like the air I was breathing into my lungs had barbs attached to it, and my heart rate began to slow. Finally, I was able to take in my surroundings again. Gravel crunched under our feet as we made our way up the graded road.

Turning my head to the side, I could see Austin silhouetted against a sun that was low in the sky. He was breathtaking. Cut jaw, strong neck, broad shoulders leading to muscled pecs, and a tapered waist. Not to mention a butt I'd seen old ladies drool over.

Austin's eyes slid from the path ahead to me. "See something you like, Firecracker?"

I fought the heat that I knew was rising to my cheeks. "Just taking in the view. It's beautiful up here."

He shook his head with a grin. "That it is. So, how were your little hellions today?"

My lips pulled into a smile. "They were awesome. Well, most of them were anyway. We're working on a creative writing project where they write about an adventure they'd like to go on with one of their heroes. Some of the stuff they've come up with is pretty hilarious. I'm going to help them make their own books with covers and everything."

Austin's face was gentle now, with heat in his eyes that had a mirroring warmth growing in my chest. "Those kids are lucky to have you."

I ducked my head at his kind words. "Thanks. They've definitely wormed their way into my heart." They had also taken over my life. Getting up at 5:30 a.m. every weekday meant no more late-night hang sessions at Liam's beach house. But he was busy recording a new album anyway, so I hardly saw him anymore. The person I saw more than anyone was Austin.

"What was it that made you want to become a teacher?"

I hummed as I thought about how to answer. "I was a total nerd growing up. I got made fun of a lot because I liked to follow the rules, and my nose was always in a book. I had this teacher in the second grade, Mrs. Barea, who saw what was happening with the other kids."

A small smile pulled at my lips at the bittersweet memory. "Mrs. Barea intervened when she could, but more importantly, she spent a lot of time with me. Encouraging me. Letting me know that it was okay to be different, it was a blessing to be unique, and that I should never follow the crowd just to avoid kids saying mean things."

I kicked at one of the rocks in the road, feeling just a hint of embarrassment about sharing my dorky past. "I've carried her words with me all these years, and I still make it a point to visit her every time I'm home. I just hope I can make a difference in one child's life the way she did in mine."

Austin threw an arm over my shoulders, pressing the side of my body against his. My stomach did a little flip. "I know you're making that kind of difference in more than one of these kids' lives," he said and then let me go.

Clearing my throat, I asked, "So, what about you? Why fighting?"

The shutters went down over Austin's eyes, and for a moment, I thought he wouldn't answer. "My dad and I watched a lot of boxing when I was growing up. It was just him and me, my mom bailed when I was three. Money was tight, but he worked extra shifts to pay for my youth league fees and gear."

My heart ached at Austin's revelation. Every time we had one of these heart-to-hearts, I got a little more insight into how Austin had become the man he was today. "As I got older, MMA was really taking off, and we got into that. He was at every one of my matches. He would switch shifts, work doubles, whatever it took. He was always there. I owe him everything. I hate that he can't come to fights as easily now, but he loves it back in Michigan."

We crested the top of the hill just as Austin finished speaking and, suddenly, we were looking out over all of Los Angeles. I couldn't stop myself from reaching out to squeeze his hand. "He sounds like an amazing man."

"He is." Austin's voice sounded just a little rougher, a little more ragged.

"Just like his son," I said, squeezing his hand again before letting it drop.

Austin turned his face towards me. "I was an asshole to you when we first met."

Chuckling, I said, "That is true. I used to call you angry mountain man in my head, but you've grown on me."

He barked out a laugh and pulled me into a tight hug. We were sweaty and gross, but I didn't even care. Having his arms around me felt like the dip in a rollercoaster and coming home all at once. I could feel his heart beating against my cheek, and when he spoke, his voice sent vibrations through my whole body. "I'm so glad you gave this angry mountain man a second chance."

I tipped back my head so that my chin rested on his sternum. "You've proved your usefulness. Like when I needed help opening that particularly stubborn jar of pickles, even though I'm pretty sure I loosened it for you."

"Mm-hmm."

"Or when I needed someone really tall to reach that light that was out in my apartment."

"You're basically saying that I could be replaced with a ladder and an increased upper body workout."

"Hmm, now that I think about it…"

Austin released me with a shove. "You little stinker."

I shot him a smirk. "Race you back down?"

He shook his head. "No, because you'll end up tripping over your own feet, and I'll have to take you to the emergency room so they can put two-dozen stitches in your face."

That little jerk. I gaped at him. But, mentally, I was plotting my revenge. "I'm not *that* bad."

Austin snorted. He *snorted*. My revenge was going to be epic, like putting pink hair dye in his shampoo. "Whatever you say, Firecracker. Whatever you say."

❦

"You're walking funny again. Another workout with Mr. Muscles?" Taylor's voice sounded from behind me as I hobbled across the parking lot.

I turned my head towards her. "He made me run hills last night. *Hills.*"

Taylor let out a throaty laugh. "You *must* be in love with him. No man is going to get me to run up a mountain if I'm not head over heels."

My steps faltered, and my stomach dipped. I wasn't in love with Austin. Sure, I was attracted to him, but we were friends. Falling in love with Austin would be a recipe for disaster. I forced myself to find a normal walking rhythm again. "Nope. Just a sucker of a friend, apparently," I said with forced levity.

"Whatever you say, girlie."

"Hey, ladies!" Taylor and I turned to see Kyle Davis jogging towards us. Kyle was a fellow teacher with a few more years on the job than Taylor and me. He was handsome in that conventional, country-club kind of way. He was also incredibly kind and just a bit nerdy. I wished he made my stomach flutter a fraction of the amount Austin did, but he just didn't.

"What are you two up to?" he asked.

"Just talking about Carter's newfound love of running," Taylor answered with a light laugh.

Kyle's face brightened. "You like to run? I go jogging every morning before school if you ever want to join me."

I groaned. "I actually hate it. I only go because my friend, Austin, is trying to get me into shape. It's not working."

He chuckled. "It'll get easier, I promise."

"I don't have high expectations. I'd just like to get through a mile without sounding like I've been smoking a pack a day since I was five."

"It's good to have goals," Taylor retorted.

"That it is. Now, someone find me some Motrin so I can make it through this day."

The only answer to my request was Taylor's howling laughter and Kyle's deep chuckle.

EIGHT

Austin

SWEAT POURED INTO MY EYES AS MY FISTS HIT THE MITTS with a precision that created the perfect *pop, pop, pop* sound that fighters longed to hear.

"That's it. Crisper. Give me a little more heat on that hook. Perfect," Mel said as he put me through my paces. A buzzer sounded. "That's time. Take a break."

I pulled the gloves from my hands, chest heaving. "You're going to kill me one of these days."

Mel sent me a slightly feral grin. "Just making sure you're ready to take Cobra down in a few weeks."

"Yeah, yeah." I gave Mel a hard time, but I was grateful to have a coach who knew exactly how hard to push. My fight against Cobra was my first big UFL fight. The prize money was great, and if I won, it was my ticket to the top international heavyweight bracket. There was no question, I had to win.

Mel leaned against the ropes of the ring we were working in today. "You eating right? Getting enough sleep? Staying focused?"

"Yes, old man. No pussy and no pizza."

Mel chuckled. "Really? Something tells me that might not be entirely true."

I turned to follow his gaze. Standing in the entryway to the gym was Carter. She wore a pale pink sundress that brought out the red undertones of her strawberry-blonde hair and made her ivory skin glow. I felt like I had taken an uppercut to the gut.

"I picked you up some boring lunch at that health food place you love," she called over the din of gloved fists hitting punching bags.

I couldn't help the grin that came to my face. "I hope you didn't force any vegetables onto your own plate."

She beamed back. "Never. I stopped at In-N-Out for Mel and me."

Mel swung down from the ring at the uttered "In-N-Out." "I told you, you're my favorite. Didn't I?"

Carter reached up on her tiptoes and kissed Mel's stubbled cheek. "Yes, you did. How are you?"

"I'm just fine, girl. Busy, but fine."

"Glad to hear it."

"I'm going to take my lunch into the office and catch up on some paperwork, but you two use the break room or sit up on the roof."

Carter handed Mel his bag of food as I dipped under the ropes. "Thanks for bringing me lunch, Firecracker." I bent to kiss her cheek, fighting a smile when I saw the color pinking them. I fucking loved making Carter blush.

"Anytime, Bulldog. Where do you want to eat?"

"Let's go up onto the roof. I could use some fresh air."

"Sounds good."

I grabbed my water bottle and led her toward the elevator. "What are you doing downtown anyway?"

Her long eyelashes fluttered as she looked up at me. Doe eyes, that's what she had. These innocent-as-fuck doe eyes that could convince me to do almost anything. "I had to run by the school to pick up some papers I forgot and thought I might as well pay my favorite fighter a visit on my way home."

"Well, I'm glad you did. You have perfect timing, I'm starving." The elevator doors slid open to the rooftop. It wasn't finished or anything, but the guys had drug some old outdoor furniture, a table, and some chairs up here so we had a place to take a break when we needed it.

"Wow, that's an awesome view," Carter said as she gazed towards the Hollywood Hills. "I keep meaning to go to the Griffith Observatory, but I never seem to have the time."

"It's pretty dope."

"You've been there?" she asked, sunlight catching the shine of her hair.

"Yeah, not long after I first moved here. The views are killer."

"I'm sure."

"Here, grab a seat." I pulled two rickety chairs up to the worn table while Carter unpacked my chicken salad and protein shake and her cheeseburger, fries, and milkshake. I would have killed for that burger.

"What? Your health food not looking so appetizing compared to my feast of culinary delights?" Carter said with a smirk.

"It's cruel of you to tempt me this way, you know?"

"You might be one of my favorite people, but I still wouldn't make myself eat kale for you. Sorry."

I squeezed her side. She squeaked. "I would never want you to torture yourself with kale on my behalf."

"Thank you. You are a true friend." She dipped a French fry into her milkshake like the weirdo she was and popped it into her mouth. "So, how's training going?"

"Good. My boxing game is strong, and my grappling is getting better with this new coach Mel brought in."

"That's great. Does that mean I might actually get to attend this fight?"

I hadn't let Carter come to any of my bouts so far, no matter how much she begged. Fights were not exactly the safest environments, and I couldn't risk getting distracted by worrying about her when I needed my head in the game. "Carter, we've talked about this."

"I know, I know. But I really want to go to this one. It's such a big deal. I want to cheer you on." She fluttered those big doe eyes at me, and my resolve weakened.

"I'll think about it."

Carter bounced up and down in her chair like a little kid, and I couldn't hold in my chuckle. "Promise?"

"I promise."

"Yes!" She shot her fist into the air. "What do people wear to fights?"

"I said I'd think about it, that doesn't mean you should start planning your outfit." My mind drifted to an image of Carter wearing a low-cut minidress that fight groupies favored. I bit back a groan.

"I just want to make sure I'm prepared in case you decide I can go."

A smile touched my lips. "You wear whatever you feel comfortable in." I paused. "But don't let Taylor dress you." The last thing I needed was Carter starting a riot by being too damn gorgeous for her own good dressed in some skimpy outfit Taylor put her in.

Carter's brows pulled together. "Why not?"

I searched my mind for a plausible excuse. "She, uh, just doesn't have as good of taste as you. Let's not worry about it just yet, I'm still not sure it's a good idea."

Carter pulled a full-on pout. "Oh, all right."

This girl was cute as fuck.

NINE

Carter

I UNLEASHED A VERY UNLADYLIKE GRUNT AS I PULLED MY bag from the backseat of my car. Christmas break could not get here soon enough. The life of a first-year teacher was no joke. I was so overwhelmed with lesson plans, grading assignments, and preparing my students for standardized testing, it felt like I barely had time to breathe. Thankfully, I had developed a routine that managed to keep my head above water and me at least semi-sane.

LA was finally starting to feel like home. I loved the kids in my class and working at the same school as Taylor was a blast. We didn't have a ton of time to socialize, but she and Kyle always helped me when I got stuck planning lessons and made the teachers' lounge a more amusing place.

I walked up the steps to my apartment and unlocked the door. Music was on, so Lexi must be home. We were mostly ships passing in the night since she was out till all hours at glamourous Hollywood events, and I had to be up at 5:30 every morning, but our roommate setup worked for the most part. "Hey, Lex, I'm home."

Lexi popped out of her bedroom, all boobs, Victoria Secret angel hair, and the most put-together outfit. She was a knockout.

"Thank God! I need your opinion on shoes!" She held up two pairs of stilettos. I pointed to the pair in her left hand. "So," she asked distractedly as she slipped on the black Louboutin's, "how was school stuff?"

I dropped my bag on one of the bar stools and sighed. "It was good, but I'm exhausted. How was work for you?"

She felt around for a hole in her ear and slid a diamond hoop through it. "Oh, great, but just getting started. I have an event at the Roosevelt tonight. Whatever boring plans you have, you should cancel them and come out!"

I leaned back into the cool granite counter; it felt great against my aching back. "No going out for me tonight. I'm going to jump in the shower and then make dinner. Austin's coming over, and we're going to listen to our latest true crime podcast obsession."

Lexi's mouth pulled tight. "You two are like a nerdy, old married couple. You might as well be watching Jeopardy while you eat dinner on your TV trays." She flicked her hair over her shoulder and turned back to her room.

"I'm cool with my nerd status, Lex," I called, heading for my own room. I peeled off my binding work clothes and stepped into the steaming shower. It was heaven and just the pick-me-up I needed.

Towel-drying my hair, I wove it into a braid down my back and took out my contacts, opting for my glasses instead. I searched out my comfiest yoga pants, fuzzy socks, and worn tee, long-ago having given up on trying to look put-together every time Austin came over. We just saw each other too much, and I was lazy.

Slipping my feet into my cozy slippers, I headed into the kitchen to prep dinner. I wasn't the best cook in the world, but I had a rotation of a dozen or so meals I could do well. Luckily, Austin was into boring food for training mode, so it was poached chicken, veggies, and sweet potatoes with no fun stuff like butter for him, and veggies and mac and cheese with all the fun stuff for me.

I was just finishing up when I heard my front door open. "A, is that you?"

Austin's dark head, still damp from a shower, rounded the corner. He wore joggers that hung perfectly from his hips, and his worn, gray t-shirt clung to his sculpted chest. Yup, still not accustomed to his hotness. "Who else would it be?" He rounded the kitchen bar and pulled me into his arms. I lived for these moments of closeness, and as I wrapped my arms around his waist, I felt the stress of the day melt away. "Tough day?" he asked.

I tilted my head back but kept my arms around his waist. My chin rested between his pecs, and he looked down at me. "I'm just worn out and ready for Christmas break. I've been going non-stop to fit in everything I need to by the end of the year."

Austin leaned down just a bit farther and kissed my forehead. "You're almost there. One and a half weeks, and you're home free."

I reluctantly let go of his waist, feeling his warmth fade. "You're right, the end is within sight. Dinner's pretty much done if you're ready to eat."

"Yeah, I'm starved. Thanks for cooking for me, babe."

Babe. Babe was a newer endearment, and I had mixed feelings about it. On one hand, it made me shiver and tingle in parts of my body that definitely did not say "friendship." On the other hand, it made me mad, as he clearly had no intention of taking our relationship to a romantic place, so "babe" just reminded me of everything that would never be mine.

I shook myself out of those negative thoughts and reminded myself that I loved Austin. He was a great friend, and I was beyond grateful to have him in my life, even if it wasn't in every way I wished it could be.

"Earth to Carter...hello..."

I swung around to face the source of my space out. "What? Sorry."

Austin chuckled. "You must be exhausted. I asked you what you wanted to drink like three times."

I forced a smile. "Yeah, super tired. Sorry. I'll take a diet root beer, thanks."

He gave my shoulder a squeeze as he grabbed drinks and put them on the table. "You still up for another podcast episode?"

A genuine smile came to my lips this time. "Do you even have to ask? I have to know if my predictions are right."

"You always think it's the boyfriend or husband."

"In over 75% of murders, the victim knows the murderer, and it's usually the spouse!" Luckily, Austin shared my morbid fascination with true crime TV shows and podcasts.

"You are such a weirdo. You're lucky I like you."

"Oh, yes, oh so blessed am I." I tucked my hands under my chin and fluttered my eyelashes at him. Austin just laughed and pinched my side, sending pleasant shivers up my spine.

Just then, I heard a door open, and Lexi sauntered out looking like sex on a stick. I couldn't help but compare my long and lean body to her curvaceous one. My shoulders drooped involuntarily. "Hey there, Austin, keeping our little Carter company tonight?" She grinned wickedly at him.

"More like she's taking care of me." He lifted his plate off the bar and set it on the table in the dining nook. "Fueling me up for my fight next weekend."

Lexi played with the long necklace that hung between her breasts. "Well, if you want to blow off some steam after you fuel up, I'm running an event at the Roosevelt tonight. Carter said she's too tired, but you're welcome to come by."

Her words were a paper cut to my heart. Not a life-threatening injury by any means, but it still hurt like a *B*. I had to remind myself that Lexi was naturally a flirt, and Austin was free to do whatever he wanted. I just didn't want to witness it. I turned away and busied myself gathering up salt, pepper, and napkins.

Austin cleared his throat. "Thanks, Lexi, but I think I'm gonna hang here with Carter."

Lexi crossed to him and patted his chest. "You're such a good *friend* to her, Austin."

Austin stepped out of her reach, taking a seat at the table. "Well, she's a good friend to me."

An awkward silence filled the room as Lexi plucked up her keys and clutch purse and headed towards the door. "I'm off, kids. Try not to have too much fun without me." The door slammed in her wake, and I headed to the table with my food.

"Your roommate is certainly forward," Austin said with a grimace.

Silently, I breathed out a sigh of relief. Visions of waking up to a shirtless Austin leaving Lexi's room had been dancing in my head. "She's harmless. She's just naturally a flirt."

"But it's rude of her to try and get me to go to a party when she knows I have plans to hang out with you."

He had a point there, but I shrugged. I didn't want to admit just how disappointed I would have been if he had taken Lexi up on the offer.

Austin took a drink of water, and I watched his throat work. How could someone make drinking water look sexy? "Just watch yourself around her. I wouldn't trust her as far as I could throw her."

I snorted. Austin could probably throw Lexi pretty dang far. "Let's talk about something else. How was training today? You feel ready for Saturday?"

Austin reclined back in his chair, his serious business look in full effect. "I'm as ready as I can possibly be, and I'm confident I'll come out with the win."

"Without getting hurt, right?" I asked, nibbling on the corner of my lip.

Austin leaned across the table and pulled my lip from between my teeth. "Don't do any damage to that pretty mouth because you're worried about me. I'll be fine. Promise."

My heart stuttered a beat at the contact, and I swallowed hard. "If you're so confident about the match, can I finally come to this one?" I widened my eyes and gave him my very best puppy-dog face.

Austin just laughed and rose from his chair to grab something from his gym bag. "Well, it just so happens that I have a fight pass right here…"

I jumped up and rushed over to him. "For me?"

Austin dropped the laminated pass into my palm and then trapped my hand. "For you. On one condition. Liam and Ford are going with you, and you have to promise to stay with one of them at *all times*. No wandering off by yourself. Deal?"

I nodded enthusiastically. "Deal! Unless I have to pee, of course. They can't follow me into the bathroom, that'd just be weird."

Austin's brows drew together as if he hadn't considered that possibility. "Well, they walk you to the bathroom and wait outside."

I let out an exasperated sigh. He was so freaking overprotective, even after I had graduated from the Austin school of self-defense.

He tugged on my trapped hand. "I mean it, Firecracker. Promise me."

At the look of genuine worry in his eyes, I decided to take pity on him. "I promise, Bulldog. Liam or Ford will be stuck to me like glue from beginning to end." I pulled my hand and the pass from between his and threw my arms around his neck. "Thank you," I whispered into his ear.

His muscles slowly relaxed, and he hugged me back. "You're

welcome. Now, let's clean up so we can listen to this next episode."

We worked together with synchronized ease, clearing the table, washing the dishes, and wiping down the counters. I settled on the couch, pulling my fluffy blanket around me as Austin set up his phone and Bluetooth speaker. He sat back on the couch, phone in hand. "Here, come get cozy." He lifted his arm up for me to cuddle underneath.

This is where things got really blurry for me. I could say "no, I'm fine over here," but I never did. It felt too good to burrow into Austin's side, to feel his warmth and strength seep into me. I relished these moments where I could pretend that he was mine, and I was his. I held onto them as long as possible, even if it was always painful when reality struck, and he went home. But for now, I just thought about how good the weight of his arm felt around me. I didn't even make it halfway through the episode before I slowly drifted off to sleep.

I woke to the feeling of being lifted. "Wha?" I slurred a half word.

"Shhhhh. You fell asleep. I'm taking you to bed."

"Mmkay." I smacked my lips and curled deeper into Austin's arms. They felt so good and strong, and I felt so safe and warm.

Austin gently laid me on my bed and pulled down the covers beneath me, tucking me in with such care, it would have broken my heart if I were fully conscious. He carefully removed my glasses, setting them on my nightstand, then leaned down and pressed a soft kiss to my forehead. "Goodnight, Carter. Sweet dreams."

TEN

Carter

THE ENERGY IN THE ARENA WAS ELECTRIC, AND I WANTED to soak in every drop. This was nothing like the gym Austin trained at. Just an hour outside of LA, this place was massive and all sorts of fancy. They had obviously cleared out all the equipment and replaced it with rows of chairs and risers surrounding the octagon. Looking at the chain-link walls that made up each of the eight sides of the fighting ring, I suddenly felt as if I had swallowed a boulder.

Liam, decked out in a low-slung hat and sunglasses in an attempt to conceal his famous profile was out in front of me. He weaved his way through the crowd, a bodyguard at his side, but kept a firm grip on my hand. Ford followed closely behind. As we made it to the first few rows of padded folding chairs, a bulky and very intimidating security guard stopped Liam. We flashed our passes. He let us through and pointed us towards our seats. In the very first row.

I twisted my fingers into complicated knots as I sat down between Liam and Ford. "Right in the middle of the action, huh?" Even I could hear the nerves in my voice.

Liam and Ford eyed each other over my head, and Liam leaned over and patted my knee. "You going to be okay watching this? We can leave if you're having second thoughts. Austin will totally understand."

That steeled my resolve. I wanted to be here to support Austin, and I wasn't going to be a baby about it. "No, I'm fine, I'm just nervous for him. I don't want him getting hurt."

Ford snickered. "He's gonna get hurt, that's the name of the game. But don't worry, Bulldog's a beast. No one's gonna take him down."

I ignored Ford's less-than-helpful reassurances and pulled out my phone to text Taylor.

Me: *Just got to the fight now. I'm so nervous my stomach hurts.*

My knee bounced up and down of its own accord as my eyes took in every detail of the chain-link fence and the floor it surrounded. The vibration in my palm brought my gaze back to my phone.

Taylor: *You're worried about Mr. Muscles? Puh-lease, you should be worried about his opponent's blood getting on your outfit.*

I snorted.

Me: *Thank you, that was just what I needed.*

Taylor: *No problem, girlie. Have fun and call me later!*

Me: *You got it! <3*

I slid my phone back into my purse and smoothed my palms over my skinny jeans just as the lights flickered, and music started to play. Across the cage, the meanest-looking guy I had ever seen lumbered toward the ring.

I grabbed both Liam's and Ford's arms in a death grip as I frantically looked back and forth between the two of them. "That's not who Austin's fighting, right? There's no way they're in the same weight class. He's huge!"

Liam's jaw clenched. "Well, A's in the heavyweight division now, but he's at the light end of the class, so he's going to have to fight dudes a lot bigger than him. But he's got speed that they don't."

My stomach sank again. This was not good. Another song began to play, and the crowd turned behind me. I saw a figure with the hood of his silk robe up, making his way down the aisle. As Austin got closer, I swear I could feel the intense energy rolling off him in waves.

I had witnessed how seriously he took his training: the hours he put in at the gym, watching any tape he could get his hands on of his opponents' fights, how he monitored every morsel of food he put into his body. But I had never seen him like this. He was laser-focused as if he were balancing on the edge of the sharpest knife's blade. It scared me, and it was hot as hell all at the same time.

He shrugged off his robe and dropped the loose shorts he had on to reveal the shortest and tightest shorts I had ever seen on a man in real life. Dear God, I needed to look away, but I couldn't quite make myself. There was no hiding that bulge now. My face heated, and I tore my gaze back up to Austin's face. A referee was patting down his face, shoulders, chest and then examining Austin's gloves. When the ref was done, Austin made his way to the cage and climbed in.

I couldn't take my eyes off him. I felt like if my gaze was on him, no one would dare hurt him. "I think I'm going to throw up."

Ford elbowed me in the side. "Probably wouldn't be the first time someone's tossed their cookies watching a fight. Just do me a favor and point your upchuck towards Liam instead of me, okay?"

Without taking my eyes off Austin, I reached over and pinched Ford's side. "Just for that, I'm aiming right at you."

The ref ushered the fighters into the center of the ring, and his voice came over the loudspeaker, "I want a good, clean fight. Touch gloves if you want to, and then back to your corners."

Austin stayed silent but extended his gloves. His serial

killer-looking opponent kept his gloves lowered but spat something at Austin I couldn't hear. My nails dug into my palms as my fists clenched. "I really do not like that guy."

Liam squeezed my shoulder. "It's mostly show. These guys all have to play to the character they're known as."

The little relief I felt with Liam's words was soon erased by the sound of the bell. The fighters circled one another, putting out brief, testing jabs. Then, Meanie erupted with a vicious kick to Austin's side, and I gasped. Suddenly, it was like another person had invaded my body, I was screaming and cursing at Meanie. "Oh, no you don't, you little weaselly fucker." And screaming and cursing at Austin, "Come on, Bulldog, get your shit together! Take him down!"

It was all kind of a blur. I think I might have had a seizure. Four minutes into the first round, right after I had screamed at Austin to "knock him the fuck out," he did just that with a beautiful uppercut to the jaw. Meanie went down like a ton of bricks, and I lost my mind. I started jumping up and down, threw myself at Liam and then at Ford, probably hugged some strangers, too. Who knows.

EMTs rushed to help the dazed fighter to his feet, and Mel rubbed a clear ointment over a cut on Austin's brow. Once the medics looked Meanie over, both fighters were once again ushered into the center of the cage. The ref grabbed each of their hands and raised Austin's over his head. The crowd drowned out anything the ref had said.

As Austin's hand reached the sky, our eyes met. My screams silenced, and I just beamed at him. He had worked so hard for this, truly paying for it with his own blood, sweat, and tears. I knew that with winning this fight, he would get the attention of the big suits at the UFL, and his dream of fighting at the top of the international stage would be just around the corner. I was so freaking proud of him.

I felt a nudge at my side and looked over at Liam. "Come on, let's go backstage before things get too crazy out here. We can grab a drink while we wait for Austin to shower and talk to Mel."

"Sounds good to me." My cheeks were hurting from smiling so hard, and my voice was raw, but I couldn't have been happier.

ELEVEN

Austin

As Mel stretched tape across my brutalized ribs, my teeth clanged together, and my jaw clenched. The pain was no joke, but I was used to it by now. "Are you sure you don't need an x-ray, boy?"

I tried to relax my jaw. "I'm sure, old man. They're just bruised."

"Watch who you're calling *old*. I could still whoop your ass."

I chuckled under my breath and then winced as the action jarred my ribcage. "I know you could, Mel."

Just as Mel fixed the final piece of tape to my ribs, the locker room door swung open, and Liam entered. "Congrats, man, that was epic! First round KO! You know the UFL is paying attention now."

I slapped his hand in a man-shake. "Thanks, man. Where's Carter?"

"She's waiting outside with Ford. I wanted to make sure you were decent. Don't need her innocent eyes being scarred for life after seeing your naked ass. I'll go grab them."

I grunted and shook my head. "Wait, was that her cursing up a storm during my fight? I normally can't hear a thing when I'm in the zone, but I swear I heard her voice telling me to 'just knock him the fuck out already.'"

Liam had to brace himself on the lockers, he was laughing so hard. I think there were tears in his eyes. "Yes, it was her. Apparently, Carter turns into a hellcat when you're fighting."

I gingerly pulled on my t-shirt. "I've never heard her curse before."

Liam wiped at the corner of his eyes. "I know, man. I've never seen her do anything like that in all the twenty-two years I've known her. I honestly thought she'd want to leave after she saw you get hit the first time, but that just unleashed the beast."

I bit the side of my cheek to spare my ribs from laughter. "That girl is something else."

Liam turned around to pull the locker room door open. "That she is. Just be careful with her, okay?" he said over his shoulder.

My brow furrowed, but before I could respond, Carter burst through the cracked door. "Oh my gosh, you were amazing! Congratulations!" She threw her arms around my neck, and I cringed when her body made contact with my ribs. She froze and immediately pulled back. "Are you okay? What's wrong? Are you hurt?" Her brows were so tightly knit, they looked painful.

I reached out and rubbed the space between her eyes with my thumb. "Calm down, Firecracker. I'm fine, just some tender ribs."

She knocked my hand away from her face, lifted my shirt, and gasped. "Austin, that looks awful. I think we need to take you to the hospital."

I pulled her hand away and let my shirt fall back down, "It's fine, Carter, I promise. They're just bruised. I know how broken ribs feel, and these aren't that bad."

She scowled, and it was so fucking cute I wanted to squeeze her. "That doesn't make me feel any better."

I pulled her to my side, fighting to ignore the bite of pain, and put my arm around her shoulders. "Come on, what I really want to do is go eat a shit ton of In-N-Out."

Carter's face brightened, and then she looked dubious. "You? Mr. No Flavor Chicken-n-Veggies wants to go to In-N-Out, kingdom of all things fatty and delicious?"

I ruffled her hair. "Yes, smartass. This is my cheat meal, so let's do it up big."

She clapped her hands together. "Yes! Finally, a real meal! Come on, boys, we have cheeseburgers calling our names!"

Ford rubbed his stomach. "You don't have to tell me twice. Let's get out of here. Are you done with everything, A?"

"Yeah, just gotta grab my bag and I'm good to go."

Quicker than I could blink, Carter had slipped from beneath my arm to grab my gym bag off the bench. "I'll carry it."

I blinked at her. "You are not carrying my gym bag, Carter. Give it here."

She pulled her bottom lip between her teeth and silently shook her head back and forth.

Liam stepped between us. "In an effort to leave here before we all die of starvation, why don't *I* carry the bag?"

Carter reluctantly handed the bag to Liam. "Fine."

I clapped Liam on the back. "Works for me. I love having you as a butler."

He smirked. "Okay, let's go."

We exited the locker room to a hallway full of people milling about. I grabbed Carter and tucked her under my arm, keeping her out of reach of any of these hooligans. Halfway down the hall, a gangbanger-looking dude stepped in front of me, and I immediately recognized him as one of my opponent, Cobra's, crew. "Got yourself one hell of a cheerleader there, Bulldog." I felt Carter stiffen at my side as he continued. "Better hold on tight. Wouldn't want her to leave you for a real man." He grabbed his crotch and flicked his tongue as his eyes roamed Carter's body.

I shoved Carter behind me and had gangbanger dude up against the wall in half a second. "What did you just say?"

"You heard me, *cabrón!*" he wheezed.

I heard shuffling behind me, and Carter saying, "Austin, stop, he's not worth it."

I felt someone grab my arms, and Liam entered my field of vision. "She's right, A, he's not worth your shot with the UFL."

That brought me back to my senses, but I squeezed the guy's throat just a little harder and leaned down to his ear. "You don't talk about her. You don't look at her. You don't even *think* about her. Or I will find you, and I will gut you." I released my hold, and he fell to the ground, coughing. I still felt rage pumping through my veins.

This was why I didn't want Carter coming to my fights. I knew something like this would happen. She was too innocent, too pure, and it radiated off her for everyone to see. She was an easy mark, and an important one if people knew how much she meant to me. I couldn't have distractions like this in my life; couldn't let someone mean this much to me. I needed space.

I spun around, about to tell Carter exactly that when I saw that Ford had been holding her back, and tears filled her eyes. Shit. The rage disappeared as if I'd been dunked in an ice bath, and the last thing I wanted was space. "Come here." I held out my hand, and she rushed to me, shoving her face between my pecs. The adrenaline coursing through my system had numbed any pain. I lifted her chin with two fingers and smiled down into her watery eyes. "Can't take you anywhere, you're too pretty for your own good."

She let out some sound, half-snort, half-laugh, and burrowed back into my chest. "Can we go get In-N-Out now? I'm hungry."

The words were muffled by my shirt, but I smiled. "You got it." I eyed the guy on the ground, still rubbing his throat, and motioned to Liam and Ford to head out.

TWELVE

Carter

TAKING IN THE FAMILIAR SMELL OF CHALK AND PENCIL shavings, I slowly made my way through the maze of desks in my classroom, returning freshly graded assignments to each student's spot. Christmas break had been exactly what I needed. A little R&R and home-cooked meals by my mama had done wonders for my energy levels, but I had missed LA. Even though I had talked to Austin almost every day I was gone, I found myself missing him most of all. I knew my feelings had left friendship in the dust months ago, but I just wasn't sure what to do about it.

My hands stilled as they reached Michael's paper in the stack. He was another person I didn't know what to do with. Something was wrong in Michael's world. He wasn't his cheerful, inquisitive, slightly trouble-making self. He was sullen and withdrawn, and his schoolwork had started to suffer. I needed to find a way to connect with him and see what was going on. I placed the last of the papers on their corresponding desks just as the school bell rang, and children started rushing through my door.

I made it through the first half of the day with no major incidents, but Michael still seemed removed, so I stopped him as he headed to lunch. "Michael, can you stay for a minute?"

His shoulders stiffened as he slowly turned around. "Sure, Miss McCarthy. Am I in trouble?"

My heart broke at the look on his face. "No, of course not. I just wanted to chat with you for a minute. Why don't you take a seat?" I motioned for him to sit in the chair next to mine. He dropped into the chair, folding in on himself as he sat silently. "How are you doing?"

"I'm fine, Miss McCarthy," he answered robotically, his eyes cast down at his hands where he picked at his nails.

"You know you can talk to me about anything, big or small. I know it's not always cool to confide in your teacher, but I promise that I will do my best to understand where you're coming from."

His throat bobbed as he swallowed. "Yeah, I know."

I smoothed my hands over my skirt and leaned down so I could meet Michael's eyes. "I'm just worried because you haven't quite seemed like yourself the past few weeks."

"I'm fine, Miss McCarthy, just tired." As he spoke, he lifted his thumb to his mouth to chew on his nail, and his shirt sleeve rode up.

I sucked in a breath as I saw a ring of bruises circling his small wrist. I instantly felt nauseous and out of my depth. I had been trained in how to recognize the signs of abuse, but faced with the very real possibility that the sweet child in front of me had been harmed, I was frozen.

Michael must have seen the look on my face because he followed my line of vision to his wrist and quickly dropped his hand. He let out a forced-sounding laugh. "You're worried about this? I tripped, and my dad caught me before I could hit the ground. But I guess I was going fast because I got this bruise."

I wasn't convinced, but I also knew that this was a plausible excuse any social worker would have to accept on a first offense. I swallowed the lump in my throat and pushed on. "Okay,

Michael. Just don't forget that if there *is* something going on at home or at school, you can always come to me."

Michael rose quickly and headed to the door, clearly eager to end this conversation. "Yeah. Thanks, Miss McCarthy."

After I had watched Michael leave, I buried my head in my hands, fighting the burning desire to cry.

"Carter, are you all right?"

I lifted my head and saw Kyle standing in my doorway. I ushered him in, and he closed the door behind him. "Not really. I could actually use your advice."

Kyle sat down in the same chair that Michael had just vacated. "Of course, tell me what's going on."

I walked Kyle through everything I had noticed about Michael, including our most recent conversation and his bruised wrist, then sat back in my seat.

Kyle rubbed a hand over his jaw. "This is a tough one, Carter. Is this the first time you've seen any physical evidence of abuse?"

I felt sick. "Yes, but he's been withdrawn for weeks now. Even before Christmas break. But I just thought he was tired from the end-of-the-year craziness. Shouldn't I report it, just to be safe?"

Kyle grimaced. "You could report it, but that might end up backfiring on you. You have no concrete evidence, and Michael denied that anything is going on. Most likely, Child Protective Services would think you're a new teacher who's overreacting. And if you report anything in the future, there will be automatic doubt. It sucks, but social workers are overworked, underpaid, and dealing with the worst of the worst. They aren't going to jump on a report of a bruised wrist. But keep an eye on things. If you see any other physical signs of abuse, or if Michael tells you anything, then call CPS and file a report."

My shoulders slumped. Kyle leaned in and rubbed my shoulder. "It could be just what he said: he tripped, and his dad caught him. Or it could be some other kids picking on him, and he's embarrassed. I'll keep an eye out for him around school, okay?"

"Yeah, that'd be great. Thank you, Kyle, for listening and for your advice. I really appreciate it."

Kyle rose. "Anytime, Carter. I was actually stopping by to see if you were going to the teachers' lounge for lunch."

"You go ahead, I'll be there in just a few."

"Sounds good. See you in a few." Kyle sent me a smile as he left.

Walking around to my desk, I pulled my phone out of my top drawer. I was grateful for Kyle's kindness and words of wisdom, but there was only one person I really wanted to talk this through with.

Me: *Hey, you busy tonight? I could use a listening ear. I'll cook you dinner as repayment.*

Almost immediately, three little dots appeared that told me he was typing a response.

Austin: *Always happy to listen to you…and eat your food. ;-) Everything ok?*

Me: *Thanks A, I really appreciate it. I'm not sure if everything is okay, but it's not about me. I'll explain everything when I see you.*

My phone buzzed as I bent down to grab my lunch.

Austin: *I'll be at your place by 5.*

Me: *See you then.*

I trudged up the steps to my apartment, feeling fatigue with every step. The rest of the day had moved at a snail's pace while my mind went a million miles a minute, running through every possible path I could go down for Michael. I had come up with no answers, only more questions and doubts. When I reached the top of the stairs, I saw Austin leaning against the railing. "Hey there, Firecracker."

My bottom lip began to tremble. "Hey," I replied.

He opened his arms to me for a hug, and I immediately went to him. As soon as I felt his arms surround me, I burst into tears.

"Hey, hey now. What is this all about?" Austin asked as he smoothed my hair down my back.

To my horror, I just started crying harder. Austin said nothing, he just kept one arm around me and used the other to gently pull my keys from my hand and unlock my front door.

He guided me inside and to the living room, where he pulled my bag from my shoulder, laying it on the floor. He then sat down on the couch and pulled me onto his lap. He silently rocked me, rubbing my back while I wept for the next ten minutes. As my tears started to slow, he said, "Tell me what these tears are about."

I let out a stuttered breath and hiccupped. "Sorry, it's been a tough day."

Austin tucked a strand of hair behind my ear. "You don't have to apologize, just tell me what's going on. We'll talk it through."

I slid off his lap, even though it killed me to do so. I couldn't think straight with his body pressed up against mine. I took a deep breath and launched into the heart of it. "I think one of my students is getting abused at home, or at the very least picked on at school, and I don't know what to do about it."

"Which student?"

I plucked a pillow from the couch and hugged it to my chest. "Michael."

Austin's eyes softened even further. "Your favorite kid."

I sighed. "My favorite, even though I'm not supposed to have favorites."

A small smile touched his lips at my remark. "Tell me what happened."

I spent the next thirty minutes explaining everything to Austin. I tried to remember every possibly relevant detail, and he listened intently to it all. "Kyle said I have to be cautious about reporting to Child Protective Services because I don't have any real evidence."

Austin frowned. "Who the fuck is Kyle?"

I frowned back at him. "I've mentioned him to you before. He's a friend and another teacher at my school. He's been teaching for five years longer than I have, so he has more experience with this kind of stuff."

Austin cracked his knuckles. "Well, he's right that you don't have any evidence and so it will be hard for CPS to do anything other than talk to Michael. And it doesn't sound like he's ready to open up."

"I couldn't get him to, and I think he likes and trusts me. I'm not sure a stranger would be any better, but they might be better at asking the right questions." I groaned and rubbed my temples. "I feel like such a failure. I couldn't get him to tell me *anything.*"

"You're not a failure, it may just take time. Plus, it very well could be bullies at school. And not to freak you out, but it could also be a gang. They start recruiting young and don't like it when kids refuse."

I could feel the blood drain from my head. "*Gangs*? In the fourth grade?"

Austin leaned over and rubbed my knee. "It's just a possibility. We don't know anything for certain. What we need to focus on is getting more information so we know what's actually going on. And to do that, we need Michael to feel comfortable confiding in you."

A warmth crept over my whole body at Austin's use of the word *we*. I no longer felt alone in this, I felt like I was a part of a team.

Austin sat back and rubbed the stubble on his cheek. "I have an idea."

"I would love any and all ideas because I currently have none."

He chuckled. "What if I came to your class and did a self-defense demonstration? You said they were interested when you told them you were taking classes with me, right?"

"Right." I hesitated. "But I don't want them trying to beat up gangsters if they're approached by them, they could get killed!"

"It's not so much about moves that I would show them. It would be more of an excuse to talk to them about different situations they might face and how to deal with them. We could cover bullies, gangs, and abuse."

"That would at least get Michael thinking and knowing he's not alone."

"Hopefully, it will be enough to encourage him to tell you what's going on."

I bent forward and wrapped my arms around Austin's neck. "Thank you," I whispered. "I don't know what I'd do without you."

He squeezed my neck. "Good thing you'll never have to find out."

I pulled back slightly but was frozen in place when I saw heat in the dark blue eyes looking down at me. My heart thudded against my ribs, picking up pace as it went. I licked my suddenly dry lips, and Austin's gaze tracked the movement, his eyes darkening. I leaned forward. The shift was miniscule, but it jarred Austin from our moment.

He dropped his hand from my neck and stepped back. "Why don't you go put on some sweats, and I'll order us some takeout. You might also want to wash your face because you look like a drowned raccoon."

My jaw slackened, and my hands flew to my face. "You couldn't have mentioned this earlier?"

Austin laughed. "There really wasn't a good moment. You were all hysterical, and then we were making a plan to save the world, so this was the first chance I had."

I smacked his stomach with the back of my hand as I got up. "Order me pad thai, I need it after today."

"You got it, babe."

I made a beeline for my bathroom, and sure enough, I looked like a drowned raccoon. There were tracks of mascara down my cheeks, my eyes looked like I had taken a van ride with the members of The Grateful Dead, and my hair looked like a small rodent had made a home there. Just great.

As I methodically wiped the makeup from my face, my mind wandered to the man in my living room. He'd said I never had to worry about being without him, but I knew that wasn't true. One day, he would get over his hang-ups with relationships. Or worse, he'd meet someone who he loved enough to make him get over them, and he would have no choice but to leave me behind.

I knew that if either of us got a significant other, our friendship would have to change. Austin wouldn't be ditching his evening plans at the drop of a hat for me, he would be ditching them for some other girl's bad day. The thought had me rubbing the space between my breasts, trying to ease the burning sensation there. What was that quote from *Sixteen Candles*? Oh, yeah. *"That's why they call them crushes. If they were easy, they'd call them something else."*

THIRTEEN

Austin

PULLING INTO A PARKING SPOT IN THE SCHOOL'S LOT, I spotted Carter leaning across her car's front seat to grab her bag, her skirt pulling tightly across her ass. I also saw that I wasn't the only one noticing. Some pencil-pushing fucker was taking an abnormally long time fumbling with his keys while his eyes were fixed on my little firecracker's ass.

My little firecracker. Fuck. Carter wasn't really mine, but somewhere along the line, I'd started thinking of her that way. I slammed my door extra hard, jarring the joker from the trance Carter's ass had him in. She looked over my way and waved. Joker looked back and forth between the two of us and stepped towards Carter. I picked up my pace.

"Hey, Austin." She beamed up at me. Fucking *beamed* like I had solved all her problems just by showing up here. "Austin, this is my friend and colleague, Kyle. Kyle, this is one of my best friends, Austin."

Kyle looked as if he had just tasted something sour. "When you mentioned your friend, Austin, I always assumed you were talking about another girl."

Carter let out a choked laugh. "Um, nope. He's very much a dude."

I smirked and extended my hand. "Nice to meet you, man."

His beady little eyes narrowed as he attempted to squeeze my hand harder. "You, as well."

Carter, oblivious to the tension, said, "So glad you guys finally got to meet! Austin, we'd better get in there so I can move the desks around and get everything ready for your presentation."

I stretched out my arm and pulled her to my side, grabbing her bag in the process. "Show me the way." She pointed towards a set of blue double doors that screamed "school," and we set off, Kyle the creeper following behind us.

As we walked through the hallways, I couldn't help but be taken back to my elementary school days, remembering all the mystery meat Mondays, and my favorite teacher, Miss Rachael, who starred in so many of my pre-pubescent daydreams. I bet Carter starred in quite a few fantasies herself.

Carter unlocked the door to her classroom and pushed it open, flipping on the lights and walking over to her desk, taking her bag from my shoulder. I took a moment to soak it all in. I shouldn't have been surprised since I had seen her crafting decorations that day I came over to apologize, but somehow, I still was.

She had covered every spare inch of wall space with hand-made posters, paper flowers, and even an intricately crafted map of the world where each country had an animal, flower, and food item drawn on it. I couldn't begin to imagine how many hours it had taken to put this all together, and I was sure she hadn't gotten paid for that time. I sure as hell never had a classroom that looked like this one. "Carter, this is incredible."

She was already at work moving the desks in the first row to the sides of the classroom. "You like it?" Her eyes sparkled with pride.

I pulled another desk to the side, following her lead. "I love it. You're an awesome teacher, you know that?"

She blushed the pretty shade of pink that had become one of my favorite colors. "Thanks, Austin. I hope so."

I reached up and brushed a strand of hair from her face, my fingers lingering on her cheek, that familiar energy buzzing to life at the touch. "I know so."

She looked down at her shoes, breaking the contact. "I should run you through how things will go today before the kids get here. They know you're coming and are super excited. Pretty much all the boys are huge UFL fans, even if they are way too young to be watching that stuff. I'll introduce you and then let you go through your speech. You'll have to use me to demonstrate on because I didn't want to send the kids home with permission slips for a self-defense workshop, just in case there's something bad happening at Michael's house."

I could tell Carter was nervous, she was talking faster and faster the way she always did when she was anxious, so I reached out, grabbed the back of her neck, and squeezed. "Hey, it's going to be okay. The kids are going to love it because they won't have to do school work for an hour. And, hopefully, it will encourage Michael to open up. But, at the very least, we'll be giving everyone some valuable information."

She let out a slow breath. "You're right."

I felt my cheeks pull into a smile. "Can you say that again? I want to record it on my phone so I can play it back to you later."

Carter slapped me playfully in the stomach. "Jerk."

Just then the bell rang, and I heard the thundering footsteps of what could only be hundreds of little terrors. Oh, shit, I hoped I could pull this off. I did not want to let Carter down.

Carter welcomed each kid in with a high-five or a funny handshake. "Come on in, everyone. If you normally sit in the first row, your desks are on the side of the classroom today. Like I told you yesterday, today is a special day because Mr. Lyons is here to talk to us about self-defense. Now, let's give him a warm welcome and show him how much we appreciate him being here."

All the kids began to clap, with varying levels of enthusiasm.

I stepped forward, and my eyes swept over each of the faces looking back at me. "Hi, guys."

"Hi, Mr. Lyons," they answered. Clearly, Carter had been teaching them manners, as well.

"I'm really glad to be here to talk to you today. We are going to cover a lot of different situations, and it's important that you pay close attention so you don't miss any important details. And if you all do a good job listening, then you just might get to see Miss McCarthy kick my butt at the end of my talk." I grinned over my shoulder at Carter, whose lips had pursed.

This sent the kids into fits of laughter, but once they were under control, I launched into my spiel. I covered how to handle school bullies, gang members, and finally if someone at home was hurting them. In each scenario, I gave them examples of who they could go to for help, and how they could recognize a safe resource. I then rewarded them with having Carter show them how to break a few different holds and get away. They got quite a kick out of their teacher pretending to knee me in the balls. I ended with a recap, asking, "Who can give me an example of a safe person to go to if you need help?"

A small girl in the second row tentatively raised a hand, and I pointed to her. "A policeman."

"That's right. A policeman or woman is a great resource. Who else?"

A boy in the first row shot up his hand, and I nodded in his direction. "A teacher. Like Miss McCarthy."

Bingo. "You got it. Teachers are a great safe place. I happen to know that Miss McCarthy is pretty darn cool, and she cares about you all a lot, so you can always go to her about anything at all." I noticed another boy, seated on the side of the classroom, whose eyes had become downcast as he stared at his shuffling feet.

Carter stepped forward. "That's right, you can always come and talk to me about anything. I'm here before and after school and during lunch. Let's all thank Mr. Lyons for coming in today."

"Thank you, Mr. Lyons!" echoed throughout the classroom.

"Mrs. Woodward, the secretary, is going to stay with you while I walk Mr. Lyons out. Can you help her get the desks back into formation?"

The students immediately got to their feet, chattering with one another as they moved desks around.

Carter made her way to the door and opened it to a gray-haired woman with a warm smile. "Thanks for keeping an eye on them, Joanne. I'll be back in five."

Joanne patted her shoulder. "No trouble at all, dear. Take your time."

Carter and I started to make our way down the hallway when she paused and grabbed my arm. "Thank you so much for doing this, Austin. Everything you said was great, and I think the kids really liked it."

"I hope it helps them." Over Carter's shoulder, I spotted a face in an open classroom door staring us down. Kyle.

Carter must have seen a scowl on my face because she turned to see what I was looking at. Immediately, Kyle's face broke into a smile, and he waved. She returned the wave and then turned back to me. "What's with the angry face?"

I slung my arm around her shoulders and started walking again. "I really don't like that guy."

She tilted her face up towards mine. "Who? Kyle?"

I felt my jaw tighten. "Yes, Kyle. He's a creeper, and he wants in your pants."

Carter let out an exasperated sigh as I pushed the door open and we were greeted by bright sunlight. "He does not want in my pants. He's my friend. You're just being overprotective as usual."

As we reached my car, I turned to face her, looking at the smattering of freckles painted across her peaches-and-cream complexion. She was pure innocence. "Just be careful, okay? I know you don't have that much experience, and I don't want you to get hurt."

Carter's body visibly stiffened, and I instantly knew I had put my foot in my mouth. "How do you know that?"

I rubbed the back of my neck and swallowed. "Liam might have mentioned something." Carter scowled. "Don't be mad at him. He was just trying to paint a picture to show me how wrong my impression was of you."

"And that picture just had to include my level of sexual experience? Geez, what is it with guys and virginity?" There was nothing I could say to that. Carter's gaze traveled to her shoes as she began shifting her weight from foot to foot. "Look, it just isn't something I want the whole world to know. It's personal."

I reached out a finger and lifted her chin so she had to look at me. Her skin was petal-soft against my calloused fingers. "It's not the whole world. It's just me. I would never judge you by how many guys you have or haven't slept with. In fact, I think it's great that you've waited."

Carter's cheeks turned pink. "It's not like I'm waiting for marriage or anything. There just hasn't been the right person or the right time. I just never felt ready."

I cleared my throat as I tried to empty my mind of thoughts of Carter letting anyone have that part of her. "I think that's good. You should listen to that voice telling you to wait. The guy you give that part of yourself to should be worthy of it."

She blushed even redder. "I should get back to my class. Thanks again for everything." Carter hesitated for a moment, and I hated that I had caused this awkwardness between us. When she reached her arms around my waist, I inhaled her faint flowery scent and breathed out a sigh of relief. "You're the best," she whispered into my chest.

"Anything for you, Firecracker."

FOURTEEN

Carter

THE SKY WAS STILL JUST A LITTLE BIT PINK, THE HUE A leftover from a gorgeous sunrise, as I headed up the walkway towards the school's main doors. My steps faltered for a second when I noticed a small figure sitting on the front steps, baseball cap pulled low. My heart sped up as I realized it was Michael. "Hey, Miss McCarthy. Can I talk to you for a minute?"

"Of course." I turned and sat on the step next to him.

As I sat, he looked up, and I saw that his cheek was puffy and turning a dark blue. "I need your help." His lower lip began to tremble.

I bit the side of my cheek until I tasted blood to keep myself from crying. Reaching out, I grabbed Michael's hand. "I will do absolutely everything I can to help you, but you have to tell me what's really going on." He nodded. "Come on, let's go inside and find a quiet place to talk. And I'll get you some ice for your cheek."

He nodded again, and on a faint whisper said, "Okay."

I stood and helped Michael to his feet. As we walked through the silent hallways, our footsteps echoed off the walls, and my heart felt like it was going to beat out of my chest. I took a deep breath, trying to steel my nerves. Michael was trusting me with his secrets, and I needed to stay strong for him.

I motioned Michael to the main office and pushed open the door. Joanne was already behind the reception desk, getting things organized for the day. "Good morning, Joanne, do you have the keys to Cindy's office?" Cindy was our guidance counselor, but our budget only allowed her to be here twice a week, and today was not one of those days.

Joanne's brows furrowed as she eyed Michael at my side. "Sure thing, honey, got them right here." She slipped the keys into my hand, and I headed towards the counselor's office.

I unlocked the door and flicked on the lights. "Why don't you grab a seat, Michael? I'm going to ask Mrs. Woodward to get me some ice." Michael nodded woodenly and sat down on the couch in the office as I headed back to Joanne. In hushed tones, I said, "Joanne, I need you to do a couple of things for me."

"Is everything okay?"

"I don't think so. I need you to call in a sub for me today, I'll need one at least for the morning. I also have a feeling I'll be needing you to call the police but wait until I give you the go-ahead on that. I'll open the door and nod if that's the case. Also, can you go to the teacher's lounge and fill a bag with ice for me?"

Joanne's eyes filled with tears as she patted my hand. "Of course, dear. You just go take care of that boy."

"Thank you, I'll do my best." I turned and headed back to Michael. When I opened the door, I found him wringing his hands. "I'm really glad that you wanted to talk to me. I want you to know that we can go as fast or as slow as you want. And if you need a break, all you have to do is ask, okay?"

"Okay, Miss McCarthy," he mumbled.

I took a deep breath, steeling myself, and asked, "Who gave you the black eye?"

Michael stayed silent for a moment and then said, "My dad."

Over the next two hours, Michael slowly told me how his dad, Joe, had begun pushing him around over the past few months, berating him for being "lazy" and "no good to anyone," and finally hitting him. It turned out that Joe had recently lost his job. This meant that he was home all the time and drinking more heavily. It also meant that Michael's mother, Sofia, often had to pull double shifts at her job and was home a lot less. Michael said that his mom had no idea his father was hitting him. Joe had threatened Michael that if he told anyone, he could get Michael's mother sent back to Mexico, so Michael had stayed silent.

I had never experienced such a vicious warring of emotions before. I felt torn in two between my grief for all that Michael had endured, and my complete and total rage at his father. When Joanne knocked on the door to hand me the ice pack, I nodded at her as a go-ahead to call the police. Now, I needed to prepare Michael to face them. "Michael, I had Joanne call the police so that we can make a report." His tiny body stiffened next to mine. "I know it's scary, but this is the right thing to do, and I will be with you every step of the way."

"They're going to take me away, aren't they?"

I rubbed a hand up and down his back. "I'm not sure what will happen, but I'm going to write down my cell phone number for you. You can call me at any time if you get scared, no matter where you are, okay?" I knew that Michael would most likely be placed in emergency foster care until his mother was cleared of any wrongdoing, but I didn't want to scare him before he talked to the police.

"Thanks, Miss McCarthy." His words were betrayed by the trembling of his lower lip.

My heart clenched. "Of course. I'm going to go out to the lobby and bring them back here, okay?"

"Okay." He looked so lost, but I knew the only way that would change was to keep moving forward.

The rest of the day was spent walking through Michael's story with the police and a social worker. I was grateful that they were all kind, gentle, and seemed to have no doubts about what Michael said. The female police officer had to take photos of Michael's face, and the faint remnants of bruising on his wrist.

I tried to get Michael to eat some lunch in the middle of all the chaos, but he just picked at his food and sipped his soda. As the police wrapped things up, the social worker confirmed my suspicions, telling Michael that she would be taking him to a temporary foster home tonight. He started to cry, and I almost lost it as I wrapped my arms around his shaking body.

The social worker assured him that he could keep his cell phone with him and that he could call her or me anytime he wanted to. This seemed to ease his mind a little, but he was clearly overwhelmed. I would have given anything to take him home with me, but I knew that wasn't allowed. I gave Michael one more squeeze as the social worker picked up his backpack, ready to be on their way.

When the door to the office shut, I slumped back on the couch and looked up at the two police officers that remained. "What now?"

Officer Clark, a kind, middle-aged gentleman, leaned forward and patted the hand resting on my knee. "Now, we get your statement and then let you go home. I want you to know that Joe has already been picked up and is currently being processed. Based on everything the kid said, his mom will probably be given custody back by the beginning of next week. Another officer took her statement earlier today, and she's beside herself. Sounds like she knew her husband was a jerk but had no idea he'd turned abusive. She's been an American citizen for over six years, so not sure what the dad threatening to send her back to Mexico was all about. He probably just said it to scare Michael."

I sighed, rubbing my temples, trying to get a little relief from the raging headache that had come on sometime after lunch. Doing my best to press on, I recounted everything I could think of to the police. When I finished, both officers thanked me and gave me their cards, telling me not to hesitate to reach out if I had any questions. Then they left, and I was alone.

It was already 6 p.m., later than I almost ever stayed. I bent down to pick up my bag and was immediately lightheaded when I rose. I leaned against the wall, realizing I hadn't eaten anything since breakfast. Crud. All I wanted was a hot bath and a warm meal and someone to drive me to both.

I pushed open the office door, and my eyes widened. Sitting on the bench opposite the door was Austin. My soul seemed to sigh at the sight of him. Decked out in workout pants and a hoodie, he rose and prowled toward me. "What are you doing here?" I asked.

He grabbed the back of my neck and pulled me into his chest. "You were supposed to meet me at the gym at five. When you didn't show and weren't answering your cell, I freaked and drove over here. Joanne told me you had to report a case of abuse and were in with the police. So, I just waited. I'm so sorry, baby."

I sighed into his chest and then inhaled the scent of clean laundry, spice, and Austin. Something about that smell just calmed me. "It was awful, A. I can't even talk about it because I'm all talked out, but it was awful."

"Come on, I'll drive you home."

"You can't, my car's here," I groaned.

"Yes, I can. Just leave your car here for the weekend, and I'll bring you to work on Monday. Do you need it for anything this weekend?"

"I guess I don't. But you'll have to chauffeur me around if I decide I need to go anywhere."

He massaged the back of my neck and pointed me towards the exit. "I'll even take you to In-N-Out on the way home."

I smiled a faint smile, my first of the day. "You are a god among men."

"I know I am."

❦

I spent the weekend soothing my soul with Ben & Jerry's and mindless television. Austin kept me company through most of it too, not pushing me to talk about anything but just lending me his silent support. Monday morning had arrived far too soon, and Austin was now driving me to school. "You ready for this?" he asked.

I blew out a breath. "Ready as I'll ever be. The social worker called me last night and told me that Michael is back with his mom. They were granted an order of protection against Joe, so that's good."

"That's real good, baby."

What was with this *baby* stuff? "Baby" was way worse than "babe," and it had me wondering if just maybe Austin was getting ready to take us out of the friend zone. I didn't want to get my hopes up, but I couldn't help longing for more. Things were so effortless with us. I knew taking things to the next level might complicate things in the beginning, but I had no doubt we could end up in an amazing place.

Austin swung his car into a spot by the front of the school. "Want me to walk you in?"

I grinned at him. "No, I'll be fine." So overprotective.

"Okay, I have a late training session tonight, but I'll see you tomorrow?"

"Tomorrow it is." I swung out of the car but leaned back down. "And thanks again. For everything."

"Anything for you."

I pushed the door shut and watched Austin pull away. As I made my way toward the school, I remembered that I had left my travel mug of stale coffee in my car over the weekend. I needed to grab that to rinse it out. I turned around and headed back towards the parking lot. Just before I reached my car, I heard, "Excuse me, do you know where I can find a Miss McCarthy?"

I turned and saw a large man who looked as if he hadn't showered or slept in days. His clothing was rumpled, and his eyes were bloodshot. I looked around at the mostly empty parking lot, suddenly uneasy. "Um, yes, I'm Miss McCarthy."

The man's gaze darkened, and I took a step back. "You fucking bitch!" His hands struck out faster than I thought possible and grasped my throat. I clawed desperately at his arms, trying to loosen his hold. Panic was rising fast. I couldn't breathe, I could barely think, and then, my vision started to go black.

FIFTEEN

Austin

A s I sat going over my training plan with Mel in his office, my phone buzzed in my pocket. I pulled it out and saw Carter's face flashing on the screen. "Hold on a sec, Mel, it's Carter calling, and she's supposed to be teaching right now."

A knowing smile spread over Mel's face. "Go ahead and take it, son. Tell her I said hello."

"Hey, Firecracker, what's up?"

A voice that wasn't Carter's filled the line, and a chill skittered down my spine. "Austin? It's Taylor."

Her sniffling sounded across the line, and my muscles locked up as I gripped the phone hard. "Taylor, what's going on? Is Carter okay?"

"They say she's going to be fine, but she was attacked in the parking lot this morning."

My whole world slowly ground to a halt, and my ears began to ring. Images flashed in front of my eyes of Carter's devilish grin as she switched the car radio to a country station, knowing I hated that shit, her eyes twinkling as she shut my car door to head into school. Why didn't I fucking walk her to her classroom? That thought jarred me back to the reality in front of me. "Where is she?" I barked.

"We're at the school, with police and paramedics. I can't leave, but I didn't want her to go to the hospital by herself. I tried calling Liam, but there was no answer, and I didn't want to leave something like this on his voicemail."

"I'm on my way." I punched the end button on my screen and fought the urge to throw my phone against the wall. "I gotta go, Mel. Carter was attacked at school. I don't know what the fuck is going on." I didn't wait for an answer, I just charged out of the gym and towards my car. All I could think was that I had to get to her.

I slammed the door to my car and took in at least three cop cars and an ambulance, lights all flashing. I elbowed my way through the crowd of onlookers as I made my way towards the ambulance. Carter was sitting on the edge of a gurney, staring off into space with what looked like an ice pack pressed to her neck, an EMT taking her pulse.

It was as though she sensed I was there because she suddenly looked up. When our eyes connected, she dropped the ice pack and tried to stand, but the EMT pressed her back to sitting. When the ice pack fell away, I saw a hideous string of reddish marks around her neck that I knew would soon turn purple, and the side of her beautiful face was clearly swollen. By the time I reached her, I couldn't seem to take a full breath. "What happened?" I choked out, my voice raw. I fought the instinct to pull her to me, to touch her anywhere because I didn't want to cause her any more pain.

Carter reached out and grabbed the side of my shirt, fisting it and pulling me closer to her. "Michael's dad," she said. Her voice was so hoarse, it sounded like someone had scoured her throat with steel wool.

I silently cursed and moved even closer to her. I gently and so very cautiously began to rub my hand up and down her back. "I should have walked you in."

She pushed her weight into my side. "Not your fault."

"Why the fuck wasn't he in jail?" I fought to control the level of my voice. Struggled to breathe evenly. With every slow pull of air, I could hear the blood roaring in my ears.

A nearby police officer heard my outburst and turned to walk over. Taking in my proximity to Carter and her clearly leaning on me, he started to speak, "He was out on bail, but he's back in custody now. His bail's been revoked, and he won't be getting out anytime soon." I clenched and unclenched the fist that wasn't touching Carter, trying to take comfort in the fact that this monster was behind bars. The knowledge did nothing to calm me. "You should be proud, though. Your girl here did a number on him. Kneed him in the balls and broke his nose."

I tilted my head down to meet Carter's eyes.

"I remembered what you taught me," she said in that same hoarse whisper that made me what to murder someone.

"You did real good, Firecracker." I turned back to the cop, jaw working. "What happens now?"

"Like I said, he violated the terms of his bail by even being on school grounds, so he's in jail. At least until his trial. We've put an order of protection in place for Miss McCarthy, and he'll be charged with assault on top of the abuse charges he's already facing."

As the cop finished speaking, the EMT chimed in. "We should get her to the hospital now to get checked out." He looked at Carter. "Is anyone riding with you?"

Before Carter could answer, I jumped in, "I am."

"Okay, let's get going." He laid her back on the gurney, buckling her in place with what looked like three seatbelts.

I cringed as she was loaded in. I fucking hated seeing her like this, all weak and helpless. But I reminded myself that she wasn't either of those things, she had defended herself and had taken that bastard down. I inclined my head toward the cop. "Can you do me a favor and give my car keys to the receptionist in the office? Tell her I'll be sending someone to pick them up."

The officer extended his hand for the keys. "No problem. Listen, man, I see that look of rage in your eyes. Don't do anything stupid, okay? Just be there for her."

I swallowed words that I wanted to hurl at the cop and instead said, "Yeah, man, I got it." And with that, I hauled myself into the back of the ambulance.

The ride was a quick one, and we were swiftly ushered into an ER exam room. I stayed close by Carter's side, bending down to gently brush the hair back from her face. "I texted the guys to let them know what happened and ask them to pick up my car from the school."

Carter blanched. "Tell Liam not to call my parents."

"You sure about that?"

She started to nod but then stopped herself, the action clearly causing her pain. "I'll call them tomorrow when my voice is back to normal."

A nurse bustled in, taking Carter's vitals and prepping an IV. Carter's eyes widened a bit at the sight of the needle, and I took her hand in mine. She squeezed it as the nurse inserted the IV. "We're just getting some fluids in you now, but once the doctor examines you, we'll get you some pain meds," the nurse said as she hurried back out.

Turning back to Carter, I saw that her eyebrows were pinched together in pain. "Your head hurt?" I asked.

"A little."

She was lying through her teeth. I kept a hold on her hand, hating that there was nothing else I could do for her at the moment, nothing I could do to take her pain away. I would gladly take a hundred hits to the head to ease her suffering. Where was the fucking doctor already?

I heard the door swing open, and a man entered who looked like he was in his fifties and was wearing a white lab coat. "Hello, Miss McCarthy. I'm Dr. Baines. It sounds like you had quite the scare. How are you feeling?"

"Not too bad," Carter croaked.

"I know your throat has got to be hurting you pretty badly, but I'm going to need to ask you a few questions. As soon as I'm done, we'll get some pain meds in that IV, and you'll feel a lot better. Did you ever lose consciousness?"

I felt Carter's hand twitch in mine. "Not really."

The doctor looked up from the chart he was holding. "Did your vision go black?"

"It started to," she said so softly I could barely hear her answer.

Dr. Baines made a note. "Did you hit your head?"

Carter briefly closed her eyes. "He hit my head against my car."

The rage inside me felt like it was boiling my blood. It took everything I had not to destroy the hospital room around me. The only thing holding me back was the fear in Carter's eyes, I didn't want to do anything that would frighten her further. I took a deep breath and made sure I wasn't gripping her hand too tightly.

The doctor clicked his pen, placing it back into his pocket and removing a penlight. "I'm going to look in your eyes to check for a concussion and then examine your throat." He moved quickly through his inspection. When he probed the swollen side of Carter's face and the back of her head, she winced, sharply sucking in air.

"Careful," I barked at the doctor.

"He's just doing his job," Carter said, squeezing my hand. "Sorry."

"Not a problem. You've got a bit of a goose egg on the back

of your head, but all in all, you are very lucky. You don't have a concussion, and I don't feel any broken facial bones, but I want to get an x-ray just in case. Your neck and throat will be sore for the next week or so. I'm going to write you a prescription for an anti-inflammatory and a painkiller, they should help. If you have any worsening pain or blurry vision after you've been discharged, I want you to come back immediately. Do you have someone who can stay with you tonight?"

"I'll be staying with her tonight and can drive her back to the hospital if anything gets worse."

The doctor smiled kindly. "Great, I'll just inject this fast-acting painkiller into Miss McCarthy's IV, write up her prescriptions, and order that x-ray."

Just moments after the doctor had left, the door flew open, and Liam and Ford rushed inside. They screeched to a halt when they saw Carter, face swollen, neck bruised. "What the hell happened?" Liam said through clenched teeth.

"A parent of one of Carter's students attacked her in the parking lot this morning." Just saying those words brought my simmering rage back to a boil. "She's going to be fine, and he's in jail, but her throat and head have her in a lot of pain, so she's not going to be doing much talking, got it?" Carter turned towards me and stuck out her tongue. Clearly, the pain meds had started to kick in. I squeezed her hand. "I'll be right back, you guys. Stay with her."

I didn't look back at Carter as I made my way to the door and out into the hallway. My sneakers squeaked against the linoleum in an annoying rhythm until I reached the end of the hall. Sucking in a deep breath, I leaned my forehead against the wall, pressing my fingertips into the cool surface, battling my desire to pound a hole into it.

A hand landed on my shoulder. Turning my head to the side, Ford filled my vision. "Hey, you okay, man?"

I pushed off the wall. "Not really. Shit, Ford, I've never been so fucking scared in my life."

"You care about her."

"Of course, I fucking care about her," I spat. "She's my best fucking friend."

Ford paused, seeming to choose his words carefully. "You ever think it's more than that? I've seen the way you look at her, how you treat her. And I know she's in love with you, it's written all over her."

I pushed at Ford's chest, harshly but not aiming to hurt. I just needed him and his words away from me. "Don't tell me that. I'm not in a place where I can be in a relationship. I need to be focused on my career. Fuck! I don't even know if I'll *ever* want that again."

Panic began to take a firm hold on my pounding heart. Images flashed through my mind at a rapid pace. Carter cooking me dinner. Carter nibbling on the corner of her lip as she tried to figure out who the killer was on whatever true crime show we were watching or listening to. Carter beaming up at me as my arm was lifted in victory at my last fight. Carter tucked perfectly under my arm as I held her on the couch.

Fuck. Carter had snuck through my defenses with her disarming innocence, and now I knew she was too close.

Ford smoothed out his shirt. "Well, time is ticking by, and I just hope you don't miss out on the best thing that may ever happen to you." With that, he turned and walked back towards Carter's room.

I just stood there, clenching and unclenching my fists, listening to the blood roaring in my ears. I could not deal with all the shit raining down on me right now. Taking a few more deep breaths, I straightened my spine and made my way back to Carter, the girl who had my insides twisted up in knots that might never unravel.

I rolled my car to a stop outside of Carter's apartment and cut the ignition. "Stay where you are, I'll come around and open your door."

"I can open the car door, Austin, it's not like my arms are broken."

I cringed at the thought of that bastard breaking one of Carter's arms. This all could have been so much worse. She could have fucking died. "Stay put," I barked out, harsher than necessary. Carter shrank back, and I reached a hand over to brush her unmarred cheek. "Sorry, I didn't mean to snap at you. I'm just pissed as hell and worried about you."

She pushed her face into my palm. "I'm fine."

"You're not fine, but you will be." I broke away from Carter and got out of the car. She waited for me to open her door, and I helped her out of the car.

We made our way into the apartment, and Carter turned to face me. "I'm going to change into pajamas."

"Do, uh, you need help changing?" Good God, I really didn't think I could handle helping Carter undress tonight—or any night for that matter. My restraint only went so far, and her sleek curves were far too tempting. Ford's words echoed in my head, and I fisted my hands. He was wrong, he had to be wrong.

Carter smiled, oblivious to where my mind had gone. "No, I'll be fine."

I checked my phone, it was already past 8 p.m. Damn, this felt like the longest day ever. I slumped into one of the kitchen barstools and massaged the back of my neck while I read over Carter's discharge paperwork one more time, wanting to make sure I knew when to give her the next dose of pain meds.

The sound of Carter's door opening had me spinning around. Hell, she was wearing a pair of those super short girlie boxers and a long-sleeved shirt that hung off one shoulder. She was barefoot, and her toes were painted a bubblegum pink. My dick twitched. Shit. I coughed in an attempt to banish images of me ripping those tiny shorts from her body. "Why don't you go climb into bed, and I'll get you a glass of ice water. That might feel good on your throat."

Carter gave me a small smile. "Okay, thanks, and not just for the water. For being with me today and staying tonight."

I probably shouldn't stay the night, but instead of making an excuse to leave, my dumb ass just said, "Of course." After filling a glass, I followed Carter into her room. "Here you go." I placed the glass of water on her nightstand and sat down on the side of her bed. I reached out and tentatively smoothed the skin around her abused throat. "I'm so fucking sorry this happened."

She shivered when my hand reached her pulse. "Stop saying that, it's not your fault."

"I want to kill him."

"Please don't. I would miss you if you went to jail." A small smile touched my lips. "Can I ask you to do something for me?"

"Anything."

"Will you just hold me for a little while?" I couldn't answer. Carter looked up at me with those wide, innocent eyes. This was such a bad idea. She kept speaking. "It's just that you make me feel safe."

How could I deny her when she said something like that? This girl could wield words the way a surgeon wielded a scalpel, cutting right to the quick. "You got it." I made my way around her bed, slipped off my shoes, and crawled under the covers. I steeled myself, trying to remember my last fight or picture the men's locker room, anything to keep my dick in check.

As soon as I lay down, Carter shimmied over and laid the unbruised side of her face on my chest. Her "thank you" was muffled by my shirt. I gently squeezed her shoulders. She was quiet for long minutes, and I thought she had fallen asleep when her voice cut through the darkness. "I was so scared."

"Baby."

I didn't know what else to say, but Carter kept talking. "I was so scared, but I just kept thinking about all the things I haven't done yet that I want to experience. All the places I haven't gone, all the people I would miss. It was seconds, but it felt like hours. I thought about you. And that's when I fought."

Her words shredded me. "I'm so glad you fought, Firecracker."

Carter tilted her face up to mine, our lips a hair's breadth apart. "I'm glad, too." Her words brought a warm breeze across my face.

I don't know who crossed the distance, if it was her or me, but suddenly we were there. The kiss was soft, but it lit a fire in my gut that I had never experienced before. My tongue parted her lips, and I fought back a moan at my first taste of her. I wanted more, needed more. I wanted all of her. And that's how I knew I had to stop. I forced myself to pull back, my lips buzzing with the undeniable and indescribable energy that was Carter and me.

"Sleep," I said, my voice rough with the desire that was pumping through my veins.

"Okay," she answered, her voice just a little bit shaky.

Fuck, what had I done? I could blame the kiss on the heightened emotions of the day, but the truth was that I had been playing with fire for far too long. Before I knew it, Carter was out, but even the sound of her deep, even breaths couldn't lull me to sleep, and it was hours before I finally nodded off.

I awoke to a delectable backside pushed into my painful erection, and I groaned. My hand was resting on the smooth skin of Carter's abdomen, dangerously close to dipping underneath her boxer shorts. Shit. I slowly rolled to my back and tried to slip my arm from beneath Carter's neck.

She shifted and started mumbling in her sleep, then I heard

distinct words. "Don't go Austin...love you." I stilled, studying her face. Her eyes were closed, her breathing still deep. She was asleep. Meanwhile, my whole body had seized up. I was suddenly hot and slightly nauseous. I needed some distance to think.

As carefully as possible, I crept from the bed and into her en suite bathroom where I splashed cold water on my face and stared at my reflection. I needed to get out of here. Reaching for my phone, I texted Liam as I swished some mouthwash around in my mouth. As I exited the bathroom, I froze. Carter was awake. I forced words to come out of my mouth, but they were stilted. "How are you feeling?"

She rubbed sleep from her eyes, and her hair stuck up all over the place. "Better."

I slipped my phone into my pocket and my feet into my shoes. "I have to get to the gym, but Liam is going to check on you in a couple hours. He said to text him if you want him to bring you anything."

A small frown formed on Carter's lips. "Okay. Are you all right?"

I shuffled my feet. "Yeah, fine. Just running late."

"Okay, if you're sure," she said. Her head was quirked to the side in that adorable way that now only compounded my nausea.

I backed towards her bedroom door. "I'll text you later. Get some more rest." I hauled ass from Carter's apartment to my car, eager to get my ass to the gym to pound the shit out of something.

SIXTEEN

Carter

AUSTIN WAS FREAKING OUT. I COULD RECOGNIZE THE look of sheer panic in his eyes. I just wasn't sure if the alarm spelled good or bad things for the future of my heart. I was hoping against hope that he was flipping out about the possible change in our circumstances and not freaking out about how he was going to tell me that kissing me felt like kissing a sister.

I tried a shower to clear my head, but it was no help. Cautiously, I slipped on my most comfortable sweats, taking care to not bump my neck or move too quickly. Heading out to the living room, I found Lexi sitting at the bar drinking her coffee. "Oh my God, you look awful!"

"Gee, thanks."

"I didn't mean it like that. Taylor left me a message yesterday and told me what happened. Are you okay?"

I continued into the kitchen, filling the kettle with water to make myself some tea to soothe my throat. "I'll be fine."

"Was that Austin I saw making a mad dash from your bedroom?"

I fought a cringe at the thought of Austin trying to get away from me. "He spent the night to make sure I was okay."

Lexi placed her coffee cup down on the counter. "Honey, are

you sure that's a good idea? I know you have feelings for him." I pulled a mug down from the cabinet and found a lone box of tea amongst all our coffee paraphernalia, trying to ignore Lexi's words.

I made a noncommittal humming sound in the back of my throat. What I wanted to say was, "Yes, all right? I'm head over heels in love with him, and I have no idea if he feels the same. Sometimes, I think he might; and other times, I think he sees me as his sister." But I didn't say that. I wanted to keep that admission to myself for just a while longer. As soon as I spoke those words out loud, there would be no taking them back.

Lexi ran a perfectly manicured finger around the edge of her cup. "I think if a guy wants you, he's going to make the first move. Especially a guy like Austin. And I don't say that to hurt your feelings. I just don't want you to get your hopes up and get more hurt down the line."

I gripped the edge of the cool granite counter top to the point of pain, using the feeling to ground me. "Mm-hmm," I answered, biting the inside of my cheek. I knew there was a possibility she was right, but I also knew that she didn't know Austin as well as she seemed to think she did.

I needed to call up my courage and talk to him, be honest about my feelings. At least then, I would know. Then, I could either jump him or try to move on, but I knew I couldn't stay in this place of limbo any longer. Especially when lip touches that seared my soul were being introduced into the status quo.

Lexi rose from her stool, leaving her coffee cup for me to clean up. "I've got to get to work."

"Okay." I washed her cup while I waited for my tea to steep, the whole time thinking about how I could explain to Austin that I had fallen in love with him.

I fell into step next to Taylor as we headed towards Ford's bar. It was Liam's birthday, and I had taken extra care in my preparations for the evening. My strawberry-blonde hair hung in soft, beachy waves down my back. I had lined my eyes in a shade of coal that made the green in them pop, and I was wearing a little black dress that made it look like my legs went on forever.

I had given it my all to make sure I felt my best because the last two weeks had sucked big time. Being forced to take a week off work to recover meant that I was super behind on everything now. Michael knew what his father had done and felt horribly guilty, no matter what I did to assure him that it wasn't his fault. And Austin was officially avoiding me. I had only seen him once in the past two weeks, and it was for about ten minutes when he and Liam dropped off dinner for me. We had traded a few texts, but he always had excuses for why he couldn't hang out. Tonight, I was getting answers. My phone buzzed in my clutch, and I pulled it out.

Lexi: *You almost here?*

Lexi had finagled herself an invite to Liam's birthday party when he had come over to hang out with me while I recovered. She wasn't exactly the person I was most excited to hang out with, but I didn't blame her for wanting to go to a rock star's birthday.

Me: *Walking up now.*

Lexi: *Great! We're in the back.*

Taylor and I made our way past the line of people to the front door where the doorman checked us off a list and let us through the velvet rope. I grasped Taylor's hand as I cut a path through the crowd towards the seating at the back of the bar. I found Liam surrounded by gorgeous women, Ford, and a few more guy friends. I leaned over the table and grasped his face, planting a smacking kiss on his cheek. "Happy Birthday, Liam."

He smiled a smile that told me he'd already had a few. "Thank you."

I held up a gift bag and let it dangle from my pointer finger. "For you. Is there somewhere I can stash it so it doesn't get lost?"

"Yeah, there's an office down the hall on the right. Austin's back there stowing some other gifts. Tell him to get his ass back out here."

Perfect. I could corner Austin's grumpy butt and get him to tell me what the heck was going on. I had grown paranoid that the pain meds I had been on the night Austin slept over had seriously screwed with my memory or perception of events. Maybe I had thrown myself at Austin and begged him to take my virginity—that would be humiliating. No matter what had actually happened, I was getting to the bottom of things tonight.

I slipped through the back hallway and found the office door. Knocking briefly, I chuckled to myself—like anyone could hear knocking over the pounding of the bass in the speakers. Hesitantly, I pushed open the door, but when it reached the midpoint of the threshold, I froze. My heart thudded against my ribs and then dropped to my toes.

Austin was there, all right. He leaned back against the desk, while a girl was on her knees in front of him, unbuttoning his pants. I did a double-take when I realized the girl was Lexi. Vomit crept up my throat. I felt Liam's present slip from my fingers as I turned and ran. I thought I heard someone call my name, but I couldn't be sure with the music blaring all around.

I pushed people aside as quickly as could to make it back to Liam's table. Taylor was sitting just across from him, and I grabbed her shoulder roughly. She spun around and took in my face. I must have looked awful because both she and Liam spoke at the same time. "What's wrong?"

I swallowed back the bile that was still making its way up my esophagus. "Lexi and Austin are hooking up in the office."

Taylor stood, wrapping an arm around my waist. "Jesus, you need better friends."

Liam leaned across the table and grabbed my hand. "He's been drinking, he doesn't know what he's doing."

I couldn't deal with Liam's reasoning right then, so I turned to Taylor. "I'm sorry to make you leave when we just got here, but I really need to get out of here."

"Of course, let's go before He-Man pulls his dick out of that skank and comes after you." I cringed at the visual, and Taylor sent me a sympathetic smile. "Sorry." Once we were out on the street, I sucked in a deep breath, trying to still my riotous stomach. Taylor still had a hold of my hand, and she squeezed it. "You going to be okay?"

"Yeah, it's just the wakeup call I needed."

SEVENTEEN

Carter

I MOANED AS SUNLIGHT HIT MY TENDER EYES; APPARENTLY, crying myself to sleep had taken a toll. I rolled over and stretched, propelling myself into a sitting position. Gazing around Taylor's guest room, I thanked my lucky stars that I hadn't had to return to my own apartment last night. Slowly, I got to my feet and meandered out to the living room to find Taylor sipping tea on her couch. "Hey, girlie, how are you feeling?"

I shuffled toward her and plopped down on the opposite end of the couch, pulling my knees up to my chest. "I feel like I'm hungover, and I didn't even drink."

"It's all the tears. A crying hangover. Just drink a bunch of water, and you'll start to feel better." She paused, bringing the cup to her lips. "What are you going to do?"

I let my head fall to my knees. "I have no idea. You know, Lexi texted me as we were walking in last night. I think she purposely timed it so I would see them together, or at least have a real good idea of what they were up to."

Taylor shook her head. "What a bitch. I know you probably don't want to hear this right now, but she's always been jealous of you and the attention those guys give you. She's used to being the center of attention and gets bitter when she's not."

"What am I going to do? I have to live with her."

Taylor set her mug on the coffee table. "Move in here. I have more than enough room."

"Really?" Taylor lived in a gorgeous four-bedroom house in the Los Feliz hills that I would kill to call home. It felt like a Mediterranean oasis, complete with a pool and spa.

"Why not? My dad got me this place as a ridiculously over-the-top graduation gift. Trying to assuage his absentee-father guilt. So, you wouldn't have to pay rent. We have the same schedule, so no worrying about roommates throwing ragers when you have to be up at 5 a.m. Plus, we have the same taste in cheesy made-for-TV movies. We are basically a match made in roommate heaven."

"Well, when you put it like that…"

Taylor clasped her hands together like a little kid. "Yes?"

"Yes. Thank you."

She shrieked and threw her arms around me in a tight hug. "Now, tell me what you're going to do about Austin because, that, I don't have a quick fix for."

My excitement about moving in with Taylor immediately dulled. I sighed. "I lay awake most of the night thinking about it. In some ways, I really do think Lexi did me a favor. I mean, our relationship is kinda messed up. It's like we're dating, except we don't have sex. I've said no to any guy who's asked me out this year because I'm so caught up with Austin. But I haven't been honest with him about how I feel or tried to set any boundaries with him putting us firmly in friendship territory either, and that's not fair to him. I mean, we're not actually dating, so he should be free to hook up with whoever he wants."

"Technically, yes. But come on, your roommate? That's not cool."

Leaning back into the arm of the couch, I tried to sort through my feelings on the matter now that I had slept on it. "He has to know I have feelings for him, right?"

Taylor sucked in a slow breath. "I would say, yes."

"If that's true, then it's super shitty of him to use my roommate to get off. I haven't kidded myself into thinking he's been celibate for the past year, but he's never rubbed my face in it, never hit on one of my friends. I always convinced myself that he just wasn't ready for a relationship with all he has going on, but that when he *was*—"

"He'd choose you?" Taylor finished for me.

I worried my bottom lip with my teeth. "Yes. I hate that I was so naïve. I was living over in dreamland, making up this whole story in my mind about why Austin hadn't made a move. It's pathetic."

Taylor leaned and patted my knee. "It's not pathetic. You fell in love with someone, and you hoped he felt the same. Every girl on the face of the planet has been there. And, to be honest, I feel like Austin has been a bit selfish. I think, on some level, he knew that if he was honest with you about not wanting a romantic relationship, you would pull back, and he didn't want to lose the comfort of having someone always there to support him. It's like he got all the benefits of being in a relationship without having to commit to one. You met all his emotional needs, and he found random girls to fulfill his physical ones."

I groaned, leaning my head back to stare at the ceiling. "No matter what the reasons are, I need some time and space away from Austin. Because if I keep spending this much time with him, I'll never fall out of love with him. Which means, I'll die a ninety-seven-year-old virgin, while he's out screwing half of LA."

Taylor chuckled into her mug. "Do you really think you can walk away from him?"

"I have to. I want to meet someone who can love me back. I want to get married and have kids one day. I can't do that if I stay stuck in this place."

"Fair enough."

I started chewing on my bottom lip again at the thought of not having Austin in my everyday life. "It's not like it's forever, it's just until I can get over him."

"That might take longer than you think."

"Yeah, but I have to try. I'm going to see if he can meet for breakfast." I reached for my phone so I could text Austin before I lost my nerve.

"Doing it in person? Wow, you really have lady balls."

I stuck out my tongue at her and powered on my phone. "Oh, shitake mushrooms." My head popped up, and I met Taylor's eyes. "I have thirty-eight missed texts."

She rose, taking her coffee cup to the kitchen. "This is going to be one interesting breakfast."

࿐

Austin

I groaned at the pounding in my head and the taste of death on my tongue. Opening my eyes, it took a few moments to realize where I was—the guest room at Liam's house. Thank God. I rolled into a sitting position and pushed myself to my feet. Everything was just a bit fuzzy, I didn't even remember coming back here last night. I glanced around, looking for my phone and keys, but didn't see either so I went in search of Liam.

I found him in the kitchen, pouring himself a cup of coffee. "Looking for this?" He held up my cell phone.

I grunted. "That and some coffee. Why do you have my cell?"

Liam sipped his coffee, just staring at me for a moment. "Because you wouldn't stop calling and texting Carter. Thanks for ruining my birthday, by the way."

Icy cold dread slid over my body as images from last night came crashing back: taking shots with the boys, Lexi cornering me in the office, Lexi unbuttoning my pants, Carter walking in, the shock on her face, the tears in her eyes, running after her, taking more shots when she wouldn't answer my calls. Fuck, I was a bastard. "I'm an asshole."

Liam's knuckles bleached white as he gripped his mug. "Yes, yes you are. I almost punched you last night."

"I'm surprised you didn't."

"Fuck, man, of all the chicks in the greater Los Angeles area, you pick her roommate? Were you trying to crush her?" The silence in the kitchen was deafening. "You know she's in love with you, don't you?" I didn't say a word. "And you're in love with her."

I jerked back. "I am not."

"Bullshit." Liam set his cup down with a crack.

"I'm not. Or I can't be. What I know for sure is I don't want to be in a relationship." I pulled at my hair as I started to pace.

"You're a fucking idiot." More silence. "Fine, man. If that's true, then you have to let her go. Don't keep stringing her along, letting her think there's hope."

My head snapped up, and I stopped in my tracks. Let her go? Fuck, no. "We're just friends, we've never hooked up." That one kiss didn't count as hooking up, even if it had set my blood on fire. Even if nothing I had done over the past two weeks had been able to erase the memory of that handful of seconds. I pushed on, ignoring the pang in my chest. "You're friends with her, are you going to let her go?"

Liam shook his head. "I've seen you two together. You don't act like just friends."

"Whatever."

A buzzing sound came from Liam's direction, and he picked up my phone. "It's Carter, she wants you to meet her for breakfast." The fist I hadn't realized had a hold of my chest loosened. Everything would be fine. I would apologize to Carter, and everything would go back to normal. Liam threw the phone in my direction, a bit harder than necessary. "Do the right thing, man."

EIGHTEEN

Carter

I SAT AT A TABLE OUTSIDE OF TOAST, ONE OF AUSTIN'S AND my frequent haunts, drumming my fingers to the staccato beat of my heart that felt like it was going to come out of my chest. I didn't have to go through with this. Austin could arrive, and I could just apologize for overreacting last night, and everything could go back to normal. But where would that get me in the long run? Nowhere I really wanted to be. I just had to resign myself to getting through the awkwardness and pain to come. The only way out was through. I forced myself to take a sip of the freshly squeezed orange juice and take a deep breath.

"Hey, Firecracker."

And just like that, it was as if someone had kicked me in the gut, stealing all the air from my lungs. I turned in my chair, finding Austin's tall frame towering over mine. "Hi." It came out as a squeak.

He reached down, pulling me to my feet and into a hard hug. "I'm so sorry. I was an insensitive ass."

I felt myself stiffen at the reminder of last night's events, and I pulled back. "Let's sit."

Austin nodded and took the seat across from mine.

I took another sip of my juice and swallowed. I just had to say what I needed to say before I lost my nerve. "I need to tell you some things."

"Okay, shoot."

I fisted my hands in my lap, letting the bite of pain from my nails digging into my palms keep me from passing out or throwing up. "I'm in love with you." Austin just blinked at me. "I know you probably already knew I had some level of feelings for you, but I just needed to get that out there first. I'm in love with you."

There was no response other than the clattering of dishes and muted conversation around us. "I've come to realize that you definitely don't feel the same way about me. I was kidding myself for a while that you might, but you don't, and that's not your fault or even something I can be mad at you about. I need to get over you. And to do that, I'm going to need to take a step back from our friendship. As much as it kills me to do it."

Austin's throat worked as his jaw clenched. "What does 'take a step back' mean?"

I pressed my nails harder into my palms. "I think it's best if we don't talk at all for a while."

"How long is a while?" He ground out each word like it was a battle for him to say them.

"I'm not sure. Can I let you know when I'm ready?"

Austin tilted his head back and looked at the cloudless, blue sky. "Is this really necessary, Carter? I mean, we've been friends for a year, never crossed any lines. I'm not in love with you, but I care about you. A lot. And I feel like you're punishing me for not loving you."

I felt a tacky wetness on my palms, and some part of my brain realized I had broken the skin there with my nails. The pain was nothing compared to the wounds his last words had inflicted. "I'm not trying to punish you." My voice was shaking. "I'm just trying to do what I think is best."

"Best for you, but not me," he said, his teeth grinding together forcefully between words.

At the end of the day, I guess he was right. I was choosing my happiness over his, but if I wouldn't fight for my myself, who would? Not him. I needed to fight for me. "I guess so. I'm sorry, Austin, I really am."

"You know what, Carter, don't call. Befriending you was a mistake. I did it for Liam, but it was a mistake." My heart splintered, sending what felt like millions of microscopic shards into my bloodstream, radiating pain throughout my body.

He stood, roughly shoving back his chair. "You've spent your entire life living in this naïve little bubble, thinking the world is all sunshine and rainbows, that everything will turn out exactly the way you want it to because you've willed it so. And if you can't have it just the way you want it, you throw it away. Well, I'm no one's trash. And it might be time for you to think about growing up."

His words left burns in their wake, but I said nothing, just stared at the chair Austin had abandoned, letting my vision go hazy. What would hurt more I wondered: to never see my best friend again, or to live my whole life standing next to the person I loved to the depths of my soul but was destined never to have? I guess I didn't have to decide, the choice had been made for me.

Minutes passed. Austin was gone.

"I guess I should go now." I spoke the words quietly to myself as though they would will me into movement. I slowly and robotically pulled a five-dollar bill from my purse to cover the OJ and set it on the table.

I rose, spotting a bloody fingerprint on the bill. How fitting. I waited for a moment, glancing around to see if Austin might miraculously return, full of apologies and amends. There was nothing. No one. So, I turned and walked away, silent tears streaming down my face.

NINETEEN

Carter
THREE MONTHS LATER

TAYLOR FLICKED ON THE SIDE LAMP AS THE CREDITS TO the movie rolled, illuminating herself on one side of the couch, and Kyle reclined in one of the overstuffed armchairs. I wish she would have left us all in darkness.

"So, now that we've officially watched every horror movie on the face of the planet, can we pretty please go out tonight? Pretend we're young and alive?" Taylor was exaggerating. We hadn't watched *every* horror movie, but we'd watched a lot.

I was desperate for anything to distract me from the pain of losing Austin. That meant dark rooms and endless screenings of films that had lots of dead bodies and zero unrequited love stories. Clearly, Taylor was done with me keeping her locked in a cold, dark room this summer.

"I'm actually pretty tired. I think I'm going to go to bed early tonight." I faked a yawn. "But you guys should go out."

Taylor threw up her hands with an exasperated sigh. "Carter, all you ever do is sleep and watch movies!" Actually, I rarely slept. The dark circles under my eyes should have been her first clue. I lay awake in my room each night, replaying my last conversation with Austin over and over, wishing with all my might that

I could just take the words back. Wishing I could have Austin back. Taylor's voice gentled. "I'm worried about you."

I swallowed back the tears that clogged my throat. "I'm sorry, Tay. I know I've been a bummer to be around this summer."

Taylor launched herself at me, pulling me into a tight hug. "You're not a bummer to be around. I just want you to start fighting to get your life back. Find your mad!"

Kyle cleared his throat, drawing my eyes to his handsome face. "Why don't I take you girls out to dinner? Mexican?"

Taylor pulled back, releasing me from her hold, and clapped her hands like a five-year-old. "Yes! Chips and queso! Come on, Carter. Please?" She stuck out her bottom lip, and I couldn't help but laugh.

"All right. I just need to shower and change real quick."

Kyle sent me a tentative smile. "Take your time, there's no rush." I had a feeling Kyle was talking about more than me getting ready for Mexican food. He had been a wonderful friend through my great summer sulk. He listened to me talk about Austin until even I had gotten sick of Austin's name coming out of my mouth. Kyle had held me as I had a sobbing breakdown on the last day of school. And he made me laugh.

"Thanks for this," I said, returning his smile with one of my own.

"Anytime."

An hour later, the three of us were piled into a booth at a neighborhood Mexican restaurant. I had a frothy margarita in my hand, and queso and guacamole were on their way. I had to admit, Taylor was right in trying to get me out of the house. As I sipped the salty-sweet concoction, my eyes traveled around the restaurant. There were groups of friends laughing, families enjoying a night away from cooking for themselves, and couples gazing into each other's eyes everywhere.

It hit me like a freight train. Life was passing me by. And I was letting it. I had never been this kind of person before: someone who brooded in a corner because I didn't get something I wanted. When I thought back to the person I'd been over these past three months, I didn't like her very much. It was time for me to check back into life.

"So," I asked Taylor, "how was your date the other night?" The surprise that showed on Taylor's face was the only evidence I needed that I had been an unbelievably cruddy friend to her lately, as well.

"Honestly? It was a total bust. He talked nonstop the entire date. Didn't ask me a single question about myself." She took a sip of her margarita. "Oh, well, on to the next one. That's the beauty of internet dating, right?"

Kyle tried unsuccessfully to hide his chuckle by taking a sip of his beer. Taylor didn't miss a thing and shot him a dirty look. "I know you're anti-internet dating, but how else am I supposed to meet someone? I'm too freaking busy!" She turned to me. "You know, I think we should sign you up. It's time."

My palms began to sweat, and I rubbed them against my jeans. "I don't know. I'm not sure I'm ready for full-out competitive dating."

Taylor snorted. "Stop calling it that. It's fun!"

"I don't really consider that fun."

"I'll tell you what," Kyle interrupted. "When you're ready to go out on a date, just tell me. I'd love to take you out."

My cheeks heated. Kyle had been hinting about his interest over the past few months, but this was the first time he'd stated it outright. "Thanks, Kyle. I'm not quite ready yet, but when I am, I'd really like that." He beamed at me. Kyle was exactly the kind of guy I needed to date. He was kind, funny, and most importantly, he had no problem telling me he liked me.

My phone buzzed in my purse, jarring me from my thoughts. I slipped it out, sliding my finger across the screen to read the message. Blood drained from my face, and my stomach roiled.

Unknown: *Austin gave it to me so good last night, my pussy is still aching today. But he's so desperate to have me again I'm just going to have to put up with a little pain tonight.*

These little gems had been popping up on my phone at least once a week since I'd found Lexi on her knees in the office of Ford's bar. At first, they came directly from her phone, but when I blocked her, they started popping up from unknown numbers and emails. I had given up trying to stop them.

Taylor snatched the phone from my hand, quickly scanning the message. "That fucking bitch. Carter, you have to change your number."

If I was honest with myself, the reason I hadn't changed my number was the tiny kernel of hope that Austin would call. But who was I kidding? His career had taken off like a rocket. He had forgotten all about me. It was time to move on. "You're right. I'll go to the phone store tomorrow and see what I need to do."

Kyle snagged the phone from Taylor, reading the message and then deleting it, all with a look of pure disgust on his face. "This should just be a confirmation that you should want nothing to do with that ape. If this is the kind of woman he associates himself with, you should count yourself lucky you got away from him."

"Yeah," was all I could say. I wanted to find more of my mad. I really did. Austin had been a prick at the end of our friendship. But even with all he'd said and did, I wasn't sure I could ever consider myself *lucky* for not having Austin in my life.

TWENTY

Austin

SMOOTH IRISH WHISKEY FILLED MY SENSES AS THE BASS beat the bar's DJ was spinning thrummed against my temples. The alcohol stung my split lip as I took another sip of whiskey, but I relished the burn. Warm and willing bodies pressed up against me on both sides. I smiled into my glass.

"Will you show me the belt you won?" one of the girls cooed.

"Sure thing, honey." I grinned at her and motioned a wobbly hand at Ford. "Where's my belt?" My words sounded just a little bit slurred.

Ford scowled in my direction. "It's locked up in the office so your drunk ass won't lose it or give it away to one of your groupies."

"Stop being a jealous pussy." I stood, and the world seemed to tilt on its axis slightly.

Ford stood, as well, reaching out a hand to steady me. "Maybe you should stop being a drunken idiot."

"Fuck you!" I swung a wild fist in his direction but missed sending a table of drinks and myself crashing to the floor.

"Jesus. Help me get him up, would you?" Liam's voice sounded far away. All I could do was groan.

"We should just leave him there. It would serve him right."

Liam bent down, appearing in the periphery of my vision. "You're a mess, you know that?" I groaned again.

"Let's take him through the back, so no paparazzi get a picture of this shit," Ford said as he helped Liam get me to my feet.

The world blurred around me as I was ushered through the crowd. The LA night air was still warm, even though it had been dark for hours. It wasn't cold or fresh enough to give me the relief I needed. "Gonna puke."

"Shit! Get him over to the bushes! I do not want this joker's puke on my favorite kicks," Ford groused.

I emptied the liquid contents of my stomach onto the poor, unsuspecting shrubbery. When my heaving finally stopped, I straightened. The world still seemed a little blurry, but I felt a whole lot better. Liam handed me a bottle of water. "Thanks." My tongue felt thick in my mouth.

"Let's get him in the car."

Ford narrowed his eyes at me. "Are you going to throw up again? I don't want any of your nasty-ass puke in my nice, new car."

"I'mmm good," I said, drawing out the *m* sound.

Ford sighed. "All right. Let's go."

Liam and Ford helped me into the back of the SUV, and I immediately laid down. The engine roared to life, sending vibrations through the seat. "Where's Carter?"

Liam turned around in his seat, gazing down at me. "What do you mean?"

"Where'sss Carter? Can't leave her here alone."

Liam glanced back at Ford, and then returned his eyes to mine. "She's not here, Austin. She's, uh, at home."

Something tickled the back of my mind. "Oh, yeah, because she left me."

"Buddy, she didn't leave you. Look, why don't you try to get some sleep. Everything will look better in the morning."

"I'm fucking pissed at her, man!" I saw Carter's beautiful face in my mind, smiling that radiant smile of hers. "But I miss her, too, ya know? She's so fucking beautiful, right?"

Liam reached out and patted my shoulder. "I know, buddy, she is. Just close your eyes."

My eyes did feel pretty heavy, so I let them slowly shut, and was dead to the world before we were out of the parking lot.

~

It felt as if a tiny elf were chiseling away behind my eyeballs. I opened my lids to find myself again in Liam's guest room. At least I wasn't in some fight groupie's bed. That had happened more times than I wanted to admit over the last few months. I gingerly pushed myself into a seated position, rubbing a hand over my stubbled jaw. Fuck, I needed some painkillers and maybe a little hair of the dog.

I stumbled into the kitchen to find Liam and Ford both sitting at the dining nook, sipping coffee. "There any more of that?"

Liam studied me with an unreadable gaze. "Yup. In the pot."

"Thanks." I poured myself a cup in the largest mug I could find and took a seat next to Ford. An awkward silence followed. "Sorry if I did something stupid last night, it's all a little hazy."

Ford cleared his throat. "We wanted to talk to you about that."

I looked between Ford and Liam, now noticing their creased brows and nervous glances. "Okay," I said.

Liam leaned forward. "We're worried about you. You're drinking more than you ever have before—"

I interrupted him before he could continue. "I know I was shitfaced last night, and I'm sorry for whatever idiotic shit I pulled. But I just won my first UFL championship. Didn't I deserve to cut loose after that?"

Liam and Ford exchanged a look. It was Ford who spoke. "You've been drinking a lot even when you're in training, which you *never* used to do. And you're fucking anything that moves."

I snorted. "So I'm having a little *fun*, what's wrong with that?"

Liam set his mug down on the table with a sharp clang. "You took a swing at Ford last night. I've never known you to do that before. And, quite frankly, if this is the new *you*, I'm done."

The few sips of coffee I'd taken settled in my gut like a lead weight. I took quick inventory of Ford's face. He didn't look hurt. "Did I make contact?" My voice came out hoarse.

"No, man. You only succeeded in taking yourself out."

I swiped a hand over my brow. "Fuck. I'm sorry, man. Really, I—" I stumbled over my words because I didn't know what the hell to say. There was no excuse for trying to deck one of your best friends just because you were wasted. I wasn't a college frat boy; I was too old for this shit.

I wasn't in total denial. I knew I was trying to numb myself. Trying to turn off those flickers of pain from missing Carter by fighting, fucking, and getting shitfaced. It had to stop. I may need a distraction, but I could throw myself into something worthwhile instead of into the bottom of a bottle.

I cleared my throat. "I hear you. I'm gonna make some changes."

The set of both Ford's and Liam's shoulders relaxed. Shit. What had I been putting my friends through these past few months? I was a bastard.

"You know—" Ford started.

"Don't," Liam broke in.

"What? He's a miserable bastard without her in his life."

My spine straightened. "What are you talking about?"

A small grin spread over Ford's face. "In your drunken state last night, you might have mentioned how much you missed Carter."

My expression went on lockdown. "She doesn't want me in her life, and I think that's for the best. I need to focus on getting my shit together right now."

"But—"

"He's right," Liam said. "He needs to clean up his act before he goes knocking on anyone's door."

My teeth ground together at the thought of Liam keeping me from Carter. There was this constant push and pull where she was concerned. A part of me that wanted nothing more than Carter back in my life. But in what capacity? She didn't deserve me jerking her heart around. And every time I thought about committing to more with Carter, a panic seized my heart. So, I was left at this lonely impasse.

The one thing I did know is that I wasn't going to drag my friends down with me anymore. I pushed up from the table. "Come on, I'll treat you both to breakfast at The Griddle. Then, we can go shoot some hoops, and I'll sweat the rest of this whiskey out of my bloodstream."

Ford rubbed his hands together like some weird combination of an evil genius and little kid. "Now that's an apology I can get behind."

Liam stood, slapping a hand on my shoulder. "Good to have you back."

TWENTY-ONE

Carter

THE FULL MOON LIT THE WALKWAY AS KYLE AND I MADE our way to the front door. Summer had slid into fall and, before I knew it, winter was almost over. I had taken Kyle up on his offer to take me out. It was now our third official date. He'd taken me to a screening of one of his favorite films and out for ice cream after. The film hadn't been my cup of tea, but the ice cream was delicious, and the company lovely.

As we reached the door, Kyle grasped my elbow. "I'm not going to ask to come in, but I would like to kiss you goodnight."

So far, the dates had ended with an awkward hug or a peck on the cheek. Asking for a kiss kind of took the fun out of it in my mind, but I should be grateful that Kyle had sensed I wanted to take things slow. "I'd like that."

His hand released my elbow and came to the small of my back. He dipped his head, eyes closing as his lips met mine in a gentle touch. I shut my eyes, trying to lose myself in the moment. Kyle's tongue dipped between my lips, but the rhythm felt out of sync. Seconds passed, but no sparks came to life.

Kyle pulled back, sucking in a breath. "Wow. That was, wow."

I bit the corner of my lip, unsure of what to say. Evidently, Kyle hadn't felt any lack of chemistry. Or if he had, he was covering it well. "Thank you again for the movie and ice cream."

"You're welcome. How about I cook you dinner next Friday?"

I twisted my fingers. I hoped these dinner plans didn't mean that Kyle was ready to move things along physically. "Um, sure. That'd be nice."

"Great." Kyle bent forward for another quick peck. "I'll call you tomorrow."

"Goodnight," I said and darted inside. Pushing the door closed, I sighed as I leaned against it.

"Is that a happy I'm-in-love sigh?" Taylor called from the living room.

I started towards her. "You couldn't hear me sigh from all the way over there."

She cackled. "No, but I could see your dramatic shoulder rise and fall. So, tell me all about it. How was date number three?"

"It was nice," I said as I plopped down next to her on the couch.

"Nice? Uh-oh, what happened?"

"No, it really *was* nice. The movie wasn't my favorite, but I still had fun. Kyle's sweet, and he makes me laugh..." I trailed off.

"But?" Taylor prompted.

"But he kissed me tonight, and there were just no sparks." I let my head fall onto the back of the couch.

"Ah. Don't get too discouraged," Taylor said as she patted my knee. "Sometimes, it takes a while for you to find your sexytimes groove with someone."

"That's true," I admitted. But I wasn't sure if that was going to be the case for Kyle and me. I had never felt the kind of attraction for Kyle that I'd felt for—I stopped myself right there. Comparing Kyle to Austin would get me nowhere. "He's cooking me dinner on Friday."

"Oooooooohhhh!" Taylor sat up, suddenly very interested. "Are you going to sleep with him?"

"What?! No! Do you think he's going to expect that? He just kissed me for the first time tonight." My stomach felt just a little bit queasy.

"No, relax. Kyle seems like the gentleman type. And if he's not, just knee him in the balls and head on home."

A small giggle escaped my throat. "Your solution is always to knee the guy in the balls."

Taylor shrugged. "What? It's a good solution."

I leaned over and enveloped her in a hug. "Thanks for being such a good friend and sticking with me through my sulky phase."

She squeezed me back. "Anytime, girlie. But I've gotta say, I'm glad we can leave the house again." I snorted and pinched her side. "Hey! Watch it!"

"Yeah, yeah." I rose from the couch. "I'm gonna grab a shower and hit the hay, I'm exhausted."

"It's all that making out, takes it right out of you," Taylor said as she waggled her eyebrows.

"Shut it, you!"

"You love me."

"Unfortunately, I do," I called over my shoulder as I headed into my bedroom.

I tossed my purse on the bed and made quick work of showering and brushing my teeth. Pulling on my comfiest PJs, I slipped beneath the sheets. Flopping back onto the pillows, I worried my bottom lip between my teeth. I knew I shouldn't do it, but the pull was too strong.

I slid open my nightstand drawer and pulled out my iPad. Tapping on the YouTube icon, I typed in a handful of words. Austin's face filled the screen in a post-fight interview. I studied the sharp angle of his jaw, the glint of his deep blue eyes. My heart contracted in a brutal squeeze. It always felt the same, a delicate balance of pleasure and pain, but I couldn't stop myself.

I tapped *next* and watched Austin decimate his opponent in the fight that had netted him his first heavyweight UFL title. A tear slid down my cheek as his hand was raised in the air. It didn't matter how many times I watched the same videos, their effect never weakened. I told myself that, eventually, they wouldn't pack such a punch, but deep down, I knew I was lying.

TWENTY-TWO

Austin

THE HALLWAYS AND DOORWAYS OF THE T-MOBILE ARENA on the Vegas strip did little to dull the roar of the crowd. I was glad. The cheers and boos did nothing but feed the beast inside. I had gotten really good at keeping that monster fat and happy over the past few months. If I didn't, ugly things happened, and I didn't want to go back there.

Swinging my arms back and forth to keep my muscles limber and warm, I paced up and down the hallway outside my locker room. When I reached a corner, I paused, hearing Liam's voice. "He's good. He's in the other room warming up." His voice held a softness and tenderness that it only had when he was talking to one person. "How's that tool you're dating?" A stone dropped in my gut. "Come on, you know you need to end it. There's no need to keep leading the poor schmuck on."

Carter was dating someone. I always knew it would happen, I was just surprised that it had taken this long. I was also annoyed that Liam hadn't mentioned anything. "All right, all right, I'll be nice. Promise. See you when I get back."

Liam rounded the corner, almost barreling straight into me. "Whoa. Sorry, dude." His eyes darted around the hallway, and he looked guilty as hell. This was the awkward place we had lived in since Carter and I had stopped talking. Liam had re-fused to pick sides, but he was damn protective of Carter.

Almost an entire year had passed, and I hadn't heard one single peep. Not that I blamed Carter. The final words I had spoken to her had been cruel and untrue. I cringed at the memory. "Was that Carter?" I asked, voice rough.

"Um, yeah."

"Who's she dating?" It burned to say those words. The idea of anyone's hands on her untouched skin made me want to kill someone. It was fucked, I knew it, but I couldn't help it.

"Are you sure you want to talk about this right before your fight?"

A hand clamped on my shoulder. "He's right, son. You need to be focused."

Liam and my dad might be right, but I didn't give a fuck. "Who. Is. She. Dating?"

Liam just shook his head. "Some teacher at her school."

I jerked my head in a nod, spun on my heel, and stalked back to the locker room. My pre-fight preparations were a blur, the deafening cheers of the crowd muted to a dull roar, the fight intros might as well have been in another language. The only thing that penetrated my brain was the sound of the bell.

I unleashed the rage I held in check every day, the fury that could only be quenched on fight nights. I let it go, unchecked and unrestrained. Fourteen seconds later, my opponent lay semi-conscious on the ground. I was almost disappointed; I wanted to feel that pain.

Minutes later, my hand was raised in the air, and I was named UFL Heavyweight Champion for the second time in a row. Liam and Ford were hooting and hollering. Mel gave me a fatherly slap on the back. My own dad squeezed my neck, bringing his forehead to mine. "Proud of you, son."

It should have felt like I was on the top of the world. It

didn't. It just felt empty.

⌒᥈

Strobe lights pulsed in rhythm with the music, I had a class of Glenglassaugh thirty-year whisky in my hand, my friends all around me, and gorgeous females flitting about. The finding myself in the bottom of a bottle had stopped, the losing myself in a nameless woman had been a little harder to cut back on. I took a sip of the heavenly amber liquid, determined to enjoy this day. To enjoy this life I had fought so hard to get for myself. This life that I had given up so much to have.

A pair of large breasts pressed into my back. "Want to take this party upstairs?" a voice cooed in my ear.

Another girl leaned in. "We both want to play."

My cock didn't even twitch. What was wrong with me? This should be every guy's dream, but all I could think was that girl two's voice was whiny, and girl one's breasts felt like boulders poking into my shoulder blades. Neither of them had a cute-as-fuck head tilt or nibbled on their bottom lip when they were worried about something or twisted their hands in complicated knots when they were nervous.

Or, hell, maybe they did, but I would never know them well enough to find out for sure. It was then that I knew I was done. Done with these one-night stands that brought release but no true relief, these faces that blurred from one to the next, faces that sure as hell didn't give a shit about me. Done.

I stood then, causing girl number one to spill her drink. "Sorry, ladies, tonight's just not the night."

Girl one huffed, and girl two pouted, neither action was very attractive. But at least when I showed no signs of reconsidering, they left. I gave a signal to my head of security, John, not to let anyone new past, and he nodded in acknowledgement.

"Dude, what's wrong?" Liam asked. Both he and Ford wore

looks of startled concern.

"I'm just over this. Can we get out of here?"

"Sure," Ford answered.

Some of my life may have gone to shit, but I had some of the best friends in the world. We exited the club, John along with Liam's security guard clearing a path. "Let's get some food," Liam suggested. "I'm starving."

"Sounds good," I said, cracking my neck.

Soon, we had found a twenty-four-hour diner and were spread out in a booth with more food than a small army would need laid out in front of us. "So, you want to tell us what's going on?" Liam asked.

I swallowed my bite of fried chicken and studied him. He was my in. If anyone could get Carter to let me back into her life, it was Liam. "I just thought this would all feel differently. Make me happier or something. But it just all feels kind of..." I let my words trail off, not wanting to seem like a total ungrateful pansy-ass.

"Empty?" Liam chimed in.

"Yeah."

"I know what you mean, man. The things you thought would mean everything to you can turn out to mean shockingly little."

I guess he would know better than most. Liam's career had only reached even higher heights over the past couple of years, but he still hadn't found that one person to share it with.

Ford cleared his throat. "Are you finally going to pull your head out of your ass and realize you let go of the one person who would have made this all fun?"

"I didn't let her go, she walked away."

"And you let her," Ford shot back.

"Liam told me not to call her!" I said, shooting a scowl in his direction.

Ford let out a scoffing laugh. "You're going to use that as an excuse? When have you ever *let* someone stop you from going after something you wanted?"

He made a damn good point. I had bowed out of the most important fight of my life because I was afraid. That stopped today. I wanted Carter back in every possible way. I wanted her in ways I'd only dreamt about. Her skin against mine, her hair raining down around me as she took all of me. My cock jerked to life in a way it hadn't in months. I had been without my girl for way too fucking long. I was finally ready to fight for her, even if I had to defeat her and my own demons in the process.

Liam must have recognized the look of determination in my eyes because he said, "You're going to have one hell of a battle on your hands. You ready for that?"

I jerked my head in a nod. "I will be."

"Good, now get to work."

TWENTY-THREE

Carter

THE SOUND OF A SLIDING GLASS DOOR HAD ME TURNING away from the view of downtown LA and towards Kyle's questioning face. "Who were you talking to?"

I forced a smile. "Just Liam."

Kyle's eyes went just a little stormy. "He's at Austin's fight, isn't he?"

My stomach sank. I did not want to get into yet another argument with Kyle about a person who was no longer in my life. To be fair, Kyle probably sensed that my heart just wasn't into this relationship. After I had finally said yes to a date with Kyle three months ago, I just kept saying yes to the dates that followed.

Our relationship was comfortable, easy, with no real drama or heartache, but there were no real sparks either. Kyle was kind and thoughtful; never made me second-guess his feelings for me. However, lately, Kyle had begun to press. Press for more of my time. Press for a more serious relationship. Press for more of my body than I was ready to give. I was starting to think that Liam was right, maybe it was time to end things. But I just wasn't prepared to throw in the towel quite yet.

"Yeah, but he's back tomorrow."

Kyle nodded his head jerkily and then reached for my hand.

"Come inside, let's watch a movie."

"Okay." Curling up on Kyle's couch while he searched for a movie he wanted me to watch, my eyes traveled over the space. Everything was utilitarian with no real heart or warmth. Granted, he was a guy, so I didn't know what I really expected.

The sofa springs squeaked as Kyle sat down, throwing an arm over my shoulder and pulling me against him. "You're going to *love* this film, it's a cinematic masterpiece and one of my all-time favorites."

A genuine smile came to my lips. This was one of the things I found charming about Kyle. He was a total film geek. I often didn't completely get or enjoy the films that were his favorites, but I appreciated how passionate he was about them. It was adorable. "I'm excited to watch it," I said, knowing I'd most likely need to fight nodding off.

I was right. Two and a half hours of subtitles would never be my idea of fun, but everyone had to make sacrifices for their significant other. Arching my back as I stretched, Kyle's eyes dropped to my breasts. I had to bite my lip to keep from chuckling. He grabbed my wrist, pulling me onto his lap and pressing his lips to mine.

There was a flicker of heat as his tongue invaded my mouth, but it quickly faded away into nothing. My mind drifted to another embrace, and I cursed myself and that stupid kiss. One that had lasted under a minute was now the bar I held all other kisses to. I was starting to wonder if I had imagined the way my belly heated and my lips tingled when Austin's mouth had been on mine. I tried to shake those memories from my mind, focusing on the feel of Kyle's tongue dueling with my own.

His hands slipped beneath my top, stroking my skin. It felt nice. But was *nice* what I should be feeling? Where were the dips in my stomach or the stuttering of my heartbeat? When Kyle reached for the clasp on my bra, I stilled his hands. He groaned in my ear. "Carter, come on." His hands worked their way back to my bra, unclasping it.

I shoved at Kyle's chest, and it wasn't gentle. "Stop it. I told you that I just wasn't ready to go there yet." My stomach twisted into knots. Something was holding me back from being intimate with Kyle. A part of me felt guilty since we had been dating for a while now, but there was a larger part that knew I had to be true to what my gut was telling me.

Kyle brushed a frustrated hand through his hair. "This is getting a bit ridiculous at this point."

"Look, Kyle, I think it's best if we stop seeing each other." The words were out of my mouth before I had a chance to evaluate or second-guess them. But as soon as they left my lips, I knew it was the right decision.

Kyle ran a hand down my back. "I'm sorry, I shouldn't have pushed. You just drive me crazy, and sometimes I get carried away. I promise to be more mindful."

He leaned in to kiss me, but I held out a hand to stop him. "I appreciate that, but I still think we should stop seeing each other. We are just looking for different things right now."

Kyle's cheeks reddened. "I don't agree. I think we do want the same things, you just have to be willing to let go of things in your past to see that."

My stomach clenched at his insinuation. "I'm sorry, but I can't do this anymore."

Kyle's face only got redder, but he took a steadying breath and kept his cool. "I'm sorry you feel that way, and I hope you will take some time to think about it."

"I will, but I don't think I'll change my mind." I rose, refastening my bra. "I really am sorry, Kyle."

He said nothing as I grabbed my bag and headed for the door.

∽

The warm mug brought comfort, along with the hands that had prepared it. "I'm so sorry, Carter," Taylor said as she settled on the opposite end of the couch.

"It's all right. I never should have gone out with Kyle in the first place."

"Don't say that. You never know when a spark will appear. Sometimes, it's *POW;* but other times, it's a delayed reaction that leads to a fireworks show. I'm just sorry this one ended with more of a fizzle. And that he was such a pushy jerk."

Swallowing a sip of tea, I said, "Well, at least I tried, right?"

"Right." Taylor's eyes studied me carefully. "Do you think any of the lack of heat is because you're still tied up in Austin?"

I sucked in a breath. We didn't talk about Austin much after those first painful months following our falling out. I had been miserable. Our little group had kind of fallen apart. Taylor had stayed firmly entrenched in Team Carter, but it was like the guys were children of divorced parents with shared custody. I gave Austin the bar, never once setting foot in there since the night I had found Lexi on her knees and had even given up Liam's Malibu beach house for the most part. But Liam and Ford made sure to spend time with me whenever they could, often coming over to Taylor's and my house so we could feed them.

My friends rarely mentioned Austin unless I had a moment of weakness and asked about him. It's not like I had a prayer of forgetting him, even if I would have tried. He was *everywhere.* Sometimes, it felt like his face was stalking me around Los Angeles, looking down on me from larger-than-life billboards. He seemed to be touting everything from Gatorade to under-wear. He'd even guest-starred on a television show. I had, of course, followed his launch into superstardom, secretly watching every single one of his fights on my laptop or iPad in my bed-room, screaming into my pillow when necessary. I think Taylor knew I did it, but she never said anything.

"I've never stopped missing him," I admitted. "I'm not sure what that says about me after he basically told me I was an over-emotional baby and to get lost. Maybe I'm just messed up in the head."

Taylor leaned forward and patted my knee. "You are not messed up in the head. And I don't think he really meant it. Everyone has said something in the heat of the moment they wish they could take back."

"Well, it's not like he's been pounding down my door, trying to apologize."

Taylor made a humming sound around the edge of her cup before taking a sip of her tea. "For what it's worth, I think you just triggered some of his deep-seated issues by getting so close to him."

"My bestie, the shrink." Taylor grinned at me over her mug. "At the end of the day, the *why* doesn't really matter," I continued. "He's not in my life, and chances are, he never will be. I just have to find a way to get past it. Kyle wasn't the one for me, but I have to keep the hope alive that someone out there will make me forget all about Austin Lyons."

TWENTY-FOUR

Austin

I OPENED THE DOOR TO MY OFFICE AND GESTURED FOR LIAM to take a seat on the couch opposite two overstuffed chairs some overpriced interior designer had picked out. "So, what do you think?" I had just finished giving him the tour of my recently remodeled MMA training center. I had bought the old gym Mel owned six months ago, sending him off into retirement with a handsome paycheck.

After buying out the businesses on the floors above, I had gutted the entire building, bringing it down to the studs before remaking it into a training facility that had all of the latest technologies, equipment, and services. It was my baby, and a way to keep my mind distracted from obsessing about Carter since giving up the numbing effects of an entire bottle of booze.

"This place is incredible, A. I'm proud of you, man."

"Thanks, Liam. I wouldn't have made it this far without your help."

Liam leaned back into the couch, resting one ankle on his knee. "I had no doubt you'd make it to the top, and here you are."

I leaned back in my own chair, my mind running through all that had happened over the past year. I'd accomplished just about everything I'd ever dreamt about. I'd dominated the UFL heavyweight division, had gained crazy lucrative sponsorships, and was now training some of the other top fighters in the world, but ever since that fight a few weeks ago, I had only grown more aware that something was missing. Some*one* was missing.

I shifted in my chair. "I'm thinking about dedicating the third floor to a youth program." I had always dreamed of starting something for kids who didn't have access to the kind of training and equipment they would need to excel at MMA. A program they wouldn't have to pay a dime for. So parents like my dad wouldn't have to work extra hours just so their son could follow his dreams. The more I daydreamed about what something like that could be, the wider the scope grew, and the grander my plans got. It also gave me a great idea for a catalyst to get Carter back in my life.

Liam cocked his head to the side. "Really? That'd be awesome."

I picked at the fabric on the arm of my chair. "I hope so. I was actually thinking of asking Carter to consult on it, but when I tried to call, her number was no longer in service."

Liam sat up. "You finally got off your lazy ass and called her?"

He was such a dick. "I'm not lazy. I was just waiting for the right opportunity and getting all my ducks in a row."

Liam smirked now, and I wanted to wipe it off his face with a nice uppercut to the diaphragm. He was eating this up. "Okay, maybe not lazy. Maybe just a little, itsy-bit scared…of a girl about half your size, literally."

"Give me a break already, would you? What's the deal with Carter's phone?"

Liam's lips pinched together, and I was suddenly on alert. Something wasn't right here. "She has a new number. Lexi was pretty persistent in sending her some real charming texts, so she had to change it."

My jaw went tight at the mention of Lexi. "Shit." A wave of dread washed over me, and something that felt a lot like shame.

"I can't believe she'd say anything to Carter."

"That girl is unhinged. She texted Carter weekly, graphic shit that would make even Ford blush."

My teeth ground together. "What a conniving bitch." Liam just stared at me. "I know, I know, it's my own fault for ever touching her."

"It is your own stupid-ass fault. I don't want that chick anywhere near Carter."

"Me either." I cracked my knuckles. "God, it kills me that Lexi's been laying into her." And it did. There were lots of things I regretted doing over the years, but number one would always be touching that snake of a female. My stomach roiled at the thought of her and how much my actions had hurt Carter. I knew I would have to tell her the whole story at some point, but I needed to get her to trust me again before I did. I could only hope that she would forgive me when she learned the truth.

"It should," Liam shot back, protective big-brother act in full effect. As annoying as it was at the moment, I was glad Carter had someone like Liam looking out for her.

"Enough already. What do you say? Will you give me Carter's number?"

Liam rubbed his jaw like he was considering all his options. "I'm not giving you Carter's number without asking her if it's cool. But before I even ask her, I gotta know where your head is at."

"I'm ready to go after my girl." That was the simple truth of it. I never should have let her go in the first place. But the fact was, if I hadn't lost her, I might have always taken her for granted just a little bit. Having lived without her for an entire year, I knew that life was just a little bit duller without her in it. I didn't laugh as often or as hard. I sure as hell didn't look at the positive side of a tough situation. I just plain wasn't as happy. At the end of the day, I was selfish. I wanted her in my life in every possible way, lighting up every dark corner.

A small grin spread across Liam's face. "You know you're going to have your work cut out for you. She thinks you never want to see her again."

"You know me, I'm not afraid to fight for what should be mine." Not anymore anyway.

"Just go slow with her. Ease into being friends first, give her some time to adjust."

I didn't want to take it slow. I wanted to throw Carter over my shoulder, cart her back to my house, and never let her leave. But that would probably get me arrested. "I'll try to go slow."

"All right, good luck, man. You're gonna need it."

TWENTY-FIVE

Carter

I SWIRLED THE SPATULA AROUND THE EDGE OF THE CUPCAKE, leaving smooth waves in the buttercream frosting. After sprinkling a few sugar crystals on top, I reached across the kitchen bar and placed it into Liam's waiting hands. "Thanks, this looks amazing."

"Anytime. You want milk or water?"

His eyes lit up like a little kid's at Christmas. "Cupcakes and milk? I feel like I'm back in Georgia, sitting at your mom's kitchen table."

I smiled as I poured him a glass of milk. "Best compliment ever."

He smiled back and took a sip. "So…I saw Austin today."

I stilled. Liam almost never brought up Austin's name, and if he did, it was usually an accident. Never anything direct like this. "He said he tried to call you and asked for your new number. He's starting a youth program at his new training facility, and he wants you to consult on it. You ready for something like that?"

I wiped my suddenly sweaty palms on my apron. I had no idea if I was ready. I had honestly resigned myself to the notion that Austin wanted nothing to do with me. And why would he? He had the world at his fingertips now. I was just a faint memory of a girl he used to know.

Because I was so sure he was done with me, I honestly hadn't thought about how I would feel if he ever came back around. My heart clenched. "I miss having him in my life. I miss my best friend. So, I guess...yes?" Liam didn't look convinced. "I just need to have better boundaries in place this go-around." I could do this. I had a year of distance on my side, and the knowledge that Austin had zero interest in me beyond friendship. This would be a piece of cake.

Liam had a look on his face that I couldn't quite read, but he pulled out his phone. "I'm going to send it to him then."

I swallowed hard, my throat suddenly dry as a desert. "Okay."

Later that afternoon, I was on my hands and knees, scrubbing a spot on the kitchen floor that nobody could see but me when my phone's ringtone caused me to jump and knock into the bucket of water next me, spraying it all down my front. "Shitake mushrooms!" I had turned my phone's ringer to the highest possible setting so I wouldn't miss any phone calls while in my cleaning frenzy.

In hindsight, it probably didn't need to be quite that loud when it was less than two feet from my face. Live and learn. Jumping to my feet, I grabbed for my phone. Austin's name lit up the screen, I guess he hadn't changed his number. My hands shook as I hit the green button. "Hello?"

"Hey, Firecracker."

With just two little words, he stole all the breath from my lungs. "Hi, Austin."

"It's so good to hear your voice."

"Yours, too." His was different, yet the same. Rougher or deeper somehow but holding that same warmth that hit me right in the belly.

"How are you?"

"Um, I'm good. Freaking out a little bit at the moment, but

good." I twisted the rag I was holding between my fingers.

"Don't freak out. I hate that this is over the phone, I want to talk to you in person. Would you meet me?"

My stomach dipped at the thought of seeing him in person after all this time. "Uh, sure. When?"

"How about tomorrow after you're done with school?"

"Okay, that works."

"Can you meet me at my gym? The same place we used to do self-defense training."

I sucked in a breath, thinking about walking into a place that held so many memories but nodded. Then I realized Austin couldn't see me nodding and said, "Yeah, I can do that."

"I can't wait, Carter. See you tomorrow."

"See you." He had hung up, but I stood there for several long seconds, phone still pressed to my ear, wondering what I'd just gotten myself into.

The sound of footsteps had me turning around as I headed out to the school parking lot. It was Kyle. I inwardly groaned. It was like he was everywhere these days. But I guess that's what you got when you dated a co-worker, and it didn't work out—frequent awkward encounters. "Hey, Carter, you done for the day? Want to go grab coffee?"

He asked me to do something at least three times a week. At first, I had said yes every so often because I wanted us to transition back into a friendship. We'd never had much chemistry, so I had thought it would be easy, but…not so much. I now politely declined every time he asked. "Hi, Kyle. I can't, I have plans."

"Oh, yeah, what are you up to?" he asked as we continued walking.

I thought about lying. Austin had not exactly been a warm and fuzzy topic during our short relationship, but I went with the truth. "I'm meeting Austin at his gym."

Kyle grasped my arm and stopped walking. "You're talking to him again?" His jaw was tight, and his fingers cut into my flesh.

I pulled my arm out of his grasp. "Just as of recently, but yes."

He ground his teeth together. "You can't do that."

I wanted to pound my head against a wall. Kyle was a great many wonderful things, but what he was *not* was the most socially adept person in the world. It was hard for him to get the message, even when I spelled it out. "Kyle, Austin and I are just friends. We've always just been friends, and we'll always *be* just friends." It hurt my soul to admit that. I continued, "But you and I are broken up. We have been for weeks. You have no say in who I spend time with." I said it in a soft tone, even though the words were a bit harsh. I needed him to get the picture, but I didn't want to be cruel.

"He's just going to play you for a fool *again*," he spat and turned on his heel toward his car.

My stomach pitched. Kyle had hit at the heart of my greatest fear in all this: that history would repeat itself and I would be left shattered. Again.

∽

I bumped my car door closed with my hip and then leaned back into it, not quite ready to face the meeting ahead. Looking up at the building that had once been so familiar, I realized I wouldn't have even recognized it if I had been driving by. Apparently, there had been brick beneath the ugly old siding, because a beautiful and expertly refurbished red surface looked back at me. It was perfect for a fighting gym. Taking a deep breath, I straightened my spine and pushed away from my car.

The pounding of my heart rang in my ears as I pushed open one of the double doors. There was a good chance I might puke on Austin's shoes when I saw him. Welcome back to my life, friend! I took in the brand new interior as I tried, in vain, to slow my heart rate. There was now a modern reception desk and seating area right as you entered, and behind the reception desk sat a woman who looked like a Brazilian supermodel. I did a double-take when I realized I recognized her. "Sofia?"

"Carter!" Michael's mother rounded the reception desk and pulled me into a tight hug. While I still saw my old student often, I hadn't seen his mother in almost a year. "How are you?"

"I'm good." My voice wavered, betraying me. My mind, already a riot of emotions, was now confused on top of it all. How long had Sofia worked here?

"I see my four o'clock is here." My body froze at the low, warm tone. Austin.

Sofia let out a soft giggle and released me. "I'll talk to you later."

I couldn't seem to make myself turn around. Time slowed. The blood in my ears roared. My heart thudded against my ribs. It was the hand at my elbow that did the trick, jarring me into motion. I spun around.

There was Austin in all his glory. Just like with his voice, he was different yet the same. My eyes traveled over his face and down his body. It seemed like he was more cut, his edges were sharper, and was it possible that he had gotten taller? But his eyes held that same warmth and spark of mischief that I remembered. Someone might as well have punched me in the stomach.

"Hey, Firecracker." He extended his arms, and I immediately walked into them. It was like I was a puppet and he held all my strings. All my reservations, my determination to keep him at arm's length, it all melted away at the first glance. While elements of his voice and body had changed, he smelled exactly the same. I closed my eyes, took a deep breath, and inhaled all that was Austin. "You okay?"

I nodded into his chest, not yet trusting my voice. When he

pulled back, I saw that we were alone. "Hi," was all I could muster.

Austin seemed to understand it would take a minute for me to relax. "Why don't we head back to my office?"

I nodded in response, and he led me down a hallway filled with life-sized photos of fighters locked in battle. When we reached a door with a gold placard that read *Boss,* he stopped and pushed open the door. His office was not at all what I would have expected. In fact, it looked like something out of an HGTV show. Everything complemented each other perfectly, and there were even throw pillows on his couch—the old Austin hated throw pillows.

A set of bookcases that housed about a dozen framed photos beckoned to me. Most of them were of Austin with an arm raised above his head, being crowned victor of a fight. I paused at one where he was surrounded by Liam, Ford, and his dad, newly earned belt slung across his mid-section. I hated that there were all these memories that I hadn't been a part of. That thought died as I came to a photo I'd never seen before. It was of Austin and me, my head was thrown back in laughter, and he was gazing down at me with utter reverence on his face. It was that look that had mixed me up inside. I felt heat at my back. "Liam took that one."

I cleared my throat, stepping away from Austin's warmth. "I haven't seen it before."

Austin held out an arm, gesturing for me to take a seat on the couch. "He gave it to me about six months after we stopped talking, right after I pulled my head out of my ass and realized what a jerk I'd been." I looked down at the hands clasped in my lap, unsure of how to respond. "I was a mess for a long time after you said you needed space, and it took me even longer to realize how unfair and cruel I had been to you. I'm so sorry, Carter—"

I couldn't do this. I didn't want to rehash all the ways that things had gone bad and why. "Austin," I jumped in, "it's not necessary for us to go back through all of this. In fact, I'd really rather not. I'm sure there are things we both regret in how things went down. Could we maybe just start from scratch?"

He blinked at me and then blinked again. Clearly, he'd had some big speech planned, and I had stolen his thunder. "Uh, yeah. Sure."

I sagged back into the couch, letting out a small sigh of relief. From the corner of my eye, another picture caught my attention, it was of Austin and my favorite student, Michael. They were holding up their fists and mugging for the camera. My jaw hung open. "That's…that's Michael." My head snapped towards Austin.

He tugged on the collar of his t-shirt. "Yeah, we hang out sometimes."

"He's never told me that." Michael and I had stayed close even after he graduated from the fourth grade. Once a week, we met in my classroom, and I helped him with any schoolwork that he was having trouble with. Or, I took him to get In-N-Out. He always voted for In-N-Out. What could I say, he was a smart kid.

Austin rubbed a palm over the stubble on his jawline. "I asked him not to. I didn't want to bring up any bad memories for you. I offered Sofia a job when I bought the place from Mel. She can bring Michael with her whenever she needs to, so he and I spend a fair amount of time together."

My mind was spinning with all this new information. Wait, were Austin and Sofia together? That would explain a lot. I wanted to punch myself in the ovaries for the disappointment I was feeling. Austin must have seen where my mind headed because he quickly added, "She's actually dating one of the fighters I'm training. A real good guy."

I hated the sense of relief I felt at his words. "That's great," I croaked.

"You know that Michael's dad, Joe, just got out of prison, right?"

My shoulders stiffened at all the memories that surrounded my attack and the weeks afterward. "Yeah, I know, the parole board notified me. My order of protection is still in place, and I really don't think he's going to be seeking me out."

"You're probably right, but just be extra cautious about locking your doors and being aware of your surroundings."

A smile came to my lips. "Some things never change, huh?"

Austin quirked his head to one side. "What?"

"You, being overprotective. Some things never change."

He shook his head, a grin of his own present. "I guess not. Speaking of, I want to talk to you about a program I'm starting." Austin launched into his vision for an after-school program that would serve boys and girls of all ages from low-income backgrounds. He planned on having self-defense and martial arts classes, tutors to help with homework, and would even serve the kids an after-school snack and dinner. He eventually wanted to provide the high school-aged kids college and career counseling, as well as matching them up with weekend jobs to build up savings.

I was blown away. "This all sounds incredible. How can I help?"

Austin had a smile on his face that looked as if it might crack his cheeks. "I could really use a second set of eyes and ears while I do the hiring. I know what to ask from a business and martial arts perspective, but not so much from a kid perspective."

I nodded. "Sure, I'd be happy to pull together some good questions to ask and sit in on any interviews."

"I was hoping you'd say that. Are you available tomorrow after school? I'm having a few potential martial arts teachers come in and teach a sample class."

I pulled my bottom lip between my teeth, nibbling on it. "I'm not sure I can do tomorrow. I have to take my car into the shop when class gets out, and Taylor is going to pick me up at the shop."

"I can pick you up and drop you off at home afterward, it's no problem."

This was all progressing really quickly. I wasn't sure how my little heart was going to handle all this togetherness time, but Austin looked so dang hopeful, I couldn't say no. "If you're sure you don't mind."

"I'm sure."

"Okay, I'll text you the address of my mechanic when I get home."

Austin rose from his chair. "Sounds good, let me walk you to your car."

I got to my feet, slipping my purse over my shoulder. Austin guided me through the door with a hand on the small of my back. Just that tiny contact stoked the embers of the fire I had thought long-ago extinguished. The chemistry I felt for Austin was still there, so what? He didn't feel the same. All I had to do was stay strong and keep my guard up. I could do it because I refused to end up back in love with a guy who was never going to love me back.

TWENTY-SIX

Carter

I COULDN'T HELP BUT HAVE A HUGE GRIN ON MY FACE AS I walked out of the gym with Austin. We'd spent the last four hours meeting with potential instructors for the youth program and discussing the candidates. Austin's passion for the project was contagious, and I found myself daydreaming about all the things the program could accomplish.

Austin paused before opening the passenger car door for me. "How about I take you to dinner to celebrate?"

I stopped myself before the automatic "sure" could pop out of my mouth. Seventy-two hours of having Austin back in my life, and I was already in danger of slipping into old, familiar patterns. I needed distance. Some space and time to shore up my defenses. I toyed with my purse strap and bit down on the corner of my lip. "I think I'd better get home."

Austin stared intently at me. "Come on, Carter, you have to eat."

I pulled my shoulders back and looked him in the eye. "I don't think it's a good idea." Austin said nothing, so I continued talking, trying to explain. "I just need to be better about boundaries." My cheeks heated at the reminder of how I'd pined after Austin in the past. I never wanted to be that girl again.

A muscle in Austin's cheek jumped as he ground his teeth together. "Okay, whatever you want."

I slipped into the buttery-soft leather seats of Austin's Range Rover as soon as he opened the door, setting my purse in my lap and trying desperately not to tell Austin I'd changed my mind. The car ride was quiet except for the sounds of the navigation system instructing Austin when to turn. My body grew tighter with each passing silent minute. I hated this awkwardness between us, but I didn't see any way around it. I wasn't willing to let myself fall back into being a total doormat when it came to Austin. I needed to stay strong.

Austin pulled to the side of the road, snagging a parking spot just a few houses down from mine and Taylor's. "I'll walk you to the door."

I pulled the strap of my purse over my shoulder. "That isn't necessary, my house is right there."

He opened his car door. "I insist."

"Of course, he insists, alpha-male overprotective nonsense," I muttered to myself as I got out. With Joe out of prison, I should have been grateful, but Austin attempting to finagle us right back into the exact relationship we had been in before was getting on my last nerve.

"What did you say?" Austin asked as he rounded the front of the car.

"Nothing." Taking off toward home, I left Austin in my wake. As I reached the gate, I saw an over-the-top arrangement of lilies and roses sitting on the steps. Our gate required a security code, so any deliveries had to be left out here. I bent down and pulled the card from the holder in the midst of the fragrant spray, it had my name on it. Quickly opening the card, I groaned when I saw Kyle's name. The card read, *Please forgive my harsh words, I just don't want you to get hurt. Love, Kyle.*

"Who are the flowers from?"

The sound of Austin's voice made me jump just a little. "Oh, just Kyle, an apology for something stupid."

Even in the dim light, I could see the tense set of Austin's shoulders, frustration seeming to radiate off him in waves. "So, no boundaries needed for ol' Kyle?"

I bristled. "My relationship with Kyle is really none of your business. You've seen me to my door, there are clearly no kidnappers or murderers about, so I think you can go."

Austin stepped back, running both hands over his buzzed head. "I'm sorry. You're right, that was uncalled for." He took a deep breath and pinned me in place with his gaze. There was a depth of emotion in his eyes that I had rarely seen before. "Can I just come in for a minute? I really need to talk to you about something. I'll even carry your flowers. I'm not sure you'll make it inside with the world's largest bouquet here."

I fought the smile that wanted to rise to my lips. "Oh, all right." Austin heaved up the vase of flowers with a dramatic groan as I keyed in the gate code.

"This is a nice place," Austin said as we headed up the walkway.

"Yeah, I really lucked out that my best friend had a killer pad I could con her into letting me live in." I winced, thinking about the circumstances that had surrounded my moving in with Taylor. Reminders of past hurts were everywhere, just waiting to jump out and sucker punch you right in the heart. Pulling my keys from my purse, I unlocked the door. "Taylor, you home? I'm back, and Austin's with me," I called out, wanting to give her a heads-up about the male guest.

Her voice echoed from upstairs, "I'm here. I'm just on the phone with my mom, be down a little later."

"Okay, tell her hi for me." I loved Taylor's mom, she was the kindest, most kick-butt mom ever, and she had raised Taylor all on her own. She had come to visit a number of times since I'd lived here, and we always had a blast. I turned around to find

Austin setting the flowers on the kitchen bar, looking around and taking in the space. "Can I get you anything to drink? Water? Beer?"

"Uh, water would be great." His hands were shoved into his front pockets, and he almost looked a bit sheepish.

I grabbed two bottles of water from the fridge and gestured towards the living room. "We can talk in there." I wondered what in the world he wanted to talk about and really hoped he wasn't going to try and dredge up the past again. I needed to keep looking forward. Plopping down on the couch, I slipped off my shoes and pulled my knees up to my chest. Austin sat down on the opposite end of the couch, and I handed him his bottle of water. "So, what's up?"

He broke the seal on his water, took a sip, then proceeded to tighten and loosen the cap systematically. My level of anxiety started to rise. "Look, I feel like I need to be honest with you about my intentions for getting back in contact." A fist closed around my heart, stopping it from pumping in a normal fashion. "I don't want to be friends with you." A combination of ice and boiling liquid began surging through my veins. Was it possible to have hot flashes at twenty-three? "I want so much more than friendship from you."

My heart stuttered, stopped, and then started beating again. "What does that mean?" I didn't want to hope. Hope was what had ultimately broken me a year ago, and I didn't want it to destroy me again.

Austin set his water on the coffee table and scooted towards me on the couch. He plucked the water from my hands, setting it next to his. He pulled one of my hands to his mouth and kissed my palm. "I've missed you so fucking much. Every day, I missed you. At first, I was too stubborn and pigheaded to come to you. Drowning in my own pride, thinking I was right, and you were wrong. Then, I saw how far I'd fallen without you, and I knew I had to clean up my act before I could bring you back into my life. But it took me a long fucking time to realize I had never seen you as just a friend. You've always been more. You've always been everything."

My mind spun. I felt lightheaded, and the hot and cold flashes were back. These were the words I had always wanted to hear. Words I craved with a soul-deep ferocity, that nothing else could satiate. So, why was fear all I felt? A panic that rocked me straight to my core.

Tears pooled in my eyes. "I don't think I can do this." They weren't the words I'd thought would come out of my mouth if Austin ever showed up at my door, heart in hand. Pain flashed in his eyes, but I was overcome by memories of all the tears I'd cried, all the sleepless nights, the painful joy of watching him fight on screen in the safety of my bedroom. My heart physically hurt. I pulled my hand from his.

Austin swiped a hand roughly across his face. "What does that mean?"

"It means, this is a lot to take in. And I'm really freaking overwhelmed right now." Tears continued to track down my face, a release valve for all the bottled-up emotions I'd been carrying around for the past year. "What did you expect me to do? Throw myself at your feet as soon as you said you had feelings for me? You really hurt me." Needing to move, to expel some of this energy, I stood and began to pace. It didn't help. When I felt Austin behind me, I whirled around. "You broke my fucking heart!"

Austin reached out like he was going to pull me to him, but he stopped himself mid-motion, letting his hands fall to his sides. "I know. And I'm so fucking sorry. I'll never be sorrier about anything in my whole damned life. I would do anything to take away that pain."

His words only made me cry harder. "Please," he begged, "please, let me just hold you."

The rawness of his voice had my resolve crumbling. I gave a small nod, and his body engulfed mine. He held me as my body shook, and my tears soaked his tee. One hand trailed up and down my spine while the other massaged my nape. As my tears lessened and my sobs slowed, his touch began to stoke flames in my lower belly. Austin whispered in my ear, "I'm sorry I blindsided you. I know it's going to take time for you to trust that this is what I really want, to trust *me*. I'm here for the long haul, I'm not going anywhere. We can take this as slow as you want."

Pulling back, I sucked my bottom lip between my teeth and nibbled. I felt Austin's hand twitch on my neck, and I knew he was fighting the urge to use his fingers to release my lip like he always used to do when I employed the nervous habit. Waves of nausea rolled through my stomach, brought on by both the idea of fully opening myself up to Austin or closing the door completely. Each road was paralyzingly terrifying. I needed time. I needed space. I needed to know, without a shadow of a doubt, that he would never hurt me like that again.

"I'd like it if we could just be friends first. We need to take some time to get to know one another again. I'm a different person than I was a year ago. You might not even like me." It was true, but it was also the only thing I could think of to buy me some time. Time to see if I could truly trust that this Austin who said he loved me now, had always loved me, was here to stay.

Austin huffed, pulling my forehead down to his. I stopped breathing. "The core of you will always be the same, Firecracker. The only thing that could change would be the toppings. But, you're right, we should take some time to get reacquainted. Just promise me you'll spend some one-on-one time with me so we can actually do that. No more bullshit about not going to dinner with me because it's a bad idea." He widened his eyes at me to emphasize his point.

I nodded slightly, the skin on our foreheads rubbing together.

"Okay." I whispered the word so softly, I could barely hear it.

"Okay," he said almost as softly. He pulled back slightly, and then he brought his lips to my forehead. They were warm and still surprisingly soft. I reveled in the contact, wished I could swim around in it for hours. All too soon, he retreated. "I gotta get out of here before I push you for more than you're ready for."

I nodded robotically, following him to the door. I was in a fog, felt as if I had taken too much cold medicine or something. Austin turned as he opened the door. "Goodnight." He cupped my cheek briefly and then released me. "Lock this behind me," he said, tapping the outside of the door. My head bobbed up and down in agreement. Then, he was gone. I pushed the door closed, flipped the lock, and then sank to the floor on my socked feet. Resting my head back on the hard wood of the front door, I looked to the ceiling for answers. It had none.

Soft footfalls sounded on the stairs, and Taylor's slipper-clad feet appeared, making their way down. She sank to the floor next to me, and I instinctively leaned my head on her shoulder. "I'm not going to lie, I eavesdropped on the last half of y'all's conversation."

"Nosy B."

"My bestie's got the love of her life sitting on the couch pouring his heart out, and you think I'm not going to listen? Pssshhh." She pinched my leg. "So, what are you thinking?"

"I honestly have no idea. I'm all over the place. Half of me wants to jump into his arms and scream 'love me forever.' The other half of me wants to run in the other direction because there's a huge chance I could get hurt. And I know it would be so much worse this go-around."

Taylor looped an arm around my bent knees, hugging them to her. "Honey, loving someone always means you're running the risk of getting hurt. But the only alternative is to completely shut yourself off from the world, and that would be one lonely life."

I sighed. "You are a wise woman, Miss Lawson."

"Don't I know it."

My ringtone sang out from the living room. "Crud, that's my phone."

"Come on, lazy bones, can't stay on the floor forever." She stood and reached out a hand to me.

I took it and grumbled, "But I like the floor, things are safer down there." Taylor chuckled and slapped my butt as I passed her. I grabbed my phone from my purse just as it stopped ringing. The screen read: *One missed call – Kyle.* "Oh, come on."

"What is it?" Taylor asked as her nosey butt leaned over my shoulder to peer at my screen. Then she snorted. "Oh, lordy, that boy can't catch a clue."

I slipped my phone into my back pocket without checking the message. "I don't know what I'm going to do about him. It's so awkward. Those flowers over there are from him."

Her eyes widened as she took in the monstrosity of a bouquet. "Whoa."

"Whoa is right. He said he was apologizing for snapping at me when I told him I was meeting up with Austin, but he signed it 'Love, Kyle.' Something like that doesn't exactly require flowers. We're not together anymore. We were barely together for three months to start with."

Taylor drummed her fingers on her bottom lip. "I'd say have another conversation with him, but all the other talks you've had with him haven't worked. I think you just need to distance yourself from him as much as possible. Don't call him back, and try to make your interactions at school as brief as you can."

"I think you're right. I'll just avoid him as much as possible."

"Of course, I'm right. Now, you want to order Chinese and watch a Lifetime movie?"

I grinned and handed Taylor my cell phone. "Sounds like perfection. You order while I go change?"

"You got it."

I bounded towards my room, feeling a burst of energy from the gratitude that filled my heart. Friends, food, and cheesy TV made everything else in life just melt away. Any and all decisions could be postponed for another day.

TWENTY-SEVEN

Carter

THE PAST FEW WEEKS HAD BROUGHT WITH THEM A TURN to a new normal. Between helping to get the new youth program up and running, and spending time with our friends, I saw Austin almost every day. He never pushed the romantic envelope, but he wasn't afraid of showing his affection either. Cupping my face in his hands, kissing my forehead, lingering hugs. I was about ready to combust, yet something was still holding me back from jumping in with both feet.

Today, I was standing next to Michael, who seemed to have grown a foot in the past year, and watching Austin do a demonstration with one of the fighters he was training. "He's badass, huh, Miss Carter?" I had told Michael he could call me Carter now that I wasn't his teacher, but he couldn't quite break the formal habit and had settled on Miss Carter.

My eyes had been focused on checking out Austin's butt, which was straining against his workout pants, so I really couldn't say anything about his athletic prowess at the moment. "Watch your language. If your mom hears you, you're going to be cleaning the house for a month." That was another thing that had changed in the past few weeks of spending my afternoons at Austin's gym. I'd gotten to know Michael's mom, Sofia, even better, and she was a gem. A total sweetheart who wasn't afraid to crack some skulls if necessary.

Michael instantly spun around, looking for his mom. The comically petrified look on his face had me busting up laughing, and Austin turning around at the sound. "Now, class, it looks like someone isn't paying attention." Austin started stalking towards me as the twelve-year-old students began to snicker.

I started to slowly back away as Austin advanced. "Now, Austin…" My voice trailed off as he surged ahead, throwing me over his shoulder like a sack of potatoes. I shrieked and laughed even harder as he ran around the studio with me over his shoulder. Just as he passed the hooting group of boys, I felt my phone vibrate in my front pocket.

Austin slowed. "Is that a phone in your pocket, or are you just happy to see me?"

I smacked his shoulder. "Put me down, you big buffoon." Austin chuckled as he slowly slid me down the front of his body, the friction causing sparks of electricity. Our eyes met and held for a moment, our mouths just a whisper apart. It would be so easy to just lean in that fraction of an inch and taste his lips. My phone buzzed again, and I jolted away. Fumbling to untangle my phone from my pocket, I almost tripped. Austin chuckled.

"Hello?" My voice sounded husky and breathless. I really hoped it wasn't one of my parents calling; I hadn't even looked at the caller ID. There was no answer on the other end. "Hello? Anyone there?" Again, no answer, but I heard shuffling in the background. Maybe it was a pocket dial. I pulled the phone away from my ear to see who it was, but it just said *Unknown*. I put the phone back to my ear. "Hello-o-o?" There was just a click in response. Call ended. Weird.

I looked up at Austin, who I realized was standing very close, brows furrowed. "Who was it?"

"I don't know. There was no one there, but I heard sounds in the background."

"Who do you think it could be?"

I glanced down at my phone's screen. "Probably just a wrong number." Something pricked at my memory, and I scowled.

"What?" Austin reached up and rubbed at the furrow that was now between my brows.

"I guess it could be Lexi, although I haven't heard from her since I changed my number and email."

Austin froze at the mention of the elephant between us. "I'm sorry she was such a bitch to you, and even sorrier that I gave her the ammunition to use."

I swallowed down the lump in my throat that felt like it was made of razor blades. "It's okay. Let's not talk about her. She's not worth it." I glanced down at my phone to check the time. "I have to get going if I'm going to have time to shower before I make dinner for you and the boys."

"Okay, I'm going to grab a quick shower here and then I'll be right behind you. Do you need me to pick anything up on my way?"

"Liam's bringing beer, so I think we're good. I'll text you if I think of anything."

"Okay." Austin leaned forward, grasping the back of my neck and bringing my forehead to his lips. At the contact, the energy between us flared to life again, all the previous tension forgotten in favor of a whole different kind of tension. He slowly pulled away, and I felt instantly colder. "Drive safe."

"Yes, oh overprotective one." He smacked me on the butt as I made my escape.

I spent the drive home daydreaming about all the ways Austin set my nerve endings on fire. When I pulled into the driveway, the gate closing behind me, I realized it was a miracle that I hadn't gotten into an accident. I sent up a silent prayer that I wouldn't be receiving any red-light traffic tickets in the mail. *No more thinking about Austin while driving*, I mentally scolded myself as I cut across the grass and unlocked the front door. Toeing off my sneakers by the door, I set my purse down on the bench at the end of my bed. Time for a cold shower to get my body under control.

I pulled my hair up into a top knot since I wouldn't have time to wash and dry it before Austin got here. I stepped under the chilly spray and jumped, okay, maybe not quite *that* cold. Reaching for my body wash to scrub away the grime of the day, I let the water cool my overheated skin. I sighed in relief when I shut off the tap, wrapping a warm, fluffy towel around my body. I patted my face dry and then reached for a cotton swab and my toner. My hand hit air. My toner wasn't where I always kept it. Weird. I looked at my vanity. It was always set up in the same way, in the order in which I used the products, but everything was moved around. A chill skittered over my skin, and I pulled the towel tighter around myself.

I opened the bathroom door and walked into my bedroom. Nothing had seemed out of place when I came through earlier, but with closer inspection, I could see that picture frames had been moved, and when I opened my bedside table's drawers, it looked like someone had rifled through them in a rush.

I had a type-A personality when it came to organization, everything in my life had an assigned place and went into that place. Austin used to make fun of me for it or try to secretly move something and see if I'd notice. I always noticed. But Austin hadn't been in my room, and Taylor would never be this careless. Even if she came in to borrow clothes, she generally left me a note. I was starting to freak out. Crossing to my purse, I slipped my phone from the side pocket and dialed Austin.

He answered on the second ring. "Hey, babe, you think of something you needed me to pick up?"

I gripped the phone tighter. "Austin, I think someone was in my room."

"What do you mean?" His words had a harsh bite to them.

"Stuff in my bathroom wasn't where I always leave it, my picture frames were moved around, and it looks like someone went through the stuff in my nightstand."

"But nothing's missing? Are you sure it wasn't just Taylor looking for something? Where is she?"

"Taylor left this afternoon to go see her mom for the weekend, and she wouldn't have moved my picture frames." Austin probably thought I was a looney tune, but I knew someone had been in here.

"I'm two minutes away, just hold tight, and I'll check everything out."

"Okay, see you in a minute."

"In a minute."

I sighed a breath of relief. Even though Austin might think I was overreacting, he was still going to check things out. I was grateful. I keyed in a text to Taylor.

Me: *Sorry to bug you while you're with your mom but were you in my room looking for something before you left?*

Almost immediately, my phone buzzed with a response.

Taylor: *No, why?*

Me: *Stuff just isn't where I left it, but who knows, maybe I'm just losing my mind.*

I didn't think I was though.

Taylor: *You've been working too hard lately. You're probably just exhausted and put something somewhere you usually don't.*

I didn't want to worry Taylor on her trip, so I agreed with her and didn't mention my pictures and nightstand.

Me: *You're probably right. Have fun with your mom and give her a squeeze for me!*

Taylor: *Will do!* <3

I jumped when I heard the buzzer for the gate and rushed to the intercom by the front door. "Hello?" I hated that my voice sounded just a little shaky.

"It's me." My shoulders slumped in relief at the sound of Austin's voice, and I buzzed him in, opening the front door before he could even knock.

He came up short on the front step. "Why are you in a towel?" he choked out.

My cheeks heated. "I had just gotten out of the shower when I realized things weren't where I left them."

"Go put on a robe while I go check the rest of the house."

I nodded and bolted for my room. I opened the top drawer of my dresser in search of my favorite pair of panties. They were the softest silk, and I wanted my comfiest things at the moment. I picked through the drawer, not seeing them. I had just done laundry yesterday and knew I had put them in here. I searched again. Nothing. Dread hit my stomach like a heavy stone. I abandoned my underwear drawer and threw on my robe. The big, fluffy one, not the sexy, skimpy one. I needed all the protection I could get. I made a beeline for the living room and almost collided with Austin. Shrieking, I reeled back and almost landed on my butt before Austin caught me.

"Jesus! Are you okay?"

"My favorite pair of underwear is missing."

Austin cursed and pulled out his phone. "I'm calling the cops, this is too weird."

I listened in a daze as Austin answered questions a dispatcher asked, providing my address and saying that we thought there had been an intruder. He kept an arm around me the whole time he talked. When he hung up, I started word vomiting. "I want to put clothes on, but I don't want to put anything on that some creepy intruder touched. I just keep imagining all the germs he might have had on his hands. I mean, it's got to be a guy if he stole my panties. I guess that's sexist, it could be a girl intruder, maybe she's a lesbian or just has really good taste in lingerie, they were made of the nicest silk."

Austin clamped a hand over my mouth. "Take a deep breath, Firecracker." He slowly removed his hand, making sure my diatribe wouldn't start up again.

I inhaled deeply through my nose and out through my mouth like they taught in the one yoga class I'd gone to. "Sorry."

"It's okay, you're freaked. Sit down on the couch, and I'll get you a glass of water." I did as he instructed and continued the yoga breathing, trying to calm my nerves. Austin brought over the glass of water and rubbed my back. "Did you get in touch with Taylor?"

"Yes, she said she wasn't in my room today, and she knows I would murder her if she borrowed my favorite pair of panties. Plus, we are not the kind of roommates who borrow each other's underwear, that's crossing a line."

"Okay, what time did she leave for the airport?"

"She had a car picking her up at 3 p.m."

The buzzer sounded, and Austin rose to answer it. I could hear the muffled conversation of the police identifying themselves and smoothed my sweaty palms over my robe to dry them. I stood as Austin led the two police officers into the living room. There was an older officer with graying hair and a bit of a paunch, and a younger one who was reed-thin and looked to barely be twenty-one. The older man, who introduced himself as Officer MacMillan, was clearly in charge. The younger man, Officer Garcia, kept glancing at Austin, apparently star-struck by the UFL superstar.

"So, Miss McCarthy, you believe there was an intruder in your home?" Officer MacMillan said as he looked up from his notepad. I talked the officers through what I had discovered, blushing crimson when it came to telling them about my missing undies. Officer MacMillan took a few notes but seemed to grow more and more skeptical. "We're going to take a look around, and then we'll come back to talk with you some more."

I nodded as Officer MacMillan headed to my bedroom, and Officer Garcia went outside. I turned to Austin, who was seated next to me. "They don't believe me."

He rubbed a hand up and down my back and then started kneading my shoulders. "You don't know that for sure. Let's just wait and see what they have to say after they've looked around." I let myself collapse into Austin's side as he continued his ministrations.

Ten minutes later, the officers returned following a brief con-fab in the entryway. "Now, Miss McCarthy, are you sure you didn't just misplace this pair of underwear?" Officer MacMillan asked, eyebrows lifted.

My hackles raised at his condescending tone. I took a deep breath, reminding myself that this guy didn't know me or my character. "I'm sure, sir. And there were things moved around in my room."

The older officer tapped his notepad on his thigh. "Well, there is zero sign of forced entry. You got a lot of spare keys floating around?"

"Just me, my roommate, and our housekeeper, who has worked for Taylor for over three years."

"Well, maybe your roommate was nosing around and is too embarrassed to admit it. We'll file a report, but there's nothing else we can do."

I squeezed Austin's knee in frustration. "Couldn't you at least dust for fingerprints?"

Officer MacMillan chuckled. "Honey, this is LA. We don't spend resources like that on a missing pair of underwear."

Austin pushed to his feet then. "I think you can leave now, but I'd like to get your badge number before you go." He had been mostly silent throughout the meeting, but now I could feel anger coming off him in waves.

Officer MacMillan smugly tossed a business card onto the coffee table. "My badge number's on the card. You know she's probably just doing this to get your attention." And with that, he turned and left. Hot tears of frustration streamed down my cheeks as I gripped the couch cushion I was sitting on.

The younger officer lingered, looking uncomfortable and waiting until his partner was out of earshot. "I'm sorry about him. He's old school, and his time on the job has made him a cynic. I'll make sure a report gets filed. It honestly sounds like it could be a case of stalking, so maybe think about changing locks, stay alert, and call if anything else happens."

Austin jerked his chin in the boy-man's direction, and he left. Austin followed him out, there was the sound of a lock clicking, and then he was back. "Stay here for just a minute, I'm going to make a couple calls." Pulling the blanket off the back of the couch, I tucked into a ball. I could hear the muffled sounds of Austin talking to someone, but couldn't make out what he was saying.

A few minutes later, he came back and sat on the coffee table, knees bracketing my legs. "I talked to a locksmith, they'll be here in an hour to change all your locks. The boys are picking up pizza and bringing overnight stuff. We're gonna have ourselves a slumber party, and if you're lucky, I might even let you paint Ford's toenails."

A faint smile came to my lips at that mental image. Austin stood and reached out a hand. "Come on, let's strip your bed and wash your sheets. Once those are done, we can start washing all your clothes." I just blinked up at him. How did he know that this was just the thing I needed? He bent down and grabbed my wrist when I didn't move. "I know it will make you feel less skeeved out if we wash everything."

I smiled for real then, feeling as if I had taken a solid hit to the solar plexus in the best possible way. This man was kind, caring, and was going to help me wash every item of clothing I owned because I was a freaked-out germaphobe. It was then that I knew I was going to let him back in. All the way in. I was going to jump off the high dive and take the risk of a big ol' ugly and painful belly flop because he was worth the risk.

I stopped walking, and because Austin still had a hold of my wrist, he stopped, too. I leaned forward and pressed a kiss through his t-shirt to his left pec, right where his heart might be. Feeling his sharp intake of breath, I tipped my head back to look him in the eyes. "Thank you," I whispered.

"Anything for you," he whispered back.

TWENTY-EIGHT

Austin

SUNLIGHT FILTERED THROUGH THE PALM TREES AS I STOOD in my open entryway, waiting for Liam to get out of his overpriced sportscar. "Thanks for doing this," I called as he shut his door.

"No problem. I'm happy to help. Having some of this stuff in place will make me feel a hell of a lot better about Carter and Taylor living in that house by themselves."

My gut tightened at the reminder of Friday's events. I hated the idea of Carter being alone for a second and hoped that getting some things in place to help her defend herself would ease my mind. "You and me both. All the supplies are in the garage, but do you want to come in for a quick drink first before I have to head to the gym?"

"Sounds good. It's hot as hell out there, and it's only April."

I ushered Liam inside and into the oversized gourmet kitchen, grabbing him a beer and me a water. "Here you go."

Liam took a swig of the dark ale. "So, how's training going?"

My hands tightened around my bottle of water. "It's going." The truth was, I had been distracted as hell. My training was suffering, and I'd fallen behind on the day-to-day aspects of running the gym. I'd spent the entire weekend with Carter and wouldn't have wanted it any other way, but that meant cancelling two training sessions and a meeting with one of my fighters.

Liam studied my face. "You seem stressed. What's going on?"

"You mean besides the girl I love thinking someone broke into her house and stole her fucking underwear?"

He narrowed his eyes at me. "Fair point. But there's something else."

I cracked my neck. "I'm just trying to figure out how to balance training, the gym, and Carter, without one of those things falling through the cracks."

Liam straightened on his stool. "You're not having second thoughts, are you? Because I may not be able to kick your ass, but I will seriously hire a hitman to murder you if you hurt Carter again."

My skin prickled at the insult. "Fuck, no. I'm just not used to having to juggle so much." I paused, thinking about how my nerve endings had felt itchy all day. "And I want today to go well."

Liam started a slow chuckle that turned into cackling. "You're nervous? Austin 'Bulldog' Lyons is *scared* of taking a girl on a date."

I scowled. "Screw you, man." I was planning to surprise Carter with our first official date this afternoon, but my stomach had been in knots since I'd decided on a plan of attack. I wasn't good at this kind of thing. I had grown up with my last girlfriend, so I hadn't really had to think about wooing her beyond getting her a corsage for prom. Could I even call Carter my girlfriend? Fuck, I was heading into pussy territory, and fast.

Liam doubled over, barely able to get his words out. "The look on your face! Fucking priceless!"

I chucked my half-full water bottle at him in response.

"Shit!" Liam caught the bottle as it bounced off his shoulder. "There's no need for violence. Tell Dr. Liam what's got you doubting yourself."

I shook my head but couldn't help the small grin. Liam was a nut, but he was also the crazy person who had an inside track to Carter's mind. I walked him through my plan for the afternoon. As I talked, his shit-eating grin got wider and wider. "She's going to love this. I gotta admit, I'm impressed with you pulling out all the stops already."

"I told you I was going after my girl. I'm not messing around." And I wasn't. It was killing me to take things as slowly as I had been, but Carter's breakdown the night I had brought her home had shown me just how much I'd hurt her. How scared she was to fully let me back in. I needed to take things at a snail's pace. And I could do that. I could do anything as long as it got me my Firecracker in the end.

What I didn't want was to backtrack on any of the progress we'd made. "You sure it's not too much? I don't want to overdo it and send her running for the hills."

"Are you kidding me? She's going to love it."

I blew out a long breath. "All right." All I could do was trust that Liam wouldn't steer me wrong, and send up a prayer that I wouldn't screw this up. I glanced at my watch. "Shit, I gotta get to the gym. I have a meeting about the media day we're doing for Eric's fight." I hated when we had to let the press vultures into the gym to open workouts, but they promoted the fights, so there was no way around it. The fans usually made it fun, though, keeping the energy levels up throughout the workout. This would be my first really massive media day as a coach, and I wanted to make sure all of the attention was focused on my fighter, Eric.

"Eric's looking good. Think he'll come out with a win?" Liam asked.

"I think there's a real good chance. For a new fighter, he's got some major skills. With a few more fights on the big stage, he'll get used to the pressure and really be able to dominate his weight class." I grabbed my wallet and keys. "Come on, all the stuff is in the garage. Just lock up when you're done. Thanks again for helping me out, man."

"Anytime. Good luck this afternoon. Just remember to pop a mint before you go in for the kiss!" Liam said with a chuckle.

I drilled him with a half-hearted hook to his side. "Yeah, yeah." I slipped out my front door and into my SUV. I could do this, I was a grown-ass man, I would not bow to the pressures of a first date.

TWENTY-NINE

Carter

I POPPED THE TAB ON MY SECOND DIET COKE OF THE DAY, and it was only noon. Monday was hitting me hard. After my terrifying Friday, the weekend had taken a turn for the better. The boys had all demanded that they spend the entire weekend with me since Taylor was out of town. Friday night, they were feeling so badly for me that I talked them into face masks and a chick flick. Saturday, I went with them to their flag football game, where Austin had proceeded to growl at any guy who spoke to me. Liam and Ford thought it was hilarious. Sunday, I cooked a massive brunch, and the boys watched sports while I graded papers. It was heaven, but I was exhausted and struggling today.

I pulled my lunch bag from the file drawer on my desk and unwrapped my sandwich. I had taken to eating in my classroom in an effort to avoid any potentially awkward run-ins with Kyle. Taylor usually joined me, but she had lunchroom duty today. A knock sounded on my door that had me sending a silent prayer heavenward that Kyle hadn't come to search me out.

"Come in." A dark, buzzed head appeared in the cracked door, his eyes sweeping the room. When he saw that I was alone, he opened the door fully. "What are you doing here?" I stood from my desk and crossed to Austin, wrapping my arms around his waist. His shirt was warm from the sun, and I burrowed my cheek deeper into his chest.

"I brought you some presents."

I pulled back and saw that he was carrying a medium-sized gift bag. "I like presents."

He shot me a devastating grin that had my lower belly clenching. "You get most of them now, but one has to wait until after our date."

My cheeks rose as a smile spread across my own face. "Date?"

Austin gestured for me to sit back down at my desk. "Yes, I'm taking you on our first official date this afternoon. Hurry home after school, and I'll pick you up around four. And wear something comfortable, like jeans."

My smile got bigger. "Okay. Now, gimme." I made grabby hands at the bag he was holding.

"Spoiled rotten, I tell you." He reached into the bag and pulled out a Taser, pepper spray, and what looked like some sort of brass knuckles with two spikes—all of the items pink. "I thought if they looked a least a little girlie, you'd be more likely to use them."

My jaw hung open. "What, no bazooka? Armed battalion?"

He tapped my nose. "Don't tempt me. Just do me a favor and carry them. Put one of them in your hand when you're walking to and from your car."

I could see the concern in his eyes and the hard-set line of his shoulders. He was worried about me. That was about the only thing that could have gotten me to carry this ridiculous stuff. "Okay, but if I accidentally maim some poor old lady or poke my own eye out with one of those spikes, you're paying the medical bills."

A smile came back to Austin's lips. "You've got yourself a deal. I've got to get back to the gym, but I'll see you a little later." He leaned across the desk and kissed my forehead. The contact carried with it a promise of much more to come. Tingles shot to my nipples, and I sucked in a breath.

When he pulled away, I could see heat in his eyes. As he made his way to the door, I saw Kyle peeking in through the window, but he quickly jumped back when our eyes met. I felt bad, but maybe this was for the best. If he saw me with someone else, perhaps he would finally realize that there was no chance for us. Austin turned as he reached for the doorknob, oblivious to Kyle's spying. "Bye, beautiful."

A blush filled my cheeks as I got out a hushed, "Bye, Austin." He was gone, and I was a bumbling mess for the rest of the day: dropping erasers, knocking over the cup of pens on my desk. I think my students thought I was drunk.

When the last bell finally rang at 3:15 p.m., I gathered up my belongings as quickly as possible and made a beeline for home. As soon as I arrived, I tore through my room, pulling my favorite skinny jeans from my dresser and tossing shirts all around until I settled on a white eyelet blouse with ruffled sleeves that made my boobs look great. I dashed into the bathroom to freshen up my makeup and hair. The gate buzzer went off just as I finished gliding some pale pink gloss across my lips. Slipping my feet into a pair of gold sandals, I grabbed my purse.

Instead of buzzing Austin in, I simply headed out the door, being extra careful to lock it behind me. His broad frame peeked out from behind the slatted wood gate, and butterflies took flight in my belly. This was it, our first real date. Would he try to kiss me? I really hoped so. All of a sudden, all my fears came rushing back. What if I had changed, and Austin didn't like the person I was now? What if he realized he wasn't attracted to me after all? My hand paused on the gate's doorknob. I didn't know if I could go through with this.

Austin must have sensed my hesitancy because low and rumbly he said, "Open the door, Firecracker." I gulped and did as he said. The door swung toward me, and Austin's eyes travelled up and down my body, stalling on my breasts—thank you eyelet top—and then moved back to my face. "You look gorgeous."

I, of course, blurted out, "I think I'm going to puke."

He started laughing so hard he had to brace himself on the gate's frame. "I don't think you mean you're actually sick."

"No, but I could be," I said, scowling at him.

Austin reached for me, but I backed away, mad at his insensitive butt for laughing at me. The evasion didn't last long, and he wrapped an arm around my shoulders, pulling me into his chest. "There's no reason to be nervous, baby. You're my favorite person in the whole world. There's no way we're not going to have a blast." I melted into him at those words; they were just what I needed to hear.

He must have felt the tension bleed from me because he squeezed my shoulder and pulled back, forcing me to meet his eyes. "Everything okay now?" I nodded, cheeks heating at the thought of my freak-out. Austin grabbed my hand, interlocking our fingers, and led me to his car. "You're so fucking adorable."

I slipped into the SUV as soon as Austin opened the door, clicking my seatbelt into place and fumbling with my purse strap. Austin got in, cranked the engine, and then reached for my hand again, placing our interwoven fingers on his thigh. He'd never held my hand like this before, and I soaked up the sensations as he traced nonsensical shapes on the back of my hand.

I took in his face as he navigated through traffic: his cut jaw with just the faintest shadow of stubble, nose with just the slightest crook in it from being broken one too many times, deep and dark blue eyes, and a Dodgers baseball cap pulled low on his forehead. He was breathtaking, and he apparently wanted me. I was going for it. Smiling down at my lap I asked, "So, where are we going?"

He turned to glance at me briefly, a devious grin on his

handsome face. "It's a surprise."

"Come on."

"You're just going to have to be patient."

"Patience is not my virtue."

Austin chuckled. "We'll be there in about ten minutes, so you won't have to be patient for long."

I let myself be lulled by Austin's gentle ministrations on the back of my hand and, before I knew it, we were pulling into the parking lot at Griffith Observatory. "I've always wanted to go here, but I've never made it."

He smiled as he swung into a parking spot. "I thought it would be the perfect spot for a picnic."

I just sat there and blinked at him for a moment. "A picnic? I love picnics!"

"I know you do." He slipped on the sunglasses that hung from his shirt collar and pulled his hat farther down his forehead. Studying his movements, I realized Austin was trying to disguise himself. When we used to hang out, the odd fight fan would approach him here or there, but I recognized that his entire world had changed within the span of a year.

With a squeeze, he released my hand, hopped down from the Range Rover, and came around to my door to help me out. He then opened the trunk and retrieved an extremely large picnic basket. With his free hand, he grabbed mine and led us toward the massive lawns that overlooked LA.

"It's beautiful up here," I said, turning myself towards him. "I think all this time, you were just a closet romantic."

"Only for you, Firecracker. Only for you." Austin stopped us when he came to a spot that wasn't too crowded but had a great view of the city. He set down the picnic basket and pulled out a red plaid blanket, spreading it out over the grass. He gestured for me to sit and started pulling takeout containers from the basket. "I got all your favorites from Joan's On Third."

Joan's made my absolute favorite egg salad and this delicious snap pea and asparagus salad, not to mention their cupcakes. "You are a king among men." I sighed, then made a grabby hands motion at him and started opening all the packages. My stomach growled so loudly that Austin could hear it, and he started laughing. I smacked his shoulder. He settled in next to me, and we started scooping food onto plates. "How was the gym today?"

"Good. Trained with a couple new guys who I think have potential."

I swallowed my bite of egg salad on focaccia and tried not to moan. "That's great. Are you thinking that you want to move towards coaching more?"

Austin was silent for a moment, and I turned my head towards him as he took a slug of water. "I think I'm going to retire from fighting at the end of next year."

I dropped my sandwich back to my plate. "Really? Why? You love fighting."

He toyed with the napkin that was lying across his thigh. "I love it, but I don't love what it does to my body. I get just as much of a high when one of the guys I train wins as when I do. It's not worth the risk of being turned into a vegetable from one too many concussions."

I was stunned silent. I had never heard Austin talk like this. He always downplayed any injury risks. I met his eyes and could see a hesitancy there like he was unsure if I would still want to be with him if he was no longer center stage. I reached over and squeezed his hand. "I think that's great. Really great."

His shoulders sagged in relief. "What about teaching? Are you still loving it?"

I took a sip of my lemonade and pondered how to answer that. "There are a lot of things I love about it, but there are a lot of things that are frustrating. I love interacting with the kids, figuring out how to best support and encourage each one, but I hate how many restrictions I have. I have to spend so much time preparing them for standardized tests. Tests that I'm not sure accurately measure anything and don't truly help them learn. And there is a desperate need for after-school programs like the one you're starting. All these kids need more support than they're currently getting, and I wish I had the freedom to give it to them. I can get away with some things, but not on a broad scale."

Austin had been listening intently to everything I had to say. It was so refreshing. Even Kyle, a teacher himself, got annoyed when I prattled on about my frustration with the system. Austin brushed a stray strand of hair behind my ear. "I think it's amazing that you care so deeply for these kids. I wish there was more I could do to help you."

"What you're already doing is incredible. I heard some of the boys in my class talking about the flyers I posted at school. They're going to ask their parents if they can join."

"I'm glad." Austin set his plate aside and patted the ground between his spread legs. I scooted over, and he leaned me back into his chest. His heart beat against my shoulder blades, as my own started to speed up.

We were silent as we watched the sun sink lower in the sky. When the horizon burned red, I tilted my face up towards Austin's. His cheekbones flared a deep pink with the reflecting sun. Austin angled his chin down and gazed into my eyes. My heart rattled in its cage, but I didn't look away.

He brought his mouth closer, millimeter by millimeter, and then it was on mine. His lips were warm and softer than I remembered. He tasted of the vanilla cupcake we had split moments ago and something uniquely him. I couldn't imagine a better flavor. He nibbled on my bottom lip before slipping his tongue into my mouth. I wanted, no I *needed* more. I needed him to touch me everywhere. Austin pulled back on a gasp. "Jesus, you're going to be the death of me." He brought his forehead down to mine as we both fought to catch our breath.

My whole body was tingling, and all my nerve endings seemed to be firing at once. If just kissing Austin could turn me into a quivering pile of need, I couldn't imagine what doing other things would cause. It might kill me. The reminder of the possibility of doing other stuff with Austin was like a bucket of cold ice water on my heated flesh.

I pulled my forehead away from his and turned back to the sunset. I desperately wanted to do those things with Austin, but I was terrified at the same time. Scared I wouldn't be any good at it, especially in comparison to the women he was used to. Petrified that I would give him my body, my heart, my soul, and this would all come crashing down around me. The cupcake I'd eaten soured in my stomach.

Austin's voice jarred me from my downward spiral of doomed thoughts. "What are you thinking so hard about over there, Firecracker?" I bit down on my bottom lip, unsure of what to say. He reached around and gently pulled my lip from between my teeth. "What's wrong?"

I glanced around to make sure that no one was within earshot. "I'm worried I won't be any good at that stuff." I couldn't look at Austin as I continued, better just to get it all out. "I'm still a virgin, and I don't have much experience with the other stuff." I could feel my cheeks getting hotter by the second. "I just want it to be good for you when, I mean, *if* we do that stuff. You have a lot of experience, and I'm worried I'll be a disappointment, and then you won't want to be with me and then I'll have to kick you in the balls for breaking my heart because I'm not good at sex." I sucked in air, out of breath from my tangent.

Austin grasped my chin, turning my head so I was forced to look him in the eyes. "First of all, we are in no rush. We are going to take this as slow as we need to. Second, based on that kiss that has me painfully hard, I don't think we'll have any issues in the bedroom." I could feel that hardness up against my backside, I instinctively wiggled. He closed his eyes and groaned. "Dear God, please don't do that, you're making it worse." I instantly stopped.

"Carter, here's the thing, I've had a lot of empty sex in my life. I wish that wasn't true now, but I have. That kind of sex is never as good as when you have a real connection with someone. When you have time to get to know someone and know what they like and don't, how their body responds to yours. I think it takes true intimacy to have the best sex, and I've never had that, so we're in the same boat."

I looked into his eyes, desperately hoping that what he said was true. "Carter, we'll take our time, and we'll *talk*. I'll teach you what I like. You'll help me figure out what turns you on. We just have to be honest with each other. Can you do that for me?" I nodded. "I need your words, Firecracker."

I licked my lips. "I can be honest."

He closed the distance and hovered just shy of touching my lips. "Good." His lips brushed mine with the barest touch, the sweetest embrace. "Now, let's get out of here before I embarrass myself." He jumped to his feet and lifted me to mine, enfolding me in his arms. "You're perfect just as you are." And then he kissed the tip of my nose.

I helped Austin put everything back into the picnic basket, and we wove through the remaining people scattered across the lawn. Once we were back in the Range Rover, Austin turned to me with that mischievous grin on his face that I loved so much. "Your last present is back at my house."

I had forgotten all about the present I was supposed to get after our date. Apparently, Austin's kisses had melted my brain. "I finally get to see your new place?" He had bought a house a couple of months ago that Liam had told me was killer.

"Yup. I think you'll like it." Before long, we were headed out of Los Feliz and into the Hollywood Hills, my body tilting back and forth as we sped through the canyon roads. Austin pulled to a stop in front of an imposing gate and clicked a remote on his visor. The gates slowly swung open, and we inched up a curving driveway.

I sucked in a breath when I first caught sight of the house. It looked like a magical Spanish villa. The driveway ended in a large circle with a fountain in the middle. The house itself had a tiled roof that met textured, white adobe walls. Balconies peeked out in regular intervals and were covered in deep magenta blooms. It was perfection.

"Austin, this place is breathtaking." I had slipped from the car before he had a chance to open my door.

Coming up behind me, he slipped an arm around the top of my chest and nuzzled my neck. "Glad you like it. You want the full tour?" I nodded. "Come on, then." He grabbed my hand and led me through an arched entryway into the house. Austin took me through room after room, all tiled floors or wide-planked dark wood filled with warm colors that made you want to curl up and stay a while. He paused at one door. "This is my room. I would go in there with you, but I'm not sure I could keep my hands off you, so you're on your own to check that one out."

I giggled and pushed open the door. There was a massive bed with a dark wood frame opposite an equally enormous fireplace. I ran my fingertips across the crisp, white comforter, imagining what it would feel like to slip beneath the sheets.

I rounded the bed and meandered towards what looked like the master bathroom. I gasped, I couldn't help it. I wanted to move into this bathroom and never leave. There was a giant bath-tub set in front of a huge window that overlooked a breathtaking garden alive with vibrant greens and brightly colored flowers. Turning around, I took in the largest shower I'd ever seen with more jets than I could count on first glance, the wall covered in intricate, hand-painted blue tiles.

It was all too much to take in. I had to get out of there, or I'd never leave. I walked back through the bedroom, not even daring to look at what I was sure would be a closet to die for. Austin was leaning against the door frame. "You like?"

"I think your bathroom gave me an orgasm."

"Lucky bathroom." He grinned wickedly and gave me a quick kiss, stoking the fire burning low in my abdomen. "On to the kitchen."

As we walked into the bright and airy kitchen, I heard a high-pitched whining sound. "What is that?" I asked, spinning around to face Austin.

"That would be your final present. Stay here for just a minute." He opened the door to what looked like a garage and disappeared.

I bounced on the balls of my feet but froze when Austin reappeared with a wriggling puppy in his arms. The sight hit me right in the ovaries. My hands lifted to cover my mouth, holding in my gasp. When the puppy caught sight of me, he wriggled even harder.

Austin bent over just as the puppy launched himself from Austin's arms and galloped towards me. I let myself crumple to the floor to catch the gorgeous puppy in my lap. He was this magical gray color that almost looked blue with just a dash of white on his chest and a set of four white socks. Tears gathered in my eyes, and my voice trembled. "He's for me?"

"All yours." I laughed as the puppy bathed my face in kisses. "He's a blue nose pit. I adopted him at the shelter this morning. Pitbulls are super sweet but protective, and most people are intimidated by them. They think he's about five months old, but when he gets a little older, we can get him trained to be a guard dog."

I blinked up at Austin, his intention behind the gift now clear.

I looked back down at the puppy's sweet face. He licked my nose. "Or we could just love him and cuddle him and not give him a job." The puppy yipped as if agreeing with me.

Austin groaned. "We have to get him some sort of training."

"Of course, but he doesn't need to be trained to be a vicious attack dog."

"Not an attack dog, a guard dog."

"Semantics."

"I give up." Austin sank to the floor next to me and the pup. "Liam dropped off a dog bed, food, and some toys that I got with Taylor while we were at the observatory, and I have his crate in the garage."

I leaned in closer to Austin. "Thank you so much for this, I have always wanted a dog."

"I know you have. And I can keep him with me at the gym while you're at work."

I smiled at his thoughtfulness and touched my lips to his. "You're the best." Another touch. Just as Austin deepened the kiss, the puppy yipped and launched himself between us.

Austin scratched behind the puppy's ears. "I think we're going to have to name you Cockblock."

"Austin!" I smacked his shoulder and cuddled the puppy to my chest. "I think we should call him Blue since he's got this blue-gray coat and those soulful eyes."

"Blue." Austin scratched his chin. "I like it."

THIRTY

Carter

I WAS PACKING UP ALL THE QUIZZES I NEEDED TO GRADE tonight when my classroom burst open, and a beaming Taylor came whirling in. "Oh my God, Carter, you will not believe this!" Before I could get a word out, she shoved her phone in my face. Plucking the phone from her hand, I stared at the screen. There, in high definition color on some entertainment news site, were dozens of pictures of Austin and me at the Griffith Observatory. Ones of us holding hands, kissing, our foreheads touching. My stomach dropped when I remembered all we had talked about while those photos were being taken.

Quickly, I scanned the article. It started off with, "*It looks like the reigning bachelor of the UFL may be off the market*" and went on to say there was no confirmation of who the woman in the photos was. When I reached the last line, and no personal details had been revealed, I breathed a sigh of relief. "Carter, you're white as a sheet, are you okay?"

"Yeah, I'm fine. I just had no idea someone was taking pictures, and we were talking about some pretty personal stuff when those photos were taken. I was freaked the photographer might have overheard, but there's nothing in the article from our conversation."

Taylor's own face paled a bit. "Oh, God, I'm sorry, Carter. I didn't even think about that possibility. Everyone has been in a tizzy about you and Austin, and I got excited when I saw your hot lip-lock on the site. Now that I think about it, it's got to be weird for you."

I handed Taylor back her phone and continued to organize my papers to take home. "It'll sure take some getting used to, but he's worth it."

Taylor did a little bounce. "Y'all are so stinking cute, I can hardly stand it! I know you gave me the date details last night, but seeing pics...holy shit, girl, I had to start fanning myself."

I laughed as I slid the last of my necessary belongings into my bag and hoisted it over my shoulder. "You are too much. I have to get going to pick up Blue at Austin's. Want me to cook dinner tonight?"

Taylor gave me a one-armed hug. "You are an angel from Heaven and the best roomie ever."

"I take that as a yes?"

"You know I never say no to food I don't have to cook."

"I've got you covered. See you tonight!" I called as I headed down the school hallway and out into the sunshine. I set my bags in the back seat and climbed in the front. My fingers slid across my phone's screen as I punched out a text to Austin, letting him know I was leaving school before I dropped my cell into the cup holder.

As I made my way through the Eastside and into Hollywood, my stomach started to churn with the anticipation of seeing Austin, feeling the heat of his body, the pressure of his lips against mine. I had become addicted to his touch. Even the innocent brushes fed a need to be as close to him as humanly possible. The desire ratcheted up a notch as I turned onto Mulholland but stalled for a moment when a black SUV appeared much too close for comfort in my rearview mirror. I glanced down at my odometer. Had I been traveling at a snail's pace while lost in my thoughts about Austin? Nope, I was going five miles over the speed limit.

LA drivers were so impatient. I tapped on my brakes, hoping the person behind me would get the message and back off. It must have just pissed them off because they pulled even closer. The windows were darkly tinted so I couldn't tell if it was a man or woman driving. My stomach tightened as the SUV gained even more ground. What was this idiot thinking? One wrong move and we would both go sailing off a hillside.

My heart thudded in my chest, and my knuckles turned white as I gripped the wheel as tightly as possible. Thoughts raced through my mind. How could I get out of this? Should I try to call 911? I glanced at my phone in the cupholder, but the idea of taking one of my hands off the wheel had my palms turning slippery with sweat. My body jolted forward as the SUV hit my bumper.

I couldn't get a full breath as I frantically scanned the road for escape options. Rock face on one side, a cliff on the other. Was this psycho trying to kill me? Hope flared as I spotted an overlook up ahead. I just had to make it to the pull off. "Come on, come on," I kept chanting to myself.

I was seconds away from the lookout. I could do this. I would make it. The SUV slammed into me again. It was as though the world had shifted into slow motion. My head snapped as the seatbelt jerked me back into my seat. I pumped the brakes in a frenzied rhythm as my car spun onto the gravel turn-off. My eyes slammed closed as I prayed I wouldn't go over the edge. Then, everything stopped.

Ever so slowly, I peeled open a single eyelid. My car had landed three feet from the edge. The tears came then, hot and vast, streaming down my cheeks. Desperately sucking in air, I jerked my head around in search of the SUV, there it sat, idling in the middle of the road. My heart thudded so hard in my chest, I could feel the vibrations down to the tips of my toes. No concerned citizen or ax murderer exited the SUV. The engine revved, and it took off down the curving road.

I closed my eyes and leaned my forehead against the steering wheel, trying to take slow breaths to bring my heart rate down to within normal range, staying that way for I don't know how long. When my heart finally slowed, I inhaled deeply and sat back. My chest burned where the seatbelt had kept me in place. Crap, that hurt.

My hand shook violently as I reached out an arm to shut off my car and unbuckle my seatbelt. Turning around, I saw that the whole back corner of my car was smooshed in like an accordion. My Prius had been no match for the giant SUV.

The only person I wanted in that moment was Austin. I started searching the car for my cell phone. It had long since left the cup holder. I was lucky it hadn't flown up and smacked me in the face. My fingers finally found it lodged under the passenger seat, and my hand continued to tremble as I unlocked the screen and searched for Austin's name in my favorites. Tapping his contact, I pressed the phone to my ear. He picked up on the third ring, and I could hear Blue happily barking in the background. "Hey, Firecracker, you get lost?"

"I was actually wondering if you could come and get me." My voice was shaking, I hated it. "Someone ran me off the road."

"Where are you?" All humor had fled from his tone.

"On Mulholland, about a mile from the turnoff to your house."

"I'm on my way, stay in the car and keep your doors locked."

"Okay."

"Do you want me to stay on the phone with you?"

"No, I'm okay, just a little wigged, but I'll be fine till you get here."

"Okay, hold tight."

"I will." A click sounded, and the line went dead. I rubbed the tender spot on my chest and willed the tears to stop. I did not want to be crying when Austin showed up.

Less than five minutes later, I saw Austin's black Range Rover tear around a curve on the opposite side of Mulholland. With tires screeching, he swung into the overlook and was out of his vehicle in a flash, leaving his door wide open. I started to open my own door before he reached it, but he flung it the rest of the way. He hauled me up against him. My chest protested the action, but I bit my lip. "Christ, what the hell happened?"

I burrowed into his chest, laying my cheek over his heart. It pounded in a staccato rhythm against my skin. "I'm not really sure. Someone was riding my tail when I got onto Mulholland. They tapped my bumper once, but I had no place to pull over. When I saw the overlook, I was going to pull off here, but before I could, they slammed into me."

"Fuck! Are you okay?" He pulled back and started running his hands over me like he was checking for injuries.

"I'm okay, really. My chest is just a little tender from where the seatbelt got me, but nothing bad."

Before I could stop him, Austin was unbuttoning the top two buttons of my blouse and examining the skin there. "You're going to have one hell of a bruise. Do your ribs hurt?" He started pressing down all around my ribcage.

I finally smacked his hands away. "My ribs are fine. I'm fine. My car, however, is not."

He grimaced as he took in the back end of my car. "Have you called the cops yet?"

I stiffened, thinking about my last encounter with the police. "Do I have to? You saw how they were last time."

He rubbed a hand over my spine. "Sorry, baby, we have to call them. You'll need a police report for your insurance at the very least."

"Crud, I forgot about that."

"Let's get you into my SUV, and I'll call them. I'll be with you the whole time, you won't be alone for a second."

"Thanks," I mumbled. I was sulking, and I knew it. Austin gently helped me up into the passenger seat of the Rover and then grabbed his phone from the console. He paced back and forth while talking to a dispatcher, but I didn't pay attention to what he was saying.

He slipped back into the car, shutting us in glorious air conditioning. "They said someone will be here in about ten minutes." Austin reached over. Grabbing my hand, he brought it to his mouth and kissed my palm. I let out a breath at the contact. "I'm so glad you're okay. Two more feet, and you would have gone over. I could kill whoever was driving that car."

"Don't tell the cops that."

"I won't, smartass." Before long, an LAPD squad car pulled in behind us. Austin squeezed my hand. "You've got this."

We stepped from the SUV and toward the two officers. They were polite while I walked them through everything that had happened. Austin grew more and more tense at my side when I described the black SUV idling in the road after crashing into me. One officer took photos of my wrecked car, while the other filled out a report.

When Austin asked if it was possible that the crash could be related to the break-in at my house, both officers looked skeptical. "LA drivers are crazy," one said. "You'd be shocked by how many hit and runs we see. The driver probably just stuck around to make sure you weren't hurt and then took off to avoid any charges. With this report, your insurance will cover everything and shouldn't raise your rates."

He said it like all I was worried about was having to pay for the damages. But I had been wondering the same thing Austin clearly was. Could this have been the same person who broke into my house? I shuddered at the thought of that person having a pair of my panties. Austin must have felt my shudder because he pulled me tighter against him.

We thanked the officers and got back into Austin's SUV, both silent as we drove towards Austin's house, lost in our own thoughts and theories. He pulled up in front of the fountain and hurried around to help me down. Ushering me inside, he guided me towards his ridiculously comfortable couch. "Stay here, I'll get you some Tylenol and let Blue out."

"Thanks." Leaning back against the couch, I felt a growing stiffness in my neck. I was going to feel like roadkill tomorrow. Whimpering sounded from the kitchen, and claws clacked across the tiles. Blue must have smelled me because I heard joyful yips as he barreled into the living room. He skidded on the floor, crashing into the couch. I couldn't help but laugh. I lifted him up with a groan, and he bathed my face in kisses. Dogs could make just about anything better.

A few minutes later, Austin was back with a bottle of pills and some water. "Here you go. I called my mechanic. He's going to come by to pick up your keys and will tow your car to their body shop. Once the insurance adjustor takes a look, we can figure out what you want to do."

I leaned into Austin, taking Blue with me, and he automatically curled an arm around me. "Thank you for dealing with all that and coming to get me."

"Of course." He toyed with a strand of my hair. "From now until we figure out what's going on, you're not driving anywhere by yourself. I'll take you to and from school whenever I can."

I sighed. "Austin, you have a full-time job, you can't be my chauffeur."

"I can do anything I damn well please. One of the perks of owning your own business is making your own hours." He squeezed my shoulder. "I need to do this. Please, let me. It's taking all my restraint not to pack you and Blue up and move you into my house."

I groaned. "It's a little too soon for that, don't you think?"

"Too soon for you, maybe. I just want you to be safe. If I'm driving you to and from work, it will go a long way to easing my mind."

"Oh, all right." I picked up Austin's wrist to look at his watch. "Crud, I need to go. I'm supposed to cook dinner for Taylor tonight."

"You're not cooking for anyone tonight. You are going to pop a few of those pills, take a long, hot bath, and relax." That sounded like heaven. "My mechanic should be here any minute, and then why don't you and I pick up dinner on our way to your house. I'll treat you and Taylor to Little Dom's." He was a dirty cheater. He knew Little Dom's was Taylor's and my favorite Italian restaurant and not far from our house.

"You had me at fried risotto balls."

"I love it when you say balls."

I snorted in response.

❧

I groaned as I leaned back in my desk chair. Almost twenty-four hours later, and I did, in fact, feel like roadkill. I had been popping Tylenol like it was my job, but my neck still protested any sudden movements. A knock sounded on my classroom door. "Come in."

Kyle opened the door, and I bit back a sigh. I did not need to deal with him today. He crossed to my desk, studying my face intently. "I just heard about your car accident, are you okay?"

Guilt swamped me for wishing him away—he was just concerned. "I'm fine, just a bit of a tender neck, but I'm sure I'll be as good as new by tomorrow. Thanks for checking on me."

"Of course. Why don't I give you a ride home today? In fact,

I can take you home until your car's fixed. I know Taylor has lacrosse practice after school. I'm assuming she's the one who brought you this morning."

The awkwardness was about to make a reappearance. "Actually, Taylor's team has off today, and Austin's going to be picking me up until my car's back in working order. But thank you for offering."

Kyle's hands tightened at his sides. "Why don't you just let him know I can take you home. I'm already here, so it makes more sense for me to take you."

"Austin keeps my dog with him at his gym while I'm working, so we need to meet up anyway." Kyle said nothing, but his fists got tighter, and his jaw locked. I got it. I really did. It was never fun when someone you had cared for moved on before you did, especially if you still had feelings for the person. But this had to stop. "Kyle, Austin and I are seeing each other now, so I'm not sure if it would be appropriate for you to be driving me home every day anyway."

Kyle's face got redder, and his knuckles were bleached white. "You said that you were just friends. That you would always be just friends."

My heartbeat quickened. "Things changed. I'm sorry, Kyle. I really am. I'm not doing this to hurt you."

"You're the one who's going to get hurt, and it'll be your fault," he spat and turned to leave, slamming the door behind him.

I inhaled deeply and slowly let out my breath. My shoulders stiffened as my classroom door opened again but relaxed when I saw it was Taylor.

"What the hell was that all about? It looked like there was smoke coming out of Kyle's ears."

I sighed. "He's not very happy about me and Austin."

Taylor let out a very ladylike snort. "Shocker. Sorry he's being an ass."

"Me, too."

"You ready for me to drop you at the gym?" she asked. Austin had not been happy that he couldn't pick me up, but he had dozens of reporters at his gym for an important event, and Taylor had promised to not let me out of her sight until I was safely ensconced in his training facility.

I stood, straightening my pile of papers and slipping them into my desk. "Yep, thanks for doing this. Do you want to come in with me? It's media day for one of his fighters, and the guy is hot," I said, waggling my eyebrows in her direction.

"Normally, you would have me at 'hot fighter,' but I've got a ton of grading to catch up on."

I carefully slung my purse over my shoulder. "Okay, next time."

"You know it."

We made our way down the hall and as we passed Kyle's classroom, a chill skittered down my spine. There had been a foreboding quality to his words that told me I hadn't heard the last from him.

THIRTY-ONE

Austin

"**W**ATCH HIS LEG! DON'T LET HIM GET YOU ON the ground!" I yelled as my eyes focused intently on the fighters circling each other on the mats. Eric was looking fierce. He had strength and speed, he just needed to be able to predict his opponents' moves a little bit more. That would come with time.

A buzzer sounded. "Time!" I called. "Eric, take five. Get some water, but stay loose."

Turning away from the mats, I was greeted by a throng of people. An over-eager reporter jammed a recorder in my face. "Eric Murphy makes the fourth fighter you're coaching now. Is this a sign you'll be moving away from the cage yourself?"

Inwardly, I cringed. I wasn't ready to announce my plans for retirement anytime soon. Outwardly, I kept a stone-faced mask. Before I could come up with an appropriate non-answer to his question, a sultry voice broke in. "He'd never stop fighting. This is his life." The woman's face was vaguely familiar. I'd seen her at fight events before. She was dressed in the smallest jean shorts I'd ever seen, a black crop top, and stiletto high heels. Fight groupie. I tried to be nice to all my fans, but some of these women could be vicious in their attempts to get a piece of me.

"I'm currently focused on my own training and coaching. Working with up-and-coming fighters keeps me on my toes."

The reporter chuckled, and the woman edged closer. I attempted to distance myself, but there was really no easy escape path. She pressed her breasts against my arm and ran a finger down my chest. "How about we take a five-minute break, too?"

Her perfume was too strong, makeup too thick. Everything about her was fake. My jaw clenched as I tried to extricate myself from her tentacles. A waving Sofia caught my eye. Her own eyes blazed with anger as she inclined her head to where Carter was standing behind the small crowd, gaze zeroed in on the breasts currently pressed into my side. Fuck.

"Excuse me," I said, pulling back, but groupie girl took a firm hold on my arm, pouting.

The reporter followed my sight line and perked right up. "Is that the new girlfriend? I'd love to get a photo of the two of you. Maybe a joint interview?"

Fuck no. I wasn't going to expose Carter to these vultures.

The groupie's face went from pouty to cruel in a flash. "That skinny bitch? Never. She can't give it to him like I can," she said loud enough to carry over the crowd.

Color leeched from Carter's face. She turned on her heel and took off in the direction of my office. Fuck. Fuck. FUCK.

I ripped my arm from the woman's stranglehold. "You need to leave, *now*. If you don't, security will escort you out. When they do, they'll take a photo of your driver's license, and you'll be banned from all UFL events." Her jaw dropped, but before she had a chance to respond, I took off, elbowing my way through the crowd.

I silently cursed myself all the way to my office. I hadn't even thought to warn Carter about fight groupies, privacy-invading reporters, or any of the downsides to my fame. Why hadn't I done that? Oh, yeah, because I wanted to paint the most ideal picture possible of what her life would look like with me. I didn't want to give her a single reason to say no to a future with me.

I paused with my hand on the doorknob to my office. Was I naïve to think that Carter could handle life as a fighter's girlfriend? She was a complete bleeding heart. Yes, she could stand up for herself when her buttons were pushed, but she took everyone's words to heart. Any personal attacks cut her to the quick. And in the world of MMA, personal attacks ran rampant.

Steeling my spine, I pushed open the door. Carter was bent over Blue, clipping a leash to his collar. "Firecracker," I started.

She turned, her face a blank mask. "I'm just going to have Taylor swing back by and get me and Blue. That way, you can be free to do whatever it is you need to do." Each word had a snap to it, whipped out with precision judgement.

She stalked toward the door, but I blocked her path. "Carter, that was not what it looked like."

She narrowed her eyes, pinning me in place with her teacher stare. "Oh? And what did it look like?"

I ran a hand roughly over my buzzed head. "Hell, I don't know! But I know it didn't look good." I sighed. "Fight groupies are a dime a dozen, and there's no good way to avoid them."

"You didn't exactly look like you were trying to avoid her. You looked like you were halfway to second base with her!" Blue let out a bark and then a low whine as if he too were pissed at me.

"Baby, I had no way out. I was stuck between her and a vulture of a reporter, and I wasn't about to climb into his lap!"

"Don't you *baby* me, Austin Lyons. Did you ask her to please stop touching you?"

I let my head fall back and searched the ceiling for answers. She just didn't get this world. "No, because that would have been a total pussy move."

"A pussy move? Would it be a pussy move if I asked a guy I didn't want touching me to kindly remove his hands?"

I snapped my head back down, moving into Carter's space. "Did someone fucking touch you?"

Carter threw her hands into the air on an exasperated sigh. "No! It's a hypothetical, you big jerk! How would you feel if you came into my classroom and found Kyle all pressed up against me?"

The temperature of the room seemed to rise as I pictured that scenario. What would follow would most likely get me arrested for assault. I blew out a breath. "I would not be happy," I said through gritted teeth.

Carter's shoulders slumped and curved in on themselves as she wrapped a protective arm around her middle. "Have you slept with her?"

I cringed, and Carter's eyes went misty. "Firecracker, listen to me." I reached out to pull her to me, but she took a step back. I fucking hated it when she wouldn't let me hold her, when she revoked that precious right. My fist clenched around the open air. "I was a total shitshow after we fell out. I slept with a lot of girls. I don't think she was one of them, but I honestly can't say that with one hundred percent certainty." Her face wore a look of devastation, and my heart plummeted.

Taking a deep breath, I pressed on. "I should have asked her to take her hands off me. I didn't think about it from your perspective. I would want to kill someone if they put their hands on you." Carter's body softened a little. "I'm not used to considering someone else when I act. I'm sorry, I'll work on it. I promise." And I would. I never wanted to be the cause of Carter's pain. I didn't want her to feel pain at all.

She took a step forward, resting her forehead on my chest. She was still stiff, but at least she was touching me. "Sorry, I was jealous."

"You're allowed to be jealous. I'm glad you want me all to yourself." She pinched my side in response, and I chuckled.

Lifting her chin with a finger, I stared into her eyes. "I'll try to be more conscious of how you might feel about female fans approaching me." I searched her sparkling green eyes for understanding. "But you are going to have to trust me."

She licked her lips. "Okay," she whispered.

I bent, brushing my mouth softly against hers. Her lips parted, and her taste exploded on my tongue. I groaned as I felt my cock harden. Down, boy. This was not the time or place. I tore my mouth away from the drug that was Carter McCarthy but pulled her into my arms, her head tucking perfectly under my chin. I never wanted to let her go.

"Just promise me you'll always tell me the truth." Her words sent vibrations against my chest.

My stomach sank. "I promise."

I knew I needed to tell her the truth about all the mistakes I'd made during our time apart, especially the one I'd had to maneuver to keep away from her today. All I needed was a little more time to cement her to me in every way possible so that she wouldn't want to leave. Just a bit more time.

THIRTY-TWO

Carter

I BOUNCED UP AND DOWN ON THE BALLS OF MY FEET, BODY thrumming with the excitement of Eric's win. This was his first fight with Austin as his coach, and he had annihilated his opponent. Austin had been beaming with pride. It had taken a couple of days for me to bounce back after seeing that girl wrapped around Austin, but I knew he was trying. And he was right, I had to trust him, or this would never work.

Liam, Ford, and I picked our way through the chaos of the crowd heading to meet Austin. As we turned the corner to the hall of locker rooms, I almost collided with someone.

"Oops, excuse me," I said automatically before looking up to see who I'd almost crashed into.

"Well, hey there, Carter." Lexi's voice dripped with disdain.

My heart clenched. "Hey, Lexi, what are you doing here?"

An evil grin crept across her blood-red lips. "Didn't Austin tell you? We work together. I see him all the time."

I tried not to panic. There had to be an explanation. There was no way Austin would work with Lexi and not tell me. I sucked in a deep breath. I trusted him. Steeling my spine, I said, "Lexi, you're jealous. And you have reason to be. Austin is the best man you could ever hope to know. But he's not yours, and he never will be. He's mine."

Liam stepped forward. "Carter is everything you will never be, and that's gotta burn. But if you don't leave her alone, and I do mean completely alone, I will ruin you."

Lexi's face paled, and Liam sent her a feral grin. "I see you know I can do it. I have contacts all over this city, and you'll have to get a job in Long Beach. Run along, and don't come back." Lexi sniffed and then took off toward the crowd. Liam squeezed my shoulder. "Don't pay any attention to her, she's a natural-born liar and manipulator."

"Let's just go find Austin."

Ford stepped up then. "He's probably in Eric's locker room. Let me go grab him so you're not accidentally flashed junk."

I shot him a forced smile as I twisted my fingers together. A minute later, a sober-looking Austin appeared. This was not the beaming smile he had been wearing after Eric's victory, and my stomach dropped. "Hey, Carter, come with me." He tried to grab my hand, but I side-stepped the grab and just stared at him. He sighed. "Let's go into one of the empty locker rooms so we can have some privacy." I nodded, and he walked two doors down and pushed it open for me.

I walked inside, arms crossed over my chest. I knew it was a confrontational gesture, but I couldn't help it, I needed the feeling of protection. As soon as the door swung closed, I asked, "Do you work with Lexi?"

Austin leaned back against the wall opposite me. "Yes, and no. She works for the UFL organization as a PR rep. She tried to get matched up with me, but I told them I wouldn't work with her. I hardly see her, but Eric got assigned her as his rep. There was nothing I could do without causing a lot of drama."

There was a burning sensation in my chest. "Why didn't you tell me?"

"I was going to, but I wanted us to have a chance to get to

204 | CATHERINE COWLES

know each other again first without throwing more drama into the midst of things. And things have been a little crazy lately."

He was right about things being crazy. Between my break-in and car accident, we had already been high on drama. But he still should have told me from the get-go. I took a deep breath and let it out. "Did you sleep with her?"

Austin closed his eyes, letting his chin fall to his chest. I died inside just a little. "Once. I told you, I was in a bad place when we stopped talking. I was mad at you—"

I cut him off, anger boiling to the surface. "So you did it to deliberately hurt me?"

"No!" He ran a hand over his buzzed head. "I just wanted to prove to myself that you didn't have any control over what I did or didn't do. And I was drinking a lot, so I wasn't making the best decisions. I wish I could take it all back, but I can't. All I can do is tell you that I'm so sorry I hurt you. Please, forgive me."

Austin reached out for me, but I stepped out of his grasp again. "I need some time." The words burned my throat as I fought the tears that were starting to gather. "I don't know what I think right now, and I need some time to sort it out."

He retracted his hand, clearing his throat. "Okay, how much time?"

"I don't know."

"This feels an awful lot like last time."

I shrank back at his words. "It's not like last time. I just need some time to get my thoughts straight."

Austin nodded jerkily, but his fists were clenched so hard, I wondered if he'd break a finger. "I'll give you time." The words sounded gruff, as though he really didn't want to say them. "But you have to know…I love you, Carter. I never wanted to tell you like this, but you need to know that. I love you."

The tears spilled over now, tracking down my face. "That's not fair." How could he say those words now?

"Fuck fair! If there's a chance you'll leave me, I'm not fighting fair!"

My stomach hollowed out, and I started crying harder. He might love me, but what good was that if I couldn't trust him to be honest with me. What good was that love when monsters kept popping out of every corner, threatening to stab me in the heart. I couldn't do this, I didn't want to hurt like this again. "I need to go home. I'm going to get Liam to give me a ride."

His Adam's apple bobbed up and down, but he said nothing. I ducked by him and out the door, keeping my head down until I reached Liam and Ford. They both took in my face with stony expressions. "Can you take me home?" I croaked.

Liam threw an arm around my shoulders. "Of course, we can."

I kept my head down all the way to the car and let my tears fall.

Days turned into a week, and I still didn't have any answers. What I did have were undereye circles the size of my fist, and clothes that were all fitting a little too loosely. Austin had clearly put Liam and Ford on operation don't-let-Carter-drive-anywhere-by-herself because one of them always picked me up from school. Today, it was Liam. I stared out the window of his Maserati. Apparently, he was even more bougie than Austin.

My phone buzzed in the purse at my feet, and I tensed. I felt like one raw nerve lately. Between trying to reason through all my thoughts and feelings about Austin and a bunch of hang-up phone calls, I was ready to snap. I brushed off the feeling and slipped my phone from the bag, *UNKNOWN CALLER*. I pressed ignore, knowing whoever was on the other end wouldn't leave a message. They never did.

"Everything okay?" Liam asked from the driver's seat.

"Yeah, everything's fine. How are things going with the new record?"

"It's coming together, but what I'm really excited about is the tour. It's been too long since I've been on the road."

I smiled, and it didn't feel as forced as it had been. I was so dang proud of everything Liam had accomplished. "That's awesome, Li, I wish I could go with you."

"I wish you could, too. Maybe you can come out for a few weeks this summer, we'll be in Europe."

"That would be awesome."

Liam pulled up in front of my house. "Want me to walk you in?"

"No, big brother, I'll be fine. Taylor's already home. They had an early lacrosse game in West Hollywood."

"Okay, take care of yourself and try to get some rest."

I knew he was worried about me, so I didn't give him any crap. "Will do." I levered out of the car and waved to him when I reached the gate, but Liam waited while I punched in the code and didn't drive off until I was safely inside the front yard.

My shoes echoed on the stones as I walked up the path. The noise sounded empty, just like I felt. Unlocking the front door, I pushed inside. "Wifey, Blue, I'm home."

"We're in the kitchen," Taylor called.

Blue took off running towards me, almost knocking me over when he collided with my legs. He was getting so big. "Hi, baby, I missed you so much today! Were you a good boy? I bet you were." I had bitten the bullet and found a dog walker who came by twice a day while I was at work since I felt guilty about having Austin watch him if we were taking a breather. It seemed to be working fine, but I was sure Blue missed Austin almost as much as I did. "Come on, let's go see what Taylor's up to."

I headed into the kitchen to find Taylor removing takeout containers from a bag. "I ordered us Indian."

"That sounds great." It didn't actually sound great, but I would try to force some down. I usually loved Indian, but my appetite had up and abandoned me, just like my stupid heart.

"There are more flowers." Taylor eyed me over the paper bag. "I set them on the coffee table, but we're running out of places to put them. When are you going to put that boy out of his misery and call him already?"

"I don't know," I answered truthfully. "I'm not sure how to get past it. Austin should have been honest with me from the start about Lexi working with him. We even talked about her once. He had the perfect opening to tell me. Now, I just wonder what other stuff he hasn't told me, and if I can trust him to be honest with me in the future."

Taylor arranged food on two plates and filled a bowl with naan. "Honey, can we have some real-talk?" I nodded, biting the corner of my lip. She continued on. "I think you're being too hard on him. You know I'm Team Carter all the way, but I know Austin wasn't trying to intentionally hurt you. It's not fair for you to shut him out completely. I think you're going to have to take a leap and meet him halfway. Tell him how you're feeling. He might be able to ease your mind."

What *was* I feeling? I searched my brain for the root of all my panic, anxiety, and uncertainty. I could only come up with one thing. I was terrified. Taking a second chance life had given you meant the risks were so much greater, the distance to fall so much further. Tears stung my eyes. "I'm scared."

"Oh, honey." Taylor rushed around the kitchen bar, throwing her arms around me. "I know you are. Love is fucking terrifying if it's the good kind."

She held me for long minutes as I pulled myself together. "I don't want to lose him."

Taylor pulled back, giving me an encouraging smile. "You won't. All you have to do is pick up the phone."

208 | CATHERINE COWLES

My stomach twisted in knots. "I will, I just need a little more time to figure out what to say. Sorry to break down on you when you have so much going on, I'm a cruddy friend."

"You are not," she argued.

I studied Taylor's face, her own eyes were lined with circles. "How are you? How's your mom?"

A few days ago, Taylor had gotten the devastating news that her mom had been diagnosed with breast cancer. She was just waiting to hear what the treatment plan was now. "She's hanging in there. I actually talked to her earlier today. They're going to start chemo in a week."

"That's good that they're moving so quickly, right?"

Taylor bit the side of her cheek. "It is, but I feel like I need to be with her when she's going through treatment, so I'm going to take a leave of absence from teaching and go back to Texas for a bit. I'm sorry to leave you when you've got all this other crap going on, but I need to go."

"Taylor, forget about me. I think it's great that you're going to be there for your mom. She needs you right now." I meant it, I would miss Taylor like crazy, but she needed to be with her mom. "I wish I could go with you so I could take care of you while you're taking care of her."

She smiled a little wobbly at me and engulfed me in another hug. "Love you, Carter."

"Love you, too, Tay. We'll talk all the time. I'm always here for you. You know that, right?"

"I know that. I'm so glad your crazy roommate stalked down the guy you were in love with and threw herself at him, so you were forced to move in with me." I pulled back slightly and just blinked at her. "Too soon?" she asked.

I burst out laughing. "Who knew we'd be thanking our lucky stars for Lexi?"

"She'd definitely be surprised to learn that."

The next day, Ford pulled his car into a spot right in front of my house, the parking gods were with him today. I looked over at him as he shut off the engine. "You don't have to walk me in, we're right outside."

"Now that Taylor's gone, we're just going to be extra careful."

I groaned in response. Liam had already suggested that I move in with him until Taylor came back. I had a feeling that while Liam's lips had been moving, it was Austin's voice coming out of his mouth. "Fine, come on." I punched in the gate code and unlocked my front door, but Ford pushed me aside to walk ahead.

"While you go check for ax murderers, I'm going to let Blue out of his crate." At the sound of my voice, Blue started whining, and I could hear his tail thumping against the metal grate. I opened the door and was immediately bathed in kisses. Laughing, I fell back onto the floor, hugging Blue to my chest. "I missed you, too."

"You spoil that dog." Ford had already returned from his rounds.

"All quiet on the western front, soldier?"

"Everything's good, smartass. You going to be okay for the night?"

"Yup."

"All right, I'm going to head out, I have some work to finish."

"Thanks for driving me home."

"No problem. Lock the door behind me."

I dutifully followed Ford to the door and flicked the deadbolt behind him. A ding came from the direction of my purse, which I had let fall to the floor when I released Blue from his crate. I dug around for my phone, and just as I grabbed it, I heard it ding again.

Taylor: *You've been outed, E-News identified you as Austin's girlfriend in those photos. I'm honestly surprised it took them this long. Thought you'd want a heads-up.*

Taylor: *On the plus side, my mom says Austin's a hunk, and you better hold on to that man.*

I sighed, deciding to text Taylor back later. "What do you say we go for a walk, Blue?"

He barked in response and started turning in circles. I knew that if I had told Ford I was taking Blue for a walk, he would have insisted on going with me, but I really needed some alone time to sort through what I was going to say to Austin when I called him tonight.

I quickly changed into workout pants and a tank, grabbing Blue's leash, my keys, and for good measure so none of the boys could yell at me, my phone and pepper spray. Snapping Blue's lead on, I headed out the door, making sure it was locked behind me.

My mind immediately drifted to Austin as I padded the pavement, pausing as Blue stopped to pee on something. When it came right down to it, any fears paled in comparison to how much I loved Austin. His kind heart. His generous spirit. And his hot body didn't hurt. No one made me feel more alive than Austin did. I just needed to make him understand that I'd kick his butt if he kept things from me that he knew I deserved to know.

I spent the next forty-five minutes releasing any anger and hurt I'd been feeling and thinking about everything that I was grateful for in my relationship with Austin. By the time I'd circled back around to my house, I felt ready to call him. I just hoped he wasn't pissed at me for waiting so long.

I punched in the gate code, and Blue tugged me up the path to the front door, excited for his post-walk treat. When I unlocked the door, Blue started sniffing the air and barking. What a weirdo. Was he trying to sniff out his treat? Instead of pulling me to the kitchen where his cookies were, he tugged me towards my bedroom, his barking growing more intense.

When we reached the door, I froze in shock. My bedroom was destroyed. Clothing was strewn all over the floor, ripped to shreds. The painting that usually hung over my bed was lying on the carpet, a huge slash through it. My bedding had also been torn to bits, feathers were everywhere. And above my bed, spray-painted in garish red was the word: *Whore.*

Blue's low growl snapped me into action, and as I turned to bolt from my room, I caught a glance of *cunt* sprayed in the same red lettering in my bathroom. I fumbled for my phone as I pulled on Blue's leash and started running for the front door. My heart hammered against my ribs, sending vibrations echoing through my body. My thumb unlocked my phone's screen as I cleared the front doorway. My recent calls appeared, and I shakily hit the first number I saw.

THIRTY-THREE

Austin

"YOU JUST HAVE TO BE PATIENT, MAN," LIAM SAID. We were at my house, having a beer after playing a little one-on-one. "Carter loves you. Never seen someone so head over heels. I honestly think it's less about Lexi and more about the fact that you weren't honest with her."

I groaned as I ran a hand over my scalp. "Carter said she didn't want to talk about the past."

Liam sent me a pointed look over his beer. "But it's not really the past if you see Lexi regularly, is it?"

Fuck, I knew it had been a bad idea not to tell Carter that Lexi was working for the UFL, but I had been so damn desperate to get us to a good place. I didn't want to ruin my shot with her. "Do you think Carter can handle being around all the groupies, the crazies, the paparazzi? I love her, man. I want to make this work." I blew out a breath. "But she pushes me away every time I screw up. She won't let me close enough to try and make things right."

"You need to give her time. She's scared, Austin. Terrified out of her fucking mind." My stomach dropped at his admission, and my heart clenched. "She hasn't said as much, but I've known Carter a long time, and I recognize the signs. You were her first love, her first broken heart. She's going to be a little gun-shy when things go wrong."

"All right. I'll try to give her some time." I'd give her another week. Tops. After that, I was coming for her whether she liked it or not.

"Just stay away from Lexi in the meantime." Liam shot me a pointed look over the top of his beer.

"There are rumors she's talking about quitting and moving to New York to work in fashion." I grinned, that had been the best damn news of my week.

"Praise the good Lord above!" Liam let a little bit of his former Southern twang into his voice. A ringtone trilled out, and he reached into his pocket, pulling out his cell. He shot me a grin as he answered.

"Hey, Carter, what's up?" The grin fell from his face almost immediately. "Get out of the house, now."

My heart stopped dead in my chest. Liam snapped his fingers in my direction as we both leapt to our feet. "Get the cops to her house now. Someone broke in."

My fingers robotically dialed 911 as I heard Liam say, "We're calling the cops and are on our way. I want you to stay on the phone with me until the police get there. Or we do, okay?"

I grabbed the keys to my Rover just as I connected with dispatch. I gave the woman Carter's address and the little information I had. "She's alone. She's all alone, and someone broke into her fucking house, *again*. You need to get someone there NOW," I growled.

"Sir, we have a unit three blocks away. They're en route now."

I hung up and gunned it down my driveway. Liam was in the passenger seat and kept asking Carter if she saw anyone, and she clearly kept saying no.

"Okay, Carter, go talk to the cops. We're ten minutes away." He knew I'd be breaking all sorts of traffic laws to get to Carter. Liam tapped the screen of his phone and turned to face me. "She said someone trashed her room. What the fuck is going on?"

I gripped the wheel so tightly, I thought it might break in two. "I don't know, but we sure as hell are going to find out."

I wove in and out of traffic, causing more than one person to honk at me, but no cops tried to pull me over. The lights on two squad cars flashed as we reached Carter's house. I threw my car into park behind the cop cars, not caring it was in the middle of the road and launched myself out of the SUV.

My eyes immediately found Carter surrounded by two cops, her arms were curled tightly around herself, and Blue stood at her side. Her head snapped up at the sound of my door slamming. She said something to one of the cops, handing the woman Blue's leash as I rounded the squad cars. I recognized that I was running just before Carter's body collided with mine. I held her tightly to me, cupping the back of her head. She was shaking, and I realized it was with tears. "I'm so sorry." Her words were muffled by my shirt and her sobs.

I held her even tighter. "Baby, what do you have to be sorry for?" I was so confused.

"I was mad at you, and I didn't talk to you all week. It was so stupid." She was barely making sense, only getting out one word between every two or three hiccupped sobs.

I trailed a hand up and down her spine. "Don't worry about that, everything's going to be fine." In that moment, every doubt about whether Carter and I could make this work melted away. Faced with the prospect of a single hair on her head being harmed, I knew I'd move Heaven and Earth to keep her safe, to keep her happy, and to keep her by my side.

Carter only started crying harder. "Why does this person hate me?"

One of the officers walked up then. "Should we call the paramedics? We might need to sedate her."

I scowled at the guy. "Just give me a few minutes." He nodded, and I lifted Carter up. She instinctively wrapped her legs around me. Walking a few houses away, I sat down on the curb. "Let it out, Firecracker, just let it out."

She continued to weep as I just held her. Looking back toward the scene, I could see that Liam had a hold of Blue now and was giving a statement to the female cop.

Slowly, Carter's sobs lessened, and she nuzzled deeper into my neck. "I love you, Austin," she whispered.

I closed my eyes, soaking up her words. "I love you, too."

"We don't have the best timing for dropping the L-bomb, do we?" Her lips stretched into a smile against my neck as she said it.

"Never a bad time to hear those words from your mouth." She pulled back, and I dropped a kiss to those perfect bow lips, lingering there.

When I retreated, she looked down at my shirt, one hand covered her mouth, but she was giggling. "Austin, I'm so sorry, I snot-cried all over your shirt."

"Got other shirts, Firecracker."

"That's good because this one should probably be burned."

I pulled her back into my chest. "You okay?"

"I am now."

"Good. You want to tell me what happened?"

Before she could answer, the female officer approached. "How are you doing, Miss McCarthy?"

Carter blushed and tried to get off my lap, but I kept her firmly in place, not quite ready to let her go. "I'm fine now. Sorry about that meltdown."

The woman smiled reassuringly at Carter. "Don't worry about it, it's completely understandable. Your home was violated in a very personal way." My arms tightened around Carter at those words. She ran a hand over my buzzed hair as if to reassure me everything was okay, but it damn well wasn't fine.

"What the hell happened?" I asked.

The officer, her name tag read *Officer Hollis*, fixed her gaze on me. "Miss McCarthy's bedroom was vandalized, and it was clearly a very personal attack. I was coming over here to let you know that given the other incidents, we've called in the Threat Management Unit. They specialize in stalking cases, and I think they will be able to best handle the situation. They have expertise and resources that the rest of the LAPD simply doesn't have."

Carter squeezed my hand. "Thank you. I really appreciate all your help. You've been so kind."

"No problem. The detective from TMU should be here in about thirty minutes, so just sit tight," Officer Hollis said and walked off.

Carter pinched my side, hard. "Ouch! Damn, woman."

She scrambled off my lap as soon as my hold on her loosened. "It would have been nice to not talk to an officer of the law while straddling you, Austin."

I grinned. "I'm sure she's seen way more scandalous things than that."

Carter huffed. "Come on, I want to go see Liam, and it looks like Blue is losing his mind since I walked away."

"Okay, let's go." I grabbed her hand, interlocking our fingers. I didn't want Carter out of my reach for a second. She was just going to have to get used to never being alone until they caught this creep.

THIRTY-FOUR

Carter

I SAT ON THE COUCH CRAMMED IN BETWEEN TWO VERY angry alpha males. Ever since the cops had cleared my room, and Austin and Liam had peeked inside, rage had been coming off them in waves. Now, silence reigned as the detective from the LAPD Threat Management Unit jotted down notes in a very cop-looking notebook. We had just finished telling Detective Massey everything about the events of the past few months. He looked up from his pad. "Have you noticed anyone following you? Have any hang-up phone calls? Received any strange emails? Anything along those lines?"

Austin leaned forward, resting his elbows on his knees but turning his face towards me. "You had that weird hang-up when we were at the gym, remember?"

I grimaced at what I now had to share. "Yeah, and I've gotten a few more this week."

Austin's teeth clenched, but it was Liam who spoke. "Why didn't you tell me?"

I twisted my fingers in my lap. "I didn't think it was a big deal at the time."

Detective Massey interrupted our back and forth. "Was there a number on your screen?"

"No, it always says *UNKNOWN CALLER*."

"Does the person say anything, or can you hear anything in the background?"

"I only answered the first two or three times. I could hear faint noises in the background, but nothing discernable. After that, I would just let any unknown numbers go to voicemail. The person never leaves a message."

Detective Massey made a few notes. "Keep letting the calls go to voicemail. You want to minimize any possible contact with the stalker. We'll pull your phone records and see if we can trace the call." I nodded.

"I want you to make a list of anyone who might have a grudge against you. Ex-boyfriends, someone who made abnormally strong advances towards you, anyone in your life you've had a falling out with. Anything you can think of. We're also going to look into the man you have a restraining order against." I shuddered as I began mentally compiling a list of people who could possibly want to hurt me. How much did someone have to dislike me to qualify for this lineup? "Austin, have you had any issues with overzealous fans or stalkers?"

Austin was strung tight, I could feel the constant flexing of muscles as we sat side by side. "Overzealous fans? Yes. Stalkers? No. The UFL and my head of security will have a list of anyone who's been banned from my fights for any reason."

"I'll get in touch with them for a list but, in the meantime, I want you to keep an eye out for any fans who are particularly angry that you've gotten a girlfriend. Since this started before any photos of the two of you were published, I'm leaning towards it being someone one or both of you knows. That doesn't mean they're someone you've been close to. A stalker can literally be anyone. It could be the barista at the coffee shop you go to every day."

Panic began to rise up inside me. Austin leaned back into the couch and pulled me against him. "It'll be okay, we're going to figure this out."

"I know it can be overwhelming, but the more information you can provide, the better. My goal isn't to scare you, but to make sure you are as cautious as possible while we identify the perpetrator. I'm seeing a clear escalation in behavior. These latest two incidents show that the unsub is turning violent. From now on, I want you to avoid going anywhere alone if possible. Keep your phone with you at all times, even in the bathroom. Can you stay with a friend for the time being?"

"She'll be staying with me from now on." Austin practically growled the words. He tilted his face towards mine as if expecting me to argue. He would get no arguments from me. I wasn't an idiot, and I was freaked. "I live on gated property and have a state-of-the-art security system. I also have security who works for me on fight weekends and when I do appearances, so I'll see about having a couple of them patrol the perimeter of the property."

I squeezed Austin's hand. "You don't have to go to that extreme." The look he threw me had me going silent again.

"It's actually not a bad idea. If you have the resources, you might as well use them. It's a better-safe-than-sorry kind of scenario," Detective Massey chimed in.

I nodded and leaned back into Austin's side. His muscles were still strung tight, but he ran a gentle hand through my hair. "I'll have my security contact you, and you can give them anything to be on the lookout for. They work with lots of celebrities, so I'm sure they're not new to this stalker stuff."

Detective Massey rose from his chair and flipped his notepad closed, the gold of his wedding band gleaming against his ebony skin. "Sounds good. Here's my card. It has my cell on it. Call me at any time if you have any questions or notice anything concerning. Carter, plug that number into your phone so you know it's me calling and aren't alarmed." It was sweet of him to think of that. Detective Massey had a fatherly feel to him. He was kind, thorough, and believed everything I told him, unlike the jerk cop I had dealt with after the first break-in.

I reached out a hand to shake his. "Thank you so much, I really appreciate your help."

"Anytime, Carter." He headed towards the door, calling out to the two officers who remained.

Austin squeezed the back of my neck. "Let's get you and Blue packed up so we can get out of here." At the sound of his name, Blue lifted his head from my feet where he was sprawled and cocked his head to the side.

Tears were brimming behind my eyes, and I did my best to fight them back. "All my stuff is destroyed." I couldn't bring my-self to search through the rubble of my room right now to see if there was anything salvageable.

Austin cursed and then turned to Liam. "Will you go pack up Blue's food, dog bed, and anything else he might need?"

"Sure." Liam rose from the couch.

"Everything other than the dog bed is in the cabinet by the back door," I said.

Liam ruffled my hair. "Got it."

Austin tilted up my face to his and wiped away a stray tear with his thumb. "When we get into the car, I want you to write down all of your clothing sizes and make a list of any girl shit you'll need for the next few weeks. And not the cheap stuff. I know you spend a fortune on the shit you put on your face. Make a list of everything you could possibly want or need, and I'll send it to my stylist. She'll pull everything together for you tomorrow morning."

I was distracted from Austin's ridiculously generous offer by one small fact. "You have a stylist?" I started to laugh, couldn't help it.

"Yes, you little troublemaker," he said, squeezing my side. "Someone has to dress me for events and appearances. I don't have time for that shit."

I couldn't picture Austin standing still for fittings, but I could imagine him spending hours browsing the racks at Saks even less. "Well, let's hope she has good taste. And, thank you, I can give you my credit card number so she can charge all the purchases to that."

Austin stared at me and then lifted his eyes to the ceiling. "Whatever you say, Firecracker."

Why did I have a feeling these charges would never make it to my card?

⁊⁏

I shuffled into Austin's house like a zombie. About halfway through the drive from my place, I'd hit a wall. I was mentally, physically, and emotionally spent. All I wanted was a hot shower and a comfortable bed. Blue padded along behind me. He hadn't ventured far from my side since the incident, and I was glad to have him.

Austin flicked on a few more lights in the living room. "Are you hungry? I can order food."

"Honestly, all I really want is a shower."

"Of course. Come on." Austin lifted the dog bed he'd placed on the floor and led me back towards his bedroom, but instead of going inside, he stopped at a room directly across from his. I suddenly felt unsure and a little insecure. Did he not want me sharing his bed? Were we not okay? When I looked up at Austin, his eyes were intently studying my face. He crossed to me and engulfed me in his arms. "Your first time is not going to be after a day like today. I'm going to put you in the guest room for now. I want you to feel comfortable."

I bit back the words that were trying to come out about

wanting to sleep with him. Maybe it would be better if I stayed in here. I'd probably drool on him or something equally embarrassing. "Okay." I hated how soft my voice sounded.

"Baby, you're killing me. What can I do?" Austin held me tighter to his chest.

"You've already done so much. I don't know what I'd do without you."

"You'll never have to find out." He rested his chin on the top of my head, and we just stood there while I soaked up his warmth and strength.

Finally, I pulled back. "I'm going to shower. Do you have something I can sleep in?"

"Of course. I'm going to email your list of necessities to my stylist, and then I'll leave some clothes on your bed."

"Thanks, Austin. For everything. You're pretty amazing, you know that?"

A small blush rose to his cheeks, making me smile. "Love you, Carter."

I would never get tired of hearing that. I rose to my tiptoes, planting a quick kiss on his lips. "Love you, too." Turning away, I headed into the bathroom, Blue following behind.

This bathroom wasn't quite as ridiculously awesome as Austin's, but it was close. I looked longingly at the soaking tub but knew if I got in, there was a good chance I'd fall asleep and drown. I shucked my workout clothes and stepped into the rainfall shower. Turning the water to steaming, I let the steady stream soothe my muscles that were tightly wound from stress. Finally, I looked around for some shampoo and conditioner. The shower was stocked with some fancy names and heavenly scents.

By the time I emerged from the spray, I was starting to feel more human. I bound my hair up in a fluffy towel, wound another around my body, and stepped into the bedroom just as a soft knock sounded at the door. "Come in."

Blue immediately put himself between me and the door but relaxed when he saw Austin. "Looks like he's got a little guard dog in him, after all," Austin said with a smile. He paused when his gaze moved past Blue to my bare legs. His jaw got hard, and his eyes blazed with heat. I swallowed jerkily and felt a tingling at my core. Oh, boy.

Austin cleared his throat. "Here are some things you can wear for tonight, I know they'll be huge on you, but the sweatpants have a drawstring you can tighten." He set the items on the bed, seeming to avoid getting too close to me.

I wanted to laugh. Alpha male determined to preserve my virtue. "Thanks for that."

He cleared his throat again. "No problem. Well, I'll let you get some sleep." Austin made a hasty retreat, and I couldn't hold in the soft giggle. I walked over the bed to see what he'd left me. A t-shirt that was worn baby soft…yeah, he was never getting that back. A pair of boxers. And sweatpants that looked like I would drown in them.

I slipped on the boxers and t-shirt, abandoning the sweats, and then went in search of a hairdryer. I found that and a brush in a drawer in the bathroom. I did a quick blow-dry while Blue shot me sorrowful looks. He hated the hairdryer and vacuum cleaner, usually bolting when I turned on either, but tonight, he was determined to stay by my side.

Switching off the hairdryer, I scratched Blue under his chin. "What a sweet boy you are." I could swear he grinned. Slipping my phone and charger from my purse, I thanked my lucky stars that my bag had been in the living room and had escaped the intruder's wrath. I had a missed call and text from Ford, wanting to see if I was okay and asking if I needed anything. Liam or Austin must have looped him in on what had happened. I shot him a quick text back, letting him know I was fine and slipped beneath the covers. The sheets were butter-soft. I let out a sigh.

Heaven. I patted the mattress, and Blue leapt up, burrowing into a spot right next to me. I shut off the light and fluffed my pillow.

As soon as I shut my eyes, my mind was filled with images of red writing and clothing torn to shreds. My eyelids popped back open, and I stared at the ceiling. Clearly, I wasn't quite tired enough. I rubbed a hand over Blue's fur, and he let out a contented snore, no trouble sleeping for him. For the next hour, I tossed and turned, unable to get comfortable. Then I started to think that I heard things outside, only to realize it was nothing. I was beginning to crack up.

Giving up, I threw back the covers, startling Blue into a standing position. "Sorry, baby," I said. "Want to go sleep with Austin?" Blue cocked his head to the side as if considering. "Come on." I patted my thigh, and he jumped from the bed.

I slowly opened the bedroom door and listened. No sounds came from across the way or the rest of the house. I bit my lip. Austin was probably already asleep. Tiptoeing across the hall, I knocked faintly on the door. Hearing nothing, I nibbled on my lip a little more. Should I just go in? Knock harder? Call his cell?

The door swung open, and there stood Austin in black boxer briefs, eyes groggy from sleep. Holy hell, he was hot. I slowly looked up from his six-pack and the dusting of hair that disappeared beneath his waistband. "Everything okay?" His voice was gruff, only adding to the overall sexiness of the image. Good Lord, someone help me.

"I couldn't sleep." My voice sounded just a little squeaky. "Do you think I could sleep with you? I promise not to molest you or anything."

Austin grinned at that. "Of course, you can." He stepped aside and pointed to the bed. "Get in, and I'll go get the dog bed." Before I could tell him that I let Blue sleep with me, he was gone. He quickly reemerged, dog bed in tow. Austin set it down next to my side of the bed and then circled around to climb under the covers. He paused just as he was about to turn off the light and glanced from me to a forlorn-looking Blue, who sat expectantly at the side of the bed. Austin's eyes came back to me. "You let him sleep in the bed, don't you?"

I sent him my most angelic smile. "I don't want him to be lonely."

Austin groaned. "He's not sleeping in my bed. Blue, go to your bed." He pointed at the dog bed. Blue whined. "Blue…" Austin had the perfect I'm-serious dad face going on, and I had to bite my lip to keep from laughing. Blue huffed but settled into his bed. Austin clicked off the light. "See, you just have to be the alpha."

"Mm-hmm," I mumbled, still trying not to laugh.

"Come here, Firecracker." Austin pulled me into his body, positioning my back to his front. Something very large and hard pressed between my butt cheeks, but I tried not to think about it. "Think you can sleep now?"

I squirmed a little. "Yeah."

"Okay, sweet dreams." He kissed the side of my neck and squeezed me a little closer to him. I let out a slow breath and closed my eyes, but as soon as I did, I was bombarded by the same images. My muscles clenched, and my eyes flew open. "What's wrong?" Austin asked.

"Every time I close my eyes, I see my wrecked bedroom. It's like I can't get it out of my head."

Austin had started drawing circles on my lower stomach as soon as I tensed up. Now, his fingers were trailing lower, and my body tightened for a whole other reason. "How about I give you something else to think about, okay?"

"Okay," I whispered. My voice suddenly sounded husky. Austin's fingers slipped below the band of the boxers I was wearing, and I sucked in a breath. He trailed his fingers lightly through the dusting of hair I had and then lower. My legs automatically opened slightly as if he were controlling them himself.

He slipped a finger between my lips and groaned in my ear. "You're already wet. So responsive." He dipped a finger inside, and my lower belly tightened. "God, you're so tight. I can't wait to be inside you." My core clenched at his words. "You like that idea?"

"Mm-hmm." It was all I could get out.

He bit down lightly on my neck. "Not tonight, but soon." Austin continued to work his finger in and out of me. My body felt like it was winding up, growing tauter, like I would snap with one wrong move—but in the most delicious way. I moaned as he added another finger. There was a slight burning sensation that melted quickly into intensity. He trailed his thumb through the wetness that had trickled out of my opening and brought it to my clit. I gasped as he circled the bundle of nerves, making smaller and smaller circles as he pumped his fingers in and out of me.

All of a sudden, I was spiraling down. I cried out as I clutched the sheets, breathing hard. Austin slowed his movements as I rode the wave of sensations, then he eased his fingers out of me and from beneath the sheets. I watched him as he brought those fingers to his mouth, sucking them clean. His eyes closed briefly. "Even more delicious than I thought."

I swallowed. "Will you show me how to do that for you?" I was sure my cheeks were as red as a tomato, but I wanted to give him the same pleasure he had just given me.

He bent his head towards me, laying a soft kiss on my lips. "Soon. Tonight, was just for you." Another soft kiss. "See if you can sleep now."

I burrowed back into Austin, the length against by backside had gotten unbelievably harder and longer. He groaned, stilling my movements. I kissed the arm that had remained under my neck. "Love you, Austin," I said softly and then fell into a deep and dreamless sleep.

THIRTY-FIVE

Austin

I AWOKE TO A DICK SO HARD IT COULD POUND NAILS, AND AN empty bed. Neither of those things made me happy. I panicked for a moment when I didn't see Carter or Blue, but then I smelled the scents of coffee and breakfast wafting from the other room and relaxed a little. She should have woken me.

I swung my legs over the side of the bed and plodded into the kitchen. The sight that greeted me was pure heaven. Carter faced the stove, wearing my threadbare t-shirt, her delectable curves peeking out from beneath the fabric, and her legs seeming to go on for days. I searched for something else to focus my attention on and remembered waking up alone. "You didn't wake me." It came out a little harsher than I had intended. I blamed the pain in my cock.

Carter turned at the sound of my voice, spatula still in hand. "Someone's grumpy this morning."

Damn right, I was grumpy. I needed coffee and then a long shower where I could alleviate some of this pressure before I had an aneurysm. "I was worried."

She bounded over, giving me a far too brief kiss and then was back at the stove, flipping some bacon. "Sorry I scared you. Your stylist left some basics for me on the doorstep and a note saying

228 | CATHERINE COWLES

she'd bring the rest by later today. Thank you for arranging that so quickly."

I froze. "You went outside? By yourself?"

Carter slowly turned around, looking just a little sheepish. "You have a security fence and a coded gate. I had to let Blue out to do his business."

"From now on, you wake me up. Got it?"

She grinned and turned back to the stove. "Sir. Yes, sir!"

"Come here, you little smartass."

"I'm cooking."

I walked up behind her, slipping my hand beneath her shirt. I cupped her soft, warm breast. Her nipple beaded as I gently swiped my thumb across it. "You are such a troublemaker," I whispered into her ear and then nipped the lobe.

Carter gave a small shriek but panted as she said, "You're going to make me burn breakfast."

I grinned into her neck. "Worth it."

She lightly shoved me away, my hand falling from her breast. "Go put some clothes on, you're distracting me."

"Fine." I smacked her ass before turning to head back to my bedroom. I quickly brushed my teeth and then went in search of clothes. As I entered the closet, I smelled something off. Flicking on the light, I didn't see anything immediately out of place, but something definitely smelled bad. I pulled on track pants and a tee. Bending down to pick up my favorite sneakers, I froze with my hand inches away from the shoes. "CARTER!" I bellowed.

She came running into the bedroom, a frantic look in her eyes, and Blue hot on her heels. "What's wrong?"

I felt bad for freaking her out, but then I noticed that Blue wouldn't make eye contact with me and wasn't following Carter into the closet. He looked guilty as hell. I narrowed my eyes at him and then turned my gaze to Carter. "Your dog shit on my favorite sneakers," I said through gritted teeth.

Carter's hands flew to her mouth as her eyes went to the shoes. Then she started laughing. "I'm so sorry, he's never done anything like that before."

"What the hell is wrong with him?"

She straightened. "Nothing is *wrong* with him. He's in a new place. He was probably nervous. And *you*, Mr. Meanie,"—she drilled a finger into my chest—"wouldn't let him sleep in the bed with us."

I grabbed her wrist and pulled her to me. "Even your dog is a troublemaker." I said it with a grin and then kissed the tip of her nose.

"Come on, I'll get a trash bag to pick up the poop shoes. Then we need to eat so I can get ready for work. Do you mind driving me?"

She had started to pull away, but I dragged her back. "Are you serious?"

Carter looked up at me with a furrowed brow. "You want to keep the poop shoes?"

"Not about the fucking poop shoes, about you going to work. You can't go to work right now. There's some nutcase after you!"

She sighed. "Austin, I have to go to work. I don't want to lose my job. You can drop me off and pick me up. I won't go anywhere alone, and I'll have my phone with me at all times. Promise."

I groaned as she shot me her please-understand eyes. "Fine, but on one condition. And if you don't agree, I'll call your parents and tell them about everything that's going on."

On the car ride back to my place last night, Carter had begged Liam not to tell his parents or hers about what was going on. She didn't want to worry them when they were currently taking care of her grandmother, who had Alzheimer's.

Her jaw dropped. "That's not fair."

"Take it or leave it."

She huffed, crossing her arms under her chest. "Fine, what's the condition?"

"One of my security guys sits in the hallway outside your classroom."

Carter glared daggers at me, but I didn't give in. "Oh, all right," she said after a lengthy stare down.

Gripping the back of her neck, I brought her lips to mine. "See, compromise?"

"More like coercion."

I grinned. "Whatever works."

"You can clean up your own poop shoes," she said with a huff, pushing off my chest and turning to leave.

After a hurried breakfast and a quick call to my head of security, John, we were on our way to Carter's school. I wasn't happy about it, but I knew John would be at the top of his game. Brushing my thumb across Carter's knuckles, I asked, "Are you sure about this?"

Carter had been quiet since we'd gotten into the car, and I was wondering if she was having second thoughts. "I can't let this person control my life. That would be letting him win."

"You're brave, you know that?" She sent me a small grin. "Just don't be too brave, okay? If anything feels the slightest bit off, you get John and call me."

She squeezed my hand. "I promise."

John met us in the parking lot, and after brief introductions, we headed inside. Carter kept a firm hold on my hand as we walked down the familiar hallway. "I need to get John a visitor's pass and explain why he'll be lurking in the hallway for the time being."

"Lead the way, Firecracker." After a few minutes explaining the circumstances to the principal, he reluctantly agreed to let

John stay. It might have been my death glare that convinced him.

As we filed out of the office, I spotted that douchebag, Kyle. Carter stiffened at my side when she saw him headed our way. Slinging an arm over her shoulders, I pulled her flush against my side. She melted into me. "Good morning, Kyle," Carter said, the picture of polite professionalism.

"Carter," Kyle greeted stiffly. "What's with the entourage?" he asked without glancing at John or me. What a piece of work.

Carter fidgeted next me, so I spoke up. "Carter's having a little trouble with a creep who can't seem to get the message, so John here is her new security detail."

Kyle's eyes darted from Carter to me and back again. "You can't be serious?" he spluttered. "If you're having trouble, it's probably one of the riff-raff *he* associates with regularly. That's what happens when you surround yourself with the bottom of the barrel of society, Carter. You need to get away from him. Surely, you can see that."

I was going to pound this prick into the pavement. John must have sensed my aim because he grabbed hold of my arm, growling low into my ear, "That's exactly what he wants." He was right, of course. This guy was probably hoping I'd take a swing at him and get banned from campus.

There was something about Kyle that had never sat right with me, something slimy about his good-guy persona. I always thought it was just that he wanted in Carter's pants, but maybe her stalker was standing right in front of us. I didn't know much about his and Carter's relationship, but Liam had assured me it was never serious. Maybe them never being serious stuck in Kyle's craw, or maybe he had deluded himself into believing their relationship was. I definitely needed to get Massey to look into this guy.

Carter stepped in between the two of us. "Kyle, enough! Don't talk about Austin like that. If you don't stop with these ridiculous insults, I'll file a report with Principal Hughes."

Kyle's face was getting redder by the second. He looked moments away from stroking out. "Lie down with dogs, and you'll wake up with fleas. I'll see you around, Carter." He stepped around Carter and stomped down the hall.

Carter's shoulders slumped. I reached out to bring her to me, but when she felt my hand, she spun around, her eyes blazing. "You baited him! You basically accused him of being my stalker!"

I purposely kept my voice low. "He could be your stalker. That guy is a total creep."

"My stalker could be anyone. Literally, *anyone*. You making things more awkward and uncomfortable with someone I work with and have to see almost every day is not helping anything."

I deflated a little at that. "I'm sorry, baby. You're right. I've just never liked that guy."

She let out a long breath. "I know. I don't like him much anymore either. He certainly showed his true colors. I can't believe I dated him."

"You dated that tool?" John piped in.

"What can I say, your boss broke my heart. I was willing to try anything to get over him." She said it with a small smile on her lips.

I grabbed her around the waist. "Such a smartass," I said, kissing her hard on the mouth.

THIRTY-SIX

Carter

I WALKED INTO THE LIVING ROOM, BLUE TROTTING BEHIND me, and found Austin sitting on the couch, knees spread wide in that quintessential *guy* stance, scrolling through something on his phone. The fading late-afternoon light hit his face just right, warming the apples of his cheeks and highlighting his cut jaw. He was beautiful. I knew a guy would never want to be called *beautiful,* but that's what he was. My heart clenched. God, I loved him.

Hearing the soft footfalls my socked feet made on the tile, he looked up. "Hey, babe, what sounds good for dinner?"

I didn't answer. Instead, I plucked the phone from his hand and set it on the coffee table. Then I steeled my nerves and straddled him. His eyes widened slightly, but his hands immediately went to my hips. "You know, I'm not all that hungry at the moment."

"You're not, huh?" Austin's fingers flexed into the flesh at my sides.

"Nope." I leaned in and brought my mouth to his. Tasting a bit of bitterness from the beer he had been drinking and that flavor that was uniquely Austin, I groaned slightly into his mouth.

He slipped a hand beneath my t-shirt, trailing up the small of my back and around to my stomach. "So smooth. I'll never get tired of touching your skin." I needed the barriers between his skin and mine gone. I took my hands from his shoulders, moved them down to the hem of my shirt, and pulled it up and over my head. Austin's eyes were fixed on the swells of my breasts peeking out from my new blush lace bra. I reached back and unfastened it, letting it fall to the floor. He continued to stare, then lifted his eyes to mine. "So damn pretty."

He skimmed his hand higher, swiping his thumb across my nipple in the way I loved. "More," I said, biting back a moan. Austin dipped his head and took my pebbled bud into his mouth. This time, I did cry out, loudly. The pulls on my nipple sent zings of pleasure directly to my clit. My head fell back as he moved to the other nipple.

He nibbled lightly. "I wonder if I could make you come like this?"

"Please." I was panting.

"My eyes! Dear God, my eyes, they're burning!"

Those words, spoken by that voice, were a bucket of ice water thrown on my overheated body. I shrieked, throwing my body forward so that my chest was pressed up against Austin's, concealing myself.

"Jesus, Liam! Turn the fuck around and try knocking next time," Austin bellowed. Luckily, my back had been to the door so there was no way Liam could have actually seen anything, but I'm sure his imagination was working overtime. I grimaced at that thought, certain my cheeks were turning fuchsia.

"You know Ford and I have keys. Why would you do this to me?" Liam groaned as Austin deftly got me back in my bra, and I slipped my shirt back over my head.

"Where is Ford, anyway?" Austin asked.

Liam had a hand covering his eyes and was facing away from us. "He was outside on a phone call when I pulled up."

Just then, the front door opened, and Ford strode in. "What the hell is all the yelling about?" he asked, sending a perplexed look towards Liam, who still had a hand over his eyes.

Liam pointed roughly in my direction without turning around or dropping the hand from his eyes. "Carter flashed me!" He sounded outraged.

"Oh, I did not, you big drama queen. And you can take your hand off your eyes now."

"Are you sure? You are like my little sister, and I never, ever want to see my little sister's boobies. Or my little sister about to go to pound town with my best friend."

Ford snorted. "Hey, I thought I was your best friend."

Before Liam could retort, Austin jumped in. "Watch it, Liam, or I'll go to pound town on your face."

Both Liam's and Ford's expressions twisted into ugly grimaces, but it was Ford who spoke. "That's just wrong, man. And some fucked-up mental imagery I won't be able to get rid of quickly."

"I'm the one who's going to have nightmares!" Liam yelled.

I stepped in between all of them. "Enough, all of you are a bunch of dramatic babies. I'm hungry, can we order some food?"

Liam pouted. "Fine, but I'm not sure I'll be able to eat."

I rolled my eyes. "Let's see what you say when Little Dom's arrives, fatty." He immediately perked up at the name of our favorite Italian place. That's what I thought.

The next morning, I was sitting in Austin's passenger seat, sipping my coffee and texting with Taylor as Austin and I pulled into the school parking lot. Last night, the boys had stayed far too late, and I had fallen asleep on the couch while they watched a baseball game. I had briefly awakened to Austin carrying me back to his bedroom and stayed semi-conscious long enough to take out my contacts and brush my teeth. I woke in the morning to find myself pinned between Austin and Blue. Austin had not been happy to discover Blue in his bed, but he was just going to have to get used to it.

As we swung into a parking spot, I spotted John waiting in the same place he had been yesterday. I waved in his direction, and he responded with a chin lift. I liked John. He wasn't the most talkative, but I could tell he was salt of the earth and took his job seriously. I would never admit it to Austin, but I breathed a little easier knowing that John was right outside my door all day. "Morning, John," I called as I slipped from the Range Rover.

"Morning, Carter."

Austin came around the front of the SUV and threw an arm over my shoulders. He always claimed me in some way—an arm around me, holding my hand, grasping the back of my neck. I loved that he wasn't afraid to be affectionate in public. It was never over-the-top, but I always appreciated it. Maybe because I had been unsure about us for so long, this clear declaration always hit me right in the feels. I pressed my body into his, hoping he'd sense my gratitude. He tilted his head down and kissed my forehead. "Let's get you to class."

"You don't have to walk me all the way in, you know."

"Last time I didn't walk you all the way in, you almost got strangled by a crazy person." John's head snapped up, and I stiffened. Austin squeezed the back of my neck to soften his words. "Sorry, baby. Didn't mean to remind you. I just won't ever take chances with your safety again."

I forced a smile to my lips. "Good thing you taught me how to kick some ass, huh?"

Austin grinned at me. "Damn straight. John, she broke the guy's nose and crushed his nuts."

John held open the main door for Austin and me. "Good for you, sweetheart."

"So you know I've got your back if anything goes down." John chuckled in response.

Austin kissed the top of my head. "My Firecracker, always causing trouble."

I grinned as I swung the door of my classroom open, but it died on my lips. The walls were covered in black and white photos with red writing: *whore, slut, bitch*. And when I saw what the pictures were of, vomit crawled up the back of my throat. It was me, straddling Austin, top off, head thrown back. My immediate reaction was that I had to get rid of them, no one could see these. I reached out my hand to the images directly in front of me, but John stopped me. "You can't touch them. There might be prints or some kind of trace evidence."

"The kids can't see these." My voice was high and panicked, sounding foreign in my ringing ears.

"We won't let them." Austin's voice was hard.

"I think I'm going to be sick." John grabbed the trashcan by my desk, and I emptied the meager contents of my stomach into it while Austin held back my hair.

When the heaving stopped, Austin handed me a tissue. I took it with a shaking hand. "Let's get you to a bathroom."

"Toothbrush. My desk." I pointed that still-trembling hand towards a drawer in my desk. John retrieved the brush, handing it to Austin.

"John, here's my phone. There's a contact for a Detective Massey. Call him and explain what happened." Keeping one arm around me, Austin handed the phone to John, who nodded. "Baby, where's the teachers' lounge?"

"Next to the office." My voice sounded foreign to my own ears. Dead.

Austin ushered me down the hall to the lounge. Following me into the bathroom, he leaned against the door as I brushed my teeth and ran a damp paper towel over my mouth and neck. When I was done, he pulled me to him and held me tight, massaging my nape. His heart pounded against my cheek, and I knew rage was flowing through his veins, but he was containing it, not wanting to scare me further.

"Those pictures were taken last night," I said softly, hesitantly. "Someone was on your property."

"I know." The words sounded like they were barbed and ripped from his throat. "I'm going to have John double the number of guys we have on duty."

I inwardly cringed, thinking of the cost, but didn't say a word. We just continued to stand there. "This is crazy." The image of all those photos and ugly words overtook my mind, and tears brimmed in my eyes. "So many people are going to see those pictures." The tears crested my lower lids and fell down my cheeks. My skin began to crawl, and my body trembled. I pushed away from Austin. "I need to take a shower."

His brow furrowed as he studied my shaking form. "What are you talking about?"

Sobs wracked me as I struggled to get words out. "I-I feel so dirty."

"Oh, baby, no." Austin pulled me into his arms again. "You are not dirty. You are everything pure and beautiful in my world. You are perfect." He held me as I cried everything out. As the tears slowed, Austin pulled back slightly and began sweeping the tears away. "You have nothing to be ashamed of. Absolutely nothing."

He cupped my face in his hands, continuing to catch any stray tears with his thumbs. When they stopped altogether, he kissed each lid and then my forehead. "I love you, Carter. We are going to figure this out, I promise you." I nodded but didn't speak, afraid more tears might fall. I knew Austin was taking this hard. I knew it killed him that he couldn't build a wall between me and anything that might possibly hurt me. I had to be strong, if not for myself, then for him.

Austin and I exited the bathroom and headed back towards my classroom. He held me firmly against him as if he could shield me from all that was to come. I paused our movement, tilting my face up to his. "Let's just wait out here." I didn't need to see those photos again. Once had been enough.

"Okay, baby." He pressed his lips to my forehead.

Within minutes, Detective Massey and other officers arrived at the school. Massey squeezed my shoulder reassuringly and then went to talk to Principal Hughes. When he returned, he pulled Austin and me aside. "We're going to put your students in the gym for now, they're bringing in a substitute, so you don't need to worry about that. The only people who will enter that room are trained law enforcement officers." I nodded, grateful for the reassurance. "Do you know when the pictures were taken and where?"

I nodded again and forced myself to speak. "They were taken last night at Austin's house."

Austin spoke next. "I had two members of my security team on hand, one at the gate, and one patrolling the perimeter of my property but, clearly, they missed this guy."

I bit the corner of my lip. "Liam and Ford must have arrived right around when those pictures were taken, maybe they saw something."

Austin kneaded the nape of my neck. "I think they would have said something if they did, but it's worth checking." He turned towards Detective Massey. "I can give you their contact numbers."

He took the numbers down on his notepad. "I'm going to send some officers over to your home to check for any shoe prints or other signs that someone was lurking outside."

"That's fine, just have John call his man at the gate, and they'll let you in. You should also talk to him." Austin inclined his head over my shoulder, and I turned to see Kyle taking in the scene.

Detective Massey was suddenly alert. "Who's that?"

"That's Carter's ex, Kyle Davis. He works here and would have access to the classrooms. We've had a couple run-ins with him where he's made his displeasure at us dating known."

I pressed myself harder into Austin's side. I hated the idea that Kyle could be responsible for all of this. Detective Massey rose, flipping his notebook closed. "I'll have a word with him now."

Just as Detective Massey departed, Principal Hughes approached. He was a kind man, but a stickler for the rules, and I was sure having police invade his school had not made him happy. "Are you okay, Carter?" he asked.

I tried to give him a smile, but I'm pretty sure it came across as more of a grimace. "I've had better days. I'm really sorry about all of this."

Principal Hughes looked down at his shuffling feet. "None of this is your fault, but given everything the police have told me, I think it's best you take a leave of absence."

My jaw slackened, and Austin's hold on me tightened. "What do you mean?"

"I think you can agree it's not worth the risk of this maniac acting out when your students are present."

I swallowed back the tears that wanted to resurface. I had given so much to this job, truly my blood, sweat, and tears. And, in a flash, it was gone. "Whatever you think is best," I said, holding back the words that wanted to come out because he was right. I would never forgive myself if something happened to one of my kids because of me.

"I'm sorry, Carter, it's just until this situation is resolved. The school year is almost up anyway." I nodded woodenly as he turned left.

Austin wrapped his arms around me, resting his lips on my brow as he spoke. "I'm so sorry, baby."

A throat cleared behind me, and I turned to see Detective

Massey. "Kyle has an alibi for last night and this morning that we are going to check out. He says a friend came over to play video games. He crashed on his couch and was still there when Kyle left for work. Also, an officer found a broken window in the classroom next to yours, it looks like the perpetrator entered the school there. There is no interior surveillance, so we are out of luck on that front. Why don't you two head home, there's no reason for you to hang around. I'll come by as soon as I've wrapped things up here and update you on what we've learned."

I nodded. It seemed like that was about all I was capable of doing this morning. Austin held out a hand to shake. "Thank you. Call my cell if you need anything from us," he said. I was silent as we wove our way through police and school staff, not meeting anyone's eyes, letting Austin guide me. A numbness had taken over. It felt as though my life no longer belonged to me but to this invisible bad guy who had stolen the controls, steering me in whatever direction he desired.

THIRTY-SEVEN

Carter

I SLUMPED BACK INTO THE COUCH AS AUSTIN SHOWED Detective Massey and his colleagues out. The police had been crawling all over the property for hours with not much to show for it. Two partial shoe prints that couldn't give them much information, and no fingerprints.

Austin and John had created a security hub in the guest house, adding additional men to patrol the property and placing cameras everywhere. It felt like I was living in a prison, a very posh and comfortable one, but a prison nonetheless. My skin was starting to itch.

Austin reemerged from the entryway. "Why don't you go take a bath and relax a little. It's been a long day."

"That sounds perfect." I rose from the couch and stretched. Austin's eyes zeroed in on my chest as the material of my blouse stretched across my breasts. I crossed to him and placed a chaste kiss on his lips as I headed for that dreamy soaking tub in the master bath. Blue plodded along behind me.

I started the water and went in search of something to create bubbles. Surprisingly, I found some bubble bath under one of the sinks. Opening the cap, I sniffed—lavender, perfect. I dumped a generous portion under the faucet. Stripping down, I left my clothes in a pile on the floor and stepped into the steaming water. I let out a sigh as I submerged my body in the foamy depths. This tub was heaven. Nothing scary or bad could exist in this tub, only warmth and comfort. I was never going to leave.

A soft knock sounded at the door, and I jolted. I must have drowsed a bit because the water was tepid, and my bubbles had greatly diminished. "Who is it?" I needed to ask since the number of people wandering around had greatly increased.

"It's me. You still alive in there? Turned into a prune yet?"

"Yes, and yes. You can come in."

The door opened, and Austin sauntered in. He knelt beside the tub, dipping his fingers into the water. "This is practically cold. Let's get you out of there." Grabbing a towel and shaking it out, he held it open for me like I was a little kid. But his gaze on my body as I rose from the water said he was not looking at me like a child. I felt his eyes roam from my face to my breasts and navel, stopping longest at the juncture of my thighs. My stomach muscles clenched.

Austin wrapped me in the soft terrycloth, slowly and thoroughly drying my arms. Then moving to my chest, where the material brushed over the tips of my breasts that had hardened into sharp points. A tightening sensation started in my core. Abandoning my chest, he dried my stomach and then knelt in front of me to run the towel over each leg.

My breath hitched as I saw where his head was positioned. He lifted his eyes to mine as he leaned ever so slightly forward and ran his nose through my small dusting of damp curls. I bit down on my lip at the erotic sight. Austin's eyes fell closed. "You smell so good."

My breath was coming faster. "Austin, I need you."

His eyes flew open again. "Are you sure?"

I had never been more sure about anything in my life. Taking this step had never felt right before. Not the right person, not the right time. I had built up losing my virginity in my mind, thinking it needed to be the absolute perfect scenario. But now I realized I didn't need candlelight and flowers. I just needed Austin. "I'm sure. I've always wanted it to be you. And right now, I need to feel alive." He placed a kiss right above my pubic bone. I let out a breath. "I'm on the pill," I started.

Austin cut me off, rising to his feet. "I've been tested. I'm clean. Can I take you bare?" I felt another clench. I nodded. He cupped my face, letting the towel drop. "I need the words, Firecracker."

"Yes," I whispered.

Austin picked me up, and I wrapped my legs around his waist, arms around his neck. "You have to stay in the bathroom," he called to Blue, who whined in response. I giggled at that. Austin laid me gently on the bed. His eyes bore into me like he was trying to commit every detail to memory. He pulled his t-shirt over his head, and now it was me taking in every ridge and curve of muscle along with the sprinkling of dark hair that disappeared below his waistband.

Austin sank to the floor, pulling me so that my butt was at the edge of the bed as he slowly pushed my knees apart. "You're so fucking beautiful. Even your pussy is perfect." His lips started at the inside of my knee, licking, sucking, kissing, and nipping. He worked his way towards my center. That cord inside pulled tighter, and my chest heaved.

I jumped a little when his tongue darted inside, but he used an arm across my belly to hold me in place. Taking his time, he lazily explored my core, teasingly tracing circles around my clit but never actually making contact.

"Austin," I groaned his name in frustration.

"Patience, Firecracker, I have to get you ready for me." He dipped a finger inside, and my hips rose up to meet it. Austin pushed my hips back down.

My head strained against the mattress. "More." I was begging.

I didn't care.

He inserted a second finger, using them to stretch me as the tip of his tongue ventured closer to my clit. Then, a third finger. It burned for a moment, but then Austin's tongue was flicking that bundle of nerves, and I was shattering as he stretched me further.

As I came down, Austin slowly removed his fingers and quickly shucked his pants. I stared in a bit of horror and a lot of anticipation at the erection that stood tall against his stomach. Austin was a large guy all around, so the size of his cock shouldn't have come as a surprise, but it did. He chuckled at the look on my face. "It'll fit, promise." He bent over me, taking my mouth in an aggressive kiss that turned tender. "It might hurt at first."

"It's okay, I want you inside me." I ran a hand up the side of his face and over his buzzed head, relishing the feel of his hair tickling my palm. I pulled him down to me and kissed him with everything I had.

Austin pulled back slightly, and I felt his tip at my opening. "I love you, Carter."

"I love you, too," I breathed.

He pushed in. The burning and stretching were back, but Austin took my mouth in a slow kiss. "You're so tight. God, you feel perfect." I couldn't speak, but soon, my muscles began to melt, and the burning turned into a different kind of fire. My hips rose of their own accord, and Austin took that as his cue to move.

Slowly. So slowly it was a delicious torture, Austin moved in and out of me. Feeling him inside me gave me a sense of completion that I'd never know before. Prickles of pleasure danced throughout my body, jumping from one nerve ending to the next.

My body jolted with a sharp spark of arousal as Austin rolled my nipple between his fingers. I didn't know it was possible to feel this much in a single moment. He gave the bud a light pinch that had my walls clenching around him. "Fuck. I knew being inside you would be heaven."

Austin began to pick up his pace, the speed causing a delicious friction that added to the riot of sensations my body was experiencing. Sweat peppered my skin as we found a new rhythm. A rhythm that had every part of me trembling. A rhythm that was too much and not enough, in the best possible way.

I fisted the sheets as Austin delved deeper and deeper, finally hitting that spot I thought was a fairy tale. He reached between our bodies and thumbed my clit, sending me shattering a second time but in a whole new way. A way that consumed my entire being. Austin cursed as he thrust one more time, throwing his head back as he emptied himself inside me.

Panting, he brought his damp forehead to mine. He rolled us so that I was now on top of him, his dick still twitching inside of me, my own body wracked with aftershocks. I sucked in slow breaths as my heart rate slowed.

I burrowed into his neck. "I had no idea something could feel that good, that intense."

Austin chuckled. "Me either." We were silent for a few minutes as he trailed his fingertips up and down my spine. "You okay?" he finally asked.

"Mm-hmm," I answered.

Austin rolled us again so that I was beneath him and slowly pulled out of me. I winced at the bite of pain. "Sorry, baby. I'm going to get a warm cloth to clean you."

I bit my lip and watched his tight butt saunter into the bathroom. Blue let out a whine as the door opened. Austin reemerged with a washcloth in hand and pressed it between my legs. A soft smile touched my lips at the tender gesture. "That feel okay?" I nodded, heat flooding my cheeks.

"Nothing to be shy about. I love tending to this body." He bent over, kissed each of my nipples and then my lips. When he removed the cloth, I saw a few dots of pink, but nothing like I'd imagined. The grin on Austin's face told me there was indeed something about taking my virginity that stroked his male ego.

I shook my head at him. "I'm hungry. I think you need to feed me."

"What sounds good?" he asked.

"Hmm, I think I need ice cream."

"Ice cream it is." Austin rose and tossed the cloth into the laundry basket. I bent and picked up the t-shirt he'd discarded on the floor. Austin emerged from the closet with a robe. Handing it to me, he said, "Just in case someone comes by." It was probably a good idea. I handed Austin his shirt and slipped on the robe.

I quickly popped into the bathroom, washing my hands and splashing some water on my face, when I heard, "BLUE!" bellowed from the bedroom. I darted back out to find Blue frozen on the bed, a yellow puddle beneath him.

My hands flew to my mouth. "Did he just pee on the bed?"

"Yes," Austin gritted out.

"I guess he didn't like being locked in the bathroom." I had to bite my lip to keep from laughing.

Austin turned his blazing eyes to me. "I'm not letting him watch us fuck. I'm not into that voyeuristic shit."

I couldn't hold my laughter in any longer, and once it started, I couldn't stop it. "I'm sorry, I know I shouldn't be laughing."

"He ruined the comforter!" But as soon as the words were out of his mouth, Austin started laughing, too. "That damn dog."

I wrapped my arms around Austin's waist. "He's a good dog." Austin was silent. "Most of the time, he is," I argued.

Austin just shook his head. "We need a dog trainer."

"Oh, fine. Let's go get some ice cream and throw out this bedding. Come on, Blue." I rolled up the comforter, and Austin took it out to the trash. Well, I'd never forget my first time, that was for sure.

THIRTY-EIGHT

Carter

THE NEXT MORNING, I WAS TENDER. BUT I LIKED THE reminder my sore muscles gave me every time I moved a certain way. I smiled to myself as I tapped out a text to Taylor. Of course, I had to tell my bestie that I had finally crossed that barrier with Austin.

She was thrilled for me and was peppering me for details I'd never give her. I hadn't told Taylor about the new stalker developments other than glossing over a second break-in at the house. She knew I was staying with Austin now, but I didn't want to worry her, since she was already dealing with so much stress, helping her mom recover from chemo treatments.

Taylor: *Just tell me how big his dick is, and I'll leave you alone. Or better yet, snap a dick pic!*

I spit my coffee all over my placemat.

"Jesus, Carter, are you okay?" Austin stood from his chair across from me and grabbed a handful of paper towels.

"Sorry," I coughed. "Taylor was being a perv."

Austin just shook his head and handed me the towels. He was used to Taylor's and my antics. "Do you want to spend the day with me at the gym?" he asked. "We can bring Blue."

"Sure." I took another sip of my coffee and succeeded in

keeping it in my mouth this time.

Austin sat back down. "I have something I want to run by you when we're there."

"What?"

"Patience, Firecracker. I'll tell you when we get there."

"Oh, fine."

We finished up breakfast and then headed to the gym with John following behind us in another car. I hated that this was the new normal, but I was grateful to have someone at our back—just in case. I found myself looking everywhere for any sign of a shadowy figure, clearly up to no good. Austin reached over and took my hand. "Everything will be okay, I promise."

"I know, I'm just so sick of looking over my shoulder."

He squeezed my hand. "We'll check in with Detective Massey when we get to my office, see if he's come up with anything."

I leaned across the console and kissed Austin's shoulder. "You've been amazing through all of this. I honestly don't know what I'd do without you."

"Good thing you'll never have to find out."

"I love it when you say that."

He smirked at me. "I know you do."

"Arrogant."

"You love me."

I scoffed, and he chuckled as he swung into a parking spot. I grabbed my purse from the floorboard and startled when my door opened. "Sorry about that." It was John.

"Not your fault. I'm a jumpy mess, apparently." I eased out of the car, only to be surrounded, John at my back and Austin at my side. They were both on guard, and it had my own anxiety level climbing.

We made our way inside to be greeted by Sofia. She was clearly concerned, but I was grateful when she kept things light. We chatted about Michael, and she fawned over Blue. Austin tugged on my arm. "Come on, let's go back to my office."

"Okay. See you later, Sofia."

"See you, *chica*."

I patted the side of my leg, and Blue followed us down the hall. When we reached Austin's office, Blue immediately launched himself onto the couch, and I took a seat beside him, scratching behind his ears. Austin shut the door behind himself and eyed Blue. "Make yourself right at home, Blue."

I chuckled. "Oh, lighten up. Why don't you sit down and tell me what you wanted to talk about."

Austin settled in the chair across from me. We were sitting in the same positions as when I saw him for the first time after our year of radio silence. I couldn't believe how far we'd come. "What would you think about taking over as director for the youth program? I haven't been able to find anyone who's right for the position, and I think that's because I'm subconsciously comparing all of them to you. You're who I picture when I think about the ideal candidate. You'd have complete creative control."

I was stunned. Of all the things I'd thought he might want to ask me, I'd never expected him to offer me a job. In many ways, it was exactly what I was looking for, working with kids but with so much more freedom and autonomy than I had while working at a public school. But, working for my boyfriend? That could be a recipe for disaster. We did have our friendship as a foundation, though. I knew how he operated, probably better than anyone, and he knew me just as well. "There's a huge part of me that wants to jump up and down and scream 'yes,' but I need to think about it. Can I have a little time?"

His face gentled from businessman-serious. "Of course. Take all the time you need."

I jumped up and dumped myself on his lap, circling his neck with my arms and kissing him lightly. "Thank you for thinking of me."

"I'm always thinking about you."

"I like hearing that." I kissed him again. "Promise me one thing."

"What?"

"Promise that you're not offering me this job just because I was forced to take a leave of absence."

Austin's face got serious. "Carter, I wanted to offer you this job as soon as I started the program, but I knew you'd never take it then. I truly do think you're the best person for the position."

I pushed my face into the crook of his neck. "Okay, I just had to be sure." He squeezed me tighter against him, and I tipped my head back. "Since I'm here for the day, why don't you put me to work."

"I can think of a few things you can work on…" He grinned down at me.

"Quit it, you dirty bird. I mean office work."

He nuzzled the side of my neck. "You take all the fun out of working together."

"If you're a good boy, I'll let you cop a feel before we leave."

"Promises, promises."

I pinched Austin's side as I lifted myself from his lap. "Come on, give me something to do."

"All right, all right," he groused.

I spent the rest of the day pouring over all the paperwork for each of the program kids that their parents had submitted. I created a file for each child and made notes in each about what programs or support might be helpful, already planning to have meetings with each one so I could get to know them better and see how we could best help them reach their dreams. Because, who was I kidding, one hour into reading about these kids, and I knew I was going to take the job. I set the last file down and stood to stretch, I was still just a little bit sore from last night and smiled at the reminder.

At the sound of the door opening, I turned and saw Austin's dark head appear. "Ready for me to cop a feel?" he asked.

I let out a bark of laughter at his words and the truly hopeful expression on his face. "Come here."

He ambled over and pulled me into his arms, easing me into a warm and seductive kiss. His hands traveled lower and, before long, they were squeezing my backside. He pulled back, a soft look in his eyes. "You sore?"

Heat rose to my cheeks. "A little," I said with regret.

"Bath for you tonight, and then I'll kiss it all better," he said with a devilish grin. "Come on, let's get out of here."

"Okay, let me just grab my stuff." He released me, giving my butt a pat as I turned away. I shot him a look over my shoulder as I picked up my purse.

"What?" he asked. "You said I could cop a feel if I was good!"

I shook my head at him and hooked Blue's leash to his collar. "Let's go. I'm starving."

Austin grabbed my hand and led me down the hall. John was sitting in the lobby, facing both possible points of entry. "I'm sorry you had to sit around here all day, John."

He smiled kindly at me. "Not a problem, it's my job, and I'm happy to do it."

"Stop flirting with my girl." Austin drilled a faux punch into John's stomach.

"Better keep on your toes," John shot back.

"Yeah, yeah. Let's go, Firecracker's hungry." He grabbed my hand again, and we headed out to the parking lot, John leading the way this time and scanning the cars for anyone unfamiliar. He circled around the area as Austin went to open the back door for Blue. A flyer fluttered in the breeze but was held in place by the passenger-side windshield wiper. I stepped forward to grab it. Honestly, did that kind of marketing ever work?

My hand froze as I brought the flyer up to read it. On the

paper in blood-red marker read, "*LYING LITTLE WHORE. IT'S TIME FOR SOMEONE TO DIE. MIGHT BE YOU. MIGHT BE YOUR BOYFRIEND. MIGHT BE YOUR STUPID FUCKING DOG.*" My hands started shaking, but it wasn't in fear, it was in fury. I'd had just about enough from this asshole.

Austin came up behind me, and I knew he'd read over my shoulder when I heard, "Fuck! You have got to be kidding me!" He started to call out for John when I heard a crack and the windshield splintered.

Austin's body collided with mine as he took me down to the ground. The asphalt bit into my knees and cheek. I frantically reached out for Blue, who had started barking like crazy at the sound.

"Shooter!" Austin yelled to John, who already had his weapon out. The only thing I could think was, *I didn't even realize John carried a gun. Where did he hide it?*

"Baby, are you okay?" Austin was still on top of me but was trying to pat me down, assessing for injuries.

"I think so, are you?"

"I'm fine."

John rushed over to us, positioning himself between us and where the shooter must have been standing. "I can't see anyone, but that doesn't mean anything. I want you to slowly get up and face the gym. Austin, you lead, take Blue's leash in one hand, and Carter's hand in the other. Carter, you hold onto Austin and then link a finger through my back belt loop. We are going to, very slowly, make our way towards the gym. Ready?"

"Yes," Austin and I both answered at the same time.

"Move." It was an awkward and slow process, but we finally reached the doors and pushed inside. "Lock these and move away from any windows," John ordered. "Can you make an announcement over the loudspeakers and let people know to do the same?"

"I'll do that now." Austin moved behind the empty reception desk to make an announcement, and John was on the phone with 911 and then Detective Massey. Within a minute, I heard sirens. Then, Austin was back at my side, examining my cheek. "Shit, I'm sorry, baby. Let me get some stuff to clean your scrapes."

He moved to walk away, but I held tight to his hand. He cupped the unmarred side of my face. "I'm just going to the desk. There's a first-aid kit in there." I forced my fingers to unlock from around his. The fear was just hitting me, the reality that one of us could have just died. My hands had started to shake, my palms were clammy, and I felt sick to my stomach. When Austin returned, he looked at me with concerned eyes. "I want you to sit down."

John walked over. "She's as white as a sheet."

"I think she might be going into shock."

Swallowing my nausea, I forced myself to focus. "I'm okay." Both Austin and John looked skeptical. "Really, I just felt a little lightheaded for a minute."

John squeezed my shoulder and then headed over to the front door where four police officers had appeared. Austin set the first-aid kit down on the couch and removed a wipe of some sort. I hissed when the alcohol touched my broken skin. "Sorry." He blew on my cheek, easing the sting. Then he knelt on the ground and lifted my yoga pants to above my knees and repeated his actions, covering all the scrapes with ointment and Band-Aids.

"Thank you." My voice was soft as police crowded the lobby. "Austin, this is insane." He sat down next to me and pulled me into his lap. Blue took that as a sign, and he jumped up next to us. I scratched his ears. "I know, Blue, everything's okay now." He pushed his head into my hand.

Before long, Detective Massey had arrived, looking harried and concerned. Austin, John, and I walked him through everything that had happened. Another officer had collected the note, which I had dropped in the chaos and handed it, sealed in an evidence bag, to the detective. Massey then took a few moments to peruse it, his eyes pinched as he analyzed the lettering. "The escalation is continuing."

I shuddered but lifted a hand and placed it on Austin's back. His muscles were wound so tightly, it seemed as if they might snap. I started to knead them with my thumb, not that it could do much. "You should look into Lexi Perkins."

My hand stuttered at Austin's words. "Lexi doesn't know how to shoot." At least I didn't think she did. I knew Lexi disliked me, maybe even hated me, but would she really go that far? Would she kill Austin just because she couldn't have him? Or me because I did?

Austin's eyes met mine. "You don't know that. Or she could have hired someone. The only thing I know is that she's crazy and has a grudge against you a mile long."

Massey jotted down a few words in his notepad. "I'll look into her. We're also pursuing the number that was calling you, Carter. It came back as a burner, but we're trying to track it at the point of purchase."

"Do you think I should leave LA for a little while? My parents have a cabin in the mountains, I could go there…"

My words trailed off when Austin's spine snapped straight. He turned to me. "You're not going anywhere. At least not without me and security." I bit the corner of my mouth, but Austin reached out and eased my lip from between my teeth. "You're not going anywhere alone, Firecracker."

"I just don't want anyone to get hurt because of me," I argued.

"Carter." It was just one word, but it sucked all the fight out of me. I knew Austin would never agree, and that his stubborn butt would follow me wherever I went.

I tugged on the end of my ponytail in frustration. "Fine."

Detective Massey cleared his throat. "For what it's worth, it would be best for our investigation if you stayed within LAPD's jurisdiction. If you can hole up at Austin's house for a week or so, give us some time to investigate, that will help. I know it's not fun to feel confined, but it might be safest."

I nodded, resigned. "I'll do whatever you think is best."

"I do think you should let your parents know what's going on and any other close friends and family that you haven't informed yet. They need to be aware in case the stalker reaches out to them in search of information. You can give them my phone number, and I'll answer any questions they might have."

"I appreciate that." I had stiffened at the idea of calling my parents, who were going to freak, but I knew it was time. As it was, my mom might murder me for not telling her sooner.

Austin took my hand in his, squeezing it in reassurance. "It's time, baby."

"I know." I let my head drop to his shoulder. "My dad is going to flip."

"It'll be okay."

The next hour passed in a blur of answering the same questions all over again to different police officers. Austin and I were now in the back of John's SUV, heading home with a police tail. I was trying to wrap up a phone call with my parents who, as I had suspected, freaked the frick out. I thought I had finally convinced them that it was best for me to stay in LA and that they should not fly out here to be with me, when my dad barked, "I want to talk to Austin."

I took a deep breath and turned toward Austin, covering the bottom of my cell with one hand. "He wants to talk to you."

Austin plucked the phone from my hand. "Hello, Mr. McCarthy." I couldn't hear what my dad was saying, and Austin's face stayed a stony mask, only muttering a few, "mm-hmm"s and "I understand"s. Finally, after a few more moments of silence, Austin said, "Sir, I'll protect her with my life. I promise you."

Then, he hung up. My body was at war with itself. My stomach wanted to heave at the thought of Austin hurt in any way. My heart, on the other hand, was doing cartwheels at the knowledge that Austin loved me so deeply.

Austin handed me back my phone, and I shoved myself under his arm. "I love you, but don't you dare do anything stupid that would result in you dying on me."

Austin kissed the top of my head. "Not going anywhere, Firecracker." I let the warmth of his kiss seep into me and closing my eyes, I fell asleep.

THIRTY-NINE

Austin

RAGE LIKE I HAD NEVER KNOWN BEFORE PULSED THROUGH my veins as the SUV wound its way through the canyon roads of the Hollywood Hills. I pulled Carter tighter against me, taking a deep breath to inhale that familiar flowery scent I loved so much. I hoped feeling her body safely tucked next to mine and breathing her in would calm me. No such luck.

Nothing could ease the burning sensation in my chest. Carter could have died today. Could have been wiped from this Earth. She would have left me with a very bleak and empty existence. My body pulsed with the need to end whoever had threatened my Firecracker. But I didn't know where to direct that anger. There were too many suspects. Nothing was in my control, and I fucking hated it.

John slowed the SUV as we approached the gate. He paused while one of the security guards plugged in the code, and the doors swung open. "You're gonna have to have a talk with your guys," I said in a low voice, not wanting to wake Carter.

John's hold on the wheel tightened. "I will. They're all carrying, but they'll be extra vigilant and start wearing vests."

"Good. I don't want anyone getting hurt."

"Not on my watch." John brought the car to a stop in front of the house. "Want me to lift her out?"

I couldn't handle having anyone else's hands on my girl at this moment, so I shook my head. "I got her." I carefully opened my car door and slipped an arm under Carter's legs.

She jolted. "What?"

Shit. She was jumpy, and with good reason. I brushed the hair away from her face. "It's okay. We're home. You fell asleep in the car. I was just going to carry you inside."

Carter's face softened. "It's okay. I'm awake. I can walk."

I sent a small smirk her way. "You sure about that?" My firecracker was a great many wonderful things, but coordinated was not one of them.

She slapped my shoulder. "Yes, you big jerk. Now, out of my way."

I retreated from the car, allowing her to exit. As soon as her feet touched the ground, I pulled her to my side. She collided against me with an "*oof.*"

"Gonna need you close for a while. Need you to be okay with that."

Carter looked up at me with those big doe eyes, eyelashes fluttering. "Okay, Austin."

I relaxed a little at her easy acquiescence. I was going to keep her locked away and under my constant supervision until this psycho was caught. My phone buzzed as we entered the house, and I slipped it from my pocket. When I read the name, I scowled at the screen. Fuck, this day just kept getting better.

I glanced at Carter, who had taken Blue's leash from John and was unhooking it. This was not going to go well, but I had learned my lesson, I was going the route of upfront honesty. "Baby." Carter rose. "Lexi's calling right now. Do you want me to answer?"

The look on her face cut me to the core—suspicion, doubt, betrayal. "Why does she have your number? Or if she had it from months ago, why haven't you blocked her? Unless you weren't sure if you might want to call her up again?"

I fought the desire to snap. Would this forever be an issue? "Carter, I sometimes had to talk to her for work. You know that." I ran a hand roughly over my head. "I thought we were past this. At some point, you have to trust me."

Carter blew out a long breath, deflating as tears misted her eyes. "I'm sorry. I don't know why I said that. I do trust you." She collapsed against my chest, and my arms automatically encircled her lean frame. She was so delicate. Yet so tough at times, that I forgot just how delicate she really was. She tipped her face up towards mine. "I really do. She just brings out the worst in me."

I brushed my lips against hers. "It's okay. Everything will be okay."

"I love you, Austin."

"Love you, too." My phone buzzed to life again in my hand. Glancing at the screen, I grimaced.

Carter stiffened in my arms but said, "Go ahead, answer it."

I nodded, teeth clenched. Hitting accept and then the speakerphone button, I greeted, "What do you want, Lexi?"

"YOU RAT BASTARD! YOU CALLED THE FUCKING COPS ON ME?!"

Great. Lexi was in full drama queen-mode. "I didn't call the cops on you. The cops are interested in you as a person of interest because of your shady-ass behavior over the past year. It's no one's fault but your own."

"You'll regret this," she seethed. "You and that goody-two-shoes bitch of yours!" The line went dead as my stomach dropped.

"She's crazy," Carter whispered.

"We need to call Massey and let him know what happened." Carter nodded, lifting a hand to cover a yawn. "I'll do that. Why don't you go lay down for a bit? I'll order us some dinner after I get off the phone with Massey."

"Okay." Carter stretched to her tiptoes, giving me the briefest of kisses. "Thanks for taking such good care of me."

"Always."

Carter shuffled off towards my room, Blue following close behind while I placed a call to Detective Massey. Thirty minutes later, I had given Massey the rundown and ordered Thai food for Carter and myself. Grabbing a bottle of water, I went to check on my girl. Easing the bedroom door open, I found her curled in a ball in the center of the bed, Blue right by her side.

My heart seized. I never wanted this woman to leave me. A tremor wracked my body as I thought about how much I loved her. I was terrified by it. But I wasn't going to let that fear keep me away from her. She was my everything.

FORTY

Carter

I SAT AT THE KITCHEN TABLE, WILLING MY COFFEE TO DO ITS job and wake me up. The night before, I had slept like the dead, and ten hours later, I was still having trouble waking up. I took another sip, and Austin chuckled. "Still not quite awake yet?" The sexy jerk had already done a two-hour workout this morning. I grunted in response, and he chuckled again.

The vibrations my phone sent across the table as it started to ring caused me to jump. I snatched it up, and then my eyes went to Austin. "It's Detective Massey."

Austin was instantly on alert. "Answer and put him on speaker."

I punched a couple of buttons on my phone's screen and then greeted, "Hi, Detective Massey, you're on speaker with me and Austin."

"Good morning, Carter, Austin. I have some good news for you."

I perked up. "We love good news."

There was a smile in Detective Massey's voice when he spoke. "Well, I love being able to give it. We tracked down the burner phone, and you'll never believe who it belongs to."

"Who?" Austin and I said at the same time.

"Joe Harker, your past student's father. It looks like he's our guy. I've seen this sort of thing happen before: anger turning into a different kind of obsession altogether." I reached across the table and tried to grab Austin's hand, but he was already on his feet and coming around. He pulled me to my feet and wrapped his arms around me, kissing the side of my face that wasn't scratched.

Massey continued talking. "Two officers located him just a few minutes ago, and they're bringing him to the TMU headquarters. Contacting you was a violation of his parole so he won't be getting out anytime soon, even if we didn't have other charges to bring against him. I'll update you as we know more, but I thought you'd like to know you can breathe a little easier now."

I squeezed Austin more tightly. "Thank you so much."

"Thank you," Austin echoed. "We really appreciate all your hard work."

"Happy to help, I'll be in touch."

With that, I clicked the end button on my screen and started doing a happy dance all over the kitchen. Austin, having had enough of this, swept me up into his arms and kissed me soundly. "You are such a goof."

"But you love me."

"I do love you." He kissed me again.

"So, what do you want to do now that we're free?" I asked.

"I want to celebrate." Austin lifted me up, and I wrapped my legs around his waist, my robe flapping around us. He set me on the counter and reached for the belt holding my robe together. As he loosened the knot, my breaths started to come faster, and my nipples tightened. Slipping the fabric off my shoulders, I was suddenly completely bare to him. He stepped back, his gaze darting over my skin. Heat came to each place his eyes touched.

"You are so damn beautiful, I'll never get enough of looking at you." He stepped closer. "Each bend."—his hand grazed my knee heading up to my hip—"each curve." He bent down, kissing the top of my breast. "Each swell. I'll never get enough." Sparks danced across my skin with each caress.

I reached between us and pulled Austin to me by his waistband. "Need to feel you." I helped him peel out of his t-shirt while using my feet to push his workout pants down. My hands roved over his torso and chest, fingers dipping into the grooves of muscles and tracing his nipples.

Suddenly, his lips were on mine again, hungrier, fiercer than before. It was like we couldn't get close enough. And then I felt him at my entrance. "Yes." It came out breathy because I was panting. He pushed inside me, moving slowly. I could tell he was holding back to keep from hurting me, but there was no pain, only a delicious stretching sensation. But I needed more. "More. Please, more."

Austin started to move, his thrusts picking up speed. His eyes burned into mine, holding me captive, drawing me into him in every possible way. This was why I had waited. Because I hoped sex could be like this. Firing every nerve ending and singeing my soul, all while making me feel seen and understood at the deepest level.

My eyes misted. The coil within me tightened. Austin reached between our bodies and applied just the right amount of pressure to send me careening over the edge. My walls contracted around him, and he grunted out his release.

Slowly, I came back to myself, Austin's forehead was pressed against mine, arms braced on either side of my body. He gently pulled himself from my body. "Was that too much?"

I leaned forward, pressing my lips to his. "That was perfect."

Austin's eyes softened as he pulled my robe around my shoulders. "Shower?" he asked. I nodded, and before I knew what was happening, Austin had lifted me into his arms and was carrying me through the house towards his bedroom. While I was wrapped in my robe, he was still buck-naked. "Austin! Someone could see, there's still security around."

"Don't give a fuck, Firecracker." I reached around and pinched his bare butt. "Hey!" he hollered.

"That's what happens when those bare buns are out for all to see."

Austin set me down outside the shower and turned on the water, holding a hand under the flow until it was warm. Then, he stepped in, pulling me with him. He reached for the body wash I used, squirting some into his palm and then rubbing his hands together. He turned me away from him and started massaging the soap into my back. "I could get used to this."

"Could you, now?"

"Mm-hmm," I hummed.

I felt his body move closer to mine, and his lips touched the shell of my ear. "Move in with me," he whispered.

I froze. "What?" My heart thudded in my ears. Had I heard him correctly?

He rested his hands on my hips. "Move in with me. I realize now that Joe is in custody there's no reason for you to stay, but I don't want you to go. I'm selfish, and I want you with me all the time." My heart seized. He wanted me to stay. Not because I was in danger, but because he wanted me with him.

I looked into his eyes, searching for…I don't know, a thread of uncertainty or doubt. I couldn't see any. "Are you sure? Isn't this a little soon?" I wanted to give him an out, just in case this offer had been made in the heat of the moment. But I was all in. There was no one I'd rather spend time with, no one else with whom I'd want to build a home. He was it. He was everything.

"I'm sure. You're my best friend, my favorite person, the love of my life. And if we can get through this past month, I'm pretty sure we can get through anything." My heart did summersaults in my chest. "What do you think?" he pressed.

"I think…" I paused, "Yes!" I threw my arms around him.

"When?" I asked, leaning into him, my lips almost resting against his.

"Today? Yesterday?"

I giggled. "Today." I was smiling so hard, my cheeks hurt. I grabbed the body wash and started a furious scrub. "Hurry up, I've got packing to do. Well, searching through my trashed stuff to see if there's anything left to pack, but you get the picture."

Austin chuckled but reached for his own, more manly smelling, soap. "Calm down, I'll help you pack."

I pushed Austin aside so that I could rinse the suds off my body, being careful not to wet the hair that was in a bun on top of my head. I didn't have time for blow-drying this morning. "You can help me with the heavy lifting, but I'll do the packing."

I looked up to see Austin had pulled a full-on pout. "I can help pack."

I bit back a smile. "I love you, but you'll just want to throw everything into boxes and call it a day. And you'll drive me nuts if you're just hanging around while I'm trying to organize things." He ushered me aside to rinse himself but didn't deny anything. "You know I'm right."

Austin turned off the water, and I stepped from the shower, grabbing us both towels. "Why don't you just drop me off on your way to the gym?" I paused as I handed him his towel. "Oh, shoot, I forgot you don't have your car." His Range Rover was currently under the care and inspection of the LAPD. "Oh, well, we can just Uber."

Austin wasn't saying much as he toweled off, just eying me. Finally, he said, "Don't be mad." Just the sentence every girl wanted to hear from her boyfriend.

"What?" I asked. Then thinking I knew what he was going to say, I kept right on talking. "I can be in the house by myself for a few hours. Joe's in custody, there's nothing to worry about." I walked out of the bathroom in search of clothes.

Austin followed closely behind me. "It's not that. I mean, I'm not crazy about you being there by yourself, but that wasn't what I didn't want you to be mad about. I got you something, and I don't want you to fight me on it."

I narrowed my eyes skeptically at him. "If this is another Taser, I think I'm good with the one you got me already."

A smile stretched over his lips. "It's not a Taser. Come on. Get dressed, and I'll show you."

As quickly as possible, I lotioned and dressed, and then followed Austin through the house. I was confused when he started heading towards the garage, but then I got excited. "Holy heck, did you get me another dog?!"

Austin scoffed, "Fuck, no!"

I pulled on his arm. "Hey, now, that would be a great gift. Blue could use a sibling." At the sound of his name, Blue lifted his head from where he was snoozing on the couch.

"That dog is a terror. I'm not getting you another one."

"He is not a terror. He's perfect."

"Keep telling yourself that." Austin paused at the door to the garage. "Remember, no getting mad."

"No promises." If this was a permanent security detail or worse, a gun, I was going to be pissed.

Austin shook his head and pushed open the door, flicking on the lights. There, in the garage, was a brand new Mercedes SUV. It was a gorgeous silver color with gray interior. I knew nothing about cars, but even I could appreciate this one. I turned my head to Austin. "Why would I be mad that you bought yourself a new car? It's your money, you can do whatever you want with it."

A grin stretched across Austin's face. "I'm glad you see it that way because I bought it for you."

My jaw slackened. "You, what?"

"I bought it for you."

My head swiveled from Austin to the car and back to Austin

again. "Y-y-ou can't," I stuttered. "It's way too much."

He stepped forward and grabbed my hands in his. "Baby, this is one of the safest cars on the market. I love you, and I want you safe and in one piece. Please, for the love of all that is holy, accept this car. Even if it's just for my peace of mind."

I bit my bottom lip as Austin stared at me with imploring eyes. I sighed, releasing my lip. "I will, on two conditions."

Austin's face brightened, but he was still cautious. "Name your terms, Miss McCarthy."

"One is that you let me donate the proceeds of selling my Prius to the youth program." Austin's jaw tightened, but he nodded. "Two, I get to drive to my house."

He laughed. "You drive a hard bargain, but I accept."

I threaded my arms around his neck. "Thank you. You are incredibly kind and generous. A little crazy, but mostly kind and generous."

He brushed his lips against mine in a touch that sent a shiver down my spine. "Get your purse, and we can get on the road. I'll grab the keys."

I shot him a devilish smile and darted for the door, excited to take my new wheels for a spin. When I reached the kitchen, I paused. "Austin, what is Blue chewing on?"

Austin had stopped at my back and was now staring at Blue. "Motherfucker! That's my heavyweight belt!" At Austin's bellow, Blue's head shot up. He dropped the belt and ran for the living room.

While Austin dashed to the belt, I stayed frozen, hands covering my mouth. "Austin, I am so, so sorry," I said through my fingers.

He stood, belt in hand. "It's okay," he ground out. "He only got the end, it's an easy fix." Then he brought his eyes to mine, and they narrowed slightly. "Why doesn't he ever destroy your stuff?"

I shot him my most angelic smile. "Maybe because you

wanted to send him to guard dog school and tried to make him sleep on the cold, hard ground."

"I bought him a three-hundred-dollar dog bed, and this is Southern California, not the arctic circle!"

"You sure you still want us to move in with you?"

Austin grabbed my wrist and hauled me against him. "Yes, even if you do come with a devil dog."

I kissed him softly. "We should really think about getting him a sister. I've heard it can help if the dog has someone to play with." Austin just groaned.

FORTY-ONE

Carter

M Y NEW CAR DROVE LIKE A DREAM. IT WAS LIKE driving a cloud. Seriously, it felt like I was floating along Mulholland. I could handle LA traffic in a Zen-like state as long as I was driving this car. As I unlocked the front door to my home for the last three years, I knew that Austin was gloating. He knew I loved the fancy-schmancy SUV and all its bells and whistles.

As soon as the lock clicked, Austin gently ushered me aside and pushed the door open. His eyes quickly traveled around the entry, living room, and kitchen. Apparently, overprotective Austin wasn't taking a vacation anytime soon. I sighed and hefted up a handful of the boxes we'd stopped to get at an office supply store. "I got these, baby."

Taking the boxes from my hands, he headed towards my bedroom. He paused at the door, taking in the carnage that had yet to be cleaned up. Cut-up clothes and other random items still littered the floor, and the red spray paint continued to cry out those awful words on the walls.

Blue whined at my side, and I shuddered at the memories assailing me. I knew that if I asked, Austin would handle all of this for me. I'd never have to see a torn scrap of clothing or angry red letter. But I refused to let myself cower in a corner. Joe was locked up. There was nothing to be scared of anymore.

I straightened my shoulders. "I need to find someone to re-paint these walls and replace the mirror in the bathroom before Taylor gets back." We'd spoken on the car ride over to the house via the high-tech speaker system in my new SUV that made it sound like she was sitting right next to me.

I could tell she was worn out from taking care of her mom, but she was overjoyed by the news that they had caught the stalk-er and that Austin had asked me to move in with him. Since he was in the car with me, she also took the time to threaten him with bodily harm if he ever hurt me. I loved my bestie and was flying to Texas to see her and provide a little TLC as soon as school was out. But first, I had to fix her house. I was not leaving *whore* scrawled across the wall as a welcome-home present.

Austin turned to face me and squeezed my shoulder. "I don't want to leave you with all this. Why don't you let me deal with it? Or I can hire a crew to do it. You won't have to lift a finger."

This man was so very sweet. I leaned forward and touched my lips to his. Staying close, I said, "I can do this." I wanted Austin to see me as a strong woman who could stand on her own two feet.

He pulled me even closer. "You're not on your own, you know? You have me, and you always will."

That hit me right between the breasts, my heart doing a lit-tle clench. "I know I do, and I'm so grateful for that. But there's nothing for me to be scared of anymore. Plus, I'll have Blue with me so I won't be alone."

Austin closed his eyes briefly like what he was about to say almost caused him physical pain. "Okay, but keep your phone close by. And promise that you'll call if you change your mind or just get bored or hungry or…anything at all."

A smile touched my lips, and I reached up on my tiptoes to give him another kiss, this one longer and hotter. "Thank you. I love you, A."

"Love you too, Firecracker." I followed him to the door, where he instructed, "Lock this behind me."

"Will do. Now, get out of here." I closed the door behind Austin and flipped the lock. Turning to Blue, I said, "Well, let's get started." I synced my phone with the Bluetooth speaker that had miraculously escaped being destroyed and blasted the country tunes Austin hated.

For the next hour, I filled trash bag after trash bag with torn clothing, ripped pictures, and shattered knickknacks. Some of the broken items were irreplaceable. I shed a couple of tears as I knelt to pick up the pieces of a shattered ceramic apple my dad had gotten me when I was twelve when I told him I wanted to become a teacher. Drying my eyes, I reminded myself that these were just things and stuff could be replaced.

My head snapped up at the sound of Blue's low growl. "What's wrong, baby?" I asked but froze when I felt the cold steel of a blade at my throat.

"Hello, Carter." I knew the voice so well, but there was a deadness in it that I had never heard before.

My brain couldn't quite wrap itself around what was happening, it was like my synapses weren't firing quite right. "Kyle? What…?" My words trailed off because I didn't know what I was going to ask. "What are you doing?" or "Why?" seemed ridiculous given the circumstances.

The blade bit into my skin. "I want you to stand up nice and slow." Blue growled again and inched toward us. "Call off that mangy mutt, or I'll slit your throat and then gut him like a fish."

Hot tears, a mix of anger, fear, and grief, flowed down my cheeks as I shakily got to my feet. "It's okay, Blue, everything's okay. Stay." Blue whined but stopped his forward movement.

Kyle jerked me back against him with one hand and used the other to throw my speaker against the wall, shattering it and leaving us in silence. "That's right, everything's just dandy. I'm just going to have a little fun with your mom here. She never did let me between those thighs."

Bile rose up my throat as Kyle trailed the knife down between my breasts. My breath came in short, staccato bursts as my vision went a little hazy. How could it be Kyle? Images of him sprawled out in my living room as we ate ice cream and watched cheesy horror movies danced in my head. I remembered our first date when he was all bumbling nerves and polite gentlemanliness. This wasn't the same person I'd known for the past two years.

Choking back the acid in my throat, I asked, "It's been you all along?"

Kyle chuckled, it was ugly and menacing. "You always did underestimate me, Carter."

"But you had an alibi for the pictures in my classroom." My voice shook, and my hands trembled as I searched for a way out. Any way out.

The edge of the knife began to tear at my top. No, no, no. This couldn't be happening. "Do you know how easy it is to drug someone, Carter? All it takes is a couple of ground-up sleeping pills in a friend's beer and, suddenly, they're feeling the need to crash on your couch for the night. But the couch is right outside your bedroom, so when the police question him, he says there's no way you could've left without him hearing something. Plus, I had told him what a conniving little bitch and cock tease you were so he wouldn't have been eager to help anyway."

My phone started to ring, but Kyle pressed the blade against my skin. "Uh, uh, uh. No phones for you." He located the cell on the floor where I had been kneeling and kicked it away.

I wanted to weep as my one hope of contacting the outside world disappeared under my bed. My stomach pitched as I asked, "And you were the one who shot at us last night?"

"Yes. I must admit, that one was fun, seeing you and those

dimwits hit the deck. I could have killed you all then, so much power in my hands. But now that it's just the two of us, I thought the knife was a little more personal. Don't you agree?"

I bit down on my lip to keep from crying out as the blade bit into my skin. "Why are you doing this?"

"Why? Why?!" Kyle grabbed my shoulder in a punishing grip and spun me around to face him, pushing me back into the wall. Blue growled again, but I held out a hand to tell him to stay back. Kyle continued on his tear. "How about because you were supposed to be mine? I gave you all of these chances to figure that out. I forgave you again and again, but you just had to go back to that ape. You never let me touch you like I wanted to, but then you just gave yourself to that heathen like a little slut."

The knife dug in deeper. "You're crazy." It came out in a hoarse whisper but clearly reached Kyle's ears because his face filled with rage. Suddenly, a hand cracked across my face, sending me crashing to the ground.

FORTY-TWO

Austin

"Hey, man, thanks for getting back to me," I said into my phone.

"They caught the guy?" Liam asked.

"They think they have him. It's the father of one of Carter's students, the same one that attacked her."

"Fuck, what is wrong with that guy?"

"He's clearly got a screw loose, that's for sure," I said as I twirled a pen between my fingers.

"You don't sound relieved."

Before Liam called, I had been sitting at my desk reading the same paperwork over and over, unable to focus on the words because my mind kept drifting to Carter. I was worried about her. I got that she wanted to prove to herself that everything was fine now, that she had nothing to worry about anymore, but something wasn't sitting right with me.

I continued rolling everything around in my mind, trying to figure out what didn't feel right. I kept coming back to the note on my car and the words used on Carter's walls. Those felt personal and sexual, not like a man pissed because he had been sent to jail after assaulting someone. "Something doesn't feel right," I admitted.

"What do you mean?"

"It's just that all the incidents have seemed way too personal for this to be retribution for reporting a case of child abuse."

Liam made a humming noise in the back of his throat. "I don't know, a lot of people would take getting sent to jail pretty damn personal."

I tapped the pen against my desk, my nerves still not settling. "I guess you're right. But it seemed like there was a sexual element to it, too. That doesn't make sense with this Joe guy."

"I hate to break it to you, A, but Carter's a gorgeous girl. It wouldn't be surprising if a creep fixated on her started to take things in that direction."

My fingers clenched around the pen, and the plastic began to crack. "This guy needs to go away for a long time, preferably forever."

"I feel you. Where is Carter?"

My hand relaxed. "She's at her old house. Packing."

"Packing?"

"Yeah," I said, grinning to the empty room around me. "I asked her to move in permanently."

"No shit?"

"No shit."

"I'm happy for you, man. Both of you," Liam said, a smile sounding in his words.

"Thanks, Li. You and Ford can help me move the fifty million boxes I'm sure Carter's filling with her shit right now."

Liam chuckled. "You got it. I've gotta jump, but I really am thrilled for you guys. So happy you finally pulled your head out of your ass."

"Yeah, yeah. I'll talk to you later."

"Later." I tapped the end button on my screen and scrolled to John's number. I didn't care if I was being paranoid, I was going to get him to sit in his car outside Carter's place until I got there.

Just as I was about to hit his name, the phone buzzed with an incoming call.

It was Detective Massey. When the words, "we have a problem," came over the line, my stomach dropped.

"What is it?" I asked as my hand clenched around the phone.

"Joe Harker isn't our guy."

"I thought you traced the hang-up calls to him." My grip tightened even further.

"We did. It turns out he was calling to make amends, but he said he kept getting nervous when he called, so he would hang up. He got sober in lockup and apparently found religion. He has ironclad alibis for at least two of the incidents. One is an AA meeting his priest leads, and the other, he's on surveillance at his job. He was in interrogation, weeping about how he'd done wrong, but that he would never hurt no one now that he's sober."

I was already up and moving, grabbing my wallet and keys and heading out the door. "Massey, I'm at the gym right now, but Carter's by her fucking self at her old place."

Massey's voice was suddenly alert and full of concern. "Austin, I called you because she didn't answer her phone."

My heart was raging against my ribs like it was doing battle to get free and get to Carter. Never again would I not listen to my gut when it told me something was wrong. Never would I leave Carter when something told me to stay. Fuck, once I knew she was okay, I was never letting her out of my sight again. "Get the cops there. Now. I'm already on my way."

FORTY-THREE

Carter

ROUGH FIBERS PRESSED INTO THE SIDE OF MY FACE AS I slowly became aware of my surroundings. I was lying on the floor of my bedroom. What had happened? My cheek was throbbing, my lip burned where it was clearly split, and the metallic taste of blood filled my mouth.

The ground vibrated with pacing footsteps. "I'm not crazy. Not fucking crazy. She's crazy. Crazy and a slut." The sound of Kyle's voice brought it all crashing back. Blood roared in my ears, and I desperately tried to keep my breathing even, not wanting to alert Kyle that I was awake.

Blue growled a low warning as Kyle's footsteps grew closer. "Shut up, you filthy mutt. I'm only keeping you alive so Carter will behave." Well, that was good to know. I needed to think. I needed a plan. How could I think up a strategy when I couldn't risk opening my eyes to see what I might have within reach?

My heart raced, and I fought to keep each breath uniform. I painted Austin's face in my mind, hoping it would calm me, the deep blue of his eyes, the sharp cut of his jaw, the feel of his buzzed head tickling my palm as I ran a hand over his scalp. I wanted to run my hands over his beautiful body every day for the rest of my life, and I wasn't going to let this asshole steal that from me.

I cracked open one of my eyes a sliver. "YOU LYING SLUT!" A boot slammed into my gut, forcing all the air from my lungs and sending pain radiating through my body. "You're a liar, just like the rest of them!"

I wheezed and rolled onto my back, clutching my stomach and trying to ease the pain. "Get up, you stupid whore." I couldn't have done it even if I wanted to. My breaths were shallow, and air didn't seem to be able to get to my lungs. "I said, get up!" Kyle jabbed the knife in Blue's direction. "Get up, or the mutt gets it."

Tears tracked down my cheeks as I stared at Blue, whose teeth were bared at Kyle in a snarl. I wrapped an arm around my ribs and slowly pushed myself up. "I should have known you were just like the rest of them, just like all the other sluts in this city. I thought you were different, but you're not! YOU'RE NOT!" He screamed the last words. Kyle was clearly devolving. "Get on the bed."

My stomach roiled, and I knew I needed to make a move now if I was going to make it out of this alive. "No," I said with all the calmness and firmness I didn't feel.

"Get. On. The. Fucking. Bed." Kyle punctuated each word with a point of his knife toward my torso.

I took a deep breath, calling up every ounce of courage and every hope for a beautiful future with Austin. I screamed, "BLUE!" as I struck out with a palm strike to Kyle's nose. There was a pinch in my side at the same time I felt a crunch of bone beneath my palm.

Kyle bellowed in pain as he flew backward onto the ground, then Blue was on him, teeth at his neck. The next thing I knew, two police officers were charging in, and Blue retreated from Kyle to stand guard in front of me, growling at the officers.

"Ma'am, are you okay?" One of the officers had a hold of Kyle, while the other was trying to approach me with his hand out in a placating gesture. "Can you call your dog off?" Between the pain in my side and the shock of what had happened, I couldn't seem to form words.

Just then, the officer whirled around, gun out, to face a rapidly approaching and ferocious-looking Austin. He looked like a true warrior and nothing, not even a gun-toting policeman, was going to stop him. "I'm her boyfriend," he growled.

"Yes," I wheezed out the word.

The cop lowered his weapon but didn't holster it. "Can you get her dog so that we can examine her."

Austin's concern-filled eyes flew to mine. "Blue, lay down," he called, his voice full of alpha authority. Blue whined but obeyed. Austin strode forward.

"I'm okay." The words came out on that same weird wheeze. Suddenly, my chest was burning, and my legs started to collapse. The last thing I saw before everything went black was the horror written all over Austin's face.

FORTY-FOUR

Austin

I SURGED FORWARD, CATCHING CARTER JUST BEFORE SHE HIT the ground. "Fuck! What's wrong with her?" I yelled at the cop like he had some sort of miraculous knowledge that would enable me to help her.

"Let me examine her." The calm quality of the cop's voice just pissed me off, but I swallowed it back. I lay Carter down on the ground as gently as possible. He immediately got to work assessing her injuries. Her shirt was torn down the middle, and as the officer pulled it away from Carter's body, I saw blood pooling around her abdomen. Vomit snaked up my throat, but I forced it back.

The next moments felt like an eternity as I knelt next to Carter's broken body while the cop applied pressure to the wound on her torso. I watched blood seep from between his fingers, fixating on the dark liquid as if I could will it back into her body. I forced myself to look away from the gore and towards her face. I stroked her hair, silently begging her eyelids to open so I could see her vibrant green irises.

"Sir, I need you to move aside so we can treat her."

I started at the voice behind me, and Blue growled low. I turned to see two EMTs with a backboard in tow. The second police officer must have already taken Kyle away because that fucker was nowhere in sight. I looked back to Carter, leaned down and kissed her forehead. "You can do this, baby. Fight." I dragged myself and Blue away from Carter, my vision going fuzzy as I stared at the medics working on my beautiful girl. How the fuck did this happen?

What felt like both hours and mere seconds later, the EMTs were loading Carter onto a stretcher. "Are you riding with us?" one of them asked.

"Yes," I croaked out. My mouth and throat felt like they were made of sandpaper.

"What are you going to do with the dog?"

I looked down at Blue's sorrow-filled eyes. "He's coming, too."

The younger EMT looked to the older one, who shrugged. "We don't have time for this, bring them both." With that, Blue and I followed the stretcher out the door. Neighbors had come out of their homes and were huddled together on the sidewalk, watching the morbid action unfold. I ignored them and hefted myself into the back of the ambulance, Blue jumping right in after me.

The lights and sirens flared to life, and the ambulance pulled away. "How is she doing?" I asked the older EMT, who was in the back with me.

This guy had clearly mastered the stone-faced response in his years on the job because he gave nothing away when he said, "Too soon to tell. I think the blade may have nicked her lung because she's having trouble breathing."

I clenched the bench I was sitting on and said nothing. We flew through LA traffic, cars thankfully getting out of our way. The rig came to a stop, and the back doors flew open. The driver had apparently called ahead because doctors and nurses already wearing gloves and what looked like surgical scrubs greeted us. The stretcher was pulled from the ambulance, and the older

EMT started shouting terms I didn't have the first clue about to the doctors.

I jumped down, Blue hot on my heels, and we took off after the team with Carter. A doctor turned, putting a palm to my chest when we reached an interior set of double doors. "You can't come into the trauma room with us, and that dog shouldn't even be here. You need to wait in the waiting room or take your dog home and come back."

My shoulders and fists clenched. "I'm not going anywhere, and this dog saved that girl's life, so he's not going anywhere either."

The doctor shook his head, exasperated. "Fine, but you can't come back here."

A nurse touched the asshole doctor's arm. "I'll show him where he can wait." The doctor jerked his chin in a gruff nod and slammed through the double doors. My eyes went to the nurse, who shook her head. "Sorry about that, he doesn't have the best bedside manner, but he's a great doctor. I'll show you where you can wait."

She led me down a hallway and opened the door to a small room with half a dozen plastic chairs. "This is a private waiting room where no one should give you any grief about your dog. If they do, just say he's a service dog, and you don't have the paperwork with you. Can I get you or your dog some water?"

I looked down at Blue, whose muzzle I realized was slightly bloody. Shit. "Yeah, some water for my dog would be great, and maybe some paper towels so I can clean him off?"

The woman gave me a small smile. "No problem, I'll be right back."

"Thanks, ma'am, I appreciate it." I sank back into a chair, the hard plastic jarring my spine. Blue shuffled over and laid his head in my lap with a pathetic-sounding whine. "I know, boy, but she's going to be okay." I dug my fingers into the rolls of fur at his neck. He shuddered at the contact. "You did a good job, Blue, you protected your mom." He cocked his head to the side slightly, looking up at me with heartbreakingly sad eyes while still keeping his head on my lap.

Blue and I stayed like that until the door opened and the nurse bustled in, water in one hand and Liam and Ford at her back. Shit. I didn't even think about calling them or Carter's parents. I stood and Liam pulled me into a tight hug, his voice was strained when he said, "Detective Massey called me and said Carter had been hurt. What the fuck happened?"

I pulled back, and Ford grasped my shoulder. I said only one word. "Kyle."

"Fuck!" Liam swung around and slammed his palm against the wall. "Is she going to be okay?"

"He stabbed her,"—my voice hitched—"and I'm not sure what else. The doctors took her back to work on her, but I haven't heard anything."

Liam's eyes were wet, and Ford looked murderous. We turned collectively to look at the nurse, who had bent down to place the water at Blue's front paws. When she rose, she handed me a roll of paper towels. "Here you go. I'll go see if there's an update on your friend. Are any of you family members?"

"No," I answered. "I'm her boyfriend, and these are her friends." The word *boyfriend* seemed completely inaccurate. Carter was so much more to me than my girlfriend. It was then I knew that, as soon as she was well, my ring was going on her finger.

Liam took a step forward. "I'm a close family friend. We grew up together. I need to call her parents, but I need to have something to tell them."

The nurse nodded, pursing her lips. "I'll see what I can do." With that, she exited, sneakers squeaking against the linoleum floor.

I sighed, leaning my head back and squeezing my eyes closed. How the hell had this happened? I couldn't stop asking the question. I'd let her down. I hadn't been there when she needed me, again. Fuck. A hand clamped down on my shoulder, and my eyes snapped open. "Don't like where your head is at, brother." It was the always insightful Ford.

"I let her down, man. I wasn't there like I knew I should have been, and she got fucking stabbed. Her lip was split, eye swollen. Her goddamned shirt was torn open." I shrugged off his hand, needing to move, needing to hit something. "That fucker touched her, and I can't even do anything about it because the cops already have him. And Carter's back there, maybe fucking dying, and I can't do anything about that either."

Liam grabbed me this time, using both hands on my shoulders, and I could sense Ford at my back. "Rein it in, A. You gotta swallow that shit down right now. Carter needs you. You have to be there when she wakes up and not in lock-up because you destroyed a hospital waiting room or punched a doctor."

My nostrils flared as I fought to get my breathing under control and reel in the rage that was now flowing freely. I clenched and unclenched my fists at least a dozen times as I breathed in and out. Liam and Ford stayed with me, at my front and back, unmoving. My brothers, keeping me grounded. I let out one more slow breath. "I've got it in check now."

Liam clapped me on the back. "Good, because I really wouldn't have wanted to get some security guard to come Taser your ass."

I tried to smile at his snarky comments, but my lips just wouldn't cooperate. Ford squeezed the back of my neck. "She's strong, A. Stronger than you think. She's gonna pull through." I nodded, and he released me.

The waiting room door swung open, and asshole doctor was back. "Greta's going to be bringing some paperwork back for you to fill out as best as you can but, in the meantime, I need to know if the young woman has any allergies."

My jaw worked. "The young woman's name is Carter and, no, she doesn't have any allergies. Now, can you tell us what the fuck is going on?"

Asshole doctor took no offense to my tone or language because he continued as if I had said: "please, sir."

"Carter is going to need surgery. She has a collapsed lung that is not reflating, and we believe the knife may have pierced the lung in a way that needs surgical intervention."

"But she's going to be okay, right?" It was Ford who spoke. I was locking it down so tightly that I thought more than one of my muscles might snap.

The doctor looked at Ford, his mask of detachment firmly in place. "It's too soon to tell." God, I hated those words. "But we'll do everything we can. She's being prepped for surgery now. I'll come and speak to you when I'm done."

I stepped forward then. "Doc?" I extended my hand for a shake. When he took it, I pulled him in close and whispered with no small amount of menace, "I love that girl. She is my whole fucking world. So you do everything you can possibly think of to help her. You get me?"

His Adam's apple bobbed as his head tilted back to meet my eyes. His mask slipped just a bit. "I get you."

"Good." I squeezed his hand to emphasize my point and then released him. He darted for the door.

Liam shifted from foot to foot, slipping his hand in his pocket and pulling out his cell phone. "I have to call her parents." He looked lost. "This is going to kill them."

I stepped towards him and reached out my hand. "Let me do it. I told her dad I'd protect her, he should hear from me that I failed."

He smacked my hand away. "Quit it with that shit. You did

everything you possibly could to protect her, more than she wanted you to. We all thought they had the guy, this is not on you."

"I knew in my gut that something was off. I shouldn't have let her stay there alone."

Liam scoffed, "Like Carter would let you tell her what she could or couldn't do. That girl is as stubborn as anyone I've ever met. This is only one person's fault, and that guy is in jail."

My shoulders slumped. I knew Liam was right, Kyle was the one to blame. I just couldn't shake the guilt that had taken hold. I couldn't shake it, but I could shut up about it, so I nodded at Liam, and he slipped from the room to make his call. I sat back down in one of the ridiculously uncomfortable chairs, and Ford sat down next to me. "He's right, you know." I grunted in response. "This is not your fault."

"I know it's not my fault. What's tearing me up is that I didn't stop it."

"Austin, there is so much shit in this world that is beyond your control. Some of that shit is really fucking bad, but some of it is really fucking good. It's always gonna be a roll of the dice. All you can do is make sure you focus your energy on the important stuff within your control."

I rubbed Blue between the ears. "I'm going to ask Carter to marry me."

A huge smile broke out over Ford's face. "That's one great thing to focus on. Make sure you get Taylor's or Carter's mom's input on the ring, don't want to get that shit wrong."

A small grin came to my face. "Definitely don't want to fuck that up."

〜

The waiting-room door opened again, and the same doctor and a new nurse entered. I could read nothing on the doctor's face. The three of us stood, and Blue alerted at my side. "Miss McCarthy has been moved to the ICU. The surgery was successful but more complicated than we expected. There was a vascular tear we couldn't see that caused some internal bleeding and a strain on the heart."

"What does that mean?" I interrupted, my hands clenched into fists at my sides.

The doctor's Adam's apple bobbed. "Her heart stopped on the table. We were able to get it beating again and find the bleeder. We expect that she'll make a full recovery, but we'll know more when she regains consciousness."

A tingling numbness had taken over my body, and there was a ringing in my ears. My beautiful, vibrant firecracker's heart had stopped beating. I was jarred from my thoughts by the nurse. "I can take you up to ICU if you're ready."

We followed the woman to a bank of elevators. When the doors opened, we stood in awkward silence with only the ding of the passing floors filling the small space. I clenched and un-clenched my fists, over and over, trying to force my body to relax, my heart rate to slow, but it did no good.

When the doors slid open again, I was right on the nurse's heels. She led us into an area where a handful of small rooms circled a nurse's station. She paused outside a closed door. "Don't be alarmed by the different machines in the room, they are just helping to support her while she recovers." I gave a jerk of my chin, and she pushed open the door.

My heart stuttered in my chest when I got my first look at Carter. There were tubes everywhere, including one coming out of her mouth that must have been helping her breathe. The split in her lip had been sutured, but the bruising around her eye and cheek had worsened in the hours since I'd seen her.

My stomach roiled at the thought of all that had been done to her. I dragged my eyes away from Carter's broken body that looked so tiny in the hospital bed and looked at the nurse. "I need to know…" I could barely choke the words out. "Was she raped?"

A soft look came over the nurse's face, and she laid a hand on my arm. "There were absolutely no signs of sexual assault." I nodded, swallowing the emotion that clogged my throat. "You can sit with her. Try talking to her. Many patients report that they could hear those around them even though they couldn't respond."

I nodded again, woodenly. "Thank you."

She smiled gently. "Of course. Just let any of the nurses at the station know if you need anything."

I edged closer to the bed, pulling a chair behind me. I sank into it—more uncomfortable plastic. A hand gripped my shoulder. "Liam and I are going to give you a minute. You want us to get you anything? Water? Coffee?"

"No. Thanks, Ford." He gave my shoulder a squeeze, and they eased out of the room. I studied Carter's form, looking for someplace I could touch her without hurting her. One hand was on top of the blankets, but it had an IV in place, and a clip on one of her fingers. I carefully pulled back the covers to expose her other hand. It was thankfully free of any tubes or injury. Her nails still carried the pale pink polish that she loved so much.

I gently lifted her arm, laying it on top of the blanket, and clasped her hand between my own. I hated how cold it felt, how lifeless. I fought the urge to climb into the bed beside Carter. Blue's paws plodded against the floor, I turned slightly to see him sniffing the air. When he caught Carter's scent, he whined and then laid his head on the bed next to her hand. His tongue darted out, licking her fingers and mine.

I couldn't stop the tears that fell, splashing onto Carter's hand, held between my own. "You can't leave me, Firecracker. I need you. Blue needs you." I got no response, but Blue lapped up the tears as my chest heaved.

FORTY-FIVE

Carter

THE FIRST THING I WAS AWARE OF WAS A FAINT BEEPING noise. The second was pain. I hurt everywhere. It seemed like even the strands of my hair held pain. I tried to tell my eyes to open, but the only thing I succeeded in doing was affecting a fluttering sensation. Suddenly, I felt pressure around my hand.

"Baby?" I relaxed slightly at the familiar voice. "Firecracker, let me see those beautiful eyes." Austin's words spurred on all the fight I had in me, and my eyes began to open. Austin's face, slightly blurry, slowly came into focus. "There she is."

I opened my mouth, which felt like sandpaper, and tried to ask what had happened, but all that came out was a "wha" and a whoosh of air. Austin quickly reached for a pitcher of water and poured some into a cup with a straw. He gently placed the straw between my lips, and I sucked down the liquid. Water had never tasted so good.

Austin started to pull the cup away, and I let out a sound of protest. "Slow down, baby, don't want you to get sick." I didn't want to get sick either, throwing up while in this much pain did not sound fun. "Try not to talk. You had a tube down your throat, so it's going to hurt for a little while." Austin must have sensed my rising panic because he grasped my hand and said, "You're okay now, everything's going to be fine."

I swallowed against the pain in my throat and mouthed, "*What happened?*" My entire body stiffened as memories came flooding back: packing up, and then Kyle. My head suddenly snapped around, causing pain to ricochet down my spine.

"Baby, calm down. You're safe." Austin crouched next to the bed, but it was the whine that came from behind him that put me at ease.

My shoulders slumped in relief. "Blue." It came out as a hoarse whisper.

"Blue's fine, Firecracker. Helped you take that fucker down. Never been prouder in my life."

A small smile touched my lips as I squeezed Austin's hand. Blue's face popped up over the edge of the bed, and Austin lifted our joined hands to rest on the top of his head, Blue's tail thumping against Austin's leg. I tipped up my face to Austin. "How is he allowed in here?" I whispered.

Austin grinned. "At first, we pretended he was a service dog. Then, Liam and I *might* have pulled the celebrity card."

I started to giggle, but pain radiated throughout my chest, causing me to gasp. Austin straightened, pressing a button on my bed. "Careful, baby. Just breathe. Slow, shallow breaths." I did as he instructed. The pain in my chest eased, but the pain on Austin's face did not.

I squeezed his hand as fiercely as I could and mouthed, "I love you."

"Fuck, Firecracker, I love you so damn much." He bent down and pressed his lips to my forehead. The contact was warm and firm, reassuring me that everything really would be okay. "Never been so scared in my life. I thought I was going to lose you." He was breathing heavily, and his eyes were glistening.

"I'm sorry," I whispered, then smiled just a little. "You're not getting rid of me that easy."

Austin just shook his head. The door to my room swung open, and an older gentleman in a white lab coat entered, followed by a woman in blue scrubs and my mom. I blinked back tears as I breathed, "Mom?"

She rushed to my other side. "Oh, baby, I was so worried. I'm so glad you're awake. Does anything hurt? Can I get you anything?"

Austin cut in, staunching my mom's verbal flood. "Her throat hurts from the breathing tube, not sure about what else."

"Oh, then don't talk, honey."

Lab coat guy, who was clearly my doctor, thumbed through my chart. "Hello, Miss McCarthy, I'm Dr. Stevens. Glad to see you awake. We did have to put a tube in your throat to help you breathe, but that's been out for the past few hours, so the pain should fade soon. I'm going to ask you a few questions, but you can just answer them by nodding." The doctor turned to Austin and my mom. "Now would be a good time to grab a cup of coffee. I'll need to do an examination, and the nurse and I will change her bandages."

I stiffened at the idea of Austin leaving. He squeezed my hand. "I'll be right outside." He turned to the doctor, piercing him with the same intimidating stare he had given the fighters he faced in the octagon. "I think it would be good if her mom stayed while you examine her, make her more comfortable, don't you think?" Austin's eyes narrowed with his last few words.

Dr. Stevens fumbled with the papers he was holding. "Sure, that would be fine if it's what Miss McCarthy prefers."

I nodded, and my mom ran a soft hand over my hair. Austin leaned over and pressed a kiss to my brow. "Be back as soon as they're done." He rose, snapping his fingers, and Blue followed him out. Apparently, those two had bonded during the time I was lights-out.

"He hasn't left your side other than to go to the restroom or talk to the police. Love that you have that kind of love, baby." God, I loved my mom. Loved that she immediately saw through Austin's gruff exterior and got how well he loved me.

She straightened as the doctor launched into an explanation of all that had happened to me, medically speaking. He poked and prodded, assessing my injuries and checking the stitches, and he also ordered another round of pain meds that he said would make me sleepy, but that rest was the best thing for me at the moment. I grimaced at the thought of losing more time, but my chest and head were aching so badly, I quickly nodded in agreement.

The doctor excused himself, and as soon as he hit the threshold of the room, Austin's face appeared in the doorway. He scooted around the doctor, who gave a disapproving look to the dog trailing behind him, and then made his way back to my bedside. "Everything go okay?"

My mom answered for me. "Everything looks good. They ordered up some more pain meds that will most likely make her sleep, but the doctor said that's what's best right now. I'm going to go find your dad and tell him you're awake."

"Thanks, Mom." My voice was a little stronger already, and it didn't hurt quite so much to talk.

"Of course, honey." She was smiling, but tears were gathering in her eyes. "I'm just so glad you're okay." With that, she hustled out of the room.

I tilted my face towards Austin. "How long was I out?"

His expression darkened, and I instantly regretted asking. "Almost thirty-six hours. Longest day and a half of my life."

I figured I should get all the unpleasant topics out of the way now, so I asked, "What happened to Kyle?"

Austin's expression went weird, and he said, "Why don't we wait and talk about that when you're feeling better?" My body went on alert. Was he not in jail? Did he somehow get out on bail? Reading my panic, Austin sat on the side of my bed and cupped the cheek that wasn't throbbing. "Everything's okay. He's never going to hurt you again, all right?"

"I need to know what happened, it's scarier not knowing."

Austin closed his eyes, and when he opened them, they were full of uncertainty. "The police took him into custody at the house. After they brought him in, they searched his apartment and found a closet full of scrapbooks. You're not the only girl he's stalked. There were notebooks dedicated to at least ten other women. There was a clear pattern of escalation with each victim, but you are the first victim where he turned violent." A shudder ran through me.

Austin squeezed my hand. "The police presented some of the evidence to him and his lawyer yesterday evening." He paused, sucking in a breath. "Baby, last night, he hung himself in his jail cell." I blinked up at Austin, having no words. Of all the things I'd thought he might say, that was nowhere on my radar. The only feeling I could muster up was relief, which immediately turned to guilt about feeling that way. Tears started to gather in the corners of my eyes. "Baby, breathe nice and slow for me."

"I-I-I hate that all I feel is relief." I was fighting the tears, knowing that if I gave in to the sobs, I would be in tremendous pain.

Austin leaned down, expression fierce as he got right in my face. "You should feel relief, and you're not going to beat yourself up about that. *I* feel relief. He was a sick fuck, and this world is a better place without him in it. That is not a kind of sickness you can heal, baby. As long as he was in this world, you would have been at risk, and I am not down with that. So, he's gone, and I'm happy about that."

I sniffled, but the tears eased. "I love you, Austin."

"Love hearing those words from you, Firecracker." He kissed

the corner of my mouth farthest away from my stitches.

As he rose, the nurse bustled in with a syringe in hand. "Here we go, this should have you feeling better in no time." She slid the needle into my IV, and a minute later, my eyelids were drooping.

⟳

"Get me out of here!" I was whining, it was unattractive, and I didn't give a flip. I had been in the hospital for a week now, and I was going stir-crazy.

"Calm down, Firecracker, the doc said there was a good chance it could happen today." Austin was reclining precariously in a plastic chair, feet resting on my hospital bed. He had stayed by my side for the past seven days, refusing to go home.

My parents, who were staying at his house, brought him a fresh change of clothes each day, and he showered in the bathroom attached to my hospital room. The staff took pity on him and rolled in a cot that he could sleep on. Once I was doing better, Blue got the boot, my parents taking him home to Austin's house.

My room looked like a florist shop with arrangements from family, friends, and co-workers. Not to mention a ridiculously large teddy bear that Liam and Ford had brought for me, which Blue had proceeded to hump. My room was a revolving door of visitors. Taylor had even flown in for a day, saying that she'd needed to see with her own two eyes that I was doing okay.

While I was unbelievably appreciative of all the love my family and friends had shown, and everything the doctors had done to help me, I needed out of this hospital. The stitches in my lip had been removed yesterday, and the ones along my ribs could come out in another week. I was ready to go home, well…to my new home.

My parents had taken the news of me moving in with Austin surprisingly well. Once the police had cleared the scene at my

296 | CATHERINE COWLES

old house, my mom had set to work finishing what I had started, packing up all my belongings. Austin had hired movers, and all my things were now waiting to be unpacked at his house.

I twisted in my hospital bed. "I'm ready to go home."

A grin stretched across Austin's face at my calling his house *home.* "I'm ready for us to go home too, but not before the doctor says it's okay. I don't want your lung collapsing again." That was the big concern, and why I'd had to stay in the hospital for so long. I had been instructed that even once I was released, I'd have to take it easy for a few weeks.

"I'll stay in bed and let you wait on me hand and foot if I can just get out of this hospital. I want food that doesn't taste like cardboard, and a bed that doesn't feel like it's a slab of concrete," I said, giving Austin my best puppy-dog face.

He shook his head and came up to a sitting position. "Don't give me that look. We do what the doctor says."

"Oh, fine, but I won't be held responsible if I lose it on some poor, unsuspecting nurse who brings me another container of Jell-O."

Austin chuckled and bent down to sweep his lips across mine. "How about, if you don't get out of here tonight, I'll see if I can get approval to bring in some outside food? I'll have Liam pick up all your favorites from Little Dom's."

I leaned up just a bit, my ribs protesting slightly at the movement, and brought my lips to his. "You are an angel sent from Heaven above." I kissed him again. "Sorry I'm being such a shrew, I think I have cabin fever."

Austin tucked my hair behind my ear. Letting his fingers travel down my neck, he squeezed it gently. "I know. I'd be going crazy too if I was stuck in that bed. We'll get you home soon."

"We'll get you home now, actually," my mom called from the doorway. "I just talked to Dr. Stevens, and he's signing your discharge paperwork as we speak!"

I let my head fall back against the scratchy pillows. "Hallelujah!"

Both my mom and Austin laughed. "She's not the best patient, is she?" my mom asked.

"It's not her strong suit," Austin replied.

"She never was, even when she was a toddler."

"All right, you two, no ganging up on the invalid," I interrupted.

My mom crossed to my bed and cupped my cheek. "Okay, I'll let you off easy this time. I sent your father to bring the car around. Austin, will you see if there's a cart or something we can use to haul all these flowers downstairs?"

Austin looked to me and then to the door. "Sure thing, Mrs. McCarthy. You'll stay with Carter until I'm back?"

"Now, I told you, call me Sheila. Mrs. McCarthy is my mother-in-law. And, of course, I'll stay with Carter."

"All right, Sheila, I'll see what I can find." Austin strode toward the door, and I stared at his butt the whole way.

My mom cleared her throat, and my eyes shot to her, a sheepish smile on my face. "I don't blame you, he does have a nice booty."

"Mom! Don't look at my boyfriend's butt, and definitely, don't say 'booty.'"

"I'm married, not dead, Carter." I choked on a laugh that still made my chest ache but not nearly as bad as it had a few days ago. My mom brushed invisible strands of hair away from my face. "How are you feeling, baby? And I don't mean your stitches."

My mom and I hadn't had any true alone time for her to assess her daughter's mental state. I squeezed her hand. "I honestly feel okay right now. I mean, I hate that this happened, for me, for Austin, for you and Dad, even for Kyle. But I don't feel scared anymore."

"I'm glad you don't, baby. But I want you to talk to me or Austin or your dad if you start feeling overwhelmed by everything that happened."

"I will. Promise," I said. Her head popped up as the rattling of wheels sounded outside my door.

Austin came in wielding what looked like a room service cart. "This was the best I could do, borrowed it from one of the candy stripers."

I bit the inside of my cheek to keep from laughing. "I'm sure that made her day."

Austin's cheeks pinked just the slightest bit. "I think I may have scared her, honestly. All she seemed to be able to do was nod and push the cart at me."

My mom stifled her own giggle as she rose. "Well, I'll start loading up flowers, and we'll get out of here."

"Woohoo!" I made a small victory motion with my arms.

Austin prowled toward my bed. "Careful with your ribs, Firecracker."

"Yes, oh overprotective one—" My words were cut off by Austin's swift kiss.

FORTY-SIX

Carter

I SIGHED AS I SOAKED IN THE FEEL OF AUSTIN'S RIDICULOUSLY soft sheets. I was so happy to be home. It was a few days after I'd been released from the hospital, and Austin and I were lounging in his bed—I guess *our* bed now—watching movies. My dad had left that morning, needing to get back to take care of my grandmother, but my mom was sticking around, knowing that I was hoping to convince Austin he could go back to work. I knew the gym and his fighters suffered when he wasn't around. Plus, I couldn't stop thinking about what my mom had said the day after I'd gotten home.

"I'm worried about that boy, Carter."

Any trace of my laughter died. "What do you mean? Why?"

She sat on the edge of my bed. "Finding you the way he did, it's marked him. I see the way he doesn't want you out of his sight. He hesitated to leave just now even though it will be for less than five minutes. You two can't live the rest of your lives attached to each other's hips."

I toyed with the edge of the blanket on my bed. I could see what my mom meant. The truth was, the first day when I woke up in the hospital, it was rocky. I didn't want Austin to leave my side. From the moment our friendship began, I'd always felt safe with him. But once I found out that Kyle was gone and was able to wrap my head around all that had happened, I relaxed. Austin was not relaxing. I turned my eyes toward my mom. "What can I do?"

She gave me a soft smile. "You're doing a lot of it already. Just seeing you rally, seeing how strong you are, that this hasn't broken you... Hopefully, over time, that will help him let go of all that happened. Not that he'll ever forget. I'm not sure he ever will, but hopefully, it will allow him to ease up a little bit. You can also get Liam and Ford to help you by getting them to invite him to do something out of the house and then encourage him to go. And, most importantly, you can be there for him when he needs to unload about how all of this has affected him."

I nodded. "Once I'm settled, I'll try talking to him."

My mom squeezed my hand. "He's lucky to have you, Carter."

With that conversation in mind, I paused the movie and rolled onto my side to face Austin. "You okay, Firecracker? Need me to get you anything?"

"I'm fine, but I want to talk to you about something."

Austin's expression went guarded. "What's up?"

I reached out and twined my fingers with his. "I love having you with me, but I know you have responsibilities at the gym, and I don't want you to fall behind because you're taking care of me. My mom's here for the next week so you can go into work."

Austin's eyes searched mine even as his jaw tightened. "The gym will be fine without me for a few weeks. I don't want to leave you right now."

Tentatively, I pressed. "You could just go in for an hour or two. That way, there's not so much to catch up on when you do go back."

His jaw got even harder, and he slipped his hand from my hold. "You trying to get rid of me?"

I sat up, ignoring the pain in my side. "No! I love having you with me. I just don't want you to be afraid of leaving because, eventually, that will have to happen."

Austin rolled off the bed. "Well, it doesn't have to happen right this damn second." I bit my lip but said nothing as he paced the room, his body strung tight. Then he whirled toward me, bellowing, "He almost fucking killed you!" Austin's chest heaved, and I said nothing. He continued more softly, his voice full of barely restrained emotion. "He could have killed you, and I just left you there, all alone."

I knew he was carrying guilt, but I had no idea it ran this deep. I eased from the bed and crept towards Austin. Slowly, so slowly, I raised my hands, cupping the sides of his face. "Baby, I was not alone." He started to argue, but I put a finger over his lips. "I was not alone. I had Blue, a dog you gave me. I had my self-defense training, tools you taught me. And when I had to draw upon my courage to fight back, do you know what I did? I pictured your face. So, I was never alone. You were with me every step of the way."

His body shuddered beneath my hands. "I love you, Firecracker. Will till the end of my days." His arms slipped around me.

"I love you, too, Austin." I rested my cheek against his chest, listening to the thudding of his heart that hadn't quite slowed.

"Wish I could fuck you right now."

I laughed softly, the sound and movement vibrating off his rib cage. "Such a romantic."

"I'm a truthful romantic."

"Whatever you say, Romeo."

Austin pulled back slightly, and I tipped my face up to look at him. His head dipped, and his lips met mine, a soft caress that slowly built in intensity. A fire began to spark in my lower belly. I moaned when he sucked my tongue into his mouth. Austin groaned as he tore his mouth from mine. "Shit, we can't be doing that. Your doctor said three weeks."

"You started it," I huffed.

He chuckled, "Your mouth is too damn tempting. Tell you what, why don't we go outside? You can lay on one of the pool loungers, and we can get some fresh air."

I sighed. "Sounds good." If I couldn't have Austin, at least I could have sunshine.

⌒⌒

THREE WEEKS LATER

I set my purse down on the counter and turned to face Austin. "You heard what the doctor said, I'm cleared to resume all of my normal activities."

Austin scowled in response, crossing his arms in front of his chest. "I think it's too soon. Take it easy for another month. There's no reason for you to jump back into work." We had been going round and round on this topic since leaving my doctor's appointment almost an hour ago.

The good news was, I was all healed up. The stitches along my ribs had come out two weeks before, my lungs sounded great, and all the bruises had faded. However, Austin would only be happy if I stayed in bed for another month, moving only when absolutely necessary. While he had gone back to work, I knew it was still a battle for him to leave me alone.

"You know, if I start working again, it's going to be at the youth program, so you'll be able to keep an eye on me…" I let the words hang, and Austin shifted slightly as if weighing his options.

"Part-time for the first month."

I adjusted my own stance, squaring my shoulders. "Part-time for the first week."

"Two weeks," he shot back.

"Deal." I let a grin spread across my face and slowly started towards Austin. "You know the doctor cleared me for something else." I watched as Austin's Adam's apple bobbed up and down. I laid a hand on his chest as his arms came around my waist. Reaching up on my tiptoes, I brushed my lips against his. "Take me to bed."

Austin groaned as I deepened the kiss, and I felt him hardening against my belly. "I don't want to hurt you."

I pulled back, looking intently into his eyes. "You won't. We'll go slow, and I promise to tell you if I even feel a twinge in my ribs."

He studied my face, and when his decision was made, he lifted me up. With a giggle, I wrapped my legs around his waist and locked my lips to his. Austin wound his way through the house we both now called home, one arm circling my waist, and the other outstretched to keep us from knocking into any walls.

When we reached the bedroom, he gently laid me down on the bed. Stepping back, Austin tore his t-shirt over his head. I soaked in the view of his muscles rippling in the afternoon light. This beautiful man was mine. Leaning over me, Austin brought his fingers to my shirt, carefully unbuttoning each button and planting kisses as he went. My heart began to pick up its pace, and as he reached the button on my jeans, my breath hitched.

Austin paused, his eyes meeting mine as he ran his thumb over the seam in my jeans. The action sent delicious sparks through my core. Before I knew it, my pants were gone, and so were his. I rose up off the bed, letting my shirt fall from my shoulders and unhooked my bra, tossing it to the floor.

Austin stared down at me, eyes full of reverence. "So damn beautiful. It almost hurts to look at you." He cupped my cheek, then trailed his hand down my neck, palm flattening across my collarbone, continuing on to cup my breast. When his thumb swiped along my nipple and then circled it, I felt a rush of heat.

Austin's hands skimmed down my sides, continuing their

perusal until they found purchase on the sides of my panties. Slowly, he slipped them down my legs and came to rest on his knees in front of me. Just a bit self-conscious, I tried to close my legs. Austin stilled my movement. "Don't hide yourself from me. Let me look at you."

I bit the corner of my lip but nodded. Austin pushed my legs open, eyes fixed on my center. His love of every detail of my body had my heart clenching. I'd never felt more beautiful. My head tilted down, watching him study me. While I was unsure at first, I was now fully on board, the sight was hot as heck.

Austin's fingers kneaded the flesh on my thighs, gradually working their way closer to my core. My breathing picked up, and as his fingertips traced my opening, a feather-light touch, my head fell back onto the bed. So very slowly, Austin inserted a single finger. He lazily stroked my walls. He was an expert in exquisite torture.

"More." My voice came out in a whisper. When he didn't give me more, I clamped down around his finger, trying to get the friction I needed.

Austin tweaked my nipple, the contact sending a jolt to my clit, but it wasn't quite enough. "Not yet," he soothed. "Soon." His thumb edged along the side of my clit, ramping up the tightening of my muscles.

"Need you inside me, Austin." My hands trailed over his broad shoulders, the pads of my fingers relishing the feel of his soft skin over hard muscle.

Austin rose, and I shuddered when I felt his tip at my entrance. He leaned over me, one hand on the bed, the other holding the side of my neck. "Tell me if you feel any pain." I nodded, hooking my legs around him, feet digging into his muscular butt. He didn't let my actions speed his movements. Inch by inch, he entered me. The stretch, the pressure, it was heaven.

I reached up, touching Austin's cheek. "Missed feeling you

inside me, baby."

His face went soft, and then his jaw hardened as he bottomed out. My eyes closed as he reached that sweet spot, I was incapable of keeping them open no matter how hard I tried. Gradually, Austin picked up speed. That cord within me twisting and tightening.

"I'm not going to last, Firecracker. You feel too good." He reached between us and circled that tight bundle of nerves, the second pass sending me flying. Austin arched back, and I felt his release deep inside me.

Relaxing back over me, Austin rolled us so that I was lying on top of him. Still connected, I let the feeling of being skin-to-skin and so very sated seep into my pores. He kissed my forehead. "Love you, Carter."

"Love you more," I said as I pressed my lips to his chest.

"Impossible," he responded.

My lips stretched into a smile against his skin. "It's nice to have that kind of competition."

Austin traced the ridges of my spine. "That it is. You feel okay? Not hurting?"

"I feel boneless."

He snickered, and the vibrations caused me to clench in response. Austin groaned. "Fuck, you're going to make me hard again, and I haven't even pulled out."

I lifted my head up and rested my chin against his sternum. "I don't have a problem with that."

Austin shook his head. "I've turned you into a sex fiend."

I grinned. "You should be thanking your lucky stars for that."

"Trust me, I am. But right now, we have to get up and get into the shower because I'm taking you out tonight to celebrate your clean bill of health."

"Really?"

"Yep." He squeezed my side and then gently lifted me off of

him. "Come on, let's go."

After showering and applying simple makeup, I slipped into a pink sundress with capped sleeves and gold sandals. "You almost ready?" Austin bellowed from down the hall.

"If you told me where we were going, I could've gotten dressed quicker," I called back.

Austin entered the bedroom as I was reaching around to fasten my simple diamond necklace. "Here, let me get that." Sweeping my hair off my back, he snapped the clasp into place, then kissed the base of my neck. His eyes met mine in the mirror. "You look beautiful."

My lips tipped in a small smile. "You don't look so bad yourself." Austin was wearing dark jeans and a button-down shirt that brought out the blue of his eyes. I twisted, and his arms came around me. "Actually, you look freaking hot."

He smirked and dipped his head to brush his lips against mine. Soft, sweet, and already so familiar, it felt like coming home. "Let's get going."

"Okay." He intertwined our fingers and led me out of the room and down the hall.

When we got in the Range Rover, he handed me a satin sleep mask. "Put this on."

I ran the smooth material through my fingers and asked, "Um, why?"

Austin started the engine and hit the garage door opener. "Because I want to keep where I'm taking you a surprise."

Butterflies started fluttering their wings deep in my belly. "All right." I slipped the mask over my face and leaned back in my seat. The drive was quiet, other than rock music playing softly over the stereo. Austin seemed to be lost in thought while I was trying to figure out where we could possibly be headed by attempting to keep up with the turns he made.

Finally, after what seemed like about twenty minutes, the car came to a stop, and Austin cut the engine. "Keep the blindfold on."

"All right." I twisted my fingers in my lap. The passenger door opened, and the warm air of a late Southern California afternoon dusted over my skin.

Austin spun me around in my seat and took both my hands. "Okay, step down, nice and easy." Of course, I almost tripped over my own feet. Austin caught me around the waist. "Easy there, Firecracker."

"It was your bright idea to blindfold me, you know how clumsy I am!" I huffed.

He chuckled, taking my hand and leading me forward at a snail's pace. "Just put one foot in front of the other, there's nothing in your path."

After a few steps, blades of grass tickled my toes. I had no idea where we were. In fact, I couldn't hear any people, a rarity in LA. The only thing I could hear was the sound of far-off traffic. Austin tugged on my hand, bringing me to a stop. Carefully, he raised the sleep mask. I blinked, temporarily blinded by the sun. As my vision cleared, I saw that we were at Griffith Observatory. Looking around, I realized there were no other people here. Then my vision snagged on a picnic laid in the exact same spot we had sat on our first date.

I tilted my face up to Austin's. "How?"

He brushed a lock of hair away from my face, tucking in behind my ear. "I called in a few favors, got this place to ourselves for a couple hours."

I beamed up at him. "You *are* a romantic."

Austin gave my lips a swift kiss. "Just don't tell anyone."

"Your secret is safe with me," I assured.

Leading me forward, I noticed that the blanket was kitted out with overstuffed pillows and the same ginormous picnic basket he'd used before. My stomach grumbled, and Austin gave a good-hearted snicker. "Don't worry, I brought your favorites from Joan's again."

"You are truly the man of my dreams." I squeezed his hand and then let it go to make myself comfortable amongst the plethora of pillows. Austin reached into the picnic basket, removing a bottle and popping the cork with a satisfying sound. "Oooooh, champagne! Fancy."

He poured the bubbly liquid into two glasses. "Well, this is a celebration."

"That it is." We spent the next hour sipping champagne, nibbling on some of my favorite foods, and laughing ourselves silly. The pall of last month's attack was finally lifting, both for Austin and me. It felt so good to have nothing to worry about, having nothing to do but soak up this time together.

As the sun began to set, I climbed into Austin's lap, leaning against his chest, eyes fixed on the horizon. I felt Austin turn his head, and then he let out a loud whistle. Jarred, I twisted around to see a small, reddish-brown puppy flying towards us, ears flopping in the wind, and pink leash trailing behind her. When she got a foot away, she launched herself at us. I immediately cuddled her to my chest, cooing, "Well, aren't you the cutest. Where is your owner?" I looked up, searching the grounds, seeing someone standing far off.

Austin squeezed my side. "You're her owner, baby. She's for you."

Tears begin to gather in my eyes. "You got us a sister for Blue?"

"Yep, I figure you've both earned it. She's a red nosed pit, just rescued from a puppy mill."

I cuddled her even closer, relishing the smell of her puppy breath. "Oh, you poor baby. Don't you worry, we're going to take great care of you. I think we'll call you Ruby. Ruby and Blue is cute, right?" I asked Austin.

"I don't know, she might already have a name. Why don't you

check her collar." I fumbled with the collar as the puppy I already knew I was going to call Ruby squirmed in my lap. I finally felt metal and spun the collar around. All air rushed from my lungs when I saw what my fingers had a hold of. Tied to the metal loop in Ruby's collar with a cream ribbon was the most beautiful ring I had ever seen. The large stone caught the last rays of the setting sun as Austin whispered into my ear two words. "Marry me."

The tears in my eyes spilled over then as I whispered back, "Yes."

Austin's arms reached around me and rested the ribbon from my shaking hands. He swiftly untied it and slipped the ring onto my finger. "Build a home with me," he continued.

"Yes," I echoed, bobbing my head up and down.

"Make a family with me."

My heart stuttered. Skipping a beat at that mental picture of little dark-haired boys with my green eyes, and tow-headed girls with Austin's sparkling blue irises. I spun around, tears falling down my cheeks. "Yes." I set the puppy down and launched myself at Austin, knocking him to the ground. "I love you so freaking much," I said between kisses. Ruby yipped in agreement, running circles around us.

Austin rolled me to my back, careful to keep most of his weight off of me. "I love you, too, Firecracker. We're going to have a good life."

My heart, full to bursting, cracked open with his final words and all I felt was warmth.

EPILOGUE

Carter
ONE YEAR LATER

TAYLOR ADJUSTED THE VEIL THAT SAT ATOP MY HEAD and flowed over my shoulders as I grinned at my mom in the mirror. She darted a hand up to her face, wiping away a tear. "Mom, don't start that, because if you cry, then I will. And then the makeup Taylor spent hours on will be ruined."

Taylor squeezed my mom's shoulder. "Don't make Carter wreck my masterpiece, Mrs. M."

My mom waved a hand in front of her eyes. "Okay, okay. You just look so beautiful. I'm so very happy for you, baby."

I wrapped her in a hug. "Thank you, Mom, for everything. I love you."

"More than words," she echoed back.

"Gah! Now y'all are going to make *me* cry," Taylor huffed.

I pulled back from my mom. "Sorry, sorry. No more sappy stuff. Promise."

Taylor reached for a gift bag on the vanity. "You still planning on sneaking in to see the groom before the wedding?"

I hadn't seen Austin since the rehearsal dinner the night before. Taylor and I had taken over one of the hotel's suites for a slumber party, staying up way too late, laughing ourselves sick while looking through old pictures from our time together as roommates. Taylor had ended up deciding to stay in Texas to be closer to her mom, so neither of us had ever lived in the Los Feliz house after my attack. While I knew Taylor's move was for the best, I missed her like crazy.

I extended a hand to Taylor, and she gave me the bag. My stomach flip-flopped as I pictured the contents. I hoped Austin liked it. "I'm heading over to his room right now."

Taylor smiled huge. "I'll text Liam and tell him to make an excuse for him and Ford to leave."

"Perfect." I paused. "I'm nervous," I admitted.

She took my free hand in hers. "He's going to love it." Her eyes held mine, reassuring me further.

"Okay," I breathed. "I'm off."

Taylor held open the door for me. I hitched up my strapless lace and tulle gown with one hand and slipped past her, making my way down the hall to the elevator. I drummed my fingers against my collarbone as I waited for the elevator to take me the two floors down to Austin's room. When the doors slid open, I let out a slow breath and moved forward.

I came to a stop outside Room 731. Slipping the bag behind my back, I reached my hand up to knock, pausing for just a second to soak in the magnitude of the moment. I rapped my knuckles on the wood.

Thirty seconds later, the door swung open, and there stood the most handsome man I had ever laid eyes on. He wore a navy blue suit, tailored to fit his muscular form perfectly. The top button of his shirt was undone, and he wore no tie. He looked fancy, but he still looked like my Austin.

While I was taking him in, Austin was doing the same to me. Our eyes locked, and we both grinned. He reached out and brushed a hand across my cheek. "Just when I think you can't get prettier." I felt that familiar color hit my cheeks. "I hope fifty years from now, I can still make you blush."

"I'm sure you'll have no trouble doing that."

His grin turned devilish. "I'm certainly willing to work at it. Now, come in and tell me why you're sneaking a peek at the groom before the ceremony."

I shuffled forward and brought the bag out from behind my back. "I have something for you." Austin cocked his head to the side, a puzzled look on his face. We'd already exchanged our official wedding gifts, so his confusion made sense. I smiled encouragingly, and he took the bag from my hand. Tissue paper rustled as his hand searched, and then he removed the small piece of cloth.

Austin unrolled the bundle, his confusion compounding until he read the words on the front of the white onesie. *Daddy's Little Fighter* with a pair of boxing gloves. His jaw dropped, and his eyes shot to mine. "Does this mean?" he started. "Are you?" His eyes flew from mine to my nonexistent belly.

"You're gonna be a daddy."

Austin dropped the bag and was suddenly moving. He threw his arms around me, burrowing his face in my neck. I felt dampness there and in my own eyes. "Just when I think I can't get any happier. I love you, Carter." His hand snuck between us, resting on my stomach. "And I love you, little guy."

I drew my head back. "It could be a girl."

Austin's eyes sparkled with unshed tears and humor. "If there's a God in Heaven, our first child will be a boy."

My brows furrowed, "Why?"

"Your beauty? I'm gonna need all the help I can get looking after any girls you give me."

❧

I relaxed in Austin's arms as we glided over the dance floor. My eyes traveled around the room, pausing on different people, letting the warmth of being surrounded by all our loved ones wash over me.

Michael was shoveling forkfuls of chocolate cake into his mouth, his eyes dancing at something his mom's new husband was saying. Earlier that year, Sofia had married Carlos, the Casanova fighter who had hit on me the first time I went to Austin's gym. Sofia had brought Carlos to his knees, and he worshipped the ground she walked on. Finally, Sofia and Michael had a man in their lives who truly deserved to be there. I knew Joe had made amends as best he could, through written letters this time, but he still wasn't in their lives. There were some things you might be able to forgive, but you'd never forget.

My eyes travelled to the bar where Ford was putting the moves on one of Austin's cousins. I giggled as I saw him blatantly check out her cleavage. Some things would never change. A few stools down, Liam was engrossed in conversation with Austin's dad and Austin's old coach, Mel. Both Liam and Ford had stayed close, the brothers I'd never had but always wanted. And I knew they'd both had conversations with Austin when he struggled to let go of what had happened to me. Easing his mind and helping him make peace with it.

Surprisingly, ever since that first day at the hospital, I hadn't struggled. I felt safe. Safe because Austin made me feel that way. This didn't mean he let up on my self-defense training, that would always be a way for him to feel as if he could keep the bad things in life from touching me. Since it meant close body contact with my man, I didn't mind.

My gaze continued on, resting for a bit on Taylor, who was sitting with her mom. I was worried about my bestie. She tried to hide it, but every now and then, I caught shadows in her eyes that hadn't been there before. While her mom was in remission, I think her battle with cancer had marked Taylor. I knew the only thing I could do was be there when she was ready to open up and be willing to help her carry her burden for a while. Just like she had for me so many times.

Austin twirled me in a spin, and I caught sight of my parents swirling around us. Both my parents and Austin's dad had been relishing the joy of their only children finding their other half. Austin swung me back into his arms, kissing me soft and slow. "Good day?" he asked.

"The best," I answered, brushing my lips against his again. Pulling back, I gazed into his dark blue orbs. "Just when I think I can't get any happier."

THE END

ENJOY THIS BOOK?

You can make a huge difference in *Further To Fall's* book life!

Reviews encourage other readers to try out a book. They are critically important to getting the word out about a book, and mean the world to every author.

I'd love your help in spreading the word. If you could take a quick moment to leave a review on your favorite book site, I would be forever grateful. It can be as short as you like. You can do that on your preferred retailer, Goodreads, or BookBub. Even better? All three! Just copy and paste that baby!

Email me a link to your review at catherine@catherinecowles. com so I can be sure to thank you. You're the best!

BONUS SCENE

Want to find out what happens when Carter goes into labor? By signing up for my newsletter, you'll get this bonus scene, plus be the first to see cover reveals, upcoming excerpts from new releases, exclusive news, and giveaways found nowhere else. Sign up by going to the link below.

www.subscribepage.com/FTFbonus

ACKNOWLEDGMENTS

Acknowledgments are my very favorite part of every book. I often will flip to the end of a novel just to read the acknowledgments first because I love knowing who helped the author along his or her journey. This first batch of acknowledgments is bound to be a doozy because guess what? This is my first book! I wrote a freaking book, guys!

There are so many people who helped me make this book a reality, but the first thank you has to go to my mom. My love of books is greatly due to all the books she read to me throughout my childhood. She also supported me in every way imaginable throughout the writing process and listened to far more book talk than she was probably interested in. Thanks for encouraging me to take this crazy path, Mom. I love you!

Lyle, thank you for being so proud of me every single time I accomplished a step in this process and helping me take this leap. I'm so lucky to have you as a soul sister!

Trisha, my bookish bestie. You walked with me through every part of this journey with me. Thank you for being a kickass combo of cheerleader/sounding board/editor/shoulder to cry on!

Getting involved in the Indie Romance world has put me in contact with some incredible women. I'm especially grateful for a few authors who took the time take a baby author under their wing. I swear, women supporting women will change the world.

Alessandra Torre, I'm not sure this book would have ever gotten finished if it wasn't for you and your amazing classes. Thank you for sharing all your knowledge with the world and for taking the time out of your busy schedule to walk me through some of the scarier aspects of self-publishing. Your encouragement and wisdom have meant the world to me!

Julia Sykes, I love that book world reconnected us. I'll never forget how excited you were for me when I told you I was writing my first book. Your enthusiasm and kindness were such fortitude to this new writer's soul. Thank you for taking the time to share all you've learned with me.

Devney Perry, thank you for taking the time to answer my millions of questions. Your kindness and generosity of spirit are unparalleled!

Social media can be a scary place, but I've been lucky enough to find two incredible communities of encouraging authors in the Alessandra Torre Inkers group and my KB101 ladies. Inkers, thank you for sharing all the different things you've learned in your own journeys and for providing encouragement and laughs. To my KB girls, thanks for sharing in the joys and sorrows of being a newbie writer. So thankful to have all of you to lean on!

Emma Renshaw, my wormhole twinsie. There aren't enough "thank you"s in the world to express my gratitude for having you on this journey. You are such a gift!

Grahame Claire, I'm so glad this crazy world of writing brought us together. Thank you for your eagle eyes, wisdom, and constant brainstorming sessions!

My fearless beta readers: Trisha, Emily, Angela, and Ryan. Thank you for reading this book in its roughest form and helping me to make it the best it could possibly be!

A huge thank you to my editors Susan and Chelle for walking me through my very first editing process. You were both so kind and helpful, thank you for guiding my path.

Nikki, TWILIGHT FOREVER! Also, thank you for taking the time to answer 500 public relations questions. I'm so lucky to have a friend like you in my life!

Michelle, thank you for answering all my many medical related questions. Hopefully, I didn't mess anything up too badly!

Lastly, thank YOU! Yes, YOU. I'm so grateful you're reading this book and making my author dreams come true. I love you for that. A whole lot!

ABOUT
CATHERINE COWLES

Writer of words. Drinker of Diet Cokes. Lover of all things cute and furry, especially her dog. Catherine has had her nose in a book since the time she could read and finally decided to write down some of her own stories. When she's not writing she can be found exploring her home state of Oregon, listening to true crime podcasts, or searching for her next book boyfriend.

STAY CONNECTED

You can find Catherine in all the usual bookish places…

Website: catherinecowles.com

Facebook: facebook.com/catherinecowlesauthor

Instagram: instagram.com/catherinecowlesauthor

Goodreads: goodreads.com/catherinecowlesauthor

BookBub: bookbub.com/profile/catherine-cowles

Amazon: www.amazon.com/author/catherinecowles

Twitter: twitter.com/catherinecowles

Pinterest: pinterest.com/catherinecowlesauthor

Made in United States
North Haven, CT
06 December 2024

61816056R00195